THE COVE

A NOVEL

TOM HUNT

PAGE PUBLISHING, INC.
New York, NY

First originally published by Page Publishing, Inc. 2018

ISBN 978-1-64214-011-8 (Paperback)
ISBN 978-1-64214-012-5 (Digital)

Printed in the United States of America

This book is dedicated to Pat Sue, Jim,
Brooke, Steve, Mena and Elsie.

A special thanks to Don Pennington and Stretch Chatham

Other books by Tom Hunt:

"Bad Water" 2013

Praise for Bad Water and Other Stories of the Alaskan Panhandle.

Charles Asher - Phi Beta Kappa Book Reviews:

"Bad Water and Other Stories of the Alaskan Panhandle is a dynamic modern reiteration of early frontier literature, it contains courage misery and resilience of a lost world...."

"The concurrent streams of apollonian stoicism and odic tenderness that run through the collection places Hunt in a league with writers such as Daniel Woodrell and Dennis Letane - a literary school with folkish, almost tribal inspiration..."

"Tom Hunt captures both the enormity and the isolation of the landscape as a parallel to the lives lived within it."

"...a seamless meditation on individualism and community, history and modernity, hope and malaise and a dozen other American paradoxes. --"

"Bad water is sure to find success in the growing aesthetic movement which gave us "Mystic River" and "Winter's Bone.""

Comments from readers

Anthony W:

"Rough around the edges, Bad Water draws you in slowly, just like southeast Alaska herself. ".... one of those rare books in which every story is better than the last." Down to earth... bittersweet, horrific, humorous and ultimately intriguing. The characters become real people to us. "...leaves me yearning for more."

Walter K:

"This is not a love story nor a mystery story, although there are overtones of love and mystery within the stories themselves. I look forward to his next book. I started reading "Bad Water" and just kept reading."

Amazon Customer

"This is a very well written collection of short stories. It emphasizes the self reliance of the people who still live in what is essentially a harsh wilderness. It also touches on the theme of people who go to Alaska to 'start over' but take their troubles with them. This is not a 'fast - paced mystery story. Nonetheless I couldn't put it down. I found the stories thought provoking and somewhat haunting."

Foreword

Harbor Cove does not exist. All of the other place names mentioned do and can be found on marine charts.

The people and events are completely fictional but the discussions regarding being able to live as you choose even in the context of an overabundance of inconveniences are real. There is also an element of Darwinism at play. Boats and weather require good decisions and a healthy dose of luck. Second chances are not to be counted on. A person has to learn the rules and the right skills.

People drift in an out of Harbor Cove but the ones that stay are not ordinary, the reasons don't matter much. They develop some unusual solutions to problems, most of which work; one way or another. Some don't. The distance from civilization is more than geographical.

Some thirty years ago or so a friend of mine was in a flight training program for pilots in the Marine Corps. In the final phases of the program, after completing all of the other requirements they were interviewed by a panel, which was selected for that specific purpose. One of the questions they asked was: "Are you normal?" Of course the correct answer is "Yes" then they move on to the next question. I've often thought that a lot of us who find ourselves in places such as Harbor Cove, if presented with that question, might have stood there staring at the floor for a long time.

There aren't any answers here and for sure no heroes.

Tom Hunt

Everyone thinks their own view of the world is
particularly sensitive.

—William Zinsser

credit to Steve Heinl

The wind has picked up by the time they enter Snow Passage, where Clarence Straits enters Sumner Straits. The white water from the waves breaking at their stern are making a discernible hissing sound before they roll under the boat. Where it narrows at Bushy Island, they begin to stack up in shorter intervals and strike the boat from different directions. She says, "It's getting rough. You better turn off the autopilot and take the wheel."

He hesitates. "Look up there." He points to calmer water ahead of them, irritated that she suggests something that he should have thought of sooner. "The water lies down right up there."

She looks nervously to the stern, folding her arms. "OH MY GOD, LOOK!"

He turns just in time to see a large log shoot end first out of the tide rip they are caught in and splash back into the water just behind the boat. Then without warning, two large waves hit them, quartering on the stern. The boat rolls hard over with the first wave. The second wave hits before it can right itself, pushing it completely over on its side. The woman falls against a chair and then rolls to the floor. The cupboard doors in the galley burst open, and dishes fly through the air. She is trapped between an end table and a large chair, stunned yet aware the boat is lying on its side. She hears of the sound of water rushing over the back deck.

Her husband frantically grabs at anything nearby—the helm, overhead hand rails, the screen on the depth sounder—as he pitches across the pilot house. When the boat ends its roll, he is still upright. He looks down at his feet to see he is standing on the wheelhouse door, looking through the glass of the door window. Between his feet is green water. Still confused, he thinks, *That's kind of pretty, the color of that water.* Then coming to his senses, he yells, "Molly!"

She calls back from the salon, "Are we sinking?"

He claws his way up to the helm and turns off the autopilot. He hangs desperately onto the wheel, turning it, but the boat doesn't respond. Neither of them can think of anything else to say; they wait in silence. Ever so slowly, the boat begins to right itself and keeps moving. When they are beyond the tide rip, it's trimmed itself and is moving toward flat water. He hears Molly scuffling around in the salon, moving furniture, muttering. He checks the bilge alarm light and the gauges on the engine; everything seems to be running.

"Hey, Molly! Can you take the helm? I better check and see if we have any water in the engine room."

She comes silently forward. The color is gone from her face. She takes the helm and stares forward. When he returns, she has the publication of the *United States Coast and Geodetic Survey* open to the page describing the secure anchorages in Sumner Straits. She puts her finger on a page and says, "We need to go here. It's a good anchorage protected from all directions."

"Isn't there any closer?"

She says definitely, "This place has fuel, water, and a store. It's a fish-buying station. We are going there. I don't care how long it takes us."

"What's the name?"

"It's called Harbor Cove."

After they set the anchor, she says, "I need to get off the boat for a bit. Give me a hand with the skiff." She rows to a float with some fuel pumps on it. She's wearing a teal-colored Gore-Tex rain jacket that she unzips as she walks up the ramp to a large deck. On the deck below a sign that says Mercantile, three men are working, weighing and icing fish. Large plastic totes are scattered here and there. She dodges the men as they move about. As she moves to the breezeway that leads to the store, a large mangy dog lies in her path. She stops and waves her hand at it, shushing at it to move. It doesn't move.

While she is pausing, wondering what to do next, she looks around the shoreline of Harbor Cove, examining the derelict boats. There is a small weathered float house at the opposite end of the float that holds the fuel pumps. Scattered along the shoreline is a collection of rundown houses and boat sheds. It's hard to tell what some of the buildings are used for, and others are just collapsed.

She looks over to the edge of the deck where a man is leaning on the railing overlooking all of this. He's dressed shabbily in patched-together clothes, smoking a homemade cigarette. He notices her looking at him and sees she is being cautious. "Where you from?" he asks.

"Port Townsend, Washington."

"Your first trip north?"

She nods, watching him carefully.

"Huh." He blows smoke in the air.

She waits for a further response, and when he remains silent, she asks, "What's it like living here?"

For a moment she thinks he hasn't heard here or is just ignoring her; she turns her attention back to the dog. He says, "I'm tryin' to think how I can explain that to you, but I don't think I can do that in a correct manner."

"Oh?"

"The best I can do is that it's real close to the bone."

"Then why do you live here?"

He shakes his head a bit. "I can't explain that to you either, ma'am. It's just too complicated. I'm pretty sure, even if I tried, that there is a good chance you wouldn't understand. It's real complicated."

She frowns.

He blows more smoke into the air. "Sure a nice day, ain't it?"

1

Southeast Alaska

Today, if you look closely into the dawn, just minutes before daylight, a boat is leaving. It is a large wooden schooner that belongs to another era. The wheelhouse is small, protected by a high bow, with barely enough room inside for one person. It has rounded corners that are made to catch as little wind and water as possible. A large anchor is snugged up tight in its chock. Nothing sits loose on deck. The trolling poles have folding aluminum stiff legs, and the captain's bunk has high sides with a leather tie-down strap so he won't be pitched out when he needs to sleep while fishing off shore. It's made for tough weather and hard work. See how it glides through the morning darkness? It's riding on the soft rumble of its engine, a ship from another time. Then it's gone, back to a fog-like silence.

At the back of the cove in a house tucked under the hemlock trees Everett sits at his kitchen table. It's littered with a dirty dish smeared with egg yolk and crumpled paper napkins. There's a bottle of Tums and a pair of rubber gloves dotted with fish scales at one corner. A piece of paper with a detailed cost analysis lies in front of him. The pencil lines dividing the columns have been drawn with a ruler; the handwritten numbers are neat and precise. Yet there are splotches of bacon grease mixed with egg yolk smeared on the paper. On the upper right-hand corner is a coffee stain. With his crooked finger, he traces his way down a column, checking and rechecking.

Every morning beginning at 3:00 AM, he carefully records the previous day's fish tickets, the receipts from the liquor store, gallons of fuel sold, and reconciles the till at the grocery store. He is here every morning early at this same spot at the table, in the same chair; habits are hard to break.

He stands with difficulty, taking a few moments for the blood to move through his arthritic hips and knees. When it hits his joints, they ache and throb. He grits his teeth, waiting for it to subside. His wife shuffles into the room, wearing bedroom slippers and a bright-red bathrobe covered in yellow flowers. She watches him with worried eyes.

He carefully places a pencil in his vest pocket, stands leaning on the table, then shoulders the front door open, crossing the porch with a rolling, unsteady gait. He picks his way carefully down a gravel path that winds through the thick underbrush of Devil's Club, blueberry bushes, and tree trunks. Partly out of habit and partly to keep his mind off the pain, he goes through his list mentally.

Will all of the crew show up for work?
Are the ones that do show up sober?
Deal with that when you get there.
Get the tills ready for business.
Get on the radio to check on the fish packer about arrival times.
Count the totes again and see if they need more ice.
Recheck the freight that's coming on the mail plane . . .

The going is slow. A fall would be easy, a stumble on one of the large exposed tree roots that crisscross the path—a broken hip. He stops to rest, breathing heavily. He leans against a steep rock face to collect himself. The sound of the rooster crowing comes through the trees.

The trail breaks over a steep shale bank just before it winds down through the rocks and bushes to the trading post. He stops again, sitting on a large quartz rock, watching. It will be his last chance to rest today. Lately he has been staying in this spot longer and longer, letting his mind wander off to other things and other places.

This morning, he watches a humpback whale dive and blow its way around the inside of the cove. It blows a ring of bubbles around a school of herring then comes up underneath them with his mouth gaping open, feeding. Even at this distance, Everett can see herring flying through the air just in front of the whale's mouth as it breaks the surface. The morning light catches the spray from its open mouth, then it slides smoothly under the surface, disappearing.

Thirty miles to the west, a small wood fish boat is on fire. At first the gray smoke just rolls out of the wheelhouse door, slowly increasing in thickness, then as the flames ignite the fuel tanks, they begin to roar, sending out great billows of black smoke. The boat, the smoke, and the flames drift on the strong tides that wash through the shallow rocky passage. You will have to look closely to see it, but as the narrow passage opens out into Sumner Straits, there is a small plastic punt with a man in it; he's rowing slowly with even, measured strokes. He doesn't look back at the burning boat.

While Everett watches the whale feed, two men and a woman stumble out of a dilapidated one-room float house moored at the far end of the fuel float. The smell of bacon drifts from one of the fishing boats tied to the float. The three of them stand for a few moments, blinking into the daylight, gazing around, searching for some sort of reference point they can use to start their day. Without looking, the two men reach for each other, holding hands like children needing comfort. Still not speaking, one of them points down the dock at nothing in particular; the other squints into the sunlight. The woman sits on a plastic chair, holding her head in her hands. The man pointing releases the other man's hand to walk toward the fuel pumps, continuing to point.

A one-legged raven jumps from the bull rail and, with a couple of wing beats, flies to perch on the wheelhouse roof of the boat with the bacon smell. The man pointing stops to pet one of the dock dogs. The other man sits next to the woman and watches the water.

Everett restarts his way down the slope, shuffling out from between the bushes that bracket the path. He can see the deck where his crew is working. Two dock hands are weighing fish that are being hoisted from a small boat, icing them in a tote. They are using a rust-covered davit that has been welded together with iron pipe to lift the fish from the deck of the boat. They wipe the fish clean before placing them in a large stainless steel pan that hangs from a scale. There are two men working; there should be three.

If Randy didn't show up today, I will fire him! I have had enough of his horseshit. If he thinks I won't fire him because I won't be able to get someone else out here in the middle of nowhere to replace him, he has another think comin'. I will get someone else out here and then I'll fire him. Ah, screw it! I'll just fire him!

He turns and looks at a group of fishing boats that are tied to the fuel float. *The coho haven't showed up yet. Better call the cold storage in Craig to see if anything is happening on the south end.*

The sound of a large generator radiates from a shed next to the gravel path. He stops instinctively to check the oil pressure gauge. Several five-gallon buckets are randomly scattered on the floor, one stuffed with grimy oil absorbent pads that hang out on to the greasy floor. Another is filled with used oil filters and dirty oil. Other buckets are filled with random trash, mostly crumpled aluminum beer cans and cigarette butts.

He taps the oil pressure gauge with a gnarly knuckle to make sure the needle isn't stuck. An oil change is needed in the next few days. Continuing on, he enters the back door of the grocery store, negotiating his way around some empty cardboard boxes that have been tossed up against a stack of sheet rock that's beginning to crumble from the constant humidity. Spots of mold blotch the top sheet.

Better get that hung on the walls pretty soon, or I am going to lose it. Damn country never does dry anything out.

He has had the same thought every morning for the past year and a half.

The store is three small aisles of canned goods: peaches, corn, a large section of beans, beets, peas, pears, and hominy. One wall is filled with glass-fronted freezers that contain frozen meats and pizza. The smaller coolers have several heads of lettuce that are starting to wilt, some apples and oranges that have been there too long; potatoes, carrots and onions are in the last. The end of the aisle, closest to the till, is all Top Ramen.

Mounted deer heads decorate the ceiling rafters. A picture of Randy, the missing dock hand, is taped to the window behind the till; three gutted deer lie carefully arranged on a rocky beach. He's kneeling by the largest deer, holding its head up by the horns, smiling. Three deer are all he can eat in one winter.

The floor is rough-cut spruce planking stained with splashes of oil and ground in dirt. Saw kerfs are visible on the surface. Glass doors lead to a breezeway; they swing both ways with a hydraulic arm. One of them is worn out, and the door swings loosely but doesn't hold in the same position as the other. This pushes someone sideways if they try to open them at the same time, something that visitors and newcomers have a hard time with until they get it figured out. The small gap between the doors allows dogs to nose their way in and out of the store. In bad weather, they will spend most of a day in the store, lying on the floor near the cash register, exuding a wispy pungent steam from their wet matted fur that fades to nothing as it rises above the counter.

Everett walks through the store, unconsciously touching the glass doors of the coolers, checking to see if they're working. The cash drawer on the till at the counter is open; he puts two hundred dollars in change in the drawer, carefully placing each denomination in its proper slot then carelessly dropping a handful of pennies, out of his pocket, in the remaining slot. He unlocks the swinging glass doors and trundles across the breezeway, doing the same thing in the small room that's the liquor store.

He finally reaches his office, unlocks the door with some difficulty because the lock is gummed up with salt air and dirt. On the windowsill is a can of WD-40. He sprays some in the keyhole. On the window is a note taped with black electrician's tape. It says, "Pat wants another $100.00 credit at the store." He puts it in the side pocket of his vest.

Now full daylight consumes the cove. Someone stirs on one of the fishing boats still tied to the float. The smell of bacon continues to move through the air. The dock dogs begin to stir, scratching and biting at their matted hair. The fleas are also waking up. The dogs move their heads back and forth, tracking the source of the smell, snuffling. The largest dog, some sort of pit bull–Siberian husky mix, is blind in one eye. The eye is an opaque blue. He walks toward the smell, stopping to dig at his matted hair but still sniffing the air. For a moment the fleas get the best of him, and he stops to bite vigorously at his hind leg, grunting with the effort. Moving on, he walks through a puddle of seawater on a section of the float that's sinking.

Beyond the dog, at the far end of the float, the raven circles down from his perch on the wheelhouse, landing on a rotting section of the bull rail. He hops down the rail, stopping to crouch on his one good leg, cocking his head to one side, looking at the dog in one direction then back at the boat with the bacon smell in the other, trying to figure how to deal with both of them at the same time. Like Everett, always calculating. The dog stands, considering the raven closely.

The phone rings, and Everett grimaces, showing what remains of his front teeth. There are wide gaps between the remaining ones. They're yellow and are dotted with fine particles of chewing tobacco. Looking here and there, he tries to determine exactly from under which pile of papers the sound is coming. After several more rings and some pawing through stacks of paper, he tracks it down. He answers abruptly, "This is Everett." He listens, frowning.

"Goddamn it. What do you mean the packer won't be here this afternoon? I have fifteen totes of fish that've been on ice for three days, and God only know how long they sat in the holds of the boats before that." He kicks at some papers that lie on the floor.

He listens again.

"OK, if that's the best you can do, we'll be ready for you, but don't be cutting my price if some of those fish are belly-burned!" He sticks his head out of the door. "Hey! Bob, Rich!"

The two men stop weighing to look his way. Rich's long blond hair is thick and unkempt; the swirls and clumps are stiff and spikey. His hooded eyes are constantly glancing here and there. Frequently he will stop whatever he's doing to look over his shoulder to see if something is behind him. He turns to face Everett, but his eyes are making furtive glances in other directions. He stands with both arms hanging in front of him. He has a feral look about him. Bob is tall and skinny, in constant motion; his incessant talking is a constant irritation to anyone who has to work with him, except Rich. Bob talks; Rich twitches and keeps an eye on everything close by. Their work is relentless because they can't stand still.

"The packer isn't going to be here until eleven tonight. I want you guys back here to help with the loading."

They nod, "OK."

"Sober."

"OK. Does this mean we get overtime?"

"How many times I gotta tell you I don't pay overtime?" He rubs his face in frustration. There's a small pause. "Where the hell is Randy?"

"Probably got drunk last night."

The two men look at each other, smiling. "Do you want us to fire him?"

"No. I want to do it myself."

"Do we get to split his salary?"

"No!"

Bob and Rich turn back to their work, glancing at each other then over their shoulders at Everett; they're chuckling to themselves.

Everett is talking to himself. "Goddamned Job Service, bureaucratic bastards, don't cull anybody out. Just send me anything that can walk, talk, or breathe. They wouldn't recognize a good worker if one walked up and sat in their lap, bunch of damn pencil pushers. Couldn't pour piss out of a boot."

As Everett starts to close the door, a young native woman wearing denim jeans and a wool jacket pulls it back open, nodding at him. "Morning." She glances at Bob and Rich. "Hey, boss, don't take any crap off the hired help." She gives him a big white toothy smile, bright in contrast to her brown skin. She walks to the far corner of the office and moves several stacks of papers, uncovering a keyboard. She quickly brings up an accounting program on the screen.

Everett plops heavily into his chair. His desk is an old oak roll top that is older than he is, and he begins to paw through the stacks of papers, stopping often to inspect one or two closely, squinting then tossing it aside. "Kasey, I need to find enough money to pay the fuel bill next week."

"Let me see what I can do." She scrolls through accounts receivable, "Hey, boss, here's something. The cold storage in Petersburg hasn't paid for that last shipment of king salmon. I'll have them transfer that money into your account, which should just about cover it. If it doesn't, I'll get some money out of the liquor store account. I have a little money set aside there."

"Don't forget to record it as a loan if you get it from the liquor store."

"Right."

He stops groping through the papers on his desk for a moment, staring at the wall. "If I remember correctly, they owe us $7,456."

"Just a second and I'll check."

He stays staring at the wall.

"Right on, boss. You still have that head for numbers, don't you?"

"Well, everything else has gone to hell." Kasey's the only person to ever call him boss, and he likes it.

"I think I remember how much is still in the liquor store account."

"You better quit while you're still ahead."

"Right." He turns back to his desk.

The VHF radio crackles to life from its perch on top of the safe. "This is the fish buyer Barbara C. We will be buying fish today and tomorrow. We're anchored at the Mud Hole in South Chatham. Standing by on channels 10 and 16."

"Must be some fish in South Chatham."

A woman bangs on the office door and mouths words through the glass, "Is the liquor store open?"

Grimacing, Everett goes to the door and shuts the door behind him. He speaks softly to the woman. "Emma, you've been hitting it pretty hard lately. Maybe you better knock it off for a while."

"I know I should but . . ." She holds her hands up; they are shaking. Her eyes show a tender look of despair; she's pleading.

Still speaking in a low voice, he asks, "Ever thought about quitting?"

She shakes her head no. Fumbling in the front pocket of her wool pants, she produces a handful of crumpled paper money.

He checks it quickly, and it's two dollars shy of a six-pack. He unlocks the liquor store and gives her the beer. "You really should take better care of yourself."

Ignoring his comment, she walks quickly away. He hears the sound of the metal tab on the can pop as she treads her way through the fish totes. A man is walking up the ramp from the fuel float toward her. She points to the six-pack. "You want a beer?"

"Sure enough."

They stay at the railing at the top of the ramp, each placing a foot on the bull rail, leaning on their elbows. He grasps the can with affection. "Sure tastes good." He takes two long gulps.

"It sure does," she says. "I've been looking forward to this ever since I got up this morning."

He nods in complete understanding.

Everett goes back to his desk full of papers and sits down hard in his chair and begins to rub his forehead. Kasey stops keyboarding. "She won't quit if you keep selling it to her."

"Now tell me truthfully, Kasey, do you think she'll quit if I quit selling it to her? I've tried cutting people off. They just get someone else to buy it for them."

"Yeah, I know, I know."

"Ain't nobody's business but hers. Sure is hard to watch though."

Kasey nods.

"Most everybody gets pretty good at makin' their own misery."

"I guess that's the case, boss."

The fishing boats still tied to the fuel float are showing more wear and tear as the season grinds on. It's been several months since the last paint job, more rust on the rigging and peeled-off patches of paint exposing bare wood. It isn't a good year; fishermen are trying to decide if the fish are just late or if they're going to show up at all. "Can I catch enough fish to pay for fuel?" is the question on everybody's mind. Many are wondering what kind of work they can get this winter to make it through to next season.

As the sun warms, the wooden float steam begins to rise. A battered aluminum skiff, pushed by a noisy outboard and with the cowling missing, comes around one of the small islands at the entrance of the cove. It makes its way to the fuel float. Large areas of paint are worn from the hull of the skiff, and the dull gray of the metal shows through. The word *Lund* is barely visible. The man in the skiff is wearing a homemade knitted wool cap, jammed on his head, holding his long hair back from his face. His hair is long and thin, tucked behind his ears and hanging down the middle of his back. It ruffles in the slightest breeze. His clothing is heavy. He wears it all year. The patches on his pants and shirt are sewn on by hand with an uneven saddle stich. The edges are not hemmed and are rough and frayed. The shirt and pants are too large for his frame; his hair and shirt billow as the skiff moves. On the front of his pants, there is loose material that folds in irregular pleats caused by a rope belt that is cinched tight on his waist.

He docks the skiff in the space left by the large schooner that left before daylight. One end of a short line is half hitched around a rusty spike that is jammed into the socket for the port oarlock. He fishes through a puddle of water in the bottom of the skiff caused by leaky rivets, pushing aside a life jacket and the broken end of a gaff hook handle. He retrieves that end of the line and ties it around the bull rail, leaving the bow and stern untied. He stands for a moment, watching the water seep around the rivets into the bottom of his boat, trying to decide if he should bail his boat now or if he can wait until later. He considers the leaking water for some time then shrugs his shoulders and walks away.

He moves slowly. His walk up the ramp is sluggish, a long striding stroll, his long arms swinging in a slow rhythm. All this is done with an aristocratic disposition that borders on arrogance. He glides up the ramp and stands on one edge of the deck that's next to the outside wall of Everett's office under the overhang of the roof. Leaning on the top rail, he rolls a homemade cigarette. Gently and with close regard, he takes a long drag, then he exhales, watching the blue smoke dissipate into the morning air. Smiling, he holds his head back so his face will catch the direct rays of the morning sun. He comes to this same spot every day at the same time.

Bob calls to him, "Morning, Arlo."

Arlo keeps his head in the same position. "A fine morning, ain't it?"

Rich whispers under his breath, "Bet he don't worry about nothin'."

Arlo hears him but doesn't change his pose. He says under his breath, "Not much." He blows more smoke in the air.

The day moves on. Folks begin to come and go to the grocery store. Some just sit, still waking up, aiming to find someone to talk with, wondering if maybe there's the odd beer in the float house that they might have overlooked, or maybe the couple at the head of the ramp might share. A drink and some conversation would be good. The man petting the dog looks up at Arlo and waves; Arlo nods in return.

Arlo hears footsteps behind him. "Hey, Sue, when did you get back? I saw you leave on the mail plane last week."

"I just got back a couple of days ago."

"What's up?"

"I had to go to the hospital in Ketchikan for a medical checkup," she says, raising her eyebrows. "I thought for sure I would need to have some sort of procedure."

"Oh."

"You damn right I did."

Arlo is silent but keeps nodding as if he understands everything. He doesn't have any idea what Sue is talking about.

Although no one is close, she lowers her voice to a conspiratorial whisper, leaning closer to Arlo. "I was spotting blood in my panties. Well, shit-o-dear, I haven't had a period for Christ knows how long. I ain't no doctor, but I can tell you that is not a good thing." The more she talks, the more she lowers her head until she is looking at Arlo with her eyes glaring intently upward from beneath her eyebrows, then suddenly, in direct contrast to her clandestine posture, she begins talking in a very loud voice.

"No, that's not good."

Arlo asks, "Did you get to see your doctor?"

"Ain't got no doctor. I just caught the mail plane to Ketchikan, figured I had some sort of cancer. So when I get on the plane, I explained to the pilot, in great detail mind you, how serious this whole situation was and that we should just skip the landing at Coffman Cove and get right down there to Ketchikan, being that I probably had cancer."

"How'd that go?"

"That rude bastard didn't even listen to me. He just sits there like he has a stick up his ass and don't even say a word."

"You don't say?"

"You see what I was up against."

"Yes, I do."

"I get off that plane and calls myself a taxi and marched right into that emergency room and just told them right out that I was there because I had somethin' serious wrong with me. You know what they said?" She looks directly at Arlo, waiting for him to answer.

"What?"

"They says, 'What is it?' I told them it was some sort of cancer. They says, 'Who's your doctor?' So I says right to that doctor's face"— she points her finger at Arlo—"'Why in the name of God Almighty do you think I came to the emergency room?' Do you know what he said next?"

"No."

"'Do you have any insurance?'" Now she puts her hands on her hips and cocks her hips to one side. "So I had to explain to them very carefully and slowly like they was a bunch of small children that 'if I would've had insurance, then I would most likely have a doctor and I would've gone to see him first, but since I don't have either one, then that's why I am standing here in this emergency room talking to you.'" She raises her hands in the air then slaps them on her hips in complete frustration. "Where do they get these people!?"

Arlo nods again. "Beats me."

"Then some little bucktoothed gal comes up to me and says, since I don't have any insurance, 'Who's going to pay the bill?' I said I didn't have any idea. Sure as hell I didn't have any money left after I had to pay my plane ticket to town, but that didn't change the fact that I had some sort of cancer that was causin' me to have blood spots on my panties."

"Then what happened?"

"They finally do some tests, and the doctor comes into my room. He looks like he's about eighteen years old, and he tells me that he don't think there is anything wrong but 'we' should keep an eye on it. I tells him how in the hell would he know if something is wrong or not, he ain't ever had no blood spots in his drawers 'sept maybe if he had hemorrhoids." She shrugs in complete frustration. "By this time, I'm gettin' real tired of explain' things to this kid that he should already know, so I didn't go into that, but I did wonder how 'we' was goin' to keep an eye on 'things' when he would be in Ketchikan and I ain't."

"I see what you mean."

She stands by Arlo at the rail, staring at the water for a few moments. "Did you read about that woman that got that flesh-eating bacteria on her face and it ate her face right off and there wasn't nothin' she or anybody else could do about it?"

"No, can't say that I did."

"Well, she got that at a hospital. It just eats her face right off, and there is nothin' anybody can do about it!"

"I'm pretty sure I never did hear about that."

Sue slices the air with an open hand with a chopping motion. "Well, she *did* get it at the hospital, and it just ate her face right off, and there was nothin' they could do about it."

"Oh."

"I better not get any of them staph infections either, damn hospitals."

Arlo smiles, showing his one tooth in front. "Is that right?"

"You damn right that's right." She looks warily over her shoulder as if someone might be standing there. "Has Everett opened the liquor store yet?"

"I believe he has."

"Been nice talkin' to you, Arlo."

Rich has been watching Sue and Arlo talk. As he walks close by with a shovel of ice, he asks, "What was that all about?"

"I guess you could say that whenever Sue gets an idea, because it's her idea, she thinks it's a good one. Just goes ahead on it, doesn't seem to sort anything out ahead of time."

Sue returns a few minutes later with a six-pack, hands one to Arlo on her way back to the ramp. Arlo is a person someone can talk to; he listens. He opens the can. It foams and drips down over his fingers and splats on the deck. It's warm, but is tastes pretty good, a fine day indeed.

At the sight of Arlo drinking a beer, the man on the fuel float stops petting the dog to watch. A fisherman calls from the back deck of his boat to the woman sitting in the plastic chair and the man sitting next to her. She is still bent forward, holding her head in her hands. "Have you guys had breakfast yet?"

She shakes her head no. The man sitting with her doesn't move.

"I have plenty. I'll fry up some king salmon. There's some beans and rice left over from last night."

The two sit silent.

The fisherman smiles. "Aw, come on. I'll fry up a couple of eggs and throw them on top of the beans and rice. I'm tellin' you right now it'll be good, never have had any complaints about my cookin'."

The two stand slowly and shuffle over to his boat, climb over the gunnel, and disappear into the wheelhouse, and the woman mumbles, "Sounds good."

The raven lands on the hatch cover and peers into the wheelhouse.

A skiff makes its way between two small islands, towing a buckskin-colored log with a pickaroon stuck in one end with the handle jutting up in the air. A tow rope is tied to the handle. As the day continues to get warmer, more people emerge from their boats. Some sit on coils of rope, on an empty bucket, or on a buoy. Others produce a folding chair or sit on a chunk of firewood, carefully selecting a spot that's free of dog droppings. The day moves on.

A fishing boat enters the cove; the captain is an older man. He ties his boat to the pilings beneath the loading boom. He removes the hatch cover and climbs down into the hold and tosses some ice blankets out on the deck. Rich lowers a tote until it rests on the deck of the boat. The older man methodically fills it with fish, tossing them into the tote. The first of them lands with a solid thunk as they hit the plastic bottom. When all the fish are loaded, he begins to clean the hold. He moves slowly and methodically. This completed, he rafts to another boat at the fuel float. After his boat is secure, he goes to his bunk and falls into a deep sleep.

Everett, sitting at his desk, takes a copy of the fish ticket from Bob. Bob says, "The refrigeration system for the ice maker quit. We're getting low on ice, and there are more boats on the way."

Everett sighs. "Third time this week." He reaches down and picks up a tool box that's nestled between his desk and the wall and shoulders his way past Bob, muttering to himself.

Bob stays standing in the doorway. "Lookin' good this morning, Kasey."

"Goodbye, Bob."

"Just tryin' to make conversation."

"Goodbye, Bob."

"But—"

"Not a chance, Bob."

He walks away, glancing back at the office door. Kasey is shaking her head as she turns to her computer and becomes lost in details. When the sound of the compressor on the ice maker interrupts her concentration, she looks at her watch and realizes it's already time for lunch. She rummages through her backpack and takes out a pint jar of canned salmon. She pops the lid off with the handle of her fork. It makes a sucking sound as the rubber seal separates from the rim of the jar. Searching through the other contents of her pack, she finds a ziplock bag filled with Saltine crackers. She crushes some of them into the jar of fish, soaking up the liquid. She eats directly out of the jar while distractedly pecking at the keyboard with one finger, making small changes on the spreadsheet. The phone rings; she holds the fork and jar in one hand and reaches for the phone with the other. "Hello . . . Yeah . . . OK . . . Thanks."

Everett walks through the door.

"They deposited that money in your account."

"Good."

Boats continue to arrive to sell fish, some with their holds crammed full, others with just a few lying on deck, covered with wet burlap sacks.

Some small children appear with fishing poles on the beach by the Mercantile. They make their way to the fuel float, chattering, moving back and forth the full length of the float, casting small silver lures, hoping to catch an errant salmon but are pleased with the occasional rock fish.

Two older children arrive in a skiff with a black plastic garbage bag stuffed with dirty clothes. They trudge unenthusiastically up the ramp and past Everett's office in grim fashion, having been told to do something in which they have no interest. When they reach the two washing machines just beyond the liquor store, they dump the clothes in without sorting them, put coins in the coin slots, jamb it indignantly into the box, and leave.

When the washing machine clicks on to the spin cycle, it begins shaking violently and begins to move across the floor. The switch that turns the machine off when the load is unbalanced doesn't work, hasn't for a couple of years. The sound reverberates down the breezeway and out onto the deck where Bob and Rich are working. *Whump, whump, whump, whump,* as it jumps around the room.

Everett struggles up from his chair, marches to the laundry room, raises the lid and rearranges the load, and watches to make sure it's balanced and working. He walks out by the generator shed and looks for the children, who are nowhere to be found. He thinks briefly that as long as he's here, he should remove the buckets and greasy rags from the generator shed. His hips hurt so badly he'll do it some other time. On his way back to his office, he stops to read the notices on the community bulletin board: "Outboard engine for sale—six horsepower, needs work, ran last year, $200.00—Dan."

"Need a case of pint canning jars, Jenny."

"Will chop firewood for canned fish or venison or money if you have any."

At the bottom is a piece of white cardboard with torn irregular sides. The writing on it is in black magic marker; it says, "Good reasons to live here. (1) The fishing is real good. (2) No road. (3) The hunting in good. (4) No cops."

When he looks up, Kasey is standing at the office door. "The mail plane will be here in half an hour."

"What do we have coming in today?"

Her reply is crisp and efficient. "There are oil filters for the generator, four pairs of Xtratuf boots, this week's lettuce and vegetables, coolant for the refrigeration units, and a hooker for Bob so he will quit pestering me."

He laughs. "You better cancel the hooker because you know what that would make me."

"Yeah, OK."

"You want me to talk to him?"

"I can handle it."

"Just let me know and I'll take care of it."

He makes a mental note to keep an eye on that; he can't afford to lose Kasey. He needs to figure out how to handle it without her finding out. *Worthless sons a' bitches.* As an afterthought, he calls to Kasey, "Tell those guys that have their skiffs tied at the airplane float, they need to move them."

She walks out of the office and crosses the deck close to where Bob and Rich are working. They glance at her as she passes. "You quit gawking at me and get to work!" At the railing, she stands next to Arlo and waves at a group of men next to the fuel pumps. "The mail plane will be here in about an hour. You need to move those skiffs."

"OK, Kasey, we got it."

Arlo smiles and nods.

She lingers next to him in the sun, relaxing for a moment. She turns to him. "Jeez, Arlo, when you stand out here in the sun and get all warmed up, you start to smell a little ripe." She waves her hand in front of her nose.

"Been havin' some problems with my water system. Guess I better get it fixed."

"If you need anything to get it done, we have lots of spare parts, odds and ends left over from other jobs. Let me know."

"I'll take a look at it tonight, thanks."

"No problem." When she walks back to the office, Bob and Rich keep their heads down.

A De Havilland Beaver floatplane arrives midafternoon. At the first sound of the engine, people begin emerging from boats, appearing from the community boardwalk and arriving in skiffs. They help tie up the plane and unload the freight. Kasey sorts through the pile of boxes and bags and private mail. People show each other what they've received and share news of recent events, all talking at the same time. Some sit on the bull rail, gesturing. The dock dogs move to the sounds of the conversations, hoping to catch a pat on the head or a scratch on the ear, or maybe someone might drop something edible.

A skiff comes into view; it's Randy. He side-ties to another skiff, walks unsteadily through it with his weight, making it bounce and roll. There's a bruise under one eye and a small cut on his nose.

Someone says, "Heard you got drunk last night."

"I suppose that would be a safe assumption most any night." He stands erect with his chin elevated, talking precisely. He has told everyone he has been to law school but decided it wasn't for him. It's accepted behavior to tell other people about your past but considered a breach of etiquette to directly ask what they did before coming north. That is their own business. But one night, after a few drinks, someone did ask Randy why he quit law school. In a rare display of profanity, he stated, in his own particular fashion, "Being a lawyer would be like spending your entire existence with your head in a cloud of somebody else's shit." All agreed with that assessment, nodding in unison.

As Randy walks up the ramp, Everett is waiting at the top, sucking bits of Copenhagen through the gaps in his teeth. "You're fired."

Randy holds one hand to his chest, displaying a posture of complete shock. "Everett, you fire me without hearing my rationale! Surely a person of your experience and background of managing people will understand that, on occasion, things may not be what they seem."

"You're fired, and that's what I understand!"

Randy continues on, ignoring Everett's comments, "You're familiar with those steps that descend that treacherous rock outcropping I must negotiate every morning on my way to my skiff? Well, the top step gave way as I was coming to work this morning. And just like that I was tumbling down those steps and onto the jagged rocks below." He snaps his fingers for emphasis and points to the blood on his nose.

Everett begins to turn away. Randy talks louder, with more passion. "I lay there on the rocks, unconscious for hours, being very fortunate indeed that the tide was on the ebb, or I would've never survived, but the very moment I became ambulatory, I treated my cuts and contusions and came to work." He points to the deck stacked with totes. "Knowing that I was particularly needed today because of the arrival of the packer from Petersburg!"

Everett clinches his jaw and retreats. As he enters the office, Kasey asks, "What happened?"

"Everyone thinks Randy got drunk last night, but I think he's just having a hard time, one of those rough patches he goes through."

"Fired him again, eh?"

"Yeah, I want to fire him, but I just can't make it stick. He's out there workin'."

As Randy walks past Rich, he asks, "How many times has he fired you?"

"Several."

"What did you do? Whack yourself in the face with a rock when you woke up late?"

Randy purses his lips while he puts on his rubber gloves, vowing not to dignify their plebeian comments with a response.

Then five boats arrive with holds full of fish, and the crew scrambles to get organized. Everett joins in to weigh fish on the hanging scale, recording the results on fish tickets—one copy for the fishermen and one copy for the Mercantile. He tries to help icing but finally gives up and stays with the scales. He sits on the steps of the ice house when his knees hurt so much he can't stand. Kasey thinks about helping, but quarterly reports are due. Instinctively, she reaches for a stack of fish tickets; there's only one.

Out on the dock, Bob is lifting a tote of fish from a boat. Everett nervously watches as the power winch grinds with a gravelly sound under the heavy load. He frantically motions the fisherman, watching from below, not to stand directly underneath. Something might give way. When the load is on deck, he turns back to the scale, dodging Randy and Rich moving an ice-filled tote. They lift the lid and begin shoveling. Before he can turn again, Kasey, now standing behind him, says loudly, "Everett!"

He jerks around. "Shit! You scared me to death." He places one hand on his chest, looking sternly at her. "Palpitations."

"Let me tell you something. If you don't die of a heart attack, I will kill you if you lose any of those fish tickets. I don't want to have to hunt you down every time I need them or find them lying all over the place. I'm trying to get the quarterly reports done."

He gives her a look of puzzled astonishment.

She lifts the flap of his wool vest, pushes her fingers into his shirt pocket, and pulls out several crumpled-up pieces of paper.

"Check your pockets."

After fumbling briefly, he produces two crumpled-up fish tickets. He hands them to her, and he begins to say something.

"Later, I'll be through in about forty minutes. We'll talk then."

The men all work in silence for the next few hours, until the last boat leaves. With the totes stacked and counted, ready for the packer, Rich and Bob sit to smoke. Randy finds things to do to keep his mind busy. There are things he doesn't want to think about.

As the day moves on, it begins to settle into the normal balance: Randy is once again employed, the mail plane is gone after leaving supplies, conversations on the fuel float fade into silence then start again. Somebody decides it's time for a nap. Everett and Kasey continue organizing details and balancing accounts, and the one-legged raven and the dogs give up on finding bacon and begin to seek other opportunities.

When Kasey and Everett begin closing the store and lock the office, it's a signal for whomever wants to assemble at the far end of the fuel float. There, just in front of the small float house, is a canvas canopy sewn onto a galvanized pipe framing. On each end of the gable is a small flag, the Alaska flag on one and the United States flag on the other. The canvas used to be a dark gray but is stained completely white with bird droppings. There are a couple of plastic chairs and several of painted bent steel, which have long been covered in rust, surrounding a plywood table. There's a wooden hand-painted sign that hangs under the gable that says Saloon.

The whole affair is shoved up against a dull-green round plastic sewage treatment tank that someone beach combed a few years back when a barge broke apart in a fall storm. Nobody needs it, but it's too good to throw away. Somebody arrives with a half case of beer and lays it on the table. Others gather and talk; some just sit and listen.

Arlo stays leaning on the cap rail, staring out over the water, and rolls another cigarette. Several ruddy turnstones move nervously along a water-soaked log covered in barnacles and green slime. They move quickly, sneaking a quick look here and there then moving on, ever vigilant to possible threats. Sometimes Arlo will have a beer at the Saloon, but not very often.

When darkness begins, he does a slow stroll to his skiff. His house is semihidden in a grove of giant spruce trees. As he comes into the gravel beach in front without slowing down, he raises the outboard at the last minute; allowing the skiff to skid up on the gravel beach. He fumbles around in the bottom of the skiff and picks up a chunk of webbing tied around a large rock. One end of a line is tied to the webbing; the other end is tied to the eye ring on the bow. He packs the rock up the beach until the line jerks tight, then drops it.

The trail from the beach is woven with large roots protruding, half buried, from the ground like giant veins bulging from stressed muscles. This is a place that never gets direct sunlight. The soil is constantly wet and soggy. Three slick-haired dogs bound down the trail, barking and wagging their whole bodies. Two of them are young, barely more than puppies. He stops to sit on one of the large roots, petting them all at once then each one individually, talking to them in hushed tones. They calm down and lean against his legs.

The house is cobbled together from planks of driftwood, some lumber Everett cut for him on the portable sawmill, used plywood, and odds and ends he scrounged from others. The foundation rests on tree roots and is propped up here and there with rocks from the beach.

The dogs follow him into the house and watch as he lights a kerosene lantern with a wooden match that he strikes into a flame with his thumbnail. He feeds them some dry dog food mixed with a thick gruel made from boiling carcasses of pink salmon. They growl and snuffle as they gulp the food. He watches for a moment. At the edge of the table is a homemade wooden box; Arlo undoes the latch, removing a can of chicken noodle soup. He eats out of the can with a metal spoon, not bothering to warm it on the stove; and when he's finished, he remains at the table, staring at the burning lamp, alternately rubbing his face with the back of one hand and then the other. After some time passes, he begins picking at the small splinters on the rough surface of the table, deep in thought. The dogs lie on their sides haphazardly under the table, ears flopping here and there. After a trip to the outdoor toilet, he lies down on his bed in one corner of the room, pulling a musty wool blanket over him. The dogs immediately leap on the bed with him. Just before he drifts off into a deep sleep, he remembers he told Kasey he would see what parts he needed to fix his water pipes. He quickly decides to do it in the morning. He puts his arms around his dogs and falls into a deep sleep followed by a full-throated snore.

Everett returns to his house well after dark, stumbling on the bumps and humps of the trail. The beam of light from his flashlight is next to useless. What little daylight remains is sucked out of the air by the trees and bushes, making the darkness so thick it feels like an extra layer of skin. By the time he reaches his house, his body feels like it's on fire.

His wife asks, "How was your day?"

"I fired Randy again. Let me see what else." He tries to isolate at least some of the details: Kasey and the fish tickets, how he can't bring himself to actually fire Randy, if he should keep selling liquor to people that drink too much, how he's going to talk to Bob and Rich about bothering Kasey, have any of the fish been on ice too long. He hates to just sit there and not have a conversation with his wife who has been home alone all day, but all he can do is look at the beer she has put in front of him. She waits a moment then begins preparing dinner. He pulls the note asking for more credit at the grocery store from the inside pocket of his vest and stares at it uncomprehendingly.

"We bought a lot of fish today, it's been a good day."

"Good."

"The packer didn't make it this afternoon. It'll be here about 11:00 PM. I'll eat later." He goes to the sofa and lies down; he's asleep in an instant.

Everett lives a tricky existence.

2

A New Roof

The VHF radio crackles, "This is the US Coast Guard, radio sector Juneau back to the call. Are you in need of assistance?"

"Yes."

"What is the nature of your problem?"

"Boat's on fire."

"Are you in immediate danger?"

"Sure seems like it."

"How many people are on board, and what are their ages?"

"Just me."

"What's your location?"

"I am at the first red channel marker at the south end of Rocky Pass."

"What is your latitude and longitude? What color is your boat?"

"Color? I gotta go, it's gettin' hot in here."

"Captain, what's the name of your boat?"

Silence.

"Coast Guard calling the vessel at the south end of Rocky Pass."

Silence.

"Pan, pan. Pan, pan. A vessel has reported from the south end of Rocky Pass that there is a fire on board. Any vessels in that area are asked to keep a lookout and render assistance."

At the fuel float, last night's dampness is being steamed from the canvas covering the Saloon. The outside walls of the float house next to the Saloon are starting to feel warm. Inside, the two men and a woman are beginning to stir, stretching an arm here or a leg there, moving or shaking this or that body part. It's an experiment to find out which joint or muscle is going to object the most. They continue testing as they trickle out onto the fuel float, a managed ritual to get some blood moving, done in complete silence. When they are all standing upright, one of them points. "Hey, look!"

Through a small cut between two of the islands on the west side of the cove, a tall, lanky man in bib overalls is rowing a small plastic punt. When he sees them, he stops for a moment then turns and comes their way. His legs are crossed and folded in front of him, his knees sticking out past the sides of the punt. His arms are long and gangly, and the oars are short; he towers above the punt. The combination makes an awkward mixture of movements that reflect on the flat water; steadily and gracelessly he makes his way to the float, to the three huddled together in the morning's dampness. The man rests with one hand on the bull rail then climbs onto the float, dangling his feet in the skiff, looking at nothing. His thick, full beard covers most of his chest; it's matted with saltwater and sweat. The hair on his head is long, falling loosely on his shoulders, hanging in careless curls. He looks to be in his late twenties, is wearing a baseball cap and bib overalls. The cap is jammed on his head, and the tightness of the hat band makes his hair stick out all the way around his head. Now he looks at them as if he's just discovered they were there.

"Just lost my boat."

There is a collective sigh as they shake their heads: losing a boat is like losing a family member or a body part.

"Fire started in the engine room, don't have any idea how, called the Coast Guard, but they wanted a bunch of details that I didn't have time to give 'em. Got too hot to stick around by the radio so just got in my skiff and started to row."

"How long you been rowin'?"

"Let me see, since yesterday afternoon, I guess. It all kind of runs together, the fire, rowin' all night, didn't think I would make it, lucky the wind didn't come up." His words are slurred from fatigue. "Yeah, been rowin' all night."

He tries to say something coherent; his lips move hidden under his thick beard. Gathering himself, he says distinctly, "Do you think it's gonna rain?"

The three instinctively look at the sky. "No, probably not."

"Hard to say."

"Well, it might." This is followed by head scratching and shrugging.

The man stands stiffly and pulls the skiff up on the dock to rest one side on the bull rail, making a small lean-to then crawls into the space underneath and is soon sound asleep. He stays asleep the rest of that day and all that night. In the morning, when he crawls out from under the skiff, someone hands him a can of beans and a beer. He quickly finishes both, twisting and bending the aluminum beer can, tearing it in half, and tosses it in the water. He nods. "That tasted real good, thank you."

"Sure."

"Well, yesterday, I had a fish boat and a future. Today I got nothin', so that means I'm lookin' for work. My name is Ralph Bodeen." When he pronounces his last name, he bites down hard on the double *e*, making it sound as if there are three, maybe four of them. "I am without resources. I need work."

There is muttering, "Work?" now head scratching, sideways glances, puzzled looks. "Yeah, well, I don't know for sure if there is any work."

"Everett has a full crew. He keeps trying to fire Randy, but that don't work very good. Randy just goes to work anyway."

The woman says, "Maybe a deckhand job will come up but sure don't know of any right now."

Someone else offers. "Yep, I believe that most everybody that fishes out of here has got themselves a deckhand."

The woman turns and yells at Arlo, who is standing at his regular spot by Everett's office. "Arlo!"

"Yo."

"This guy is lookin' for work, just lost his boat. Any ideas?"

Arlo points to the ramp to the community walkway just beyond the fuel float and a small house that sits next to it. It's sided with rigid pink insulation. Arlo addresses Ralph Bodeen. "The lady that lives in that house has a bear that has been hanging out in her blueberry bushes and sleepin' on her porch. She offered me a hundred dollars if I would shoot it, but I really don't want to."

"You mean that place?"

"Yep."

"Thanks."

Putting his skiff in the water, Ralph Bodeen rows to the beach just below the pink house and scrambles over the rocks, through the tangle of blueberry bushes to the front porch. He notices several piles of fresh bear droppings as he moves through the brush; the droppings are the same color as blueberries. He knocks on the door. An elderly woman answers the door. The wrinkles on her face run vertically from the corners of her eyes to under her chin. It's a face of someone who has spent their life outdoors.

"Yes?" She holds the door just partially open, wondering.

Removing his hat, he holds it to his chest, covering the lower part of his beard, a token of respect. "Ma'am, my name is Ralph Bodeen. My fish boat has just burned up, and I don't have any money or prospects."

She nods.

"Them folks over there on that float"—she looks that way to see that they are all standing together next to the Saloon, watching—"tell me that you will pay a hundred dollars to have someone kill a bear for you."

She opens the door a little wider, assuming a businesslike demeanor. "He is a nice enough bear, but I can't have him sleeping on my porch. The other night he was trying to open the front door. I have tried everything I know to make him leave, but he's a young bear and I have come to believe he's not very bright. Nothing has worked. I'd shoot him myself, but my shoulders hurt so bad from arthritis I don't know if I could hold a gun good enough to kill him, and I wouldn't want to wound him and then have him go off somewhere. That would just make things worse." She hugs herself, sighing a loud sigh, then tilts her head in the direction of the community boardwalk, which abuts her house. "Over there." She points to where another walkway snakes through the trees joining it. "Just the other side of that walkway that Mary built. Look, you see right there." She points a crooked finger. "The one with the deer skulls nailed to it."

"Yep."

"Well, just stay on the boardwalk and just up that little hill. It turns to the left a bit. Right there on the water side is a patch of blueberries. That bear is taking a nap in those blueberry bushes. I just checked on him a few minutes ago."

"Do you have a gun?"

She turns into the house and reappears with a 30:30 Winchester lever action rifle. It's covered in rust.

"Does it work?"

"Did last time I used it, it's loaded."

He jacks the lever down, opening the magazine, looks into the breach, and sees a shell in the chamber. She hands him four extra cartridges. He walks up the boardwalk, and just where the woman said he would be lies the little black bear, rolled up in a ball sleeping. *About a year old*, he thinks. Leaning on the handrail, he watches the bear breathing, its chest moving up and down rhythmically. Sharply he says, "Hey!"

The bear raises its head to look at him. *Blam!* He shoots it between the eyes, quickly ejecting the casing into the air, catching it with one hand. The bear slumps limply, staying in a ball as if it is still napping. Ralph Bodeen walks back to the pink house, where the woman is waiting for him on her porch. She hands him a hundred-dollar bill; he hands her the gun and the spent cartridge. "I saved the brass. I didn't know if you reload them or not."

"Thank you." She turns back into the house. He walks off the porch, deep in thought.

Another woman is waiting on the boardwalk. She moves in front of him when he tries to walk past, forcing him to stop. She is a thin woman with skin so white it verges on incandescent, wearing loose cotton pants that just barely hang on her hips. The top of her rubber boots come slightly below her knees. The pants have been cut with pinking shears just at the top of the boots. The boots flop against her shins when she takes a step. Her flannel shirt is missing a button or two. There are streaks of gray in her hair; she is angry.

He takes his hat off, holding it over his chest. "Ma'am."

"What have you just done!"

He looks over his shoulder. "I just shot that little bear up there in that blueberry patch."

"You mean that baby bear that has been living here this spring?"

He looks away for a moment, staring out over the cove. "Well, I guess I don't rightly know for sure, but the one I shot might be a year or so old, maybe two years. Now that I think about it, if his momma's not around, he must be closer to two years." He scratches his head. "Yep, I would say two years old."

"DAMN YOU, DAMN YOU, DAMN YOU! That bear was just taking a nap in the sun! He wasn't hurting anything." Tears well up in her eyes, which further frustrates her. She shakes her clinched fists in his face. "Why in the world would you want to shoot that little bear?"

"For a hundred dollars."

"What!"

He points to the pink insulation showing through the bushes. "My boat just burned up and I am without resources, and that woman over there paid me a hundred dollars to shoot that bear."

She begins to sob loudly as her face floods with tears. She staggers to the handrail, gripping it tightly with both hands. "It was just a little bear." She is begging.

Ralph Bodeen walks back to the pink house and knocks loudly on the door. The woman in her knitted shawl opens the door just far enough to poke her head out.

"Yes?"

"There is a woman over there," he nods in the direction of the sobbing noises, "she don't think shooting that bear was such a good idea."

"That's Mary. She lives on that point over there just across from the fuel float. It's just that she believes everything has a soul. She's one of them Buddhists or some such thing. I don't know exactly, but it's one of them Eastern religions."

"Well, huh?"

"She also just lost her youngest sister in some senseless accident. The poor kid was just walking home with her friends, and some guy has a stroke or some such thing, veers off the road and onto the sidewalk, and she is dead, just like that. One minute she is talking to her friends, and the next minute she is dead. Now that don't make any sense at all. It don't matter how you look at it. That's all I know about it except it happened somewhere in California. Mary is a real nice woman. It's just that she is a little shaky right now."

"Well, huh?" He watches Mary sobbing through the bushes for a moment before turning back to the lady in the shawl. "Do you have a butcher's knife and a hatchet I could borrow? I would like to butcher that bear. The salmon ain't in the creeks yet. It should be good eating, probably taste like blueberries."

The woman looks at him, askance. "Well, as much as a bear can taste like blueberries."

"Yes, ma'am, I do understand that they can be a little on the gamey side. You gotta treat 'em right."

She disappears into the house and returns with a large butcher's knife and a whetstone. "The hatchet's over there." She points to a pile of wood and a chopping block with a hatchet stuck in it.

He places the stone in the front pocket of his bib overalls, and with the butcher's knife in one hand and the hatchet in the other, he turns back to the boardwalk. Mary is still standing at the hand rail, sniffling and wiping her eyes. Looking up, she sees Ralph Bodeen with the butcher's knife and the hatchet. "OH MY GOD! No! No!" She turns running to her walkway, disappearing among the trees, continuing on to the beach in front of her house. He hears her yelling in the distance, "Help! Help!" When she reaches the beach, she yells to the group standing at the end of the fuel float, still staring in the direction of the gunshot.

They turn when they hear her. "What's goin' on?"

"That man has a big knife and a hatchet, and he killed that bear!"

44

One of the men says, "You mean he killed that bear with a knife and a hatchet, shit! I never did hear of such a thing."

"No, you dummy, he shot that baby bear, so I confronted him, then he comes walking toward me with a big knife and a hatchet. He's a crazy man, and he's after me, so that's why I am asking for help, get it?"

"Where is he now?"

"Right behind me, up there." She looks toward the trees and points to just above the high-tide line. Do something!"

"You mean he has a knife and a hatchet and a gun and he's crazy and you want me to do something?" He looks amazed.

"Yes, goddamn it." She walks backward into the water, keeping her eyes on the tree line.

There are puzzled looks and shrugs from the group; a muffled discussion follows. A man from a fish boat comes out on the back deck. "I'll go take a look and see what's goin' on." He rows his skiff over to the access ramp and walks slowly up the incline to the boardwalk. When he reaches Mary's walkway, he stops and studies it carefully. It is cobbled together with shaved poles and driftwood, sectioned off with a gantry every twenty feet or so. Nailed to the crossbeams of the gantries are bleached deer skulls staring out into nothingness with their hollow eye sockets. Several small mounds of smooth stones are placed randomly down its full length. The whole affair meanders impulsively through the trees and bushes. The man finds it puzzling to think about but considers it for a moment before moving on until he finds Ralph Bodeen, who is taking the entrails out the bear. They are warm and silky on his hands as he lifts and pushes them out onto the ground.

"Howdy."

Ralph looks up at the sound of the voice. "Howdy."

"What's goin' on?"

"Thought I'd get the guts out of this bear before it started to go sour."

"That's a good idea. What are you gonna do with it?"

Ralph reaches way up into the chest cavity with both hands, grabbing the esophagus with one hand, holding the knife in the other. With a short quick stroke, he cuts it far up inside the throat. He stands with blood dripping from his hands and arms, turning to face the man standing on the boardwalk. His shirt sleeves are pulled up beyond his elbows. The butcher's knife hangs casually from the ends of his fingers. "I am going to smoke it and eat it. I am a man without resources. Fall is coming, and steps need to be taken to get through the winter. I have a hundred dollars. I can buy some rice and beans, matches, and toilet paper." He hesitates for a moment then smiles a short smile. "I lost all of my toilet paper when my boat burned up. I have no time to lose."

The man nods in agreement. "Well, it's a start, and we"—he nods at the fuel float—"will help out with whatever we can. It won't be much 'cause whenever we get some money ahead, we pretty much drink it up, but we can give you a hand with some of the little things you might need. Just let us know."

"Thank you, and now that you have offered, I can use some line so's I can hang this bear meat in a tree and smoke it before it goes bad."

"That won't be a problem. I can get it for you. Everett has some canning jars and lids for sale, and I'll scrounge up a canner from someone." The man turns to leave then stops. "That woman that lives on the point over there thinks you was after her with that knife and hatchet."

"Yeah, that's what I figured. She's fairly jumpy, and I didn't get a chance to explain anything. She's kinda hard to talk to."

The man shrugs.

Ralph points with his bloody arm and hand. "You see that walkway she built?"

"I did."

"Can't figure that out."

"Me neither. I'll tell her that you're just cutting up the bear, going to smoke it and eat it, don't mean her no harm." The man nods. "I'll explain that to her."

"I'd appreciate that. I'll get this carcass skinned out some where's so she don't have to look at it. Looks too much like a human without the hide on him. She might think it's somebody she knows. She might be one of them Buddhists or somethin' like that."

"That wouldn't be good."

Ralph Bodeen turns to his work, making a smooth straight cut with the point of his knife just under the skin down the inside of one hind leg. After making the cut, he lays the blade flat against the inside of the skin, carefully slicing the fat from the hide. The man returns to his skiff and begins to row back to the fuel float. Mary is still waiting, waist deep in water, and is beginning to shake from the cold.

"He just gutted that bear and is skinnin' it. He's gonna smoke it and eat it. He didn't mean to scare you, but you left so quick he never did have time to explain that to you."

"Eat it?"

Someone at the end of the fuel float says, "He just lost his boat. He is a man without resources." The man looks pleased with himself for making a correct assessment of the situation.

Mary turns, trying to hurry out back to the beach, but is held back by the depth of the water. When she walks ashore, the water sloshes out of her boots. She staggers to a log and struggles to take them off.

For the next few days, Ralph Bodeen lives in a makeshift lean-to just above the high-tide line. It is made from his plastic punt and a blue tarp with a few freshly cut spruce limbs placed on top. The bear is cut into quarters and hangs from some limbs of the tree he sits under. The skinned front quarters do look like the shoulders, wrists, and forearms of a human hanging eerily in the trees. There is a low smudge of smoke coming from a small fire. The smoke permeates the bushes and trees like a thick fog, obscuring the whole scene except when small puffs of wind randomly expose portions of the hanging meat. Ralph Bodeen sits patiently, poking the fire with a stick, occasionally placing a green bough carefully on the coals, watching the smoke curl up into the trees. After a few hours, he stands to poke the meat with his finger, testing its progress. Then he holds his nose close to the meat, sniffing.

One evening a large yacht noses its way into the cove. There are people on the bow, taking pictures and talking. One of them sees Ralph sitting in his bib overalls, smoking the bear carcass. They quickly turn and leave.

By the time the late spring storms blow in from the Gulf of Alaska, Ralph Bodeen has proven to be handy and resourceful: he hires out to sand and paint boats and whatever carpentry jobs need done. There is no job that is too small or difficult for him to accomplish. He shows up on time, sober, and works hard. When he's not working for others, he fashions a tent with a floor and half walls from used lumber and driftwood. The covering is made from tarps that are stretched over a frame of poles cut from the forest. There is a small barrel stove made from a twenty-gallon oil drum that sits at the rear of the tent. Just inside the front flap is a cupboard enclosed in seine web that allows air to circulate freely, keeping the contents cool. One shelf is stacked full with canned bear meat, another with canned salmon. Under his bunk are two sacks, one of rice and one of beans; the bear's skin is on the floor. With the woman's gun, he has killed two deer, and they are also smoked and canned in jars.

His camp is tucked in on the far end of a finger of water that lies between two rock outcroppings. The rocks and tall trees, combined with the impenetrable tangle of bushes, provide protection from all sides. His small punt is anchored with a rock just off the gravel beach. He takes showers at the Mercantile in the shower provided for fishermen but is often seen bathing in the ocean near where his skiff is anchored. His naked body is covered in thick black hair, bone thin, with his ribs and backbone poking up from under his pale white skin, starkly contrasting with the muted grays and greens of water and trees.

The one-legged raven has been hanging out at his camp, and Ralph feeds it scraps from his meals. It will sit on the ridgepole of the tent and watch him bathe. He has named it Captain Ahab. Sometimes when he's bathing in the stillness of the morning, Ahab, perched on the ridgepole or sitting hidden in the trees, will make a sound like a large drop of water striking a flat surface; it's a solitary, isolated, prehistoric sound that almost echoes through the trees. In the silence, the sound is unnerving and freezes him in midmotion; after waiting and watching for a moment, he continues.

Everett makes his daily trip down the trail to the Mercantile with his list and a dozen eggs under his arm, stopping at his favorite rock by the trail, watching morning come over the flat water of the cove. He wonders how something like a view gets so closely attached to someone like him. Kasey arrives every morning in her skiff, marching up the ramp to the office to immediately begin sorting through the invoices, shaking her head and muttering. Arlo assumes his position at the railing, lighting a cigarette and blowing the smoke slowly into the air. Rich and Bob yell over the edge of the dock to awaken a captain who has fallen asleep, waiting to sell his fish. Every morning the two men and a woman emerge from their small float house at the end of the fuel float, slowly moving their arms and legs. The dogs stir and scratch. The one-legged raven hops from the bull rail to snatch some tidbit from between the deck planks of the float. The dogs notice and begin sniffing for other opportunities. The days become longer. Ralph fits into the cadence of the cove.

When Ralph and Mary meet on the boardwalk, he always removes his hat, holding it to his chest, saying, "Ma'am," and she nods formally in return. The cove is too small and remote to support a feud. If things go sour, there isn't any help other than what you can deliver yourself. Things get worked out or just get lived with; just like the weather, they're bound to happen, so it's just a matter of how a person deals with them.

The cove is a good harbor, but there are some storms that blow so hard they touch everything: williwaws accelerate down mountains, uprooting trees, causing havoc and destruction. One such storm slams into the cove, rocking boats tied at the fuel float. Folks lurch out into roaring darkness, tying extra lines on their boats. It's so loud they yell in each other's ears to be heard. The howling masks the sound of large trees being blown over. Their large root balls jut up in the air, clinging to rocks and dirt. That night the wind blows, the cedar shakes from the north side of the roof of Mary's boathouse; it's slicked clean with just the one-by-twelve-inch boards that sheet the rafters left. They glisten in the wetness, and water drips heavily through open seams. The large drops strike the floor below with a noisy thudding.

When daylight breaks, Mary is standing in the pouring rain, looking at the damage, her clothing soaked, her hair plastered to her head and face.

This has been a tough year. My baby sister, that little bear, now this. What could possibly be next?

She turns at a sound behind her to see Ralph Bodeen, equally wet and bedraggled, standing, holding his hat to his chest. Rain is pelting down on his thick hair.

"Ma'am."

She looks at him in complete exasperation. "I was just standing here, thinking what else could possibly go wrong for me, and here you are."

"Ma'am?"

"Oh, never mind." She turns walking toward her house in long gangly steps, holding her wet hair to one side of her face to keep it from her eyes. Her free arm swings in an exaggerated arc, boot tops slapping against her shins, lips pursed, her head tilted to one side.

Ralph Bodeen slowly turns as she walks past him so that he is always facing her. As she reaches her porch, she turns back to him with a puzzled look on her face. He stays standing there in the rain with his hat held to his chest.

"What are you doing here?" she demands.

"Pretty bad storm last night. I come to see if your outfit made it through OK."

Irritated, she says, "As you can see, I lost the shakes from that side of my boat shed roof."

"Yes, ma'am, I do see that."

Still riled, Mary asks snidely, "And how did your outfit come through the storm?"

"Blew the canvas off the roof, but I got it back together, after a fashion. It'll work."

She looks at him, squinting her eyes. "OK, now that we have all of that sorted out, you may be on your way." She points in the direction of his camp.

He says abruptly, "I can fix it."

"You just said that you had everything put back together. I assumed that meant your camp is already fixed."

"I was talkin' about your roof."

She puts her hands on her hips. "I don't have any money or material for such a project."

"All I need is some roofing nails. I can make the shakes."

"I can't pay you."

"Oh, things will work out."

She is suddenly aware that her clothes are wet and clinging to her body and her small breasts. Grasping the wet cloth with both hands, she gathers some of the loose material and pulls it over her front, folding it in a determined way. "I'll not be trading anything for a roof, mister, and you don't even think I will."

He stares at her, and when he realizes the meaning of what she's saying, his face flushes a bright red. He stuffs his hat firmly on his head, making his wet hair flare out to the sides. He turns to leave; she sees that the side button of his OshKosh bib overalls is undone, revealing bare skin where his underwear should be. As he walks away, his pant leg rides up, showing he isn't wearing any socks. The red in his face has migrated down his neck, disappearing beneath his shirt. The embarrassment is complete.

As he starts through the trees at the edge of her property, she calls out, "Mr. Bodeen, Mr. Bodeen!"

He keeps walking.

"Mr. Bodeen, please come back!"

He stops, turns, and walks back to stand in front of her, takes his hat off, and holds it to his chest.

"Ma'am?"

She folds her hands in front of her. "Mr. Bodeen, I fear I have misjudged you and your intentions. It seems I have been hasty in my discernments." The rain increases, creating a rumbling sound as it strikes the porch roof. He blinks the water out of his eyes.

"Ma'am?"

"Would you like a cup of coffee?" She motions to a wooden bench on the porch.

He hesitates. "This ain't goin' exactly the way I thought it would."

"Have a seat." She motions again to the bench. When he sits, he sits on the front edge of the seat, hat in hand, ready to leave in a hurry if need be. She disappears into the house and returns with hot coffee. He stands to take the cup, waiting until she is seated before he sits back down. She examines him in silence. His wet skin is beginning to steam from the heat of his body, but he doesn't seem chilled at all. The steam rises in twisting columns then disappears. The redness begins to leave his face, but she can see that he is still very nervous.

"Maybe we should try to make a new start. Things didn't begin very well."

"Yes, ma'am."

"I'm afraid I didn't react very well, did I?"

"I don't talk too good."

"Yes, well . . ."

He blurts out, "Don't make no sense t'all losin' your baby sister like that. I don't care how you slice that up, it still ain't right." He's embarrassed all over again at his awkward attempt at conversation.

She looks at him closely. "Word does get around, doesn't it?"

He nods uncomfortably.

"How should I call you, Mr. Bodeen?"

"It don't matter to me, ma'am."

"Then Mr. Bodeen it shall be."

"Ma'am."

They sit without talking, sipping coffee, watching the rain. Mr. Bodeen places his cup on the floor as he stands. "Ma'am, I best be goin'."

"Mr. Bodeen, thank you for your kind offer to put a new roof on my boat shed, but I feel a person should pay their own way. It breeds independence, you know."

"Yes ma'am." He hurries away.

The storm is followed by a few good days that allows people and things to heal, dry out a bit, repair damage, and the critical process of comparing this storm to other storms. "Remember that storm that hit us over in Beauclerc a few years back? By golly, we couldn't even stand up; bet it blew over a hundred."

"I do remember. I believe it was in September or maybe early October, never seen anything like it."

"Yep, it was a bad one. We were lucky to ride that one out, dragged anchor all night."

"Jesus, I hate that."

The weather stays mild and sunny for days, and soon the talk of storms peters out and drifts on to other things: "Have those Neck Lake silvers showed up yet?" "Have the wolves thinned out the deer?" "How high will the price of fuel be this winter?" "Does all of this good weather mean that Mother Nature is just resting up for some real nasty stuff?" These discussions at the end of the fuel float at the Saloon question the very nature of things; it's important. Most evenings the one-legged raven sits on the sewage treatment container, cocking his head from side to side, listening to these conversations.

Unexpectedly, the sunny days continue. Mary sits on her porch when her daily routines are complete, enjoying the sunsets. She tries to take advantage of this time to use her porch as a place to meditate in the evening but finds it difficult. The shed roof with its shingles blown away somehow competes with her concentration, so she meditates about the roof. One day she skips her morning routine and makes her way through the woods to Ralph Bodeen's camp. As she breaks over the small ridge overlooking the cove, she sees that he is bathing in the ocean, up to his chest in the water, rinsing soap from his hairy head and shoulders. Huffing, he blows the water away from his mouth and nose as it cascades down over his head. He bends forward, ducking his head under the surface, and repeats the process. The sound is magnified because there are no other sounds. Mary thinks he looks like a bear searching for salmon when he ducks under the surface. The one-legged raven perched on the ridge pole begins making a clicking noise with its tongue. Suddenly Ralph Bodeen stands very still. Mary steps behind a tree and calls out loudly, "Hello, the camp!"

"Hang on till I get some clothes on." He gingerly walks over the gravel in bare feet, taking a moment to towel dry with part of an old blanket and puts on his coveralls. "OK, ma'am, I'm dressed."

She steps from behind the tree. "I apologize for coming unannounced, Mr. Bodeen."

"Don't know how else you could do it."

"Yes, of course."

"What's goin' on?"

"I have been thinking and was wondering if you had time to come over for a cup of coffee this afternoon. I would like to talk to you about your idea for a new roof on the boat shed."

"OK."

"What time could I expect you?"

"Toward evening."

Just before sundown, he walks out of the trees, the raven following along. The bird perches on a branch nearby.

Mary nods in that direction. "Looks like you've made a friend."

"Yes, ma'am, I call him Ahab because he's just got that one leg. He's good company, he don't hardly say nothin'."

"Would that be as in Captain Ahab from the novel *Moby Dick*?"

"Yes, ma'am."

"Well, Mr. Bodeen, you seem to have many more components than one would think at first glance."

"You were sayin' about the roof?"

She considers the change in conversation and him for a moment. "Yes, a couple of things come to mind. One is I would like to know how long it would take you to replace the roof. Another is I am still not willing to accept a new roof as an act of charity, so some sort of recompense will be needed to be figured out, and one final thing is, are you a drinking man?"

"Well, huh. Everett has a shake fro, I have a few rounds of cedar to make shake bolts at my camp, so with makin' the shakes and puttin' 'em on, I think a day or two this side of a week would do it." He forges ahead, "Yes, I do like to have a drink or two when time or money allows, but I'm not a real good drinkin' man like them folks." He points to the Saloon and the group huddled under the canvas top, around a half case of beer. Most are engaged in animated conversation. One woman is taking a long drag from a marijuana cigarette, holding the smoke in as long as possible then exhaling with a loud "Ahhhhhhhh!" She exclaims loudly, "Whoa!" then reaches for a beer. He keeps pointing. "That's what I call some pretty good drinkin' men."

Mary smiles. "When you say 'drinkin' men,' I assume you mean that to be inclusive of the ladies as well?"

"Yes, ma'am, and I hope you get my meaning. I consider the comment universal."

"I do, Mr. Bodeen. What about compensation?"

"Well, huh."

"You may think on it if you like."

"I have thought on it."

"And?"

"Are you one of them Buddhists?"

"I have been reading and studying about Buddhism for some time now, and I'm hoping to learn more, but I don't know if I could honestly say I actually am a Buddhist, but I'm certainly headed in that direction."

"That walkway of yours with the deer skulls and all of that other stuff, is that some sort of Buddhist deal?"

She looks a bit chagrined. "Actually, that is left over from when I aspired to learn more about sorcery. I thought I wanted to be a sorceress, but I wasn't able to completely understand all I needed to know. I kind of like the walkway though."

"Would that be like a witch?"

"No, I am not a witch, and I must admit the whole idea sounds quite eccentric. What does this have to do with compensation for the new roof?"

"Well, ma'am, I don't rightly know much about that whole deal, but I'd guess there is all different kinds of Buddhism just like any other kind of religion. I've heard that some of them think that all things have a soul, even worms and stuff like that. So, a person is supposed to be nice to everything so's when a person dies, they won't have to come back as a bug that lives in a horse turd, or somethin' of that nature."

She grins. "That is the general idea, but I think for me it's more like if I try to do right by others, I will be better off, you know, things will go better for everyone."

"Can anybody act that way if they want to?"

"Mr. Bodeen, I wish more people would act that way. The world would be a better place."

"Well, ma'am, wouldn't that be a reason I could build you a new roof without askin' nothin' in return?"

She gives him a thoughtful look. "My goodness, Mr. Bodeen, you are much wilier than you appear. It seems you have managed this conversation in such a way to get the results you desire."

"Ma'am."

"I'm sure you are well aware that you present a difficult situation for me. On one hand you challenge my beliefs regarding how people should treat each other, and yet on the other you challenge an idea that I cherish, which is I do not like being in anyone's debt."

"Things never do seem to line up like they should, do they?"

"I guess you're right about that."

"And things can get complicated real quick."

"Of course."

She watches him look at his feet. Finally he speaks, "Well, ma'am, it seems like we know what the rules are, so maybe we could just git started and figure somethin' out after we git goin' on it. It'd be nice to get this done before the weather gets too ugly."

"I have another request."

"Ma'am."

"Either one of us can call this off for any reason, no questions asked."

"It'll just be a few days, but if that's what you want, we can do that. I'm sure glad you ain't no witch, ma'am."

"Yes, Mr. Bodeen, I am as well." She stands and smiles a full smile; her teeth are uneven and crooked.

Early the next morning, Mary awakens to the sounds of Ralph Bodeen hammering some of the remaining exposed shingle nails back into the roof of the boat shed, a roofing hatchet in one hand and a flat bar in the other. He works his way systematically back and forth, pulling loose nails with the flat bar, hammering others flush into the boards, preparing the surface for new shingles. After making a final inspection, he climbs down the ladder to begin splitting shakes from the cedar bolts he brought from his camp. He uses a limb with a large knot on one end as a mallet to strike the blunt edge of the fro, expertly splitting off the new shakes, stacking them neatly.

Mary watches from her porch, sipping coffee. "Mr. Bodeen, I have asked Everett to order some galvanized shake nails. He tells me they will be on the next mail plane, which is tomorrow."

He calls back over his shoulder, "That is when I will need them, ma'am." He turns back to his work and doesn't stop until dark.

The gang on the fuel float is watching. Someone proposes a thought that has been on everyone's mind. "What do you think is goin' on over there at Mary's?"

"Looks like Ralph is fixin' to put a new roof on her boat shed."

"I know that. What I meant was, do you think anything *else* is goin' on?"

Now they all watch Mary sitting on her porch. There is silence and a couple of raised eyebrows. "Well, I don't know. She hasn't had anybody around since she ran that guy from Wrangell off a few years back. I'd be surprised if . . ."

The days go by; they continue to observe Mary sitting on the porch while Ralph methodically splits shakes, nailing them into place. There is speculation. "They sure don't talk much."

"He ain't much of a talker."

"Mary can hold her own in the talkin' department when she gets goin' on something."

"Don't seem like there is much goin' to me but him a-workin' and her a-watchin'."

It's early evening when he nails the last shake in place and climbs down the ladder and collects an armload of trimmings and leftover shakes. He packs them to the porch where she's sitting, placing them next to the front door.

"It'll make good kindlin'."

"Yes, it will be the best kind of kindling. Would you like a cup of coffee?"

"Yes, ma'am."

He sits on the edge of the bench. She turns her chair, facing him. He removes his hat, placing it at his feet. "Mr. Bodeen, have you given any thought as to how we are going to resolve the final terms of our arrangement regarding the roof?"

"Some."

"I have as well. Shall I make my proposal first?"

"Sure."

Darkness is coming quickly. She steps into the house and returns with a Coleman lantern, hissing as it throws off light. "I want to show you something in the boat shed."

He follows her through the side door of the shed. She stops in the back part, which used to be the workshop. Old workbenches are strewn with rusty bits and pieces of iron. An old donkey engine that used to power the cable drum sits in the middle of everything. Scattered randomly are parts of rudders, an old engine block, shaft bearings, and brass fasteners. The cable on the drum is one rusted mass.

"Mr. Bodeen, on occasion I will float my skiff in here on a high tide and place it on one of those skid logs." She points to two parallel logs that run from inside the boat shed down the beach, stopping below the high-tide line. "When I do, it's just for minor repairs and bottom painting, which I don't do very often. This area where we are standing is not used at all, as you can see. I propose that this area could be converted into a usable living space by someone like yourself that has all of those kinds of skills and knowledge. My proposal is this: as compensation for the new roof, you repair this space and live here until you move on, whenever that may be or you may come and go if you like. This could be a small apartment that would be a refuge of sorts."

He looks about inspecting the space, takes his hat off, and holds it to his chest. "Ma'am, I hadn't rightly considered anything like this."

"After seeing your present camp, I was thinking that something of this nature would be more comfortable, particularly when the snow comes this winter."

"Yes, it would."

They both stand looking around. "Mr. Bodeen, I seem to have taken over this conversation and have neglected to ask you about your considerations for compensation."

"I was thinkin' about somethin' a lot different than this."

"What is it?"

"I was thinkin' I could get a dinner once in a while. I get real tired of my own cookin'. I like bear meat, but there is a lot of it."

"That could be arranged as well."

"Yes, ma'am."

She holds the lantern closer, and when all of the shadows disappear from his face, he begins to flush red. "Mr. Bodeen, I have another suggestion, since we seem to have made an agreement on a just compensation. I think rather than shaking hands on our transaction, we should confirm it with a short dance."

"Ma'am?"

"Do you dance, Mr. Bodeen?"

"I do, but not very well and not very often."

"Then we should do just fine, because neither do I."

"Do you mean right now?"

"Yes."

"There ain't no music."

"Just a moment." She hurries back to the house and returns with a battery-powered CD player, punches the Play button, and places it on the workbench, making room among the rusty litter, sweeping it aside with her forearm.

Music comes exploding out of the boat shed, rolling out and expanding over the water. "*I was dancin' with my darlin' to the Tennessee waltz . . .*"

The crew at the fuel float is stunned into silence as they watch them step awkwardly through the lantern's light. She is wearing a thin nylon skirt that falls just above her knees. Her skinny, thin white shins are swallowed up by her red rubber boots. They slap against her legs as she steps gracelessly to the music. She looks up at him with a large smile. "I think that is a very fine roof, Mr. Bodeen."

"Yes, ma'am."

"*I remember the night and the Tennessee Waltz . . .*"

Their shadows bounce off the walls and floor, making intricate, angular shapes that move quickly from one place to another as they move to the music.

3

Human Development

Sometimes things get out of whack, they don't work
out, isn't anything to put your finger on, so just
hunker down, make the best of it, ride it out.

Neil scoops up the change from the bar. "That's it, guys. I'm tapped out, classes tomorrow." On his way out, he puts a quarter in the electronic slot machine. Lights begin flashing; bells ring. *Jackpot!* The payout is eighty-five dollars. He turns to his friends still at the bar. They are staring at him with eager anticipation. He doesn't know anybody with eight-five dollars to spare. He couldn't afford the ten dollars he just spent on beer, but they continue to stare at him. Without saying a word, he takes the payout from the bartender, places it on the bar, and orders drinks.

Before he knows it, the lights are blinking for the last round and his friends all thank him.

"Way to go, Neil."

"Well done." They raise their glasses in salute.

They all look shaky to him with slurred words and unsteady feet. Neil thinks he probably looks just like them. He drives home slowly, taking the back streets, focusing on just one thought. He has a class at 8:00 AM. Crammed in there is another thought: the teacher's program at Eastern Oregon University doesn't like their potential molders of young minds' names showing up on the police report, not to mention jail.

Just as he parks in front of his mother's house, a police patrol car turns onto that street. As it approaches him, it slows to a crawl, shining its spotlight on his car. Neil quickly lies down in the front seat. The windows of his car illuminate to an incandescent white under its intensity. It's a small town, and the police know who he is, and this is the shift that focuses on drunk drivers. They keep the spotlight focused on his car as they move slowly past. He lies still until he is sure they are gone.

The house is an older style with high ceilings and narrow stairways. It makes creaking sounds when the temperature changes. It's dark and empty. Upstairs in the bedroom, he sets his alarm, undresses, and leaves his clothes in a pile on the floor. The cold sheets feel soothing.

So far so good.

As he closes his eyes, the screen door on the front porch rattles and slams shut. There are voices mixed with shuffling sounds. He squints at his alarm clock; it's 3:00 AM. He hears the footsteps and soft words move into the living room; the hushed words continue. Then his mother's voice becomes audible.

"Take him over to the couch and get him comfortable."

"No, no, I don't want to sit down. I need to keep moving." It's a man's voice in pain, halting, grunting.

"Just to get you comfortable."

"Need to keep moving."

Neil gives up any hope of sleep, pulls on his blue jeans, and descends the creaky wooden stairs. In the living room, his mother and two other people are standing in worried silence. Neil recognizes the man; it's George, the drummer in a small band that plays once in a while at the nightclub where his mom tends bar, the Broken Wheel. During the week, he drives a logging truck, owns his own truck, makes a living but just barely. He's down to one trip a day to the local mill from Lewiston, Idaho, and it's a long day. It's all he knows, and he's too old to change. On Saturday night the band plays at nearby small towns where there are a few places left that country music is played, and one can still drink whiskey. Often the late-night conversation, oiled by a few drinks, is how the times used to be better, no shortage of logs. The men were stronger and the women much better looking.

Remember Billy Garrett? I am tellin' you right now he could change a tire on his log trailer while it was piggybacked on his truck. I mean, just lift it up, stick it on there. Didn't even break a sweat. Then there is that guy up there in Wallowa County . . . Now folks are goin' to health spas and drinkin' some green shit out of a blender, all the other stuff is goin' away, and there ain't nothin' a person can do about it.

George gets a gig when he can. When he leaves the house, he tells his wife it's for the extra money to make ends meet. She knows this is only partly true; she knows that this is a part of himself he can't give up. She sees a middle-aged man trying to keep that particular window open, just a bit, but he just can't let it go, and she puts up with it.

The white streaks in his hair are stained yellow with smoke. His skin is puffy and beginning to sag; his jawline is gone. Now he is standing in the middle of the living room with his legs apart, leaning forward to brace himself by grasping his thighs tightly with both hands as if he's expecting a strong headwind. He tries to stand and straighten his shoulders, but the pain forces him immediately back forward. His face is blue; his neck is white and bloodless. He speaks with gravelly, shallow breath. "Pain in my back."

Neil stands aside, watching him for a moment, waiting for him to collapse. The smell of whiskey and cigarettes is strong on his breath. "How's it goin' there, George?"

"Not good."

"What happened?"

George glances quickly at the other woman in the room; she looks quickly away. His mother catches the exchange, nods at the other woman, then looks evenly at Neil. "This is George's friend Irene." Irene is wearing a terry cloth bathrobe that mostly covers her silk pajamas; beneath her silk pajamas is nothing. Her face is a flat, unreadable mask. George emits a sharp moan and falls to his knees, clawing the carpet.

Angry now, Neil says, "OK, Mom, what the hell is going on?"

"George was at Irene's place and—"

Irene bluntly interrupts, "I'm a nurse, and George is having a heart attack."

Neil asks incredulously, "What the hell is he doing here?"

His mother responds as if she is attempting to explain something very basic, like why water runs downhill. "Well, for goodness' sake. We didn't want him to die at her place. His wife would be furious." She lights a cigarette.

George claws at the rug and moans.

"What about the hospital? Why isn't he at the hospital!?"

"Think about that, Neil. Irene can't check him in and have the receptionist ask her a bunch of questions, now can she? Well, his wife would certainly find out who she is and what's going on, now wouldn't she?" she exclaims.

Neil turns to his mom and asks a question that he is pretty sure he already knows the answer. "Why don't you take him to the hospital?"

He can see the slight flush of embarrassment under her heavy makeup. "She doesn't like me very well either, you know. We thought you could take him." She waves her hand that holds the cigarette.

Neil turns to George, who is still clawing at the carpet. His breath is now coming in short bursts. "Dammit, George, no one wants you to die at their place, so it looks like you and I are going to the hospital."

He carefully helps George to his feet, and they slowly shuffle out the door onto the sidewalk. There are patches of snow with skiffs of ice beneath. Neil's feet slip and slide as he grapples to maintain a firm grasp on George as they negotiate their way to the car. George curls forward in the front seat, resting his head on the dashboard, continuing to moan. Neil's mother and Irene are standing on the front porch. His mom calls out in her best maternalistic manner, "Now be careful, honey, these roads are very treacherous." The comment is so incongruent to what is going on that he stands there with the car door open, staring at her. She continues on in a fashion that is reminiscent of a conversation spoken over toast and coffee. "Do you have any classes in the morning?"

"Yes. Hey, Mom, I have to get going here. George is having a tough time."

"Oh, right, you know I think Irene and I will go down to Stockman's and have a nightcap to settle our nerves." Then as an afterthought, "What class is it?"

"Human Development," then under his breath, "assuming there is any of that going on."

She turns to Irene. "He's going to be a teacher, you know."

Irene looks at Neil with a puzzled expression.

Neil slams the car door hard because in the cold weather, the latch doesn't always work, and after two tries, it finally catches. As he puts the car in gear, he turns to George, who is still groaning, and says, "You run with a tough crowd, my friend." He tries to pick up some speed, but the car fishtails on the icy pavement as it moves down the street. The bare limbs of the elm trees that line the street are stark in the cold light of the streetlamps.

Neil has spent all of his twenty-two years in small towns, and the one thing that he knows for certain is that secrets are next to impossible to keep. Keeping that in mind, he gives the receptionist at the admissions desk accurate information to her questions, just not all of it.

"No, he's not family."

"He's a drummer in a band at the Broken Wheel."

"I don't know who is paying."

He gives the woman George's wallet; she paws through it, finding his driver's license and a hunting license. "It says here he lives in Baker City."

"Great."

"Do you know if he has any insurance?"

"No."

She asks again, "Who is going to be responsible for payment?"

"I don't know."

"Well, we can't just admit someone without the proper information."

Neil leans over and speaks loudly in George's ear, "George, who is going to pay for this?"

No response.

"He can't talk, ma'am."

"Does he have a wife?"

"I believe he does."

"Her name please."

"Don't know her name."

George is still bent over, grasping the counter with both hands, and begins discharging long odiferous farts. The front doors swing open with a burst of cold air, and a man walks purposely into the lobby. He acknowledges the receptionist with a nod.

"Doctor, I'm having a problem here. We are having a difficult time getting the proper information on this man."

The doctor looks at Neil then goes to George and watches him closely, putting his finger on George's neck. He abruptly points directly at the receptionist and says in a loud voice, "You call upstairs and get a wheelchair down here right now and get this man to the emergency room!" He puts his finger again on George's neck, searching for a pulse. "This man is in cardiac arrest!" Almost instantly, a nurse is jogging down the hall with a wheelchair.

The doctor turns to Neil. "Has this man been drinking?"

"Yes."

"Heavily?"

"A good chance of that."

"Does he smoke?"

"Yes."

"Do you know this man?"

"Not really."

"How do you happen to be the person bringing him to the hospital?"

"I woke up, and he was in the living room."

The doctor has a puzzled look on his face as he tries to sort out all of this information and somehow organize it in his mind; then he turns on his heel and strides quickly after the wheelchair.

As Neil walks to his car, he notices the sky is beginning to show some early light. He checks his watch. It's 5:00 AM. His first class, Human Development, is a class in which he has already accumulated three unexcused absences, and three is all he gets this quarter; a fourth means he loses the credits. If he goes to sleep now, he will never be able to wake up. He's been awake almost twenty-four hours. He will need some coffee.

He drives to Stockman's bar, where there is a café in the front of the building and it's always open. It caters mostly to men that work on the railroad who come in all hours of the day and night, when their shift ends. They eat at the lunch counter and at the wooden booths that line the opposite wall. The other early-morning customers come in for breakfast after the bars close to get something to eat before they go home to their wife or girlfriend who has long since fallen into a restless, angry sleep, waiting for the sound of the front door closing.

The bar is in the back, and it has a federation of loyal customers. They are serious drinkers who don't need any peripheral distractions such as live music or the kind of distrust strangers bring. The bar opens at 9:00 AM. A few customers come in early for a shot and coffee just to get their day off to the correct start. Most lift their first drink of the day reverently; only their fingertips touch the glass. There is a large jar of pickled eggs on one end of the bar that has been there for months and is still full. Once in a while someone will glance up at the mirror on the back bar to see who is sitting behind them at the tables but never at their own reflection. The music on the jukebox hasn't been changed for years. If anyone plays a song, which isn't very often, it's likely to be Willie Nelson. The semidarkness smells of old obsessions.

Neil pushes through the front door, and there is an old man sitting at the far end of the lunch counter. He doesn't look up at the sounds of someone coming through the door but continues to stare at his coffee cup. His long hair is plastered to his head, combed with his fingers and pulled straight back while it was dripping wet. The ragged ends rest on the collar of his shirt. It has dried in coarse, crusty rows. His hair and the first two fingers of his right hand are stained yellow from cigarette smoke. A homemade cigarette hangs from the corner of his mouth, and smoke is curling up over his head and past a sign that says No Smoking.

The cook, who is also the waitress, is a friend of Neil's mother. "Hey, Neil, how's it goin'?" She leans against the counter in the space between it and the cash register. The white linoleum floor tiles in that narrow space are worn down to their sticky black subsurfaces from the thousands of trips she has made between the grill and the booths attached to the far wall, delivering ham and eggs like a nurse, administering medicine for curing the initial steps of a hangover.

"It's going OK."

Neil continues walking toward the old man at the end of the counter. "Emmitt, is that you?"

The old man turns, squinting at him. "It's me, Neil Osborne."

The man continues to look at him with a deep frown, puzzled.

"Remember when I was in high school we worked for John Witherspoon out on Cricket Flat, you drove that semi-truck to deliver hay and I stacked it with bales?"

A light of recognition crosses his eyes. "Neil, my goodness, yes, I do remember you now. How are you?"

"Oh, fine, I've been going to college."

"By golly, good for you, must be about done by now. It's been a few years since we worked for John." He stands and offers his hand.

"I'm pretty close, if I can pull it off. I should graduate this spring. I had to lay out a year because I ran out of money, worked in the woods that year."

Emmitt looks at him very closely and talks in a stern voice. "Well, you know that there ain't no future in the woods or ranch work, and I can tell you for sure there ain't money hidin' anywhere on a cow. I ought to know, I've looked at both ends of enough of them." He chuckles at his own joke.

Neil looks worried. "You need a place to stay?"

"Nah, I got a little place over at North Powder, and I'm drawing some social security. I get by OK. The lights on my pickup don't work too good, so I'm just waiting for the sun to come up so I can drive home." He gives Neil a half grin. "Need to sober up a bit too, just waiting for the sun to come up so I can drive home." As he starts to sit down, he stops in midcrouch and looks at Neil. "You're up kinda late for a school night, ain't ya?"

Neil nods.

"You better not screw this school deal up, or you might wind up like me sitting in a rocking chair on the front porch, staring at an empty street, waiting for your social security check to arrive. Ain't nothin' wrong with that, but you can do a lot better." Emmitt has always had a sort of sense that allows him to understand people without knowing any of the details.

Neil looks at his watch. "Right, and I better get going. It's been good seeing you, Emmitt." He turns to the waitress. "I need a large cup of coffee."

As she pours the coffee, she asks, "Did George, the drummer over at the Broken Wheel, have some problems tonight?"

"Yes, he did."

"He gonna be OK?"

"I don't know, but he didn't look too good to me. Did Mom and Irene come in earlier?"

"They came in about an hour ago and the bartender was still cleaning up, but he locked the door and let them stay." She tilts her head in the direction of the door just beyond where Emmitt is sitting. A paper sign hangs on it with a string taped to the jamb; it says Closed. A loose end of the string is casually wrapped on a nail.

"Are they still in there?"

"Yep, you gonna have breakfast?"

"No thanks." He takes his coffee and leaves.

Back at the house, he gathers his books for the day's classes then drives to a parking lot at Eastern Oregon University. He sits, waiting, watching the sky come to full daylight, smoking cigarettes and nursing his jumbo-sized cup of coffee; he quickly falls asleep. He jerks awake when his cigarette burns down to his fingers. When he flinches and shakes his hand, ashes spew down the leg of his pants. What's left of the coffee spills in his lap. Slapping at his pant leg, he attempts to clean off the ashes but rubs them into the fabric, leaving smears and stains. When he is fully awake, he looks down at his wet crotch. "Oh, great." In frustration, he throws the coffee cup and cigarette butt on the floor boards on the passenger's side and lies back, resting his head. Just before he drifts off, he thinks, *The hell with it. I'll figure something else out.*

Suddenly he awakes to loud banging sounds on the window. Someone is yelling, "NEIL, NEIL! WAKE UP!" It's his friend Jim. When he sees Neil is awake, he lowers his voice. "Class begins in five minutes." He points in that general direction. Neil gathers his books and laptop, walking briskly after several other students hurrying to get to class on time. He looks at his wrinkled clothes and wet pants and gives up all hope of looking presentable. He looks bad and is pretty sure he smells worse. There's a small group of students standing by the front door that watch him as he walks past. He sits in the back of the room as far back as he can get. Everyone else is in the front of the room.

Conversation fades as the professor enters the room; she is a small orderly woman that, above all, considers the task of training teachers the most righteous of all professions. She's an icon at Eastern Oregon University and has been at the forefront of shepherding the small university through good times and bad. She is there every step of the way with her hair pulled back in a tight bun, unrelenting, to elevate it from a regional teacher's college to the small university it is now. She's part of the school's DNA. Dr. Addison also takes a justified pride in developing each of her students as individuals because, she believes, all of them have something to offer. She teaches them as she would like them to teach. She says frequently, "Every student has potential, and it is a teacher's obligation to unlock that potential." She is, however, not so sure about Neil Osborne.

Now she lays her books on her desk and surveys the room. "Mr. Osborne, would you care to join the rest of the students?" Her voice comes down hard on the *t*.

"No, ma'am."

"Mr. Osborne, I have frequently asked you not to address me as ma'am."

"Sorry, no thank you, Dr. Addison."

"You are part of this group, you know."

"Yes, I am aware of that, Dr. Addison."

She stiffens her neck, and with a look of curiosity on her face, she asks, "Then why aren't you joining the group?"

"I don't smell very good, Dr. Addison."

He doesn't say what he is actually thinking, which is that the smell is just a symptom. The real reason is that he doesn't belong here, in the hallowed halls of learning, with this group or any other group. When you come right down to it, he is some sort of imposter with marginal grades that's here under false pretenses, and sooner or later, there's a good chance he'll be exposed for what he is—someone who is more at home with the residents of Stockman's lunch counter or the band members of the Broken Wheel lounge late at night, than discussing the evolving behaviors of young children. His motivation is a better job; it's specific and personal. He is certain that Dr. Addison already knows this.

She straightens her back and continues to stare at him. "I will see you after class, Mr. Osborne." She turns to the other students. "Can any of you tell me what are some typical behaviors we may expect from fourth graders?

Several hands pop into the air. Dr. Addison points to one.

"Their motor skills aren't fully developed, so they might unexpectedly fall out of their desks."

"Now can you tell me, given that this is the case, what are the implications of these behaviors as to how this would affect the way they learn?"

The class is silent. Then some quiet discussions begin to float through the group. Dr. Addison waits patiently, letting them continue their exchanges.

Neil raises his hand, and Dr. Addison acknowledges him. "It seems like their physical development would be closely related to some other abilities like attention span, time on task, how well their eyes track the lines on a page, things like that."

"Class, what do you think of Mr. Osborne's comment?" An engaged discussion follows as the class exchanges different ideas related to Neil's comments and what they would mean in practical terms. Neil doesn't remember for sure where he learned that particular bit of information but is pleased that it is being considered. He listens for a moment, interested, but soon falls asleep with his head in his folded arms.

Dr. Addison is gently shaking his shoulder. "Mr. Osborne, you have fallen asleep." He raises his head, giving her a blurry-eyed look, then rests it back in his arm. She shakes him more vigorously. He jerks awake but doesn't have any idea where he is, thinking he's in the front seat of his car. His mind races to organize his surroundings into some logical order; this is definitely not the front seat of his car.

"Please, Mr. Osborne, you have fallen asleep, get ahold on yourself." The students of the next class are drifting into the room in small groups, glancing in his direction as they take their seats.

The fog in his brain begins to lift. "Ah, Dr. Addison, how are you?"

She rocks back at the smell of his breath. "I am well enough, thank you. Would you follow me into the hallway please?"

He follows dutifully behind her. They move to a secluded corner of the main hallway. "Mr. Osborne, as you will learn in the years to come, trying to understand the essence of a particular person is an unqualified gamble, but nonetheless I am undeterred." She has a determined look. "I must be honest with you and say that you test my theory that all students have the potential to succeed. I still think that you have potential but, I confess, that it might not be as an elementary school teacher. For one thing you need to be an example to your students, your community, and your profession. This sort of thing," she spreads her hands to indicate his general condition, shows significant lack of self-regard. This will not do. I should think if you were to arrive at school to teach children in this same condition in which you find yourself today, you would risk a high probability of termination. Mr. Osborne, I have come to think you are hard-wired to do things in the most difficult manner possible.

Neil thinks this would be a hard point to argue. "I have had those same thoughts."

She folds her hands back in front of her, pursing her lips. "I have been going through student files and yours in particular. It seems, as of this moment you, Neil Osborne, hold the all-time university record for unexcused absences for someone who is still here." She takes a deep breath. "The strange thing is that your grades are pretty good for someone who is not here much."

The next moment is completely unexpected. Dr. Addison moves closer to him and smiles a soft, sincere smile, a smile like your grandmother gives you when you go visit after a long absence. "Mr. Osborne, one of our tasks as an institution of higher learning is to create a product that will perform in the classroom in a somewhat reliable manner at a high level. It goes somewhat like this; we put our considerable brain power together, work our little butts off to develop an outstanding curricula, and even if I do say so myself, it's a pretty good one. However, there is one thing you can count on, as sure as the sun comes up every morning. Along comes someone who doesn't fit into all of this careful planning all of us have labored so diligently to put together. In other words, the wrong kind of human shows up, someone who lives on the edges of this culture we have attempted to construct. You are one such person, Mr. Osborne."

"Yes, Dr. Addison, I would have to say that I am well aware of that."

Neil sees what has been said of Dr. Addison is true. She is interested in all of her students. For him this is not the best news. He's just been trying to slide through as best as he can, without drawing too much attention. He leans against the wall in resignation.

She stops smiling and continues, "I happen to think a carefully constructed curricula leaves very little room for rebels, but to be quite honest with you, that is a shame, because without people who think differently, we would be a whole lot slower to change, which brings us to a whole other set of different difficulties. I firmly believe we need some nest kickers around to keep the stuffy old folks on their toes. Many students go to great lengths to show that they are different, but you, Mr. Osborne, truly are different."

Neil is completely confused; she knows he's confused.

"Mr. Osborne, why do you think I have chosen to have this conversation with you aside from my well-known penchant for gleaning the potential from all of my students?"

Neil thinks for a moment. "You're trying to teach me something?"

"What do you think that might be? Just consider for as long as you need, no right or wrong answers on this one."

"I don't know."

"Yes, you do." The smile comes back. "Take your time."

Neil looks nervously about the crowded hallway, looking for a way to get out of this. She says, "Seriously, this is a free one. Just say what you think, take a crack at it." She is still smiling.

"Maybe you're saying that, sometimes, I'll have students that don't fit the mold, and I, because of who I am, should have a better understanding of how they think and that might give me an advantage other teachers might not have."

"Now you see that is a very good answer. Others will come to you, but that one will do nicely. Now that is a narrow thread on which to hang a career, so please remember you still need to make it through spring quarter, and you know as well as I do that you have very little wriggle room. So, as you are rumbling your caravan down that particular road, Mr. Osborne, you will do well to keep it out of the ditch."

Confused and relieved at the same time, all Neil can blurt out is, "Did you count me absent today?"

She takes a deep breath. "Well, your response did stimulate a very robust and productive discussion and," she raises her eyebrows, "you didn't snore much." She looks stern again. "I will not cut you any, slack Mr. Osborne, and you will do well by yourself to remember that fact."

"Thank you, Ma—Dr. Addison."

"Good day, Mr. Osborne." She walks briskly away. The fading sound of her heels clicking on the tile floor leave a faint trail of echoes. She is shaking her head slightly. Then in what appears to be an afterthought, she turns and walks back to Neil. Ignoring his smelly breath, she holds her face close to his, speaking in hushed tones, "That man you delivered to the emergency room, the drummer that plays at the Broken Wheel where your mom tends bar, is he going to recover?"

Neil is stunned into silence.

"The receptionist at the hospital is my roommate. This is a small town indeed, isn't it, Mr. Osborne?" She quickly turns and leaves.

He feels fatigue beginning to creep its way through his body. He has two more classes today, but he knows he doesn't have a chance to get through them awake. He has only one unexcused absence in one of them, two in the other. It's a matter of picking the least worst of two bad choices, go home and get some rest or try and get through the two classes without making a spectacle of himself. He goes home to get some rest.

When he walks past his mother's bedroom, he glances through the open door. She is sleeping on top of the covers, a small slobber drips from the corner of her mouth. He kicks his shoes off and flops on his bed, instantly asleep. When he passes her room in the morning, on the way for coffee, she hasn't moved a muscle.

The kitchen table is in front of a large single-pane window. Sitting with the warm cup cradled in his hands, he feels the late-winter cold coming through the window. The heat from the coffee creates a foggy patch of steam on the lower portion of the glass. The temperature has dropped overnight, forming a covering of hoar frost on the bare stems of the rose bushes that line the sidewalk. The frost crystals make the stems thick and heavy. Morning light produces a mixture of shapes and shadows; it's a bizarre and primitive landscape.

What he would like to think about is nothing, that's all, nothing; just clear his head for a while, but it's impossible. He sips coffee, but random thoughts keep bubbling up from somewhere.

George looked damned near dead at the hospital, probably won't make it. How do people wind up the way they are? Do they subconsciously plan the way they live? Are they in control of any of that? Do they just do their own day-to-day stuff and not consider how it will turn out, or do they just get up every morning and do it all over again and wind up somewhere, whatever it happens to be? Are they overcome by circumstances? Are they going along doing the best they can and have bad luck, medium luck, no luck at all? How long was Mom going to be able to keep her particular window open?

He tries to think back through it all again to some sort of starting point or conclusion or think of some way to even begin sorting it out; he can't do it.

It looks to me like you're going to have to figure this out all by yourself, and Emmitt is right, just don't screw it up.

A few days later, his mom announces she is going to Portland to do "some shopping with her friends."

George lingers on in the hospital with tubes sticking out of him. When Neil visits him, he is asleep, his skin white and shiny like wax. Sometimes he acts as if he wants to talk, lifting one hand or moving his head back and forth, lips moving but without sound; he stops and lies still again. On his way down the stairs, Neil asks the receptionist if George has had any visitors.

"His wife called and said she was making arrangements to stay here in La Grande to be near him, but we haven't seen her."

"Has the doctor said how George is doing? He doesn't look very good to me."

"We can't give that information out to people who are not relatives. You'll need to talk to the doctor about that." She quickly finds something else to do.

Neal hurries out of the hospital back to the house and takes a shower to wash the thoughts of death and sickness from his mind. As he reaches for a towel, the front door slams open, banging against the wall. A voice yells, "Hey, is anybody home?"

It's not a voice Neal recognizes. He wraps the towel around his waist. "Just a minute."

A large woman is standing in the living room with a suitcase on the floor beside her. On the floor on the other side of her is a fifty-pound sack of potatoes in a burlap bag. It's resting precariously on one end, so she steadies it by grasping one ear of the burlap sack with her hand. She is wearing a brightly colored loose-fitting dress made of polyester that clings to her bulges and crevasses. Her stiff, wiry hair is bleached a bright yellow.

"I'm George's wife, Rose. Your mom called and told me I could stay here for as long as I wanted." She nods to the sack of potatoes.

"I brought these to help out with the food." Her free hand is resting on her hip, and she's breathing hard from the effort of packing the potatoes and suitcase from her car.

The shopping trip was well planned.

Neil, still trying to figure out what the hell is happening, just stares at her. Thinking he doesn't understand, she repeats herself, mouthing the words slowly, "I brought some potatoes to help out with the food."

"Mom's in Portland for a while, for a week or so, she thinks."

"That'll be fine," she says with an edge to her voice. "I'll just make myself at home." Then she notices he is just wearing a bath towel. Her eyes widen slightly as she looks him up and down. He retreats to the bathroom, calling out over his shoulder, "I just remembered I have a class in twenty minutes."

She yells through the door, "Your mom said it was OK if I stayed here. She called me last week, the day after George got sick!"

"Go ahead and make yourself at home. The spare bedroom is at the top of the stairs. It's the door on the right." His bedroom door is the door on the left; he hopes the lock works. Bolting from the bathroom, he snatches his books from the coffee table and hurries to his car.

His mom's "shopping trip" becomes two weeks then three weeks. George's wife does make herself at home. She visits the hospital several hours a day and is at the house when she's not there. Neil lives at the library from first thing in the morning until it closes at night. The large woman with the sack of potatoes is another reason to take his own advice and make things work.

His friends watch him with concerned amazement. Some are convinced he has been overcome by some mysterious influence or some sort of creepy personality change. They throw broad hints at him, suggesting he has had some sort of breakdown. His instructors are equally stunned; he doesn't lose any credits for unexcused absences, nor does he drop out of school or fail any classes. He gets things done in a reasonable manner and, amazingly enough, has perfect attendance for spring quarter. He ignores them all, which only creates more speculation. By disregarding their comments, he becomes even more isolated, which is just fine with him. There are too many things that are out of a person's control, so maybe people do just make it up as they go along.

His mom's shopping trip stretches into additional weeks, and upon her return, an uneasy peace develops at the house. Neil continues to live at the library, and Rose spends most of the day with George. His mother works all night and sleeps all day. Just after his mom leaves for work, Rose arrives from the hospital. When they do see each other, the tension between them is visible. Neil can't figure out if it's because Rose thinks his mom and George had been an item at one time or if his mom, being a bartender at the Broken Wheel, represents all those things that George left home for on Friday nights. He decides not to dwell on any of that.

As spring quarter winds down, Neil makes frequent visits to the Job Placement Service on campus. They have a difficult time finding an opening for him. He isn't surprised but still hopes something will come up. Finally, they call and they want to talk to him. In one of the back offices, an older man slouches in his chair. The top two buttons on his wrinkled shirt are undone, and parts of his lunch are sprinkled on the front. "Mr. Osborne, I want you to know we have worked very hard to find you placement. However, we have found it somewhat difficult because of the lack of recommendations from your professors, and of course, your grades aren't the best. Although you may find it somewhat implausible, Dr. Addison has been a central figure in finding a position for which you might be suited."

"Yes, that is interesting."

The man rubs his forehead. "How would you feel about going to Alaska?"

"If that's where the work is, I'll go. Where in Alaska?"

"In the southeastern part of Alaska. There is a section called the Panhandle. It's an archipelago made up of several thousands of islands and very few people, small towns, villages, and some of the settlements are just places where some people live that aren't really anything. They just live there. Almost all of the work is seasonal, related to fishing. There are small schools at many of these locations. Mr. Osborne, some of these places are isolated, very isolated. The administrative body that oversees this school is called the Southeast Island School District, and they need a teacher for one of these schools."

"A teacher, you mean one position?"

"Yes, that is correct."

"There is one school left that needs a teacher, and to be quite honest with you, this position has always been difficult to fill."

"Why is that?"

"I've not been there, so I can't speak about it with any firsthand knowledge, but I will tell you what I do know from what other people have said. Some of this has been from teachers we have placed at this school, who have made it a point to come to me after they taught there, to share information they thought would be useful to others who have no knowledge of the area. People such as yourself, Mr. Osborne. One such person, who came to me share their experiences, left for Christmas break and couldn't make herself return for the remainder of the year."

"What did they do about school?"

"They didn't have school the remainder of the year, and that was just fine with everyone."

"It seems like the local school board could have figured something out."

"Mr. Osborne, there is no local school board."

"What?"

The local people are ingrained in, let's see, what's the phrase that was popular in the 1970s, alternative lifestyles. Yes, I think that would be an appropriate phrase. There is no local government, no agencies of any sort, no police, no PTA, no organized committees of any sort, no roads. It's my distinct impression that most issues are dealt with by just making things up as they go along. You will be completely on your own, Mr. Osborne."

"Huh."

"I don't wish to seem as if I am overly harsh here. I am simply repeating what I've been told by others who have been there. There is one other thing you need to know."

"Go ahead on it."

"The weather is terrible."

"Cold?"

"Not like northern Alaska. It's rainy and windy. The wind will blow with hurricane force several times a year. They measure moisture by the feet of rain a year with short dark days in the winter." The man holds his hands apart, estimating twelve inches. "Feet."

"Anything else to add to the list?"

"Now that you asked, yes. We don't know for sure if there will be any school there this fall."

"You don't have anyone else that is interested in this job, do you? They can't fill the position, can they?"

The man shifts uncomfortably in his chair. "Yes, that is correct, Mr. Osborne."

"When will they know?"

"There are seven students registered now, and they need ten. We don't know when that will happen. On occasion they will collect enough students that will go to school until October 28, which is the official count day, then some will drop out. It provides a teacher for the remainder of the students for the rest of the year, but to accurately answer your question, we don't know for sure if or when it will happen."

"So it's like putting shills in a poker game."

"I wouldn't know about that, Mr. Osborne."

"What's this place called?"

"Harbor Cove. There is a small grocery store and liquor store at a place called the Mercantile. The owner buys fish during the fishing season and sells them to fish processors in one of the larger towns. That's about it, Mr. Osborne. Are you still interested?"

"I guess it won't hurt to keep my name in the hat, doesn't sound like I have much competition, but I won't count on it."

"That would be a wise move, Mr. Osborne."

4

Lynnwood

"Ed, who's turn is it to pick up the dirty dishes?" A short, wiry, red-headed woman moves through the house with alacrity, brushing her teeth with one hand, poking school lunches in backpacks with the other, surveying the dirty breakfast dishes on the dining room table.

"Marcia's."

Ed lowers his newspaper, peering over the top of the page at his seventeen-year-old daughter sitting on the other side of the room, texting on her phone. When she glances up at him, he tilts his head toward the dining room table.

"It's Michael's turn," she says.

He folds the paper in his lap and looks directly at her. "Here's the way I see this situation. Number one: If you don't change your story quickly, you will be struck by lightning from above for not telling the truth to your father." He points to the ceiling. "So just stay on that side of the room, because when you explode into tiny bits of protoplasm, I don't want to get any teenage girl juice on me. He holds up two fingers. Number two: Let's assume you get lucky and you're not just a small, smelly puddle of plasma pooled up on the sofa. In what, I estimate, will be less than a minute, your brother is going to give your mother some of his patented middle-school guff delivered in a medium condescending tone, something like, 'Don't bother me, I'm dealing with my own stuff here.'"

"But, Dad—"

He holds up his index finger, stopping her in midsentence. "By the time your mother gets him sorted out, she will be at threat level orange. Right after that, she is going to make another pass around the house, through the kitchen and into the dining room. At that point, if those dishes are still on the table," he nods again at the table, "she will be as mad as a sack full of weasels."

Marcia tries again, "But it's Michael's turn."

"Good luck." He raises his newspaper.

The mother's voice fills the whole house from the back hallway as she yells through the bedroom door. "Michael, you better get it in gear, or we'll all be late!"

Silence.

"What time do you catch the bus home after soccer practice?"

"Hold on a minute. I'm busy with something, jeez!"

Ed looks at Marcia across the living room with a "What did I just tell you?" look on his face.

She stops her fast walk down the hallway and turns in midstride. "Michael J. Simpson, you answer me right now and you do it in a civil manner. If I come through that door, the first step is going to cost you your cell phone for a week. The second step will be two weeks. Are you getting the picture, am piercing the void?" She is waving her toothbrush at the closed door.

A muffled sound comes from the other side of the door.

"I can't hear you!"

"Five o' clock." The tone is dismissive.

She stops waving the toothbrush but is still talking loudly. "When I get home from work, I will expect you to be at the dining room table with your homework in front of you at least partially done."

More muffled sounds from the other side of the door.

"By God, that's it. I have had enough of your lip!" She starts toward the door, but before she gets there, it flies open. A thirteen-year-old boy is standing there with his curly red hair hanging in his face. "OK, OK, OK, I get it, yes, Mother," he says respectfully.

She brandishes the toothbrush in his face. She doesn't notice as it drips on the carpet. "Your dad and sister are waiting in the living room."

Marcia pouts but begins picking up the breakfast dishes. Ed calls out in a loud voice, pronouncing each word distinctly, "Hey, Nancy, Marcia is just about through with cleaning the table."

Mom walks into the room, beckoning with her arm. "Come on, you guys, if we don't get going before six thirty, the freeway at Totem Lake will be gridlocked by the time we get there, and we'll all be late."

"I'll be right there as soon as I get the dishes in the dishwasher."

As they leave the on-ramp and join the other cars, Nancy sits with her arms folded, gazing out the window, watching the constant stream of cars in the other lanes. There are cars filled with people just like them, on their way to work, dropping their kids off at school, telling them they better get their homework done, trying to get the bills paid, negotiating schedules, trying to have dinner when everyone is there, and falling into bed completely worn out.

In the car beside them, a young couple is fighting. The woman red-faced, is jabbing her finger at the man. He's staring straight ahead without any expression on his face. Nancy can see his jaw muscles flexing as he grinds his teeth.

"Nancy!" Ed's voice startles her out of her trance.

"Shit! Don't scare me like that." In the back seat, Marcia and Michael don't react to the sound of their mother's cursing. They're used to it. They continue their video games without pause.

"Don't let getting to work ruin your whole day."

She begins defensively, "I'm not," then catches herself when she realizes she has been folding her arms so tightly they ache. "No, no, you're right. I better relax, or I'll be all worn out before I even get there." She leans back in her seat and stares straight ahead. A large truck and trailer is ten feet from their front bumper, throwing the remains of last night's rainstorm from its tires onto their windshield. The wipers keep most of the water off, but a thin film of road grime remains on the glass, reducing visibility. The trailer sways back and forth as it rolls over low spots in the road. She folds her arms again.

Ed speaks without looking at her, keeping his eyes on the traffic. "What's going on at the office?"

"We have been working for months on that bid for the red iron for that new parking garage on Federal Way. Everything is just about ready to go, and it should be just a matter of running the numbers again to see if we've dotted all the I's and crossed all the T's. It goes to bid next Tuesday."

Traffic slows to a crawl then stops. Nancy explodes, "Son of a bitch! Now we are all going to be late. I guess we're going to have to leave the house at five AM to get to work on time. Shit! Everyone says, 'Oh, you will get used to it.' What a load of crap that is. We've been doing this for ten years, and it just keeps getting worse!" She slams the inside of the car door with her forearm.

She sits glowering out the window then digs her cell phone out of her briefcase. "Hello, Ray? We're caught here on 405 between Lynnwood and Totem Lake. It looks like we'll be here for a while, so I'll be late for work. I'll probably miss the morning meeting. If you just e-mail me the paperwork on that bid for the parking garage, I'll work however long it takes to wrap it up tonight."

"Ed, you and the kids go ahead and start dinner. Maybe I can catch a ride with someone headed our way, or if I can't, I'll catch that bus that stops at 124th. You can come get me."

"I'd rather you didn't take the bus if it's late. I don't think that would be a good idea at all. I'd rather drive all the way downtown again if it comes to that."

"Sure, I'll call you when I find something out."

Ed looks in the rearview mirror. "What do you guys want for dinner?"

They answer simultaneously. Marcia says, "Pizza"; Michael says, "Sausage and eggs."

Ed gives a thumbs-up.

Nancy continues to look out the window, shaking her head. "All of you are going to die of clogged arteries, and it will be very soon." They all fall into an uncomfortable silence as they inch their way down the freeway.

As Nancy arrives home that night at seven thirty, she walks slowly through the front door, dropping her coat and briefcase into the first chair she comes to in the living room, walks to the sofa, and flops down. Ed watches her for a moment and asks, "Red or white?"

"White."

He brings her a large glass, placing it on the coffee table close to her left hand. He sits on the other end of the sofa, asking one of those questions that he is pretty sure he already knows the answer. "How'd it go with the bid?"

"It was fucked up like Hogan's goat."

"What!"

"It was—"

Ed interrupts, "I heard. Where do you get those kinds of things?"

"I think maybe it was one of Dad's, can't remember for sure, but sure describes the bid."

"What about it?"

"Someone had put in last year's cost of materials and last year's overhead. The numbers just didn't look right to me, so I started checking around and wound up going back through everything." She sips some wine. "You know how the price of steel has skyrocketed and everybody received raises this year. We would've lost our butts on this one. I'd like to get my hands on whoever that was."

"Good for you. I hope they appreciate what you've done."

She smiles. "I'm thinking bonus." She clenches her fist.

Ed waits until she settles down and begins to relax. When she's part way through her second glass of wine, he says, "Michael told his soccer coach today that he wasn't going to play anymore. He quit the team."

She quickly sits up straight on the couch and leans forward to stand. "Where is he? We're going to see about this."

Ed holds up his hand. "Now just a minute. We need to talk about this before you go off on him."

She sees the concern on his face and sits back down on the sofa. "OK," she says attentively.

"I could tell when I picked him up from practice today that something was wrong. He looked absolutely miserable. I decided not to push it and just wait until he brought the subject up. On the way home, he said he told the coach he wasn't going play anymore."

"Why?"

"I didn't say anything or ask any questions. I just said OK."

"But, Ed, there are other things involved in this. He can't quit something just because it gets too tough for his liking. When you start something, you're supposed to finish it. You just can't quit because it gets too hard. There's such a thing as commitments that go along with being a team member. Beyond that, what's he going to do from the time he gets out of school and when we pick him up after work? Is this about some trouble with the coach or some of the other players?"

"I don't know. I'm just saying he feels pretty bad. I've not seen him like this. I think we should just give it a rest, let him deal with it. We don't want to react in a way that will make the whole thing worse. As far as the after-school thing goes, I can take a break from work to pick him up. He can hang out with me. There's an empty office just down the hallway from mine where he can do his homework. I don't think it'll be a problem. I made a couple of calls, and it's fine, really."

"I guess that's all well and good, but I still want to know what the hell is going on." They hear a noise and turn to see Michael standing in the kitchen, watching them. After an awkward silence, Michael says, "Nothing is going on with the coach or the other players. It's just that I'm not a very good soccer player." He smiles and points to his feet. "Look at me, I'm a short, pudgy guy with big feet. I must have the biggest feet in the history of junior high soccer. Oh, I might also mention that in addition to being very long, they're also very wide." He moves his head in an exaggerated nod that makes his long red curly hair flop up and down. Giving a small wave, he turns and walks down the hall.

Nancy winces but tries to continue to keep the moment light. She says as he is moving away, "Don't forget the red hair, Michael."

"What?"

"Have you ever seen a really good soccer player with long red curly hair, not to mention the big feet?"

He shakes his head and smiles. "No, now that you mention it, in fact, I think I read somewhere that there's actually a rule about red hair and big feet that relates to how much playing time is allowed." He closes his bedroom door behind him.

Nancy sinks back into the sofa with tears in her eyes. "Shit! I was just hoping he would find something he could be really good at."

"Why?"

"Ed, we have been through this time and again. He seems to be just going through the motions with us, with school and just about everything else. I worry that he might be depressed or something. It's such a tough age. It would be good if he could find something he could get really excited about."

"Well . . ."

She holds up her hand to stop him. "I know, I know we have been through this a hundred times. You always say, 'What's wrong with being average? Leave him alone and he will find something.' Dammit all anyway. I'm worried about right now, not ten years from now." She slaps the arm of the sofa and begins to cry.

Ed sighs heavily and says evenly, "I suggest you keep your voice down and stop crying. It's not going to help. If he decides to come out here and sees you like this, it will only make matters worse for him. You know how he is. He'll start taking responsibility for your feeling bad. Now, why don't you go to the bathroom and get yourself straightened up. It's been a long day, and we have plenty of time to talk this over."

She makes a snarling expression with her lips. "As much as I hate to admit it, you're right." She takes her glass of wine with her as she leaves.

He yells as she is closing the bathroom door. "What kind of pizza do you want?"

"I want sausage and eggs. We might as well all die together."

Ed walks to Michael's bedroom door and bangs on it with his open hand. "Marcia cleaned up the breakfast dishes, so it's your turn to take care of the dinner dishes. Come on and set the table, and I'll start cooking the sausage."

"Hey, Dad, what about the rule that says something about clumsy redheads handling dishes?"

"Pele could have done it with one of his big toes, come on and get with it."

The sausage hits the hot pan with its distinct sizzle. Michael begins setting the table when the phone rings.

"Hello . . . Who? . . . Just a minute."

"Who is it, Michael?"

"I can't tell for sure. I can barely hear him because his voice is so soft, but I'm pretty sure he said 'Grandpa.' I think he's calling from Alaska."

He takes the phone to the bathroom door. "Hey, Mom! Your dad is on the phone."

"I'll take it in here."

Ed rolls the sausage back and forth in the pan then begins cracking eggs into a bowl with cream and beating them with a fork. Marcia comes into the kitchen, pulls a toaster out from one of the back cupboards, and begins making toast. When it is all done, they sit around the table, waiting. Finally, Ed calls out, "Your supper is getting cold."

"That's OK, you guys go ahead. I'll be there after a bit."

Michael cleans the dishes, leaving a plate for his mother. He and Marcia go to their room. Ed turns on the television. After the evening news, he goes to check on Nancy. She is sitting half dressed on the edge of the bed, wiping her face with a cold washrag. For a moment he thinks he will sit next to her and put his arms around her, but he is not certain if she's sad or angry. Being sad gets a hug, but being angry gets a question. He plays it safe with a question. "Was that your dad on the phone?"

"Yes."

Ed also knows that anger gets to the center of things very quickly, but at the cost of there being some collateral damage, he asks very softly, "How's he doing?"

She looks at him, her eyes smoldering. "Do you know how many times when I was growing up that I would lie there in my bunk on that tugboat, smelling the bilge, and wish for a normal childhood, things like an ordinary house with a sidewalk so I wouldn't have to slosh through the muskeg to go anywhere, some friends who are right across the street, a trip to the store that didn't involve getting in a skiff with an outboard that always needed some tinkering with before it would start, maybe a summer that I could go to art camp instead of helping tow logs with that old beat-up tugboat?"

"He couldn't help it if your mom died. He just did the best he could."

"I don't blame him, but I did wish, on more than one occasion, that my dad was just a normal dad."

"Why did he call? He doesn't call much."

Nancy begins to wilt out of her anger. "He's had a stroke."

"Oh no! How is he?"

"He sounds really old. If he hadn't told me who he was, I would've never recognized his voice. He doesn't sound like the same person. His voice is so soft. You remember how he sounded when he yelled, you could hear him clear across the cove. It doesn't seem like he should be old. How in the hell did he get old?"

"Is he in the hospital?"

"No, he was for a while, in Juneau, I think, but he's back at the Cove. He called from the satellite phone at the grocery store. He says his left arm doesn't work very well, but he's getting better at figuring things out. I just can't see how he will manage all that there is to do on the boat and the house."

"Hey, maybe this will get him out of there, and he'll finally admit he needs some help, live someplace where there's somebody around to take care of him."

Her temper flares up again. "Goddamn him, Ed!" Her voice trails off. She is shaking her head and clenching her fists.

"No?"

"Any normal person would come to that conclusion, but you know what he's doing? He says he's working very hard, doing everything his physical therapist tells him because he has a contract with Alaska Logging Corporation to beach-log a raft of logs that broke loose in a storm."

"He can't do that."

"They told him that, but he insisted, saying he would hire someone who was just as experienced as he was to operate the tug.

They agreed, and he says they've been very clear, very precise about who he hires. If who he hires can't meet all of their specifications, they will cancel the contract and the logs have to be recovered by the end of August."

"That's a tall order."

"Not only that. Whoever he hires has to know that area, be familiar with the tides, and basically do everything he can do: fix all of the breakdowns, raft logs, have a bunch of experience running a tug in Southeast Alaska, know all of the tides and currents of that particular area, where good anchorages are, what a weather report means. In other words, all of those details that need to be taken care of before they collectively become a big deal. They also specify it has to be someone who isn't a heavy drinker so they won't go on drunk for a week after they get their first paycheck. He says they're going to enforce the contract to the letter."

"You mean they want a tugboat captain that is highly qualified for just that area? You should relax. They're never going to find someone with all of that kind of experience. There are some good people around, but nobody is going to be able to measure up to all of that. Nobody knows what Owen knows about Sumner Straits and the outside of Prince of Wales Island. It looks to me like there isn't anything to worry about. They know he can't find anyone with those qualifications, and the job has to be completed by August. Unbelievable! He has to find someone in the next six weeks or so if the job has to be done by the end of August. I can't believe he agreed to all of that. You must be right about the stroke affecting him."

Nancy rubs her face with both hands. "You know, Ed, as it turns out, he can find someone who would just fit the bill. He only had to make one phone call."

Ed's face shows an expression of sudden understanding. "Aw, Nancy."

"Yep, that would be me. They didn't know about me."

"Come on, be realistic. You just can't pack up to Alaska and go beach logging. That would be way too complicated. Actually, it would be way more than that. I mean, with your job and with the kids in school, we need to be realistic about all of this."

"That's what I said."

"And?"

"He said we can get it done if we catch the high tides in late May or June. We can get the bulk of the logs off the beach on those tides with just the skiff, then get the ones that are hung up and a couple of bundles that didn't break up at the end of June. He thinks we can do it in a month or so."

"Actually, that does sound possible, not that I'm saying it's a good idea or anything like that."

"I know, I know. I need a little help here. I don't want to go back there to all of that, but you should have heard him. He not only doesn't sound like the same person. I mean, the way his voice sounds, he was actually asking for help. I don't remember him ever asking for help. He had a hard time doing it."

"What did you tell him?"

"I would think about it."

Ed thinks, *Oops.*

Ed leaves the bedroom door ajar as he walks out. "You better come get something to eat. I'll put your plate in the microwave."

In the living room, Nancy picks at the food on her plate that sits on the coffee table in front of her. Each of them is lost in their own silence. Michael comes shuffling into the living room barefooted with his red curly locks hanging uncombed over his face and down the back of his neck. He flops down in an overstuffed chair with his back against one armrest and his feet hanging over the other. He stares at his bare feet, announcing, "The kids at school call me 'feets.'"

Nancy looks up. "Are they being mean when they say that?"

"I don't know for sure. I don't think so, they're just teasing. Some of the girls call me short-round, and I think they're being nasty." He instinctively squeezes the fat roll on his stomach. "Can you tell me of at least one pudgy redhead with big feet that became famous?"

"That's an easy one, Winston Churchill."

"Did he have big feet?"

"To tell you the truth, I don't know, but he was definitely pudgy."

Michael looks at his mom, staring at her still-unfinished plate of food, lost in her own thoughts. "What's the matter, Mom?"

"Your Grandpa Owen had a stroke."

"Did he die?"

"No, but he said he can't use his left arm very well."

"Oh well, I guess it could have been worse. Can he get along OK with that?"

Nancy looks at Ed; he says, "Go ahead and tell him the rest of it."

Nancy carefully recounts the phone conversation, explaining as best she can some of the decisions that face her. She ends with pointing out how it all rests with her because she is the only one who's qualified under the contract with Alaska Logging Corporation.

Michael leaps to his feet, causing his hair and stomach to bounce and jiggle; he is astounded. "Mom, you never told me any of that stuff. Holy crap, you can do all of that stuff? Run a tugboat, tow logs, yank logs off the beach!" He stares at his mother with an open mouth.

"Michael, it's not that intriguing. It's mostly just a lot of hard work and miserable weather. Please don't romanticize this. I couldn't wait to get out of there."

She sees the look in his eyes and tries again. "I'm serious, it's not what it sounds like. It's . . . it's . . ." she gropes for the correct words, "it's very difficult. More than that, it's grim and arduous in ways that are impossible to explain to you." Nothing she says even gets close to getting through to him.

"You can work on engines?"

"Yes."

"Can you run a chainsaw?"

"When I was younger, if I had to."

"My god! You're a logger!"

"Not really, more like a deckhand."

"Why didn't you tell us that you did all that stuff?"

"I was afraid you would make too big of a deal of it." She juts out her chin and gives him a hard look. "Like you're doing right now. It's not a good way to live or make a living. You'll have to trust me on that."

Marcia is standing in the kitchen. Michael says, "Marcia, have you been listening to this? Our mother's a closet logger." They both laugh.

Nancy is still glowering. She leans back on the sofa in resignation. "I told you I grew up in the Cove, and I've told you what it was like living there in the isolation and bad weather. I just didn't think I needed to go into all of the details. Beach logging was just a small part of what we did. Mostly we towed small rafts of logs from the log dumps at the logging camps to ships loading them for export or to some of the small mills around the Panhandle.

"The logging camps were built on floats, so we towed them when the camps relocated. Of course there were always small barges with equipment that needed to be moved and fuel barges coming and going to town. We stayed busy, sometimes busier than we wanted to be. Being a deckhand generally means working long hours in nasty weather and, in our case, with marginal equipment. There's one thing I know for sure, I can't sit here in this comfortable setting to which we are all accustomed and make you understand how miserable it can be. Your dad and I have worked very hard to ensure you won't have to go through anything like that. We're are glad that's all behind us."

They both turn and look at Ed. "You did it too?"

"For a year or two, that's how I met your mother."

Marcia looks at Michael in mock horror. "The secret lives of Ed and Nancy!"

Michael asks, "Is that why we don't ever visit Grandpa Owen?"

"That's part of it, yes."

"Why doesn't he ever come visit us?"

Nancy begins to vacillate. "Your Grandpa Owen is just a different sort of person, is one reason." She looks up from her plate. Michael is sitting cross-legged, staring directly at her. His elbows are resting on his knees. Marcia is sitting on the arm of a chair.

"How?"

"I don't know if I can explain it. For one thing, he doesn't care about things that other people care about."

"For example?"

"He doesn't care what kind of clothes he wears or how they look, what other people think of him or what they say about him. He found a pair of cheap coveralls washed up on the beach with someone's name written on the back, large letters in magic marker, 'Bob Ohmer.' He wore them for years. He's not much on casual conversation. He likes isolation and miserable weather and that damned old tugboat, which is older than he is, by the way. When you come right down to it, the boat is not only what he does. It's who he is. He hates going to town, and I don't mean a town like Seattle or Lynnwood. I mean a town that only has one gas station and two bars, most people wouldn't even call that a town. He's never told me much about himself, but I think he grew up somewhere in northern California, but I don't even know that for sure. I don't know anyone who likes being around other human beings less than he does. He's just so damned content with being peculiar it's somehow annoying."

"Is he grouchy? Is that why he doesn't like being around other people?"

"No, he's not grouchy at all. I don't know any particular reason, I guess. I wish I could explain it better, but to tell you the truth, I try not to think about it, so I don't."

Michael won't let it go. "So he doesn't go to town or talk to other people, just sits there by himself and looks at the end of his nose?"

"No, no, he goes wherever there's work. There are always things to be done on boats, particularly on an old wooden one. Something needs fixed most every day."

Michael has a puzzled look on his face. "How big is the Alaskan Panhandle?"

"It's about the size of Florida."

"Let me get this straight. Grandpa can just walk out his front door, start his boat, and go anywhere he wants in the Panhandle?"

"That's right. Well, I guess, technically he could go anywhere in the world. It's the Pacific Ocean but the Panhandle for sure."

"Anytime he wants?"

"Sure, weather permitting of course."

"Why don't we ever call him?"

"He doesn't have a phone."

"Does he have a computer?"

"No."

They all sit watching each other. Nancy can tell Michael is intrigued by their conversation. She doesn't want him to be interested, but he is. Ed is watching closely.

"Him not having a phone isn't the only reason you don't talk to him much, right?"

"I think that's a fair statement."

"Is Grandpa Owen short and red-headed?"

"Yes."

"A bit pudgy?"

"Yes."

Michael rises and walks to his bedroom. When he's leaving, his dad can see a small smile on his face. Ed says, "I'll bet you a hundred dollars he's in his room right now on Google Earth, checking out the Alaskan Panhandle."

"Shit, shit, shit!"

"Just a word of caution, the more evasive you are about this, the more interested he will become."

"I just want him to have a normal life and do what other kids do—go to school, hang out with his friends, have pimples, do arm farts in the lunchroom, just be a kid. That's all I want. The last thing I want is for him to become a deckhand on a tugboat and start hanging out with the guys on the fuel float, drinking beer."

"Jeez, Nancy, you're going down that road way too fast. Slow down and give Michael some credit. He just asked a couple of questions about his grandpa."

"But he's just a kid."

"Hold on a minute here. It seems to me we were just talking about how worried we were that he's lost interest in soccer and we were upset about him saying he's pudgy and has big feet. Now you're worried that he's too interested in something?"

"Ed, you know perfectly well what I'm talking about."

"I do but I'm not sure you've come to the best conclusions. You haven't said you're even going to Alaska, yet and you've got Michael hanging out on the fuel float drinking beer with the guys."

In the next few days, their routine is punctuated by Michael appearing out of his room with printouts of maps and charts of Southeast Alaska, presenting them to his mother with a series of questions. "Have you been to Haines?" "How about Sitka, Wrangell, Craig, Port Alexander?" "Show me some places you've anchored." "Is this a good anchorage?" "What is a fathom?" "What's a knot?"

She patiently and calmly answers all his questions, and when he's done, he disappears back into his room.

The next Friday afternoon, when they arrive home, Marcia and Ed hang back on the front porch while Michael and Nancy enter the house. They hurry back to the car and retrieve a marine chart from the trunk. They hurry to the living room and unroll it on the carpet, placing an empty coffee cup on each corner. After Nancy changes clothes, she enters the living room to see them on their hands and knees, scrutinizing it with focused interest. She comes to look over their shoulders, and when she realizes what they are looking at, she says, "Dammit, Ed, will you just leave this alone."

Marcia says, "This was my idea, Mom."

"Marcia, why would you want a chart of"—she looks more closely, checking to see exactly what chart it is—"Sumner Straits?"

Marcia kneels on the floor and points to a place on the chart with an inordinate amount of interest. "This place here, Exchange Cove, has a spot up here in this corner that's marked log rafts. Are there log rafts there?"

"Not anymore, that area has already been logged, but they did keep them there. That little corner of the cove is protected from weather. But what are you—"

Marcia interrupts, "So, Mom, how long would you estimate it could take to tow a raft of logs, say, a raft of two boom logs wide and fifteen boom logs long, to the mill in Wrangell?"

"What? How did you know about . . . ?"

"Oh yes, you would go when the tide was flooding of course, so you would pick up about three knots when you go through that narrow spot between the bottom of Wrangell Narrows and St. John's harbor, don't forget that."

Nancy's eyes narrow to little slits. She puts her hands on her hips. "Ed Simpson, you put her up to this!"

Marcia reaches out and tugs on one of her mother's arm. "Mom, Mom, I forgot."

"It's been a dry summer, so the current from the Stikine River isn't as swift as it usually is, maybe a knot and a half or something like that. You'll have to factor that into your estimate."

Ed says, "That should be an easy problem for an old salt like yourself." Seeing the quizzical frustration on Nancy's face, Ed and Marcia erupt into loud laughter. Ed bends over and grabs his knees. Marcia rolls on the floor.

"You both think you're so funny."

"Come on, you have to admit we had you going pretty good."

The three of them sit and begin to relax. "I admit I bit right into that one. I was thinking, 'How in the hell did Marcia know all of those details, the number of boom logs in a raft, the tides in that stretch of water between Exchange Cove and Wrangell?'"

"Dad just told me he worked one summer for Grandpa Owen."

Nancy frowns at Ed.

"I know we agreed not to mention your growing up there, but since she already found out some of the details, I figured it was OK."

"That was the summer I broke my leg, the summer we met."

"When I first saw you standing on the deck leaning on a pike pole, I was a goner. It was love at first pike."

"Shit-o-dear, Mom, you never told us you broke your leg. How did you do that?"

"It slipped down between two logs when I was trying to run across a raft. I kept going, but my leg stayed right in that crack. Watch your language, young lady."

Marcia shakes her head in disbelief at both of her mother's comments. They sit in silence for a few moments, then Ed speaks. "Your dad called me at work today. He wants to know if you would call him back with an answer. He needs to try and find someone else if you can't make it."

"I get it now. After he called, you and Marcia cooked up this little scheme to try and soften me up a little bit before I called him back."

"That was part of it."

"What's the other part?"

"Marcia and I have been talking, and we think you should go help your dad."

"Ed, you know I can't do that."

"Mom, you have to, and that's all there is to it."

Marcia's directness irritates her. "You think so, do you?"

Ed says, "Actually, there's more to it than that. Not only do we think you should go, we also think you should take Michael."

"No, no, no, and no."

"Just hear me out. I have talked to Michael's teachers and the principal, and they say if he works some extra time before he leaves and takes some stuff with him, he can keep up. If he needs some help, you can help him or maybe the teacher there."

"You mean if they have one."

Ed ignores her comment. "You have a whole bunch of vacation time because you never take any time off work, and you have just saved the company a whole pile of money on that structural steel bid. We think you don't have any good reasons not to go, so it's really up to you and how you want to deal with your dad. The details of this whole thing will work."

"What do you mean 'deal with my dad'?"

Ed grimaces, knowing he needs to tread lightly. "From where I'm sitting, it seems like there might be a couple of things you need to put to rest or at least try to put to rest." He looks away.

"You mean with my dad?"

"Yes."

"Jesus Christ, all I've ever said is that I wanted a normal childhood and that wasn't possible because my dad was so weird or something like that. That didn't sound right, but you know what I mean."

"I do. Sometimes, or I should say often, when you talk of it, you seem angry. I don't know exactly why. Nevertheless, it's as if there is some sort of unattached blame floating around that doesn't ever get tethered down. It might not be a good deal if he died without you two talking again."

"I guess I can't argue that, and I do think about it more than I should, but there is no getting around the fact that growing up like that was so one dimensional. I can't bring myself to say it was exactly medieval, but it was close, without a doubt nineteenth century." She looks at the floor. "I'm having a hard time putting all of that into words. I'm always talking around the edges of whatever it is that is pissing me off. All I can say is that growing up like that was abnormal. That's all there is to it."

"Hey, Mom, there's no argument there. However, it doesn't sound like Grandpa Owen is going to be around much longer. This might be the last go-round. Maybe if you went up there, you could talk him out of this idea and help him figure out what to do next." Marcia brightens up with a smile. "That would be the normal thing to do."

Nancy looks at Marcia and points her finger. "One thing I do know for sure: Grandpa is not moving to town unless he is tied up, dead, or completely paralyzed." She pauses. "Well, dead would do the trick."

"Sounds like he's working on that, Mom."

Nancy shakes her head in desperation. "I suppose Michael has told everyone at school he's going to Alaska to work on his grandpa's tugboat."

"I think, in all fairness to Michael, he's been saying he 'might go,' as in there is a chance of it happening."

"When did Dad say he would call back?"

"Tonight."

"OK, Ed, how would you describe Michael's feelings about this?"

"I've never seen him so excited."

Nancy walks to the living room window, which looks out at the tall fence, which blocks the view of the neighbor's house. She says distractedly, "Don't forget to put the trash receptacles out by the curb. Tomorrow is Thursday."

"OK."

"I'll go talk to Michael's teachers so we can get his schoolwork organized."

The next day, Nancy walks into Michael's homeroom just before lunch. The class is still seated, and there's a low murmur of voices. She has intentionally come when all of Michael's classmates are within range of her voice. She speaks to the teacher loudly enough to be heard by everyone. "I'm here to talk about what schoolwork Michael needs to do while he's in Alaska, working as a deckhand on his grandfather's tugboat." The murmuring stops; all eyes are on Michael. He is staring at his mother.

"He will have hours of work to do on deck and will be required to stand on wheel watch, but during those long hours, when we are towing a log raft in all kinds of weather, day and night, he will just have to sit down at the galley table and do his schoolwork."

Michael is stunned. Nancy asks the teacher, "Isn't it about time for lunch?"

"The bell hasn't rung for lunch yet, but Michael's mother and I do need to get started organizing his schoolwork for his trip to Alaska, so do you all think, if I excuse you a few minutes early, that you could help us out by going to the lunchroom quietly?" Heads nod emphatically.

"OK, quietly then."

As the last of the students enter the hallway, the teacher walks to the door to watch. He motions to Nancy to come watch. As the class moves away, Michael is surrounded by the other children. Questions are flying back and forth. They can see Michael's red curls bobbing up and down in the middle of the group as he turns to answer each question.

The teacher turns to Nancy. "Well done, now let's get our deckhand's work together."

5

Going Back

You can hear the plane before you can see it. Kasey yells from the railing next to the office. "Move those skiffs from the airplane float, mail plane's coming!" She points at the sky.

Folks begin to stir—the few sitting at the Saloon, the two men and the woman from the float house at the far end of the fuel float, a couple of fishermen from their moored boats. They cluster around the fuel pumps. Bob and Rich stop icing fish and watch from the deck railing. Kasey stands to one side, waiting to sort the freight. The pilot steps on the float as the plane glides into the dock, tying it off to a cleat. Nancy and Michael wriggle out of their seats past the boxes of mail and freight and stand expectantly. They are all silent for a moment. Two older fishermen, standing by themselves, begin to smile.

"Well, well, well, talk about surprises."

They all begin to talk at once. "Holy smokes! I thought you was never comin' back here."

"What happened? You get run out of Seattle?"

"Times must be tough in America if you're comin' back here."

"You don't have to tell us what you did, just let us know how soon the cops are gonna be here so we have time to hide out for a while." There is sniggering, the sound of a can of beer being popped open.

The pilot begins handing boxes of freight out of the rear door to Kasey; she sorts it into small piles.

"Hey, guys, how you all doing?" Nancy holds her hands in the air in mock surrender. "No cops after me that I know of anyway. I didn't know I was coming myself until a couple of weeks ago."

One by one they step forward to shake her hand. She says, "This is my son Michael."

"Nice to meet you, Mike."

"Hey there, Mike."

"About time you got up here and looked this place over."

Mary, standing next to Ralph Bodeen, waves from the back of the gathering. "Hey there, Nancy."

"Mary, oh Mary!" Nancy walks to her; they hug affectionately. They stand that way for moments, then Mary puts her hand on Ralph's shoulder. "This is my friend Ralph Bodeen. He's living in my boat shed for a while."

"Pleased to meet you, Ralph. Mary and I go back a long way. I spent a lot of time with her when I was growing up."

He removes his hat. "Ma'am."

"When we get settled, I'll come over and we'll catch up."

Nancy starts back through the group, shaking hands, patting people on the back. As she gets back to Michael, she asks, "Where's Rusty? Did he move on? I didn't think he would ever leave here."

They all go quiet for a moment, then someone says, "He's dead."

Nancy gets a puzzled look on her face. "What!" She thinks for a moment. "Couldn't have been that old, was it some sort of accident?"

Arlo holds his hands in the air and shrugs. "He just died. We found him in his sailboat lying on the floor. He was just dead, didn't show up at the Saloon for a couple of days, but we didn't think much about it. You know how he used to just hole up for a while to think about stuff. He'd been dead for a while though, started to puff up some. We called the state trooper in Wrangell, but he was out of town on something else. They said it would be at least a couple of more days before they could get out this way. We told them he was puffed up and we didn't know if he would explode or something if we left him too long. They said it couldn't be helped, they only had a couple of officers and they were all busy. We offered to let the air out of him and stick some ice in him, but they said not to touch the body till they got here, but we packed some ice around him and threw a tarp on him anyway. We're pretty sure he would've exploded if we hadn't done somethin'."

"Jesus!"

"They had a hell of a time gettin' him out of there, pretty smelly." Everyone nods in agreement.

They all stop talking for a moment. Finally someone turns to Michael and says, "Well, it ain't no secret who he's related to."

Michael looks at his mom curiously; she remains silent.

Kasey finishes stacking freight and holds a box wrapped in brown paper up in the air. "Bob, Rich, there's a package for you."

They look at each other. "What the hell? We didn't order anything. Rich, did you order somethin'?"

"Not me."

"It has your names on it, right here." She shakes the box at them. "Better come and get it."

They walk down the ramp and around the group clustered together, watching closely. "Kasey, I'm tellin' you we didn't order nothin'."

"You better open it up and see what it is then."

When they remove the wrapping, on the outside of the box is a picture of a life-size figure of an inflated naked woman, blond, blue eyed.

After a short silence, the group explodes into laughter. "Whoo-ee, Bob, I didn't know you had a girlfriend!"

"You been holdin' out on us, you devil."

"My goodness, Bob, I'll have to admit she's quite a looker."

"Yeah, won't give you any back talk either."

When the noise subsides, Kasey looks at Bob evenly. "Now you can stop pestering me."

Chagrined, Bob places the package on the pile of mail and starts back up the ramp. Rich picks up the package and follows.

Michael is watching closely, his eyes moving quickly from the two men to Kasey then back again. Nancy whispers in his ear, "We'll talk about this later."

He looks up at her. "It's OK, Mom. They're just joking around. You can buy them online."

"Michael!"

"Well, maybe not that one. He took the package with him."

Nancy looks at him, astounded.

"I'm just kidding, Mom." She doesn't look relieved.

Someone in the crowd laughs. "Sounds like he's got it figured out to me."

Nancy gives up on the conversation and glances toward the mouth of the cove. "Where's Dad?"

"He'll be here in a minute."

She hears the sound of an outboard as a skiff comes into view. Standing in the stern is her dad, short with large rounded shoulders; his left arm hangs straight down, his hand loosely grasping the tiller. He turns the skiff by leaning on the tiller with his leg. She sees him lean with his body. Until now it hadn't occurred to her that he would look so different, have difficulty doing something so routine as running a skiff. Even from a distance, he looks old.

Nancy instinctively reaches and pulls Michael closer to her, protectively. He doesn't notice; he's watching the approaching skiff intently as it turns parallel to the float. Owen reaches over the tiller with his right hand, shifting the engine into reverse, backs it into the float, shifts into neutral. He flings a line over the bull rail, reaching under it with his right arm. The skiff moves away from the float, but he stops it by leaning on his elbow. It's awkward and difficult; they all watch in silence as he ties a couple of half hitches. He manages to sit on the railing. Grabbing his left leg with his right hand, he swings himself onto the deck, kneels on his right leg, then stands.

He walks to Nancy with a rolling limp. He hugs her with his good arm. "Good to see you, Nancy, I didn't think you'd come."

"It's good to see you, Dad."

"You must be Mike." Owen reaches down and removes Michael's cap, ruffling his curly red hair with his hand. "Well, I'll be damned." His smile shows two gold crowns on his front teeth. Taking off his wool cap, he shakes his head, showing off his own shock of red hair. He takes a step back and looks at Michael's feet. "Yep, sure enough, those feet are way too big for a short guy like you." He laughs out loud.

Nancy watches. She is also taken by how much they are alike, down to some of his small facial expressions, even how Michael had latched on to the idea of going to Alaska. Researching all the small details, learning to read marine charts, poring over them for hours on end were exactly the ways her dad confronted new ideas. She looks down at Michael; there's a large smile on his face.

She understood the excitement that he felt about going to Alaska to see his grandfather for the first time, but she was also sure that once he discovered the isolation, no television, no Internet, saw the broken-down shacks and derelict boats, people living on the fuel float with their missing teeth and patched clothes, he might change his mind. When it sinks in that he doesn't have any of the comforts that she and Ed have worked so hard to provide them, he will understand.

"Well, Dad, it looks like you have had quite a time of it." She nods at his arm.

"Sure enough, but you can't let it get the best of you, eh? Gotta keep on it, gotta' think about the things you can do, not the things you can't." He clinches his left hand, making a fist. "See, I still got a little grip in that left hand." He hesitates and smiles a crooked smile. "Ain't much good for anything though."

Michael walks from his mother's arm and begins gathering up their luggage and placing it in the skiff. "Where do you want this, Grandpa?"

"Up near the bow."

When they are all seated in the skiff, Owen speaks to Michael, "Why don't you sit back here next to me?" He pats the seat opposite him at the stern. "We'll just go slow for a while, till you get the hang of things. When we need to turn to the port," he points a finger, "you just push on that tiller a bit and help me out. If somethin' doesn't go right, don't worry about it. We can always stop and figure it out. It's one of the advantages of running boats." The skiff disappears around a point; so does the sound of their voices.

6

The Meeting

When lumber comes out of the planer, it's cradled on parallel chains that hang on metal frames. It moves slowly but steadily to be sorted and stacked. The night shift compels Neil to think the whole rest of the world is sleeping while he's working, and in the morning, when his shift is done, the rest of the world is just getting started. In the darkness just beyond the floodlights, the town is asleep; working on the dry chain offers a kind of privacy that belongs, he thinks, just to him.

After work he stops by the Stockman's for a cup of coffee and breakfast. The waitress is always glad to see him and catches him up on most of the local gossip. Next he goes to Safeway to shop for something for dinner and lunches, then on to the post office. Once his errands are done, it's on home to get some sleep. There is comfort in the routine. Even at his young age, he has a leery distrust of surprises.

The idea of teaching in Alaska seems like a distant thought, maybe just settle in and work at the mill. What the hell, he can work some overtime, buy a house, get some sort of a rig, go hunting, get married, have a good life. All that sounds pretty damn good to him right now. When he's honest with himself, graveyard shift on the dry chain seems like an uncomplicated, down-to-earth way to live. The demands of school have disappeared: test deadlines, class schedules, assignments, trying to fit into somewhere he doesn't belong; all of that is gone. Write the whole college thing off as a good idea that didn't work; it happens all the time.

This morning after going through his morning routine, he enters the house quietly through the back door into the kitchen, and his mom is sitting at the table by the window, still wearing her cocktail dress.

"Hey, Mom, how's it going?"

"Oh, fine, I went out with a couple of friends after work and just got home a while ago. I haven't seen you for a while. I thought I would just wait up until you came home so we could visit a bit." She is still a little boozy, in a wary sort of way. She stubs her cigarette out in the ash tray. It takes several jabs trying to subdue the smoking embers, so she gives up and leaves it with several other butts. She's been waiting for more than just a while.

Neil watches her closely, knowing this is going to be more than just a "catch up on things" conversation. He isn't going to ask but will wait until she tells him.

"How's it going at the mill?"

"Oh, just fine, I'm liking it just fine."

"It's been hard for me to get up to see George, you know, with one thing or another. Have you had a chance to see him?"

"It's been a while, I thought he looked terrible."

"I heard he might be able to go home pretty soon, but I don't know that for sure, still having some problems I suppose." She seems evasive and looks out the window. "Well, I don't know for sure, but as you can tell, Rose doesn't care for me a whole lot, but I hear from others he's doing a little better although not by much. They're saying he'll never be the same again." She waves her hand and raises her eyebrows. "But you know how people talk. Sometimes the things they say aren't even true." She says it in a manner as if Neil might not understand.

"I'm sorry to hear that. He seems like an OK guy to me."

She changes the subject. "Now what are you doing at the mill, exactly? Do you like it?"

"I'm working on the dry chain."

"Is it hard work?"

"Not really, Mom. They have machines now that do most of the stacking. I mainly just keep an eye on things."

They sit without talking while he waits for the real conversation to begin. She plays with her coffee cup, tilting it from one side to the other. "When George went to the hospital and I went to Portland a few days later on my shopping trip, did I mention that while I was there, I met this man I really liked?"

"Nope."

"Anyway, I did, and we have been communicating with each other, and we've decided to take things a little further than just being friends."

Neil leans forward on the table, looking directly at her. "OK, so when's he moving in?"

She looks at him with her eyes open, a calculated expression of shock. "I didn't say he was moving in. I just met him a month or so ago."

Neil looks at her sternly. "Come on, Mom."

She lights another cigarette and in resignation says, "He has some personal things to taker of, so it will be a couple of weeks."

"Is he married?"

"Not anymore."

"You're not going to marry this one, are you?"

She acts shocked again. "Goodness, Neil, how would that look? And you know how people talk."

"People are going to talk no matter what. That's just how people are, but putting up with that is a lot easier than going through a divorce, just get them out of the house."

"I don't know. I think I love him."

"Mom, to be truthful, it doesn't matter to me whether you're married or not, but we have been through this several times now. I think you like the falling in love part much better than you do the rest. You love the romance part. After that, it gets harder."

"We'll see."

"Actually, the timing is just about right. I've been looking at an apartment up by the college. I'll be moved in there by the time he gets here."

"Honey, you don't have to move."

"I'm making pretty good money at the mill. I'm out of school. It's time to get on with things. Good of you to offer though."

"Any word on the Alaska job?"

"They're waiting to see if there will be enough kids to pay for a teacher, then we'll see if I get hired." He looks at his watch. "As a matter of fact, I haven't talked to the placement office for a couple of weeks. I should do that today."

She looks hurt and nervously rubs at the pencil line that is part of her eyebrow. He pats her on the shoulder and leaves.

As he enters the placement office, the man behind the desk smiles and waves. The man and Neil have become friends through his frequent visits and being the last of his class to be looking for work. "Mr. Osborne, your timing is impeccable. I have just received word from Southeast Island School District. It seems as though they might have cornered enough children at the Cove to warrant a teacher. Also, you may be pleased to hear that you did have some competition. You have been selected over the only other applicant, who is from some place in Georgia I can't even pronounce."

"Thank you for the vote of confidence." They both laugh. "When do I start?"

"September 10."

"Housing is provided, right?"

"There's an apartment in the school building."

Neil thinks for a moment. "Is the apartment available anytime, or do I need to wait until school begins?"

"As far as I know, it's available anytime, but I don't recall anyone ever asking that question until now. This is a job people take and are only there for one year. They arrive late and leave early, they use this job as a way to get their foot in the door so they can move on to something better in the district or any other place. A stepping-stone as it were, but I don't see why you couldn't spend part of the summer there. Just remember this place is right out in the middle of nowhere. Another thing to consider is you won't get paid until the end of September, but sometimes they will give you draw on your first check on the fifteenth."

"I kind of know where this place is. I've checked it out on a map. What's the best way to get there?"

The man scrutinizes him a bit. "If you're asking what is the cheapest way to get there, if it were me, I would take a bus to Bellingham, Washington, catch the Alaska State Ferry to Wrangell, Alaska. From there you might be able to get some sort of seat on a float plane that is making a freight run to the Cove. That could be four or five hundred dollars."

Neil winces at the price.

"You might get lucky and catch a fishing boat going that way or maybe a fish packer. That wouldn't cost anything."

"I could take some camping gear just in case I need to lie up somewhere."

The man chuckles. "Make sure it's waterproof."

The night before he leaves, Neil goes to the Broken Wheel where his mom is behind the bar. There are several people sitting on barstools, but the tables around the dance floor are empty. They all turn and look as he enters the room.

"Neil, how are you?"

"Heard you graduated."

"Way to go, Neil."

"Good to see you. I hear you're headed for Alaska. I've always wanted to go to Alaska."

He sits at a stool on one end of the bar. His mom comes to where he is sitting and places her hand on his arm. "Hi, honey, are you all ready to leave?"

"All set. The bus leaves at five in the morning."

"I'll buy you a drink. What would you like?"

He gestures at the half-full glass sitting on the shelf behind the bar. "I'll have whatever you're having."

"VO and water."

She slips a glass from a small rack next to the sink and picks up the bottle without looking, mixes the drink while surveying the other drinks on the bar to see if anyone is ready for another, turns slightly, and slides Neil's drink to him. The routine is all done without thought or calculation, years of practice. "Anybody need a refresher?" She turns back to Neil.

He hands her his car keys. "You take the car and do what you want. It's not worth anything, so it really doesn't matter. There are some books up in my room, but they're not worth anything either."

"Do you need a ride to the bus depot in the morning? I can just stay up after my shift ends and take you."

"I have all of my things in my backpack, so I'll hike down there. It isn't far."

She looks at the keys. Neil watches as she continues to examine them closely, finally realizing this is more than just a conversation at the bar. She becomes momentarily frozen by her thoughts.

Someone calls out from the other end of the bar, "See ya, Neil, you take care of yourself."

"Be careful."

"Let us know how it goes."

His mom says, "Call me when you get there to let me know you're OK."

"I don't know how all of that works yet except there isn't any cell phone coverage, but I'll get something figured out and let you know. I can call you from Wrangell, but after that, I'm not sure."

Just before he gets to the door, he hears her say, "I'll buy a round."

The bus arrives in Bellingham, Washington, just as daylight is breaking. At the Alaska State Ferry terminal, passengers are standing at the car ramp, waiting to board dressed in flannel shirts and rain gear. A light rain is falling. As the ship leaves, he stands on the aft deck, watching the white incandescence of the wake boil at the surface. Somehow he feels relieved.

Three days later, they tie up in Wrangell. It is 10:00 PM and quickly getting dark when Neil walks up the metal ramp to the parking lot. The drops of rain are large and thick; it's raining so hard the drops explode when they hit the pavement and the water bounces back up in the air. The few passengers who disembark with him are met by friends or family who quickly take them away. Other people scurry down the ramp and onto the ship. He takes cover in the entryway to the ticket office. When the last agent leaves, he asks, "Is there a camp ground nearby?"

"No, there isn't." She hurries through the rain to her car.

Neil stands looking into the closing darkness until it surrounds him. He sighs, shrugs his shoulders, unrolls his sleeping mat and bag on the concrete, and crawls in. It's quickly soaked in water, but his body heat warms it enough to fall asleep.

In the morning, he is awakened by a policeman poking him in the shoulder with a large flashlight. "No camping here. You need to leave."

"Right, right." Neil clumsily crawls out of the sleeping bag. His wet clothes stick to the inside of the bag, making it awkward and slow. He tries to explain, "Got in on the Taku late last night, didn't know what else to do."

"It's not a big deal, but you can camp up in the woods across the road if you want. That's where a lot of the transients stay." He points his flashlight to a hillside beyond a road.

"I hope I'm not here that long."

"And you're here because?"

"I'm trying to get to a place called the Cove. I guess that isn't its real name. People there just call it that, and there's a store there, some sort of business buying or selling fish."

"Why do you want to do that?"

"Schoolteacher."

The policeman examines him for a moment. "This your first job?"

"Yes."

"Huh."

"I'm looking for the cheapest way to get there. I've been told I might be able to catch a fishing boat going that way or a fish packer, but I don't know much about that, never been here before. I think a plane ride is too expensive. Do you know of any boats headed that way?"

The policeman rubs the side of his face with the flashlight. "Mmmmmm . . . not right off hand, put your stuff in the car. I'll take you to a boat harbor. You can start by walking the docks and asking around."

"Thanks, that'll be great."

The policeman is frowning when Neil gets in the car. "You know, it's none of my business, but do you know anything about the Cove?"

"Just what I've told you."

"It's not a place I'd go on purpose, but I'm in a different line of work than you are. I don't necessarily want to discourage you, but let me tell you about something that happened on my shift last year. We were notified that a medivac by float plane was going to arrive one morning from the Cove and we were to meet it when it landed, so we rounded up an EMT and headed down to the float plane dock. This guy gets off the plane; his hand is all bandaged up with gauze and black tape. The EMT asks, 'What happened?'

"The guy says, 'I got shot.' Some folks had been partying the night before. This guy gets in a fight, the other guy pulls out a rifle, and when they struggle over the gun, it goes off and shoots this guy's finger off.

"The EMT cuts the gauze and tape off his hand, and sure enough, the ring finger on his left hand gone. There's some bone sticking out of the wound, and vein or artery is kind of hanging down into his palm. We have a small medical clinic here in Wrangell but only one doctor. It's about 5:00 AM, so the EMT tells this guy that the clinic won't be open until 9:00 AM, so is there someplace he wants to go and wait, thinking maybe he has a friend or relative in town. The guy says, 'No, but I'm really hungry, maybe we could get some breakfast.' I've never seen anything like it. We had a hell of a time convincing him that wouldn't be a good idea because the doctor was going to have to give him an anesthetic and they don't do that on a full stomach. So we interviewed him, and he sat there talking to us like it was a traffic ticket or something like that. I asked him if he was going to press charges. 'No,' he said, 'he's a friend of mine, we'll just work it out.' As far as I know, they did, we didn't hear another word about it, never seen anything like it. I just thought that story might be useful information for someone like you who is going to live there."

Neil says, "I hope I don't have him in class."

The policeman stops at the boat harbor. "Good luck."

Svarre Olsen is old. He has fished out of Wrangell his whole life, all eighty-five years of it. He doesn't fish hard anymore, from spring to fall, like he did for years, but he still fishes the peak of the coho and king salmon runs out of the Cove. He anchors out in some of his favorite spots on occasion, but mostly he ties up at the fuel float at night. He has quit counting the seasons he might have left; the thoughts of being unable to fish and not being out on the water are thoughts he concentrates on keeping out of his mind. To die on deck would be all right with him. His wife doesn't like him to talk about that. She is afraid it might be some sort of premonition. That's fine with him; he doesn't want to talk about it either, so they don't. But of course, they both think about it. Once he said he couldn't figure out why it mattered at all because when you're dead, you're dead regardless of where the body was, but that didn't go over very well.

He has had the same boat for over fifty years, made of old growth fir, two-inch planking that has been renailed twice. It was built in 1938 before plastic boats and when there were still many good carpenters and lots of good wood. It draws seven feet of water when it's full of ice and fish. The wood below the waterline is pickled from the saltwater. Svarre likes its heaviness as it moves smoothly through the water. It lies—well, rolls—slowly in heavy weather, squatting down into the swells when wind gusts strike. He long lined with it when he was younger in just about any weather. When other fishermen talk about it, they always include the phrase "A good sea boat." One thing Svarre knows for certain, the boat is still a whole lot tougher than he is these days.

The storm from last night is over; the day is warm and sunny. He sits on the hatch cover, tying leaders and sharpening hooks. When he straightens up to stretch his back, he sees a young man walking down the float toward him. His clothes are wrinkled, and the sleeping bag perched on top of his backpack is soaking wet; so is the young man.

You can always tell the ones who just arrived from down south. They all have backpacks, hiking boots, and rain gear that is worse than useless.

The young man walks to the end of the float and watches the gill netters lined up to sell fish at the cold storage plant. He stares into the milky green water that has been colored by the freshwater from the Stikine River. He sticks his hand into the freezing water and leaves it there, feeling its coldness, and when he pulls it out, he holds the small puddle that remains in his hand, looks at it up close, then tastes it. He stands there for the longest time, cocking his head from one side to the other as if he is trying to grasp a smell or trap a sound. When he turns back up the float, he begins to scrutinize Svarre's boat.

Svarre doesn't look up but concentrates on making up the leaders; it will be the same conversation that happens every summer when these people arrive from down south.

"How long have you lived here?"

"How is fishing?"

"What kind of fish do you catch?"

His indifference doesn't seem to matter to the young man who walks over to his boat.

"Hi."

Svarre continues to tie a hammered brass spoon to a leader, nodding in response but continuing to ignore him.

"Oh, sorry, you're working." He turns to leave.

And because the conversation takes this unexpected turn, Svarre says, "That's OK, I'm just finishing." He coils the leader in a circle around his hand and lays it beside him.

Then the young man asks a new question, pointing east to the mountains behind town. "What's over there?"

"Nothin'."

"I mean, if you just keep going."

"There's still nothin' except trees, bears, deer, moose, mountain goats, glaciers, and all of that, but no towns or people, if that's what you mean."

The young man stares east for the longest time. "Perfect." He refocuses on Svarre, "This sure is a nice boat."

"Thanks."

He points west. "Same thing that way?"

"A few people, but not many until you get to Japan, whole bunch of people in that neck of the woods."

"Sounds good to me."

Svarre studies him for a moment. "Generally, young fellas like yourself who are walking the docks in hiking boots and backpacks are looking for a job."

"I have a job. I'm the new teacher at a place called Harbor Cove."

"Yeah, well huh."

The young man points one arm west and one arm east simultaneously and looks at Svarre. "So what you're saying is that in both directions, there's nothing out there but critters and trees and damn few people."

"That's about it."

The young man smiles. "I don't know why that sounds so good to me, but it sure does."

Svarre points west. "Harbor Cove is that way."

"That's where I'm trying to go."

"You can catch an airplane."

"Yes, well, a plane ride is kind of expensive. School doesn't start until September."

A boat makes its way into the harbor, slipping into view from behind the breakwater. Neil turns to watch it closely with fascination. Svarre recognizes the look; the young man is captivated.

"You ever been on the ocean?"

"No, sir, I have, never seen anything like it or been in country like this." He shakes his head.

Svarre smiles at the young man's enthusiasm and reaches out his hand. "My name is Svarre Olsen."

"I'm Neil Osborne."

"I'm headed to the Cove in a couple of days. You're welcome to ride along. It'll save you an air fare."

"Great, I'll work on the boat or do whatever you need done to help out."

"Not much to be done, but we'll see."

The morning they leave, Neil is waiting eagerly next to the boat when Svarre arrives. When the engine rumbles to life, Svarre points to a line at midship that is tied to the dock. "When the tide is at this stage, it will pull the boat to the stern, when we untie, I don't want to be bumping into any of those boats behind me." He points to make sure Neil looks at the boats to their stern. "I want you to do exactly as I say so we won't have any problems." His tone is intentionally direct and severe. He wants to see Neil's reaction. If he shows any hint of anger, he will tell him he has changed his mind. He's too old to be dealing with any crew problems after they leave port.

Neil notices the change in attitude. "Just tell me and I'll do it."

Svarre continues on with his cranky demeanor; his instructions are impatient and abrupt. "You stand by this line here." He points again at the tie-up line at midship. "I'll get the bow and stern lines."

Neil climbs on board and stands at midship next to the cleat on which the rope is fastened, and waits. Finally, he says, "You know, Mr. Olsen, if me going to the Cove with you is going to be a problem, I can figure something else out. I appreciate the offer, but something else will work out."

Svarre begins to untie stern line and says evenly but with less of an edge to his voice, "No, I think it will work out fine. It's only about a six-hour run. I think you can stand me that long."

They catch the outgoing tide, and that, combined with the currents from the river, they make good time at nine knots. The day is clear and the water is flat. Neil stands on the back deck, looking at the jagged mountains beyond town, up the river and into Canada. The jagged skyline looks as if the mountains have somehow been broken off at the tops rather than formed. They completely fill the horizon, forming a wall of ice and snow and rock. The only break in the wall is where the Stikine makes its way through to the ocean.

All this is void of anything human. The view is visceral, and in some strange way, Neil feels an enormous sense of relief. He turns to look forward. Svarre is standing behind him.

He points with an old gnarled finger. "I never get tired of looking at that." He turns back into the cabin.

Neil has thousands of questions but decides to keep them to himself, and Svarre doesn't offer any comments or information. They both become content with the silence.

As they enter the Cove, Neil sees Everett's buildings first then studies the others, the unfinished houses and the derelict boats that are either sunk, anchored, or rafted to the fuel float. The large sign saying Mercantile hanging from just below the gable of the largest building dominates the scene. There is a group of people sitting under a small canvas roof at one end of a float, watching as they tie the boat to the float. They are dressed in frayed and threadbare clothes; all are unkempt. A woman calls out, "Svarre, how's it goin'?" One of the men has a finger missing from one hand.

Svarre doesn't respond until the boat is tied and the lines are checked, then he says loud enough for all to hear, "I brought you the new schoolteacher."

"Way to go, Svarre, and just in time for the meetin'."

Svarre calls back, "I thought it might be handy to have it at the school so's more people would have a place to sit down."

"You mean the ones that ain't standin' up and yellin'." The group laughs, looking back and forth at one another.

Neil turns to Svarre. "Meeting?"

Svarre points to Everett's office. "Go on up there and ask whoever's in there about the meetin'."

"Thanks for the ride."

"Sure." He turns and disappears into the wheelhouse."

Neil thinks as he ascends the ramp, *I don't think he's in any danger of wearing out his vocal chords.* He slings his pack over his shoulder and opens the door of the office. Kasey says sharply without turning her head, "There's three boats ahead of you, so you'll just have to wait your turn."

Her abruptness startles him. "Well then, as soon as I get a boat, I'll get in line."

She turns to look at him over her shoulder. "What do you want?"

"Svarre Olsen told me to ask whoever was in this office about some kind of meeting. I don't know anything about a meeting, but somehow I get the feeling I'm involved in it, and I don't have a clue as to how or why."

"Who are you?"

"Neil Osborne, I'm the new teacher."

Kasey turns all the way around in her chair, facing him. "You're early. Most teachers arrive late and leave early. We all get real nervous at Christmas break because a couple of times, teachers have gone south for the holidays and didn't come back. What are you doing here so early?"

The question catches him completely off guard. It's a simple question but unexpectedly troublesome to answer. He anxiously sorts through his mind for some sort of response, but as he does that, it triggers more thoughts than he can process while he's standing in this strange little place that's somewhere out in the middle of nowhere.

"It's the only job I can get" would be a good answer, but that's not the sort of information a guy wants to offer up his first day in town. He hopes it will be a better job than working on the dry chain the rest of his life? Maybe it is and maybe it isn't. He just doesn't know about that—yet. It might be that it was just one boyfriend too many. Perhaps he just thought too much about how and why people become the way they are. Or it was just the idea of getting out of town and doing something different. In that case, anything might be OK. It could be the "will just check this out and leave before school starts if things get too strange."

Kasey is frowning at his long silence, so he gives the only accurate answer he can come up with. "I don't know for sure."

"Fair enough."

"About this meeting?"

"Yes, well, there isn't a short answer to that question." She points to Everett's desk. "You better have a seat. Do you have some idea of where you are?"

"Close to the north end of a fairly large island called Prince of Wales, I believe."

"Right. The Cove is a remote settlement, probably more so than the rest of the island because it is not accessible by a road of some sort. Most of the rest of the island has been logged over the years. They have to get to the timber to cut it, and then they have to get the logs to saltwater so they can be towed to the mills. All of that requires a road system. All of the other little towns and places like that they can drive around to hunt and fish and visit each other. Logging brings good jobs and all that, and that's their business. They like being on a road system, and that's good enough for me. If that's what they want, good on them.

"The Cove is not a town or a village or anything. We are not organized. We don't want to be organized, and we like it that way. We like it here because we don't want to be any of those things, because it isolates us from all those other people who wouldn't like the way we do things here anyway. For certain, they wouldn't want to live here. We like it just fine the way it is; roads bring civilization, whatever the hell that is."

"This has something to do with the meeting?"

"Yes, every year or so, the Forest Service, a.k.a. the "Feds," sends someone over from Juneau to hold a meeting to ask us if we want a road. We always say no."

"I take it that isn't the end of it?"

"For some reason, they keep coming back time and again like a little kid who thinks if she keeps asking the same question over and over, her parents will get tired of listening to her and change the answer."

Neil says, "That's probably not the reason."

Kasey frowns. "It's not?"

Seeing her frown, Neil immediately backs away from his statement. "Yeah, I don't know, since I just got here. I have no idea what's going on."

"What do you think the reason is?"

He deflects her question. "Pardon me, but I didn't catch your name."

"Kasey."

"Kasey, this is my first teaching job, and I have only been in Alaska a few days, and I have only just arrived here in the Cove less than an hour ago. The last thing I want to do is involve myself in some affair which I know nothing about. I have lived in small towns my whole life, and if there is one thing I know for sure, it's that keeping your mouth shut is a very valuable skill, and it's what I intend to do."

"Since you are such a greenhorn, whatever you think is going to be disregarded anyway so it would seem to follow that there wouldn't be any risk in telling me what you think, right?" She smiles, and her white teeth flash bright next to her brown skin.

Neil gives up. "Whatever the reason is that they keep coming back is something that they don't want you folks to know about, or they would have already told you."

"That's an interesting thought, and I'll tell you, just so you'll know, you're already involved. The meeting is being held at the school in two days. I'm guessing you'll need to be there."

He sighs and rubs his head. "How do I get there?"

"Here I'll show you." He follows as she walks outside, dodging her way through the activities of the men buying and icing fish. She stands next to Arlo.

"Arlo, this is the new schoolteacher."

Arlo puts his beer on the cap rail and holds out his hand. "Pleased to meet you."

"You bet."

Kasey points to the beach, which circles around from in front of the generator shed, making a small bight that connects the Mercantile to the boardwalk. "Now here is what you do: go out through the back door and walk along that beach there." She points again. "Go past that house with the pink insulation on the outside of it. Then you go up the boardwalk past that other boardwalk that comes in from the left hand side, the one with the skulls nailed to it."

"Skulls?" He looks perplexed.

"Yes, skulls." Seeing his expression, she continues on to explain, "Deer skulls." Then in an attempt to be precise says, "Well, there is one bear skull."

Neil shakes his head incredulously. "Well, of course, that would explain everything. A person should always have at least one bear skull to balance out a bunch of deer skulls. Makes perfect sense to me."

Neil looks at Arlo, and they both smile. Kasey catches the exchange and looks sharply at them, then goes back to her instructions. "Then you'll go up a little hill, and as you come down off that, there will be a set of buildings on the left. The larger building is the school, and the small building, the one closest to the boardwalk, is the library. The big building closest to the beach is the gymnasium, the middle building is the school building. Your apartment is in the back of the school building.

"Great."

"Arlo is the maintenance man. He works on the generator that supplies the power for the school. Is the generator running, Arlo?"

"Runs good, just hit the start button. It's the red one just above the battery, says START."

Neil asks, "How do I contact you if I need something fixed?"

"I'll be right here." He pats the cap rail.

"What if I want to read at night after I turn the generator off?"

"They's a little inverter connected to some batteries, be OK for a light or two, not the whole outfit though. That should do ya."

Neil retrieves his gear at the office and makes his way along the beach. As he walks, clams squirt water in the air. He stops, poking the rocks and gravel with the toe of his hiking boot, then kneels down digging with his hands. Finally he reaches down into the hole to retrieve a clam. Holding it in the palm of his hand, he examines it closely, tapping the shell, testing for hardness, holding it close to his nose, smelling, then puts it back in the hole, carefully filling it. He climbs through the bushes past the pink house, stopping to examine Mary's walkway, standing with one hand on his hip, scratching his head with the other.

Arlo says to Kasey, "He sure is a curious fella."

"You know, Arlo, I do believe you're right. I don't know what to think about that—yet."

The library is unlocked, and the door is wide-open. It's a small building made of thick cedar planks that have been manufactured to look like logs. The roof and sides are covered with a thin layer of green mold. Under the eaves are patches of thick green moss. Behind the library is a deck fenced and covered with webbing from a seine net, and inside the webbing is a rusty basketball hoop mounted on a post made from a tree trunk.

Inside the library are two young girls smoking cigarettes, who look to be thirteen years old, maybe twelve. The younger one looks at him over the top of the cigarette she's holding with two fingers. She pointedly blows smoke in his direction.

"What do you want?" she says.

"Just checking out the library."

"Not much of a library." She rolls her eyes and takes a long drag on the cigarette.

The books on the shelves are largely paperbacks. The few chairs and tables are covered with a layer of dust and grime. Cigarette butts are ground out on the floor. Neil sits at the small table and picks up a book that is lying there. It leaves a shadow in the dust. He flips through the page with his thumb. The two girls watch him now with growing unease.

"No, it's not."

"You here on a fishing boat?"

"No."

"What are you doing here then?"

"I'm the new schoolteacher, thought I'd take a look at the library."

They look nervously at each other then at the cigarettes in their hand. One says defensively, "Well, this really isn't a school building, it's a library."

They wait for his reply, but he continues to look at the book for an uncomfortable amount of time.

The older girl says, "Teachers don't last very long here. They can't stand living the way we do."

Neil smiles at her. "I guess you girls just came in here to read some books?"

They hurry out the door with a quick look over their shoulders.

The school has one classroom. Neil counts fifteen desks, sits in one, and looks around the room. There are a couple of jump ropes hanging on the coat hooks just inside the door. One rubber boot with the top folded over sits beneath the ropes, and a red rubber playground ball lies carelessly in one corner of the room. On the teacher's desk is a white metal box with a large red cross on the top. He raises the lid; it's full of gauze, bandages, disinfectants—everything needed to repair minor cuts, bangs, and bruises. It's pretty obvious he will be responsible for all sorts of things that aren't related to teaching kids. It also occurs to him there aren't any doctors or nurses within a couple of hundred miles. He makes a mental note to get some books on emergency medicine.

He takes a moment trying to sort through these thoughts but doesn't know where to start then decides he'd better get the meeting out of the way first.

He finds the custodial closet and begins cleaning. From all the mud and leaves on the floor, it looks as if the door to the school is never locked. There's not going to be much time to get things in shape for the meeting. As he works, a couple of the locals drop by. "Anything we can do?"

"To tell you the truth, I don't know what's going on. I think I'll just clean the floors and let it go at that. It won't take long, thanks."

"Just let us know if there is."

"Thanks.

"We think that'll work just fine." They give a small salute and leave; he forges ahead with the mop.

7

Screwed

The next day, a float plane arrives with a representative from the Federal Forest Service. He rents a room from Everett immediately on arrival and stays to himself. When he walks down the fuel float, the crew at the Saloon become unnaturally silent. He returns to his room after watching Bob, Rich, and Randy buy fish. Neil is just putting the finishing touches on the classroom. He carries a bag of trash to the porch, and the Forest Service man is standing there, nervous and guarded. He says, "Who are you?"

"I'm the new schoolteacher."

The man nods at the trash. "Getting ready for the meeting? I didn't realize there was a teacher here yet."

"Got here yesterday, I came early."

The man frowns. "Why would you do that? Generally, teachers—"

Neil interrupts, "Right, I've already been told, come late and leave early."

"At any rate, thank you for hosting the meeting."

"No problem."

"I think this will be a better place, and having a teacher present will lend itself to more civilized behavior. Last year we had the meeting in the grocery store. What a mess, unruly actually."

"Like I said, I just got here. We'll see, location might not matter."

"You're not going to allow beer, are you?"

"To tell you the truth, I hadn't thought about that. I didn't realize I was in charge."

The man becomes agitated. "But this is a public school building. You can't have alcohol in a public school building."

Neil shrugs.

"Well, if word gets back to the central office that you allowed alcohol in a school, you could be in big trouble." The man looks knowingly at Neil.

"I'll see what I can do."

"This is a public building," the man insists.

Neil puts his face up to the man's nose, close enough to smell aftershave lotion and stale coffee. "And I seem to be in charge of it, don't I?"

They stand like that for a moment, then they hear the sound of distant voices, rubber boots squeaking on the wet boards growing steadily louder as people come toward the school. "And if that is the case, then you'll have to give me a chance to handle this. I'll see what I can do." Neil can see the man's jaw muscles flex as he clinches his teeth.

A light rain is falling through the coming darkness. Small groups and couples make their way from the community boardwalk to the school. Where the walkway comes alongside the school, the lights from the windows illuminate the figures, but they are still little more than moving shadows. Neil watches a tall man with long, gently curling hair and OshKosh bib overalls emerge from the dark. With him is a skinny, almost frail woman wearing rubber boots that flop and rub against her bony legs. The drops of water on their clothes and uncombed hair sparkle as they move into the light. The crew from the Saloon stops talking the minute they see Neil.

The man from the Forest Service is in the classroom, standing by the teacher's desk, rechecking some papers. Kasey and Arlo nod at him as they pass by. Kasey says, "Everett can't make it tonight, he's all wore out."

They are followed by an old man who has had a stroke. His left leg doesn't work well, but he is moving with determination and without help. He's accompanied by a younger woman. Neil can't figure out if she is a daughter or a young wife. The young man with them is short with a whole head of curly red hair. He is definitely related to the old man with the bad leg and one arm that hangs unnaturally at his side. They all greet him with a smile and a handshake. "Hi, I'm Owen, this is my daughter Nancy and my grandson Mike. We have a place in the back bay." As he talks, he circles his good arm behind him, pointing in that general direction, through the trees that surround the playground. The young man says boldly, "We are beach loggers."

Others trickle in, and as they approach the door, they ritually stamp their boots and beat the water from their clothes with their hats. Most of them go to the back of the room and lean against the wall, staring forward from beneath the bills of their hats and tousled hair.

Neil notices the man from the Forest Service standing behind the teacher's desk, getting ready to speak with a dogged look on his face. Neil walks quickly to him, extending his index finger. "Hold on just a second." Then he turns to address the crowd gathering. "My name is Neil Osborne, and I just arrived a couple of days ago and was told about this meeting upon my arrival. I'm the new teacher. I'm not sure what's this is all about, but I guess the school is the best place for it. I did what I could to get ready on short notice." He turns back to the man from the Forest Service. "This gentleman has asked me to ask you not to have any alcohol or dope at this meeting, reminding me that this is a public building and booze and dope are not allowed." There is a murmur in the room. Neil goes on, "I don't know what to say about all of that, but if word of it gets back to town, it could cost me my job, I suppose, and I'd rather not get fired before I even start."

Someone calls from the back of the room, "Yeah, someone might call the cops." There is general laughter and amusement.

"Somebody gonna pat us down?"

"I volunteer to administer the rapid eye test to anyone who looks suspicious." A woman holds up her finger, squinting her eyes, examining the others closely.

"OK, but start with yourself."

She waves her finger rapidly in front of her nose then says with disgust, "Wouldn't you know it. I flunked my own test." This causes generally merriment and guffawing.

Finally, Randy says, "Come on, you guys, give this guy a break. Sneaking a drink at this meeting isn't going to make you any smarter." He fumbles in his coat and brings out a half-full pint of whiskey and a small bag of marijuana and walks to the porch, placing them on one of the outside windowsills. Others reluctantly follow suit until the windows are lined with pints of whiskey, baggies, and cans of beer. They return to the room and settle into an uncomfortable silence.

The man from the Forest Service begins talking. "My name is Jack Wilson. Most of you know me from the meeting we had last year. You all know what this meeting is about, so I won't go into that, but just let me summarize the Forest Service's position again for the record. The Forest Service feels that since most of Prince of Wales Island is on a road system, it should offer that service to every small community, in particular the more remote villages, when it is at all feasible.

"Surely the benefits are obvious. For example, just being able to drive a vehicle to your place of residence instead of packing all of the things you need for daily life up the beach and through the woods would be a huge advantage. Being able to drive to Craig for something as simple as shopping for food would be easy. Under the present conditions, it must take a couple of days to take care of those things that most people consider routine, such as seeing a doctor or dentist."

Someone says loudly, "Who needs a dentist?" Again general laughter breaks out.

They begin showing what is left of their teeth to one another. One of the women says to the man next to her, "Hey, Bob, tell me what a nice tooth I have." They bend over laughing and grabbing their sides.

Jack Wilson is exasperated. "You make fun, but this is a serious issue. Your lives would be safer and easier if you were connected to a road system—that is a fact. The Forest Service is willing to do this as an amenity for this community. This is a significant and well-meaning offer." His rebuke quiets the noise, but as he begins to speak again, Kasey interrupts, "You have left out a couple of fairly important things."

"I have?"

"Yes, but let's start with this. We don't want a road."

"Doesn't what I have just said seem reasonable? There isn't any arguing that road access would make things nicer and easier, not to mention the possibilities for more commerce." He points directly at her. "And what about old people? Aren't they at a disadvantage and at risk here? Surely they would like more available health care."

"You'll have to ask them."

"It seems obvious."

Kasey folds her arms and cocks her head to one side. "What I want to know is, is this one of those meetings where you go back to Juneau thinking you came out here to give the 'locals' a say in a decision that they really have no power to change? That the Forest Service is going to go ahead and do what they damn well please, like build the road anyway? You go back to your office, file the paperwork—'six public hearings were held, gathering input from the local community'—then build the damn road anyway. In the end, it doesn't matter what we think, which makes this meeting your average run-of-the mill bullshit."

"The Forest Service takes this process seriously."

"You didn't answer my question."

"Well . . ."

Kasey presses on, "OK, I know you aren't the one who makes this decision, but let's put it this way: If they want to, the Forest Service can build this road whether we like it or not, right?"

"Well . . ."

"Isn't that right?"

"Yes, but that doesn't mean we will. We take all of this seriously."

Randy speaks from his spot close to the door. "Roads go both ways."

Jack Wilson looks puzzled. "Yes, they do."

"All you say about roads making living here handier may be true, but it's the stuff that will come in from the other direction that scares me. Randy raises his finger in the air dramatically. "Hah! The opprobrium!"

Someone says, "Randy is all messed up again. He always starts using them big words when he gets messed up. Let me explain it to you in terms you can understand. Here's what the deal is. Them cars have people in them from God knows where. Every one of them has a head full of ideas of how things should be. Them loggin' roads is connected to the ferry terminal in Hollis, which goes to Ketchikan, which has a ferry from Seattle, which is connected to the whole goddamned world. It will be the end of this place." Now the man addresses the line of people on the back wall, "You remember that time some woman got off one of them yachts and cleaned up the fuel float, organized every little thing on it?"

"Yep, I sure do, couldn't find any of my stuff for a couple of weeks."

"That's just a small sample of what we are going to have to deal with around here if a road goes in."

"People like that come from places where they spend their life sittin' in a car, sittin' in their house, or sittin' in an office. They hire somebody to mow their lawns so's it will look just like everyone else's lawn, spend three or four hours a day drivin' on a freeway. They have to get permission to put a new porch on their house, they have to be careful where they go at night and," he is overcome by what he has just said, "I could go on all night."

Then he's rejuvenated by another thought. "And another thing is, they're experts at writin' rules. That will be the next step after the road lets'm just drive in here. They'll start writin' rules, and then if you have rules, they're gonna enforce 'em. Any second grader knows that to pay for enforcin' all those rules, you gonna need to have taxes." He points individually at every person in the room, ending with Jack Wilson. "So we will end up with somethin' we don't want in the first place *and* end up havin' to pay for it *and* have to take all of our gear off the fuel float.

"Them people in those cars with their ideas of how everbody else should live just like they live will be all over this place. At first they'll say how quaint it is, or somethin' like that, but then they'll want to start makin' it like wherever it is they came from. Christ-O-Riley, they'll be crawlin' all over this place. Shit, look at us, look how we live."

Randy holds both arms out as if he is presenting the whole group to an entirely new audience. "We don't stand a chance against those kinds of people and all their ideas. We're hopeless against such things. That's why we're here in the first place. What's here will be gone. It's not the cars, it's all them ideas that's in'em that's gonna do us in."

Nancy thinks about their morning's commuting on the freeway and leans over, whispering in Mike's ear, "He's right about that."

Owen is leaning on a metal stool to steady himself. "Hi there, Jack, how you been?"

Jack Wilson perks up with recognition. "Owen, I thought that was you. How have you been getting along?"

Owen motions to his left arm. "Slowed down a little bit but still gettin' around, mostly. I've had to hire some help." He looks at Mike and Nancy, then around the room. "You all know I've been in the log-towing business for most of my life. Jack is in charge of permitting roads on Forest Service land. We've known each other for several years, and we are both connected to the logging business, have been for some time. Almost all of my work is connected to Alaska Log Corporation, it's their logs I tow." He looks directly at Jack Wilson. "Jack, you better tell'em what's going on in Juneau, you know, the talk about the latest land swap that's being pushed by the timber lobby."

"But, Owen, nothing's been decided. It's just talk, and most of it just a whole lot of speculation, street talk. Damn, Owen, you're putting me in a tough spot here. I have nothing to do with the legislative end of the logging business."

"Come on, Jack. Do you mean to tell me that a timber lobbyist hasn't ever contacted you to see how the permitting process is or what's being planned for the next couple of years?"

"Sure they have, but that's just how it works."

Someone standing on the porch, sipping on a beer, says, "We understand that, just give us an idea of what's goin' on."

Owen presses the point. "Jack, you know as well as I do that in terms of people, this is a small state. They're going to find out soon enough. You better tell'em. It'll be better if you tell'em."

"OK, OK, but I'm stepping way out of my department by what I'm about to tell you, and I want you to know that I will be called on the carpet when this gets back to the department. Please remember that what I'm about to tell you is nothing more than conversations circulating around Juneau."

The room is dead quiet.

"The Cove is right in the middle of ten thousand acres of prime old growth timber. Most all of the economically feasible timber on the remainder of the island has already been logged. There are some rumors that the timber lobby is gearing up to ask the state to trade some of the timberland that has already been logged for the timber that's here.

"To be quite honest with you, the access road in my proposal will come right along the edge of that ten thousand acres. It would make logging that piece very economical. The rational goes something like this: Logging is critical to a healthy economy in Southeast Alaska, logging will bring good jobs to remote areas, good jobs will improve marginal living conditions, logging will be a better use of the forest and its resources, and logging has been on the decline for twenty years. Alaska Log is the only logging company still operating, and we need them to stay in business. There is also a general notion that the swap will make better use of available natural resources. That's all I know."

Randy yells at the top of his lungs, "WE ARE SO SCREWED!"

Suddenly it feels like all the air leaves the room, boiling out the door and open windows, bursting forth into the darkness. Nobody moves, then slowly they begin to trickle out the door, collecting their things from the windowsills and porch railing.

A woman stops in front of Jack Wilson and asks, "Better use of resources?"

"That's what they believe."

She yells sarcastically at the people leaving the porch, "Wait a minute! You can all come back now. Everything is going to be fine!

All they're doing is better utilizing resources! Can't you dummies see how that will make everything OK?" They continue leaving.

Jack stands stone still. She gives him a patronizing smile. "Even when you try to explain it to them, they just don't seem to listen, do they?"

When Owen leaves, he says, "It's decent that you told'em."

Neil and Jack stand in the empty room, at a loss for what to do next. Jack says, "That didn't go at all like I thought it would."

"Don't look at me. I just got here."

Jack stands up straight, and smoothing his clothes with the flat of his hands, he speaks as if he is still addressing the gathering, "Now, ladies and gentlemen, to attend to the issue of my ongoing hypocrisy. I just happen to have a pint of whiskey right here in the inside pocket of my jacket." With a flourish, he holds up the flask with two fingers, grasping it by the neck. He moves it back and forth slowly as if he is making some sort of demonstration. "Mr. Osborne, may I offer you a drink?"

Neil smiles and shakes his head. "Sure."

They sit outside on the steps that go down to the gravel playground, watching the reflection of the night sky on the water, trading sips on the bottle. Jack takes off one of his boots and begins to scratch between his toes. The rain soaks his shirt, but he doesn't seem to notice. He takes of his other boot and continues to dig. "Every fungus known to modern science seems to grow in this country."

Neil sits, saying nothing.

Jack says to the darkness, "Sometimes I really hate my job."

The night becomes blacker. Neil grunts and looks at the near-empty pint of whiskey and then finishes it. "At the risk of getting fired from my first real job before I even start it, I will offer a proposal."

"What's that?"

"I have another one of these." He points over his shoulder at the school building. "In there."

Jack laughs and shakes his head. "It's beyond me how word of that would ever get back to the central office."

When Neil returns, he offers the first drink to Jack. He cracks open the seal as he removes the cap and tips the bottle toward Neil. "Have you ever seen anything like these people?"

"Not exactly, but pretty close."

8

Liz

To the southeast side of Ernest Sound is Vixen Harbor. On the northwest side of the entrance of the harbor, a finger of land runs out into the sound. It starts in the trees and blueberry bushes then gives way to alder trees that give way to patches of eel grass. It disappears into the water as it changes to rocks and kelp. When the salmon are running, seals bob their heads above the kelp, getting gulps of air to dash out of the cover for a chance at their next meal.

On that finger of land where the inner harbor forms into a protected pocket that is the anchorage, on a patch of white gravel surrounded by eel grass, a woman sits on an army surplus duffel bag, staring at the water. The tide is on the flood, slowly creeping up the beach over that patch of dry gravel. The gravel holds the leading edge of the water, rolling it under, slightly making it stand up, giving it a rounded look.

She is lean with stringy muscles that stand out on her forearms. Veins protrude from under her skin, standing up as if they have been chiseled there. She is bone-tired, lost in thoughts that run together and compete with each other for her full attention. She can't hold on to one thought long enough to give it proper consideration before another slips through her shield of concentration to present itself with all of its possibilities. Her mind keeps darting off in different directions.

She shifts her weight on the duffel bag but does it carefully, somehow thinking that any undue movement might attract his attention. She doesn't want him to come near her; she doesn't want to give him any vague excuse to talk because there is always the possibility she will stay. *Goddamn it anyhow!*

Behind her, the first long shadows of evening start moving away from the tree line some two hundred yards away. She tries again to watch the tide wash over the gravel as if it might become some sort of meditation that will allow her to deal with her thoughts. *That's right, I'll start there. I'll just watch the tide.* It's a transient hope. After she watches the water move over a section of the quartz gravel, her mind begins to wander again. *That job I had in Kirkland at Salty's restaurant was a good job, made more in tips than I did in paychecks. Nice people to work for, we were a good crew.*

He's going to need to check that bilge pump—bet it blew a fuse last night when the water came in over the gunnel and through the scuppers.

Too tired to wake up.

Hope I don't have to sleep on the beach tonight.

I'll sleep in the damn bushes before I go back to that boat.

"Now let's see what makes that water stick to that gravel. Do they call that viscosity or friction?" She says these last words aloud, and the sound of her own voice makes her jump. Then she thinks that even if she does have to spend the night on the beach, it won't matter much. Just one more day in all of the other days.

Two, maybe three, hundred yards behind her toward the back of the harbor is an old wooden double-ended fishing boat built in the 1920s, rigged for salmon trolling. It's thirty-two feet long, and its wooden trolling poles are askew at odd angles. The stern rests on land far enough above the water so the cockpit and power gurdies are covered by the low-hanging limbs of a large hemlock tree. The bow lies straight down the beach toward the water. The boat is rolled over on its starboard side. Several of the twenty-pound lead trolling weights that had been loose on deck are now resting on the scuppers inside the starboard rail. They are caught between the ribs that form the framing of the gunwale after they come through the deck.

The incoming tide is just beginning to creep up the bow stem. Several small trees near the boat have been cut with a chainsaw. The whiteness of the fresh cuts stands out among the grays and greens of the remaining foliage, out of place. The trunks of the cut trees are bucked up into short lengths and lie next to hull of the boat. They will prop the boat upright when it begins to float on the incoming tide.

Another line runs at an oblique angle from the top of the mast to a large cedar to which a come-a-long has been attached. Another line runs through a scupper. A long limb lie on the outside of the hull. It has been tied to the end of that line so that any pressure will be distributed the full length of the limb. A third line runs from the anchor windless down the beach toward the woman.

A man dressed in a wool sweater and green rain gear holds the end of that line. Any distinguishing features of his face are covered with bushy hair and a beard, except for the eyes, which are dark and darting. He is looping the line with half-hitches around a large rock. When that is done, he walks to the boat and ties an eye in the line, threads the free end through it, and pulls all the slack out of the standing line.

He turns and looks at the woman sitting at the water's edge. Heat from his body causes steam to rise from his head and arms, wispy clouds that quickly dissipate. He stays there for a moment, judging the distance to her. He shakes his head and thinks, *It really doesn't matter how far it is. She just as well be a hundred miles away.* He turns and walks back to the edge of the woods.

Soon the sound of a chainsaw comes rattling out of the trees and over the water. The sound is loud in the miles of silence—sudden and startling. The woman doesn't turn around; she just hunches her shoulders forward as if she is protecting herself from something. After a moment, she looks the other direction at the vastness that is outside of the harbor then back at those things that are right there before her. *How did I get here?* She looks around again as if she is expecting an answer. There isn't any, but she holds out the hope that maybe she can find the path that led her here then backtrack to some sort of beginning. She holds her head in one hand; her thoughts are still coming in bits and pieces. Was it yesterday that they were in Petersburg or the day before? *When was it that she really began to wonder?* All those thoughts are still at arm's length, just out of reach. She looks at the patch of gravel. It's now covered by the tide, and it's moving close to her feet. She looks back at the boat and says aloud, "I guess I haven't been very honest with myself."

She stirs at the sound of the airplane's engine. The sound of the chainsaw stops, and the man walks out of the wood. He looks up and shades his eyes with one hand from the glare off the water. He locates the plane then walks over to stand by the beached boat. Her joints are stiff and unyielding, and it takes her a moment to get things moving. Only then does it occur to her that she's been sitting there since first light. She stands slowly and stretches. She says, "Well, I called a plane, and that has to be a good first step."

The plane finishes its downwind leg, banks into a turn and drops over a line of trees at the far end of the anchorage, flares out, and lands in the remaining few hundred feet of water, skimming on the flat smooth surface. It begins moving toward the beached boat.

The woman walks toward it, motioning with her arms for it to come to her and not the boat. She wants the pilot to know that she is the one to be picked up. The plane veers toward her. Opening the door, leaning out to watch for rocks in the water, the pilot strains to see over the nose of the plane for the edge of the beach. After he shuts the engine down, he uses a canoe paddle to turn the plane around and back it into the beach. When he looks up, she hands him her duffel bag.

He nods toward the boat. "What happened?"

"Lost our anchor in that storm last night." She stands with one hand on the wing strut while he puts her bag in the belly pan. Separately she hands him her rain gear. Almost as an afterthought, she dips the soles of her rubber boots in the water, one by one to clean them.

The pilot nods toward the boat. "Can he use some help?"

She cocks her head to one side and considers him for a moment. "Well, I think so." She gestures toward the careened boat and at the man who is now ratcheting on the come-a-long, putting pressure on the mast. "What do you see there?"

The pilot can see now that the question is much more complicated than he intended. He also sees that she is angry, tired, and hurt. But she won't let it go. "What do you see there?"

"Listen. I didn't mean anything by that comment. I just wanted to know if he needed any help."

She won't let it go. "What do you see there?"

He shrugs his shoulders.

"What you see there is an old wooden boat lying on its side that has been in need of major repair for God knows how long. On the starboard side of the hull, there are two or maybe three broken ribs. I expect that now the starboard planking is so racked that it won't hold caulking for an entire season and probably not that long if it's out in some tough weather." She points to the man on the beach. "But when he gets back to town, he will cork the seams then smear some concrete in them to hold it there and try to get another season out of it."

The incoming tide lifts the plane from the beach, and it begins to drift away, but the woman doesn't notice. "And the broken ribs? He took two two by fours and nailed them across five ribs, including the broken ones, and nailed them down tight. His hammer wasn't big enough to suck the broken ribs back into alignment, so he scrounged up a big boulder from the beach and beat on it until they came back into place."

"That's a good idea."

She struggles to talk to the pilot tolerantly, trying to smile, but it isn't quite a smile; it's more of a grimace. "Yes," she says slowly. "That is a good idea, but wouldn't it have been a better idea if he had remembered to trim ten feet off the anchor cable every once in a while so it wouldn't rust from the inside and break in a storm and then your boat might get blown up into the trees?" Anger is beginning to creep into her voice. "If a person did something as simple as that, then you wouldn't need to have these 'good ideas' about hammering your boat together with a rock you picked up off the beach. I'm tired of those kinds of good ideas."

Just the hint of a breeze moves the plane slowly toward the beached boat. She still doesn't notice. "If he gets back to town in one piece and if the caulking holds and if the nailed-together ribs hold, he could get another three seasons or more out of it without any major work. Don't you think that's a good idea?"

The pilot looks away.

The man on the beach walks rapidly down to the rock with the half-hitches around it and adjusts them to take more slack out of the line. He is more animated now; the incoming tide is moving up the bow stem, just beginning to float the boat. He hurries to look in the hold to see how much water is coming through the seams then quickly goes to the come-a-long and begins pumping the handle.

The woman on the plane is watching the pilot closely; she knows what he's thinking. "Go ahead and ask him if he needs any help."

"We better get going, lady. The plane is moving."

"Don't you think leaving is a good idea?"

The plane drifts on and is now just a few yards off the beach where the boat lies. The man comes down the beach to stand nervously at the edge of the water, facing the plane, thinking there must be some difficulty. He glances impatiently over his shoulder at the boat then back at the plane. He waits anxiously for a response to his presence.

The woman leans close to the pilot, placing her face close to his. She speaks softly to him. "Ask him if he needs any help."

The pilot gives up any hope of getting out of this mess easily. He looks at the woman with resignation. He asks, "Could you use some help?"

"Thanks for the offer, but I think I have her figured out."

"You sure?"

"Yep, pretty sure."

"OK."

The pilot looks at the woman, trying to catch some indication that he has pursued the conversation far enough to keep her satisfied. *Just keep her calm.* It's just forty minutes back to Ketchikan; that's all he needs. It'll be dark soon.

The man on the beach watches the woman closely now, but she acknowledges nothing. He waits a bit and walks back to the boat. The woman becomes less guarded as the distance between them increases. The tension visibly slips from her face. Quickly she looks disheveled, and for the first time, the pilot can see there is tenderness at the edge of her eyes. He says, "OK, let's get out of here."

The plane coughs then starts; he turns it into the wind. As it lifts from the water, he makes a turn toward Clarence Strait. As he makes the turn, he glances at the woman to see if she takes one last look at where she has been; everyone takes one last look after the plane takes off. She looks in the opposite direction. The plane drones on, and she sits in silence. In a few more minutes, he will be able to see the edges of Ketchikan. All he wants to do is get back to town before dark.

He notices her hands for the first time as they lie in her lap. They are large hands for a woman, rawboned, red, and swollen. She stares forward but begins to talk. He slides the right earpiece of his head phone set back off his ear to show her he is listening. She rambles as she talks; her voice is worn and threadbare. She reminds the pilot of prospectors he's picked up after they have spent years in the wilderness, distant and wary but still wanting to hear a voice even if it's their own.

"Do you know how many coho I can clean in a day, that is, if I work most of the night?"

Don't say anything just let her talk.

He sees Ship Island in the distance and checks to see if any weather has started to move in on the south end of the straits during the day.

She continues, "How long do you think a person can go without sleep or on just a couple of hours a day?"

The pilot grunts, "Uuuuh," then fiddles with his headset.

"No, the real question is, how long can you just patch things up? How many broken ribs can you fix with used two by fours? How many seams can you patch with concrete and caulking to get by for 'just a couple of more seasons'? How many times can you talk about how things are going to be different when you really know they never will be? You know, 'next year' . . . make love in a bunk that is next to a 671 GMC diesel that smells like oil and exhaust. A float house would be fine, a plain old ordinary float house, with a bathtub for Christ's sake!"

The pilot drops the plane to just above the water. He doesn't need to, but he hopes it might be a distraction; it isn't. They are a barely visible speck in the landscape, no more than a small insect. She is silent for a moment but starts again. "I am tired and feel like I've been patched together just like that boat."

He points over the nose of the plane. "We're just about there."

"Oh." She looks up and watches the houses on the edge of town flicker by.

He raises the plane to avoid the boat traffic close to town, and he begins his final approach. She asks, "You know when you ask him if he needed any help?"

"Yes."

"And he said, 'I think I've got her figured out.'"

"Yes."

"Did you think he was talking about the boat?"

"Yes, I did."

"So did I."

When they tie up to the float below the air taxi office, she leans her duffel bag against her leg and asks, "How much?"

"I'll just charge you a seat fare. I was coming back from the mail run anyway, two hundred and sixty dollars."

She takes out a roll of hundred dollar bills from the front pocket of her shirt, peels off three, and hands them to him. "That's close enough, and it's worth every penny." She slings her duffel bag on her shoulder and instinctively looks at the sky to the southeast, from where all the bad weather starts.

The pilot calls after her as she walks up the ramp. "Where are you headed?"

She yells over her shoulder, "South!"

Thomas Basis is completely plugged with seine boats. Every stall is full. On the end of float 5, they are rafted two and three boats deep. Most are from Washington, and they are getting ready to go south—home.

There is a loud knock on a wheelhouse window followed by a small pause then several more knocks in rapid succession. A sleepy-eyed, rumpled, unshaven young man fumbles with the galley door and stumbles out on deck, clad only in sweat pants that drape tenuously on bony hips. A woman is standing on the bull rail of the finger float with her arm cocked back, ready to knock again. He mumbles, "What?"

"I notice that your nets are stowed in the hold."

He looks over his shoulder. "Huh?"

"And your seine skiff is on deck."

He rubs his face with both hands, making his hair stand up on his head. "Uuuuuh, yep, sure is."

"You guys are from south, right? I see your home port is Blaine."

As the young man's mind begins to clear, he sees a woman wearing Carhartt pants and a wool shirt; the sleeves are rolled up to the elbows. The cuffs of the pants are neatly tucked over a pair of red BF Goodrich rubber boots. A rubberized duffel bag lies at her feet on the finger float. Her eyes have that glazed look of someone who is bone tired.

"What do you want?" He looks again, noticing her hands. They are large for a woman—rough, calloused, covered with a red rash from handling fish.

An older man sticks his head out of the wheelhouse window. "We are done for the season. Don't need any crew."

"I'm looking to work my way south. I'll scrub, cook, take my turn at wheel watch, whatever it takes. I'm sober, work hard, and won't cause trouble. I've had a lot of experience on boats."

"Did you crew this season?"

"Yep."

"What boat?"

"An old wooden troller called the *Silver*."

The older man considers her. "Did you fish out of Wrangell and Meyer's Chuck?"

"Yep."

"Oh, right, I remember seeing that boat. It looked in pretty tough shape."

"It is."

"It looked like it could have sprung a plank at any time."

"It did."

"Sink?"

"It dragged anchor during that storm last Monday and is on the beach in Vixen Harbor. The captain is working on it. He's got a couple of two by fours from the hay rack nailed over three broken ribs on the starboard side. My guess is that he'll patch it back together and float it on the next big tide. If it stays afloat until he can get to town, he'll sister up the ribs, smear some concrete in the seams, and finish out the season."

"And you're not there helping because?"

"It's funny you should ask that question because that's the exact same question the pilot, of the float plane that picked me up, asked. So I made the pilot ask him if he needed any help."

"What'd he say?"

"'Thanks for the offer, but I think I've got her all figured out.'"

"Did he?"

Her eyes get hard. "Me or the boat?"

"Coast Guard on the way?"

"I don't know for sure but he hadn't called them when I left."

The older man stands resting one leg against the cap rail, watching her. She waits for a moment then turns to gather up her duffel bag. "Do you know of anyone else who might need an extra hand for the run south?"

"You can go with us."

"I can?"

He can see the relief on her face. "Sure, I had a couple of guys that had to fly south for family stuff. Where you headed?"

"Any place in Puget Sound."

"Put your gear on the top bunk in the fo'c'sle. The bottom bunk is yours. You better get some rest. You look beat."

As she climbs over the railing, he adds, "It's right next to the engine room."

"I'm used to that."

He turns to the young man. "As long as we're all up, you better put on some coffee and untie the lines. I'll fire up the engine, and we'll get out of here."

She falls into the bunk with all of her clothes on and is asleep immediately. When she awakens, it's to the sound of the engine. The boat is rolling in a light swell. She hears the swishing sounds of water moving past the hull. When she enters the galley, the rumpled young man in sweat pants is slicing potatoes and onions into a large plastic bowl. He glances over his shoulder at her. "You had a good sleep. We're just about to across Dixon Entrance. The coffee cups are in that cupboard." He points with the knife.

She leans one hip against the counter to steady herself against the roll of the ship as she pours the coffee. Seated at the galley table is another crew member reading a book; they nod at each other. "I'm Liz."

He smiles. "Steve."

She looks at the large bowl of sliced potatoes and onions. "Is there anything I can help with?"

"I was going to have meatloaf for dinner. The stuff is in fridge, and there's another bowl under the sink. You can put that together if you want."

Liz puts the egg, hamburger, and bread crumbs in the bowl, mixing them together, squishing it through her fingers. The galley is warmed by the large iron stove. With the door latched open, there's a view of Cape Chacon and the ocean beyond. The engine rumbles along in its steady rhythm. Somehow that combination all of drone of the engine and the warm stove is a comfort to her. Steve goes back to his book; the rumpled young man melts a cube of butter in a cast iron frying pan. The onions and potatoes sizzle when he dumps them in the hot pan. For the first time in what seems like a long time, she begins to relax.

During the next couple of days, Liz and the crew settle into a routine of sleeping, reading, fixing meals, and talking of fishing—boats, weather, working on the ocean.

One morning as they sit over coffee, Steve asks, "What are you going to do this winter, Liz?"

"I'm going to find a different line of work. I'm done with Alaska. I'm done with fishing."

The two men glance at each other. The rumpled young man says, "You seem like you're all worn out, sounds like you've been through a rough patch, but maybe you'll feel different when you get all rested up."

"Right now it feels like I'll never get rested up. I've been tired for so long it seems like it's baked right into me, clear through and settled in. I think I'll get some simple job like waiting on tables someplace where the tips are good. I'm ready to call that a living. A regular paycheck sounds pretty good right now." Her tenor is inflexible, and the two men stare at their coffee cups.

"How long have you fished in Alaska?"

"Right now it seems like forever."

"That's a long time."

"You know, the first few years I just couldn't get enough of the place. It was the independence of fishing, the learning how to fish. Then there is the geography of the place. I mean, that alone . . ." Her comments taper off into silence as she turns and looks out onto the back deck. "A couple of years we wintered clear out of town, just anchored up someplace, we spent one winter tied to the fuel float at the Cove. Just fished when the weather allowed. Then I couldn't get enough of it." She seems sad.

"So all of that went sour on you?"

"Pretty much."

"I'll bet you could crew on this boat. I'll bet the captain would hire you. We can tell you know your way around a boat. You ever seine before?"

"No."

"It's not like trolling. We don't work every day all season, three four days a week maybe. It all depends on the season and how many fish show up. You know how that all works."

"I do, thanks, but no."

"I'll bet you'll pick it right up."

"I'm going to move south and get a job and live like any normal person would. I need to get some stuff sorted out. I need to get settled, somehow."

The captain clumps down from the wheelhouse and pours himself another cup of coffee. He leans against the galley sink and looks at each of them. "What's goin' on?"

"We've been trying to get Liz to work on the boat next season, but she says she's done with fishing and Alaska and she's gonna stay south and get a regular job. She says she's gonna be normal."

The captain frowns. "What kind of job?"

"Anything, it doesn't matter. I'll sling hash, pump gas, keep books, anything to pay the bills until I can get reorganized."

"Done with Alaska?"

"Yes, I am."

"OK, I'll tell you what, I'm going to take the boat to La Conner to have the engine worked on. It'll take a few weeks to get the mechanic over there and to get the work done. These guys are taking off as soon as they can because they haven't seen their girlfriends or families for a few months. And I haven't either as far as that goes. You can live on the boat and keep an eye on things while you look for work."

"I don't know. I guess I don't have any place in particular I need to be. I could get in touch with my sister, but I would just as soon put that off as long as possible. I don't know though. I don't want any favors. I have some money saved up, so I'll be OK for a few months."

"It would be a favor to me to have someone looking out for the boat. I wouldn't have to drive up from Blaine to check on it or worry about a bilge pump quitting, not to mention vandalism. If you feel like you aren't earning your keep, you can start on some sanding and painting. I'd consider that a bargain."

As soon as they tie up at La Conner, an older model pickup truck arrives in the parking lot, driven by a young woman. The two young men vault out onto the dock. They throw their gear in the back and clamor into the front seat. In what seems like seconds, they are gone.

Later that evening, the captain's wife arrives. She stops short when she sees Liz. Recovering slightly, she says to Liz, "Well, he did say that he picked up an extra deckhand to help run the boat south, but he neglected to say it was a woman."

Liz thinks it's best to stay silent.

The captain appears at the door; his wife points at Liz.

Completely ignoring the moment, he says, "This is Liz. She's going to look after the boat so I can spend some time at home. Sure is good to see you, honey." As they turn and walk away, he puts his arm around her shoulders.

The wife gives one last glance back at Liz while she is saying, "The hot water heater broke yesterday. The principal at Bobby's school has been calling, something about him getting in fights with his classmates. You need to take him fishing with you next year. He's getting too much for me to handle, and another thing, the guy that was supposed to come and paint the house two weeks ago hasn't shown up yet. He hasn't called or anything, won't answer his phone, I'd like to get my hands on him. Now tell me again who that woman is."

The captain stops walking. "Whoa, you are supposed to say, 'How are you, honey?' before you start telling me everything that's wrong."

Liz returns to the galley, and she tries to remember the last time she was completely alone. Suddenly she is very tired; she folds her arms on the table and cradles her head in them, falling into a deep sleep. When daylight breaks, she is still at the galley table. Her back and shoulders hurt. She thinks, *Well, here you are.*

She takes a shower and drinks a couple of cups of coffee then walks along the waterfront to the business district. She instinctively looks at the yachts moored under covered storage. They are tied to every available spot on the many floats. She doesn't notice any commercial fishing boats and wonders if the boat she's on is the only one. The yachts look expensive. Just off the waterfront are rows of condominiums stacked two and three stories high. The small patches of lawn in front of them are perfectly groomed. The sidewalks are swept clean, and on the shrubs, there isn't even a leaf out of place.

She peers through a measured rows of poplar trees, windbreaks for the flat manicured tulip fields. The downtown waterfront has several restaurants: Nell Thorn Restaurant & Pub, the Waterfront Bistro, the La Conner Seafood and Prime Rib Restaurant. She stops and watches through the window of the Waterfront Bistro. It's busy with waitresses and busboys scurrying back and forth. When she walks through the front door, she hears the hum of conversations from the tables, sounds of waiters taking orders, dishes clanking as they bump against the trays. Just inside the door, a young man greets her. He is dressed neatly in a white shirt and black pants. "How many in your party?"

"Oh well, actually I'm not here to eat. I'm looking for work. Are there any openings?"

In his best customer relations demeanor, he says, "No, I don't believe there are any openings. The season is winding down. It's fall, you know." He has a curious expression on his face as he looks her up and down. He unconsciously takes a step backward as if to distance himself from her.

"Are you in charge of hiring?"

"No, I'm not, but the manager isn't here. I'm quite certain we're not hiring." His lips are pursed.

A couple walks into the waiting area. He quickly turns to them and asks, "How many in your party?"

"Two."

He extends his arm with his palm up. "This way please." When he walks past Liz, he frowns at her.

She doesn't have any better luck with the young woman at the till. "No, ma'am, the summer season is ending, so most all of the places will be cutting back, will even be closing until spring." The young woman is shifting her weight from one foot to the other; she looks uncomfortable.

"Oh sure, I should have realized that. It's just that I haven't been south for a long time."

"South?"

"From Alaska."

"I see. Well, that explains it."

Explains what?

When Liz is walking back out the front door, she stops to look at her full reflection in the glass; it startles her. There, looking back at her, is a middle-aged woman in Carhartt pants and a wool shirt. The rubber boots she is wearing are spotted with bottom paint. The long, slightly curly hair is flecked with gray; it is unkempt and unruly. She holds up the backs of her hands toward the glass. Their reflection reveals a network of blue veins that are popping out from the skin; her fingernails are worn down past her fingertips.

No wonder she called me ma'am. I look like I'm forty years old. Wait a minute, I am almost forty years old. How long have I been fishing? Has it been ten years, fifteen years?

In a voice louder than she intends. She says, "HOLY SHIT! LOOK AT YOU!" The sounds in the restaurant stop. When she looks behind her, they are all looking at her. She shoulders her way through the door, shaking her head. She walks along the waterfront, saying over and over, "Forty years old, forty years old, forty years old." She can't seem to stop. When she arrives back at the boat, she sits on the back deck, watching the water. It's flat and gray, shiny like polished stone. She sits for a long time. She sighs deeply, takes her phone from her pocket, and dials a number. "Hey there, Elsie. This is Liz."

"Oh my god! Liz, where are you!"

"I came south on a fish boat. I'm in La Conner."

Her sister begins yelling at some other people in her house. "Hey, you guys, this is my sister Liz on the phone. She's in La Conner! What are you doing in La Conner? I thought you were never going to leave Alaska? What's wrong?"

"I was thinking I would try something besides fishing."

There is short silence. "Well, I hate to tell you I told you so, but you know what I've always said about you being up there fishing. What a waste of a smart woman like yourself, chasing around in boats. I mean, like I have always said, you can do anything you set your mind to."

"Yes, you have said that many times."

"Well, now that you've finally come to your senses, we are going to get you settled and get your life reorganized. You're going to come stay with us. We still have that little apartment. It's yours. You will have all of the privacy you need. Where are you staying now?"

"On a seine boat. I'm looking after it while the captain is spending some time with his family."

"You just tell him that you're going to stay with your sister so he'll have to make other arrangements."

"I can't do that."

Elsie continues talking, ignoring her comment. "Here's the deal. Bernie is in San Francisco this week, hammering out the details on a contract with Safeway. It's a huge contract consolidating all of the feed lots in Northern California that supply beef products to all of their major outlets, you know, like I mean all of them. He stands to make a lot of money on this deal, Liz, the biggest *ever* for us. I mean a lot of money! When he gets back next week, I'm going to come and get you, and we are going to restart your life. I'm so excited!" She giggles.

"Elsie, I'm not going to move in with you."

"Oh, don't be so proud, this will be fun."

"I'm not going to move in with you."

"Just give me one good reason why."

"It wouldn't work."

"Sure it would."

"OK, I don't want to."

With sadness in her voice, Elsie says, "But I only want to help."

"Elsie, you are one of the nicest people I know, but the problem in this whole deal is me, as you pointed out earlier in this conversation, and this shouldn't be any revelation. I don't have very good judgment. I've been just going along all these years not paying attention to some important details. I think the phrase is 'kidding myself.' I just think I need some time to sort all of that out.

"Come on, Liz, we can make this work."

"I think what you're talking about would only complicate things. Living with you and being involved with how you and Bernie live would be the same as being in a different country, for me anyway. Too big of a change too soon. I'll call you when I get things sorted out."

"How long will that be?"

"I wish I knew. I'll talk to you later." Elsie continues to talk as she disconnects.

Well, that takes care of the question of what the hell are you going to do now?

Liz goes to her bunk and fishes around in her duffel bag, bringing out a partially full fifth of whiskey. She takes it to the galley and pours a shot in a water glass.

She sits on the cap rail at the very back of the fantail, sipping as she looks at the harbor. The whiskey helps. She begins to relax, begins to think she will just take things as they come. She has time to sort this out even if she is forty years old. She still has time to make something work. She looks again at the hundreds of yachts, the manicured fields, and condominiums. It seems so very civilized here, well managed, even the dirt. She takes another sip from the glass.

Start with something. Go to a beauty salon and get a major do-over. Get the hair done, get the nails polished, get some makeup, new clothes, clean up the language. Just get your foot in the door somewhere and make it work, a nice office that's warm, dry, and well lighted. A place that is nice and bright even on dark rainy days. Just think there won't be any more days of standing in the cockpit, getting your ass kicked in snotty weather, staying out on the grounds because the fishing is so good you can't afford to go anchor up. No more running all day and night, because of some rumor you heard on the dock, to get to a hot bite that may or may not happen. No more falling into the bunk with all of your clothes on after eating a can of cold beans because you're so exhausted you can barely hold the spoon. No more working twenty hours, daylight to dark. What you need, Liz, is some nice job where someone will just tell you what to do and you just smile and nod, collect a paycheck—simple.

She looks west across the narrows at a small harbor and the houses with their windows glowing in the coming darkness. She is just thinking about going to get the binoculars for a closer look when an aluminum skiff appears, parting the flat water. She watches as it makes a slight turn, leaving a parabolic shaped wake, the skiff comes right toward her and slows to a stop when it's alongside.

The man driving the skiff doesn't nod or wave; he just says, "Hi."

She nods cautiously.

"Is the captain aboard?"

"No, he went home to Blaine."

"Did he say when he was coming back?"

"Not for sure, he's going to have some work done on the engine, an in-frame rebuild, I think, said it would probably take about a month."

"Did you crew for him this season?"

"No, just came south with the boat from Ketchikan. I'm looking after things so he can spend time with his family. It's part of the deal. I can get in touch with him if you need to talk."

"No, no, it's nothing like that. I generally see him when he's fishing on the north end of the Panhandle, Icy Straits, and that country, but I didn't see him this year. I guess all of the pink salmon were on the south end, so I just came over to visit, you know, just to say 'howdy.'"

"Sure."

He bumps the outboard into reverse to keep the boats from banging together. "So you didn't crew for him?"

She shakes her head no.

He cocks his head to one side. "You look like you've spent some time fishing."

"You mean worn out."

"Hey, it's hard work."

"I worked on a small troller."

"Which one?"

"The *Silver.*"

"Sure, I saw that boat a few times when I was fishing out of Ketchikan a couple of years ago. It looked like—"

"I know, I know, it looked pretty tough, like it might spring a plank at any minute." Her voice has an edge to it.

He holds his hands up, trying to calm her. "I didn't mean anything, just trying to make conversation."

She rubs her forehead, sets her drink on the cap rail, and covers her face with both hands. He lets the skiff drift back close the bigger boat and holds on to the rub rail with one hand and waits. She stays with her face covered for long moments, and when she drops her hands, there's the beginnings of a smile on her face. "I'll bet when you came over here to say hi to the captain, the last thing you expected to find was some edgy woman on the back deck drinking whiskey."

"I'm not going to get into that conversation. I'm not as dumb as I look."

"OK, let's start over. Can I buy you a drink?"

He laughs. "That's the second thing I didn't expect when I came over here."

"Well?" She holds her glass up in the air.

"I'll have a beer. I go downhill pretty fast if I drink whiskey."

"It comes with a price. I feel like I need to get some things off my chest, so I'm thinking it might be easier if I tell a complete stranger who won't feel responsible for how things turn out. I get a free talk, and you get a free listen and a beer to boot. Best of all, you won't be around reminding me why the whole deal falls apart."

He laughs again. "OK, let's give it a go. I can always cut and run. I'm good at that."

"I'll bet you are." She goes to the galley and returns with a can of beer. She hands it to him as he climbs over the rail.

"Your name is?"

"Eric."

"You fish alone, Eric?"

"Yep, I fished a little double-ender called the *Gull* for a few years, just sold it and bought another one, fiber glass, a little bigger."

Recognition lights up her face. "Oh right! I remember you wintered in Thomas Basin one year, didn't you? I thought you looked familiar. You were tied up to that little barge and hung out with the folks at the transient zone until the spring of that year, right?"

He nods cautiously. "Right."

"It had that weather vane that said 'Jesus Saves' on one side and 'Smoke dope' on the other. When we went on the grid in the Basin that winter, I couldn't help but notice that whole lash-up."

Eric shakes his head in amusement. "I asked him what that weather vane was all about. I was curious if he had any hidden meanings. He said, 'I just figured that it covered about everything.'"

"What did they call that guy that owned that barge? Wasn't his name Big? Wore a life jacket that didn't fit him everywhere he went, even to the grocery store. That was it, wasn't it?"

He nods cautiously. "Right."

"You were the guy that had all of those books on board. You were like the lending library for the Basin that year."

"Yep."

She stares at him curiously for a moment. "I'm Liz."

"Hi."

Liz deliberates for a moment. "We were moored at city float that winter but spent some time at the Potlatch, have a beer and catch up on what's going on. You know, the routine."

"Yep."

"I thought the *Gull* was a nice boat."

"It's a nice boat, but you know how it is with wooden boats. They take so much more time and money, and it wasn't real big either, twenty-eight feet. That's OK for day fishing but pretty small for the outside. This other boat is forty-two feet. It'll be a lot less work to maintain and more comfortable in tough weather."

"I get that. Are you sure you're ready to hear this part of my story?"

"I guess I won't know until I hear it."

"I'll give you the short version."

"OK."

"Gordy Bolling and I went partners on the boat and permit. I sold my hand troll permit and threw in some cash for my share. The whole idea was to buy an old beat-up boat for a good price, since we had spent most of our money on the permit. The plan was we would fish where we could and save up to buy a better rig, like you did. Once that was done, we could expand our range, fish the outside, maybe even get up to the Fairweather grounds. I've heard stories of some huge catches of king salmon out there. One guy told me he had 250 fish opening day, and he had a breakdown about halfway through that.

"I thought that would be a nice life, maybe make enough money so we could travel in the off season, stay ahead of the maintenance, stay on top of things instead of just fixing stuff when it broke, try and get out of that cycle where we were always one step behind. We never did get ahead of that." She stops talking to look at the evening shadows on the water.

She sighs and begins again, "Well, we were never able to get enough money together to do anything but live. The common description of the *Silver* was the one you gave, 'Looks like it could spring a plank at any moment.' And it's an accurate assessment. If it blew much over twenty knots or so, we would stay at anchor, missed too many fishing days. But we kept at it, fixing things that should have been replaced, doing repairs ourselves that should have been hired out, telling ourselves, 'Just one good season is all we need—we'll get over the hump next year.' It never did happen, but somewhere in all of that clutter and confusion, years slipped by. I guess we just got used to it, and then at some point, I became a deckhand instead of a partner. The dumb thing is it was a long time before I realized it. I can see now that it was an idea that wasn't going to work from the start, but somehow that particular thought slipped right by me, not only that I spent several years working my ass off trying to make it work anyway. If that isn't a definition of poor judgment, one doesn't exist. I'll bet if you look up *poor judgment* in the dictionary, there will be a picture of me right beside it." She shakes her head in disbelief.

Eric folds his arms while he holds his beer in one hand. "Blame yourself?"

"For not getting it figured out sooner, you damned right I do."

"OK."

"What?" There is a touch of anger in her voice.

"Go ahead and feel any way you like, be angry or not, that's up to you."

"I do seem a bit pissed off about it, don't I?"

He shrugs. "Are you going to get drunk tonight?"

"To tell you the truth, I hadn't thought about it one way or the other." She is still crotchety. "You want another drink?" She looks at her empty glass.

"Actually, I don't, but you go ahead. I haven't talked to anyone in some time, so running into an Alaskan that fishes is a treat."

"What do you mean you haven't talked to anybody for a while?"

"I'm not very social, to tell you the truth. I have to honestly say I'm fairly peculiar that way."

Liz goes into the galley and returns with the mostly empty bottle of whiskey. She holds it up to the deck light. "Not enough left here to do much damage, luckily."

Eric nods in agreement.

Still holding the bottle in the air, Liz leans toward Eric, narrowing her eyes to mere slits in her cheeks. "And you there, Mr. Eric, whatever-your-name-is, why is it you spend so much time by yourself?"

"I like to keep things simple."

"Like your own company, is that it?"

"That's pretty much it."

She leans even closer. "So are you running from the law or something like that?"

Eric is quiet for a long time then says in a serious but careful way, "I don't think the law is after me."

Liz takes another sip of whiskey. She is beginning to slur her words. She leans back in a gesture of mock relief. "At least we got that out of the way."

"Hope so."

They continue to talk on of people they know in Alaska, people that work on the ocean, work the seasons, connected by boats. As the night gets dark, the lights from town spread out farther over the water.

"I think I'll head back to the other side. You OK here by yourself?"

"I'm fine, the booze is beginning to wear off. I'll get a bite to eat and hit the rack. Thanks, I'll see you later."

He smiles. "If I see you later, then I wouldn't be a stranger, would I?" He slips over the side of the boat like a shadow; his skiff disappears into the darkness.

9

Home

Nancy has somehow expected some changes or at least some gaps in her memory. There are some changes. The planking on the wheelhouse of the tugboat has been redone with some red cedar, but it's still the same old boat moored at the same old, rickety dock right there in front of the house. The spotlight looks new, but the old brass bell is still on the wheelhouse.

She mentally goes through the litany that her dad repeated over the years. *Built in 1916 back when there was lots of old growth timber, lots of good carpenters. She's built—built to last. She's forty feet long, wide and high at the bow then swoops down lower and narrows to a rounded stern, which lets her move through water so effortlessly she barely makes a wake. Good on fuel.*

Nancy automatically begins thinking about a checklist. Some of the planking above the waterline is swollen from the years of being constantly wet. Those places are having a hard time holding paint. The wooden letters on the bow say *Nancy* and are faded and checked. Then she begins checking through the details that could cause breakdowns or injuries: rusty turnbuckles on the mast stays, the anchor. *Is the shackle on the anchor wired to keep it from working its way loose? How about the anchor cable? Does it need trimmed back to something solid? Are any of the through hull fittings leaking?* She is still doing it. She can't stop, almost like she has never left.

"Hey, Mom."

She turns, still frowning. "What?"

"You didn't tell me the boat was named after you."

"I guess I didn't. It just didn't seem important, I suppose."

He has been watching her closely and continues to stand next to her, glancing back and forth between her and the boat.

She continues, How long it's been since the last coat of bottom paint? Need to take a good look at the engines to check for oil and water leaks, need to see if the engine starts when it's cold. Do the stuffing boxes need repacked? How many hours are on the raw water impellers? Check for soft wood below the waterline. Dad was never very regular at oiling the steering transit in the lazerette, better check on that. It's a list that never ends.

She turns to Michael. "Why don't you go see what Grandpa is up to?"

A light rain begins to fall as she goes aboard the boat. The moisture makes the air feel thick. In the wheelhouse, she can smell the mold and mustiness. It permeates the space, mixing with the smell of oil and diesel. She feels its heaviness on her skin and clothes. The galley is littered with dirty paper plates. There's a half empty can of pork and beans next to an empty can of chicken noodle soup. She remembers now that when she was young, working with her dad, when they were too tired to cook, they would eat those same things, whatever was handy. Many times they wouldn't bother to heat it up in a pan, just sit there, spooning it silently out of the can, the cold fat in the pork and beans sticking to the roof of her mouth.

"Hey, Mom, you on the boat?"

"Come aboard and check it out."

He stands next to her. "You know, Mom, those people at the meeting were pretty upset about that logging road being built to the Cove."

"They sure were."

"Grandpa's a logger, isn't he?"

"Yes, but it's not the loggers that're the problem. They're just working folks making a living the best way they can. What they're worried about is what the road brings, all of those things that most of them are here to get away from."

"Oh, civilization, so we're civilized and the people that live here aren't?"

Nancy thinks for a moment. "Mike, this is going to be a bad explanation, but it's the best I can do on the spur of the moment. There are millions of people who live just like we do. It's a good way to live. But I guess they get to thinking if it's a good thing, then why wouldn't everybody want to be that way?"

Mike asks, "Even if they don't want to?"

She gives his head a gentle push. "You ask way too many question for a pudgy redhead. Go ahead and look around, ask me some questions about the boat."

He slowly makes his way through the galley and the wheelhouse then on to the engine room. He calls out, "A GMC-871, right?"

"Right."

"I've been doing some homework."

"I can see that."

She joins him, watching as he inspects the engine, looking closely, touching the things that get his attention. "Mom, is there supposed to be water under the engine?"

"As long as it's in the bilge and not on the floorboards."

"Where does it come from?"

"If it's freshwater, then there're some leaks in the deck. If it's saltwater, then it's probably from the stuffing box on the prop shaft. It's supposed to leak to keep the shaft cool while the engine is running.

"What?"

"I'll explain that to you later."

"How do you know if the water is fresh or salt?"

"You could taste it."

"Looks pretty gross, Mom."

She gives him a stern look. "All of the real deckhands, I mean if you want to be a real deckhand, you gotta taste it as well as scratch certain body parts."

He shakes his head and smiles. "Nice try, Mom."

She laughs. "Just spit in it. If the spit dissolves, it's saltwater. If it doesn't, its freshwater."

"There you go again."

"No, that works."

He leans over the bilge and spits a huge gob of spit into the bilge just behind the engine and watches. "I'll be damned."

"Watch your language, young man!"

"You swear all the time."

"All right, you little bastard, how does the saying go? Do as I say not as I do." They both break out laughing. He stands next to her, and they stand there quietly for long moments, looking at the engine room. He looks at her as she slips into more deep thoughts.

He says, "Looks like we have our work cut out for us, doesn't it?"

"Jesus, Michael, I don't know what to think about all of this, to be quite honest with you. I just don't see how it's gonna work."

Michael quickly changes the subject. "Hey, Mom, you know all those people that were on the float when the plane landed."

"What about them?"

"They all called me Mike."

"And?"

"I think Mike is a better name for a deckhand than Michael."

She smiles. "Then so do I."

He takes her hand. "Let's go check out the boatshed."

Mike turns and squeezes by a door that is hanging crookedly from one hinge. Inside is the jumble of a lifetime of living on the water. Rusty tools litter the workbench. Rusty parts are leaning in the corners—parts of hydraulic pumps, several worn-out shaft bearings, a wooden vice made from two planks, a large band saw with the blade missing, a stack of five gallon buckets left over from oil changes, an old engine block from which parts have been salvaged. In the middle of the floor is a pile of chain. Mike asks, "What's all that chain for?"

"Those are called boom chains. They connect the boom logs together, so when you get a bunch of logs and you want to make a raft, the boom logs are connected with these chains. They make a sort of floating fence to keep them together."

Mike frowns. "Huh?"

"A boom log has a big hole in each end of it that the chain goes through."

"Well, I'll be . . ." He wanders off to inspect the workbench.

Near the back of the building are some smaller pieces of driftwood stacked on the workbench. The pieces are randomly sized and shaped. There is also a stack of smooth stones. One stone has been broken in half, showing a fossilized leaf at its center. Some of the pieces of wood have scribbling of words and numbers. One flat rock has a rudimentary compass rose scratched on it.

Mike holds up a piece of wood to the light that's coming through the window. "What's this?"

He's holding a weathered tree root that has been covered with a thin sheet of copper, carefully nailed into place with brass nails that are beginning to turn green with corrosion. On another place where the root makes a sharp turn, there are lines drawn on the copper that are evenly spaced following the curve of the wood, like contour lines. On a flat space between the fingers of the roots' spread, there are some faint numbers that can't quite be made out.

Mike looks at his mom. "Does this mean anything?"

Nancy points at the piece of wood. "You mean that?"

"Yeah, but the rest of it too."

She rubs her face with one hand. "Just doodling, just doodling. Everybody doodles just to let their mind wander, put down in some manner, whatever thought that trickles into your mind."

"Sure, but this seems like it's more than just some absentminded doodling."

"Well, that's my explanation. You'll have to ask your grandpa for his, good luck with that."

"You mean because he's had a stroke?"

"I don't know about that, but I don't think you would've gotten any kind of answer even before the stroke. You can go ahead and try, but don't hold your breath for some sort of clarification. Sometimes he would get an idea and let's say he thought it was a pretty good idea. He would maybe talk about it a bit, maybe even come to some conclusion as to whether it was a good idea or not. One time I remember he was thinking about getting a bigger boat to expand the business to towing barges, like delivering fuel to remote areas. He and I talked about it, over and over, then he went to the shop and spent the next couple of days in there, messing with stuff like this." She waves her hand at the pile of driftwood and rocks. "I don't know. I was just a kid, didn't even think it was unusual, didn't know any better. It didn't occur to me that most people didn't live like this, until later.

"Anyway, he didn't say much about anything else while this was going on, but one evening he came back to the house, sat in his chair, and started reading from a book of poetry aloud. We spent that evening reading to each other. After dinner I asked him if he had decided anything about a new boat. He said he didn't think he would buy a new boat. When I asked why, he said that the distance between getting a good idea, even if it's for all of the right reasons, and actually making it work is cluttered with the shadows of problems a person doesn't even know about yet."

"Oh, I get it, things usually don't work out like you think they're gonna when you first get an idea."

Nancy doesn't answer; she just stares at Mike.

He continues, "Just like what we are doing up here, right?"

"You know, Mike, I've not been paying close enough attention to you."

"What do you mean?"

"I just haven't, that's all."

"Grandpa doesn't seem like someone who would be interested in poetry."

"You aren't the only one who can't figure him out, including me. For example, he will just say things out of the blue, as if they just popped into his head at that very moment, but as he continues to talk, it's evident he's been giving the idea careful consideration even though what he says is completely unrelated to whatever has been going on at that moment. It can be disturbing, it makes people nervous and edgy." She chuckles. "Then if he thinks, if whatever idea it is, it's a good idea, he gets going on it, and he can't leave it alone until the idea wears out or he does. He just can't help it."

Now Mike is watching his mom very carefully. "Huh."

"I suppose poetry would be something you would have to talk to him about, but in the winter the evenings are long and we would read to each other. You know Mary, the woman I hugged on the dock?"

"I could tell you liked her."

"She would come over and stay with me when Dad was out working and I couldn't go along. Anyway, she got us started on poetry."

"Mary's nice woman, isn't she?"

"The best as far as I'm concerned." She motions to the house. "What do you say about checking out the house, maybe get a bite to eat?" She follows him as they walk on moss-covered boards that lie over muskeg. The edges of the planks squish water out to the side as they step on them. She says, "I can't figure out if I should say thank you or not."

After dinner, Owen has a marine chart unrolled on the table, showing Mike what some of the details mean, what a compass rose is and how to use it, what a fathom is, the beginnings of how to navigate. Then he makes marks with a pencil where the logs are scattered on the beaches at the western entrances of El Capitan Passage. He waves his good hand over the chart as he talks. "Most of the bundles broke, so the logs are scattered clear out to the western tip of Kosciusko Island. Some are over on the south side of Hamilton Island. We will have to wait for the biggest tides at the end of May to get the bundles, but the single logs we can start on as that cycle starts to build. That'll give us a week or so to jump on things."

"Grandpa, how big are those tides in May?"

Owen makes an awkward move for the tide book with his left hand, forgetting it doesn't work. Mike retrieves it, opens it to the month of May, and hands it to Owen.

"There's a couple that are about nineteen feet or so. Yeah, it looks pretty good for about a week or so. If we start early on the singles, we should be OK."

Nancy leans back away from the table and watches her dad with her arms folded in front of her. Owen stops talking but stares at her. She looks away.

He's silent for a moment then says, "This ain't gonna work, is it?"

She looks sad. "I don't see how it can. I mean, just dealing with the boom chains and chokers, not to mention running a chainsaw or jacks. You can't do that, Dad, and Mike is only fourteen years old. I know he'll work at it, but we need to be realistic about this. When you and I worked together, you did all of the heavy work and I ran the boat, except the summer Ed worked with us."

Owen begins massaging his left arm then rubs his bristly beard and says with resignation, "Yep, you're right, we don't be needin' someone to get hurt or killed, bunch of damned logs ain't worth that."

Mike says, "Hey, wait a minute! Do you mean we went to all of this trouble to get me out of school and get up here and we aren't even going haul one log? How's this possible?"

Nancy and Owen look away. He slides his chair back and leaves the house.

"Well, Dad, I suppose if we're honest with ourselves, we would have to say we knew from the beginning this wasn't really going to work, didn't we?"

"When I got this idea, I really didn't think Mike would come along, and I sure didn't figure he would be so excited about the whole thing. I can see how disappointed he is. I just thought you and I could get together for a while, you know, with the stroke and all, I just figured we might be running out of time."

She looks directly at her dad. "I wasn't going to come, but Ed said it would be a mistake if I didn't, then Mike was all excited about it and wouldn't have it any other way. I have to admit, it if hadn't been for that, I would've probably not come." She frowns. "Ed also said that whenever I talked about living here, which wasn't hardly at all, I got angry. I think he was a little worried about that. Maybe I would regret it down the line if I didn't see you at least one more time."

"Ed's a good man."

"Yes, he is."

"You've always had a pretty good temper. I worried about that a little myself when you were growing up."

Nancy looks uncomfortable. "You mean like the time I took after that kid with a gaff hook after he called me a skinny little bitch?"

"There were other times as well, but yeah, that's a good example. Now, as long as we're being honest, to tell you the truth, I figured Mike would be one of those bratty city kids who think they know everything when they really don't know shit. I mostly thought you guys would get up here and the last thing he would want to do is be a deckhand. So we wouldn't be faced with really needing to go beach logging and least of all disappointing him by saying we can't because he isn't able to do the work. I see now that's not the case." He begins to play with the spoon in his coffee cup, pushing back and forth on the lip of the cup, deep in thought; he mumbles under his breath, "Just another one of my bright ideas. Well, let's just try and make the best of things as they are. I'll show Mike how to run a skiff. Maybe we'll do a little beach logging for firewood. That might work out. It would be chance for he and I to spend some time together. I could show him the country a bit. What do you think about that?"

She is distracted, keeps glancing at the front door that is still ajar from when Mike left. "Sure, Dad, that might be a good idea." She turns and leaves, walking over the planks on the muskeg. The light from her small flashlight seems frail in the complete darkness. What light there is in the sky reflects off the water. She hears the sound of chains rattling in the boathouse.

As she enters, the beam from her flashlight rests on Mike. He's dragging a boom chain from the pile they had looked at earlier. Two chains are by the door with one end hanging outside. He has the oversize link that's on one end of the chain grasped in both hands. His feet are spread apart and firmly planted on the floor. He's lunging backward against its weight. Each effort moves the chain a foot or so. He takes a couple of steps backward, taking the slack out, then he lunges back and repeats the process.

"Mike, what are you doing!"

"I'm moving these boom chains. You better be careful. There are a couple by the door." He throws himself backward again, grunting with the effort. The chain rattles, and he takes a deep breath and starts again. Between deep breaths, he says, "You might trip on them." His voice is hard.

"What are you going to do with them?"

He turns toward her as far as the weight of the chain allows, squinting into the light. "I'm going to drag the rest of these over to the door where those other two are, then I'm gonna drag all of them down the dock and then I'm gonna put them on the deck of the tugboat."

"That's a hundred feet. You can't do that. You're having a hell of a time just getting them to the door."

"Maybe I can't, but I'm gonna do it anyway," he says matter-of-factly.

"I'll help you."

"No, you won't."

"But—"

"It can't work that way, Mom, or it won't work at all. Grandpa said if I can't do the work, then we won't go beach logging. I'm going to find out if I can do it, and I'm starting right now."

"But—"

"I was sitting right there when you and Grandpa were talking. The two of you can't do it, and I'm the only other guy here."

"Mike, honey, this can be dangerous work. I mean what you're doing right now is a good example, working by yourself at night. Just one slip and you're in the water between the boat and the dock, maybe crack your head on the side of the boat on the way down. That's it, you're dead."

"I guess that's part of the whole deal, isn't it?" He gives a hard tug on the chain and makes an angry, growling sound.

"Mike, let me tell you something, please!"

He stops growling.

"What I'm about say is important. You need to listen carefully. I promise I won't go on about it, but here's the deal. There are lots of folks in this country with years of experience who don't take unnecessary risks. They're experienced and careful, and they still don't make it home. This is tough country."

"OK, I'll be careful."

She holds up her hand. "How about a couple of ideas?"

He stands silently still, holding the chain.

"If you do manage to get the boom chains down the dock next to the boat, you'll have to lift them about three feet in the air to get them over the rail and onto the deck. That will be very difficult."

He gives another yank on the chain and begins growling again.

"No, no, I'm not going to try and stop you from trying and I'm not going to help you, but there's a set of steps at the end of the dock. What I'm suggesting is that you could maybe slide them up next to the boat. I think, maybe, that by taking one of a chain and pulling it up the steps as far as you're able, then you could do the same with the other end and bit by bit get it onto the deck."

"OK." He resumes pulling the chain.

"Another thing, when you get out on the dock, you need to wear a life jacket."

"OK."

"I'm not going to help you, but I am going to stay here and hold the flashlight. I won't say a word unless you want to know something."

"OK."

For the next few hours, without a pause, he jerks and pulls the chains from the pile to the door of the boathouse, down the dock next to the boat, then pushes the steps up to the boat. Finally resting, he sits on the bottom step, leaning forward with his elbows on his knees. Nancy shines her flashlight beam on his hands. Blood is dripping from them. She waits, letting him catch his breath. "We can finish this in the morning."

"I'm going to do this tonight, and in the morning, we're going to get up and you're going to teach me everything you know about this tugboat. Then you're going to teach me how to run it and then . . ." He wipes his hands on his pants and grabs one end of a chain. He struggles but finally gets one end on his shoulder. He staggers—alternately angry, silent, stumbling, lunging, cursing, locked in mortal combat. The chain links begin to show traces of blood. She remains silent, watching, and wonders about this change that's come over her son. He tries to climb the steps with the chain on his shoulder while he looks at the water between the boat and the dock.

"That's not a good idea, Mike."

He shrugs it off his shoulder, and it clatters loudly onto the dock. She shines the light on his face. It's dirty and sweaty; his teeth are clinched tight. Nancy hears the door of the house open, her dad's uneven step clumping over the porch. He examines the scene below him—Nancy holding the light, Mike bracing himself for another try. "Are you guys all right?"

Nancy answers, "Ask Mike."

"Well, Mike?"

"I'll be done once I get these chains on deck."

"You gonna give him a hand, Nancy?"

"No."

Owen remains on the porch. He says, "Huh."

Mike continues. He slips while pulling a chain from the top of the steps and falls, disappearing over the railing onto the deck. Nancy starts forward to see if he is injured, but he quickly reappears and starts again. As daylight breaks, he drags the last boom chain over the rail. Standing next to the pile in a trance, he instinctively reaches down and grabs a chain and begins to pull.

"Hey, Mike, you're done."

"Oh yeah, right." His words are slurred with fatigue.

Nancy motions to him. "Come on, we better get your hands cleaned up so you won't get them infected. We're a long way from a doctor."

With a swollen finger, he points at the boat. "Tomorrow we start getting the boat ready." When they reach the house, Nancy dresses the cuts on his hands. He stares straight ahead when she dabs them with alcohol, and she takes him to his room. There's a metal army surplus cot shoved up against one wall. Instead of blankets, a sleeping bag is unrolled on the mattress. When she returns later, she sees that he has plopped down face-first on the sleeping bag and is sound asleep.

In the morning, over coffee, Owen asks, "What's goin' on with Mike?"

"I haven't seen him like that before. He was really pissed off. Got his neck bowed. There was no talking him out of it. Like me I guess?"

"Jesus, I hope he doesn't have a temper like yours."

"Come on, Dad."

"I'm just sayin' . . ."

She interrupts, "Anyway, Mike has been having a tough time at school. It's nothing serious, but Ed and I are worried about it. We think he needs to feel like he belongs with his friends. He quit the soccer team because his feet are too big and because he's short and pudgy. So it was a big deal when the kids at school found out that he was going to Alaska to work as a deckhand on a tugboat. His classmates thought that was pretty exciting. So when we decided last night that this couldn't be done with just the three of us, he got it in his head that he's the one holding the whole thing back because he can't do the work necessary to rig the logs."

"Huh, I'll be damned."

They both turn at the sounds of footsteps coming from the back of the house. Mike is standing there in a T-shirt stained with dried sweat marks; his hands are still swollen and bruised. "What time is it?"

Owen answers, "About nine o'clock."

"You let me sleep in!" he says accusingly.

Nancy begins, "But, Mike—"

Owen cuts her off with a raised hand. He says brusquely, "All right, kid, you don't leave me much choice, so here's the deal. You're right, if this is gonna work, we need a genuine deckhand, and right now you ain't one."

Mike looks at his grandpa closely.

Owen turns to face him. "Here's how it's gonna work. We have about a month before the high tides, so between now and then, you're gonna have to show me that you can learn fast enough and do enough fast enough to be of any use as a deckhand. And another thing you need to know is that bein' a deckhand isn't like bein' involved in any kinda democratic process. So you better get used to doin' exactly what you're told to do."

Nancy is alarmed by his bluntness. "Dad!"

He turns to Nancy. "I'm not gonna feed him a bunch of bullshit. That would just guarantee that none of this would work. Not only that, Mike would know it was bullshit. Wouldn't you, Mike?"

"Yes."

"If you're not ready in a month, we ain't gonna do it, nothin' personal, that's just the way it's gonna be."

Mike continues his grim stare. "So let's get started."

"While your mom is getting breakfast, I want you to go to my bedroom. On the back wall next to the window is a pair of black wool pants with red suspenders. Put the pants on, adjust the suspenders to fit, grab a pair of socks out of the top drawer of my chest of drawers. They should fit, our feet are about the same size. The pants will be a bit too long, so take the pair of scissors from my nightstand and cut the legs off so they're about four inches above your ankle. When that's done, come on back here, and we'll have breakfast."

Mike quickly disappears to the back of the house.

Owen turns back to Nancy. "You and I can't make this work, and I don't think, for one minute, that Mike will be able to take up the slack. If we just tell him that up front, then it would be easy to just blame us, but if we go through this, then I'll bet he'll find out all by himself it ain't gonna work. That way we tried, and all came to the same conclusion, you know, together."

"But, Dad, he's just a kid."

"Of course he is, and you ought to know better than anyone that I ain't much of a parent."

"I didn't say that."

"That's not necessary. Anybody in their right mind would know this ain't any way to raise a kid." Owen waves his hand at the room. "I mean, look at this place. I was lucky it worked as well as it did. I was lucky you were a tough kid."

Nancy is frowning.

"I been thinking about all of this since last night, watchin' Mike struggle with them chains, tryin' to sort this situation out. It's not what I expected to happen or, God knows, wanted to happen, but it's all I could come up with, it's all I know. This is all I've ever done. You're the only kid I've ever had. Your mom was only around long enough to get you born. I couldn't have done any of it if Mary hadn't been so much help. I didn't know squat about raising a kid, still don't. You know what I really thought when your mom was pregnant?"

Nancy's voice is muted. "No, Dad, I don't."

I just thought we would live here, and well, I don't know exactly, but live here and work: hunt, fish, read some books in the winter, tell some stories. You know, be like a family." Owen looks dour. "Shit, that didn't work out at all like I thought it would!" Looking at Nancy and seeing the expression on her face, he pats her on the shoulder. "I guess that's true of a lot of folks, one way or 'nother, ain't it?"

Mike returns and stands next to the front door, expressionless. "What next?"

"On the back deck is a hatch cover. Remove it and you will see a steering transit. It's a metal, half-moon bracket that the steering cable fits in. It's mounted on a shaft that goes through a bearing. When you turn the helm, it moves back and forth with the cable. Its purpose is to keep tension on the steering cable. On the work bench in the boat is a container of grease." Owen holds his hand off the table, showing the approximate size of the can. "I want you to smear the grease, with your hands, completely cover the transit and cable. Make sure you pay particular attention to the bearing."

"Got it." Mike begins to leave.

"One more thing."

"What?"

"Be careful when you're greasing the cable. It's old, and there is bound to be some broken strands sticking out. They'll poke holes in you."

Mike nods and leaves.

10

Randy

For the past week or so, Neil has made a point of keeping to himself, going through the library, starting the generator just for the practice, and taking an inventory of basic school supplies, enjoying the solitude. Most mornings he lies in bed, not looking at the clock, for whatever reason, before he decides to get up. Today he lies with his hands folded behind his head, looking at the walls and ceiling. Like all the mornings since he has been here, the first thing that stands out for him is the lack of sound. It's absolutely quiet. He's not sure if he's ever been anyplace so quiet.

He says aloud, "Hey, it's sure quiet in here." Then he smiles at his own quirkiness. He surveys the room. "Would you look at all of this mold?" Throwing back the covers, he walks out of the small apartment into the classroom; he stands with his hands on his hips as he turns in a full circle.

"You need some vinegar, my friend."

He answers himself, "How much do you think you need?"

"Let's see, enough for the classroom, the library, and the apartment. Two gallons will do nicely."

"Don't forget the porch."

"Right, make that three gallons."

"Don't forget the receipt."

"Off to the Mercantile."

He starts out the door. When the cool air touches his skin, he suddenly realizes he's naked. Quickly returning to the apartment, he gargles some mouthwash and spits it in the kitchen sink. He skips brushing his teeth, takes a cursory sniff of his armpits, slips on yesterday's T-shirt, pulling at the bottom of it with one hand while trying to smooth the wrinkles out with the other, splashes some water on his hair, and with a brush, parts it down the middle. The excess water runs down the side of his face and neck.

When he reaches the end of the community boardwalk where the ramp connects to a float, he veers off and makes his way through the underbrush, thrashing his way through the salmonberry bushes. When he reaches the beach, he begins to check under rocks and kelp to see what types of creatures are there. Beyond, at the opposite bank, he scurries up the rocks and comes to the trail that leads to the back entrance of the Mercantile. The door to the store is locked with a Closed sign in the window. He glances at his wrist, only to realize he has forgotten his watch, then he realizes he is not even sure what day of the week it is.

Some small things are shifting around in his mind. He hasn't thought about home or any number of the hundreds of other things that seemed so important to him just a few weeks ago. The notion that he considered staying in Oregon to work at the sawmill seems particularly odd and completely unconnected to anything here.

He wanders out on the deck among the fish totes just outside Everett's office and lights a cigarette. The flags on the Saloon are limp in the morning calm; the small table and deck beneath are littered with empty beer cans. The fuel float is deserted except for a couple of sleeping dogs and a one-legged raven. Silence once again closes in on him.

He sees a ball of herring gathered near the surface of the water. They flash bright silver in the morning sun. An Auklet dives under them, forcing them to boil to the surface in their attempts to escape being eaten. Once they are at the surface, some kittiwakes dive through the air to feed on them. The feeding birds drive them into a tighter and tighter ball. A seal lingers nearby then makes a pass through the fish. They disperse but very quickly regroup. The fish become more and more frantic, unable to escape or change their behavior.

Neil leans on the rail, wondering why they just don't all take off in different directions and meet up later.

Out of nowhere a strong, firm voice says, "They will come here, you know they will. It's just a matter of time."

Startled, he looks behind him at the fish totes. The ice house then steps back to see down the breezeway between Everett's office and the store, nothing.

The voice comes again, this time filled with concern and trepidation. It floats up from behind the freight shack by the fuel pumps. Neil steps sideways a few steps. He sees Randy sitting on a five-gallon bucket with his hands folded, hanging between his knees. A few feet away is another five-gallon bucket. The one-legged raven is perched on its lip, watching Randy. Randy leans forward toward the raven. At times he makes a gesture with his arm or points a finger to emphasize a point. He's deeply involved in the conversation; it's a determined effort. The raven cocks its head to one side, crouches on its one leg, and rolls one shoulder lower than the other while it continues to listen. Neil watches closely as the raven appears, at times, to nod its head in agreement.

Now Randy speaks in hushed tones and leans forward a bit more. "They will come. That guy from the Forest Service is right. All of the things he talked about will happen; they're happening now. I can hear the car doors opening and closing, see the people pointing. Nothing can stop all of those words he used at the meeting. Those words were flying around the room. I can see them hanging in the air, floating around the room, lying on the floor, drooping from the light fixtures, everywhere. I don't know if you noticed, but some even tried escaping out the door, but those all died there on the porch. Those words were meaningless. But the ones that gathered on the teacher's desk are the ones that will do the most damage, the ones that didn't try to escape, the ones that said, *All of this is for your own good.' 'The road will make your life easier.' 'The road will make you safer.'*

"Those words will make their way back to Juneau, and that's what those people, sitting behind their desks, will listen to. That's what they want to hear. They think they're normal. They'll say help those people: *'It's for their own good.'*"

His voice changes to a lower pitch and takes on a mocking tone. He raises his eyebrows and smiles a counterfeit smile. "Just think of the possibilities. We must all start now saving our money to buy a car. Now." He points directly at the raven, "Let me be the first to inform you of a very important fact: Cars are more than just a means of getting from one place to another. Yes, that is correct. They show everyone who you are and how you fit into the larger scheme of things. Oh my god!" Randy grasps his head with both hands. "They show your socioeconomic status, your position in the community. They're a continuing advertisement for who you are." He holds his arms out wide, nodding at the raven. "And you, raven, what kind of car will you have? Remember, it will reflect your station in life. It will say you are someone who rises above the everyday struggles of existence, someone who's in touch with all that goes on here in the Cove."

The raven rubs his beak on the edge of the bucket as if he's sharpening it.

"See, I knew it. I knew you would agree. Let me see, it will be the kind of car that says things like 'I am independent. I am self-sufficient. I am the silent communicator who cares enough to listen.'"

Randy ponders for a moment while he rubs his chin and laughs. "I've got it! You need a BMW. That will show people who you are. But it will need to be some subtle color that doesn't stand out. We don't want anything loud or obvious for you."

Neil begins to feel like he's peering in someone's window, watching their private life. He walks down the ramp toward Randy and the raven, treading heavily as he goes. The ramp sways and rattles, making his presence known. He comes into full view of Randy and the raven. He stops, standing there, watching and waiting. The raven stays on the bucket.

Randy continues. He points to his head. "I can see it coming."

Neil says, "Hey, Randy, how's it going?"

Randy looks at him. "Hi, Neil, I knew you were up there even though I couldn't see you."

"I didn't mean to eavesdrop. I was just waiting for the store to open."

"That's OK, everyone knows I'm crazy."

"They do?"

"They don't say anything, but yeah, they know."

"No problems though?"

"Could be, but things are working out here better than anyplace else I've been. Everett knows there are some days I just can't manage. Rich and Bob tell him I've been drinking. They think that sort of covers for me, and he pretends to fire me for being drunk, but I can tell he knows it's something else. It all kinda started when I was in law school, so that didn't work out." He chuckles to himself. "I knew it must be serious, because there isn't a stranger bunch of people than lawyers."

"So you're mostly OK then?"

"Yeah, mostly. I guess most folks have something they have to sort through. It's just a matter of the amount and the degree of what they have to put up with. All of that works out, but sometimes someone else moves in with me. I wake up, and there he is," he points to his head, "living in there. A shadow that's giving me advice and suggestions on how to solve things, and at the same time he's some sort of electrical charge that attracts all of my feelings. It gets difficult. I don't really know how to deal with him or anything else. On top of that, I still have myself to deal with." He raises his hands in frustration. "What's really frustrating is that he knows things that the rest of us doesn't know."

Neil asks, "He does?"

"There are things going on right now, things I know are not really happening, but nevertheless, they are still the truth."

"Jeez, Randy, you lost me on that one."

"Right, it wears me out when I try to solve those problems with reason. There he is, set up there in my head, kind of like he was born with me when all I was doing was just going about my own business."

"Wears me out just hearing about it."

Randy sits up straight on the bucket, holding both hands in the air. "Yeah, it's like walking around in mud, but even after all of that, there are times like right now when everything is crystal clear. That's how I knew you were up there by the totes listening even though I couldn't see you."

"Huh."

"Yes. On the other side of all that, when it's good, it's really, really good. I'm not kidding you, it's very attractive. It goes way beyond curiosity, beyond compassion. It doesn't require thought of consideration or consequences. You just run free with it. It's very clear that some of the things are really happening and some aren't, but they all are very real." Randy watches the edge of the water as it moves up the rocks nearby, and says matter-of-factly, "I was born this way. That's all there is to it." He nods knowingly at Neil.

Neil nods back.

"Randy, it's time to go to work!"

They both jump at the sound of Kasey's voice.

"The *Sea Roamer* is coming in with a load of fish. They just called on the radio, caught a bunch of king salmon in south Chatham. We need more ice in the totes." She turns away then stops and returns to the railing. "It would be a good thing if you were up here working when Everett shows up. He likes it when you're working when he shows up. Randy stands stiffly, brushing the front of his wool jacket, and says to Neil out of the corner of his mouth, "Well, she's right about that." He raises his chin and nods his head while he walks up the ramp. It's with a sense of purpose. He stands in front of a tote, putting on his rubber gloves slowly and carefully before he disappears into the ice house.

Kasey stays at the railing and says to Neil, "Cup of coffee?"

Neil is staring at the raven, still trying to figure out what has just happened, sorting out his conversation with Randy.

She shouts, "Neil!"

"Jesus, what!"

She laughs. "You're deep in thought there, fella. I hope you're not catching whatever it is that Randy has."

"Me too." He points to the raven, which is now watching him closely. "Randy was," he hesitates, "having a pretty involved conversation with this raven?" He hadn't meant to ask that kind of a question, but it just came out that way.

Kasey looks at him seriously. "Would you like a cup of coffee?"

He perks up. "Sure." He looks back at the raven as he's leaving.

She motions him toward the office and is pouring the coffee when he enters. "Sit where you can." He hesitates, looking at Everett's desk. "It's OK, he won't mind. I really don't think he'll be in today. He worked about eighteen hours yesterday. That's a lot for an old man, he's pretty beat up. I just told Randy that to get him back to work."

Neil looks out on the deck where Rich and Bob have appeared, and the three men are busy getting organized to buy fish. "Just to get him motivated?"

"He needs to stay as busy as he can. He'll be screwed if he just sits around all day."

"Keeps him from thinking too much about other things?"

"It's more complicated than that, but he knows what's going on. He's actually a pretty smart guy. My guess, he didn't flunk out of law school. He just couldn't get all of those things sorted out in his head. Probably went off on one of his 'journeys'"—she makes quotation marks with her fingers—"once in a while and school suffered for it. Everett manages to walk a fine line with many things here. He does with Randy as well. Everett can't afford to have someone who doesn't pull his own weight, and Randy wouldn't put up with being pandered to. So when Randy doesn't make it to work, which isn't very often but still more than most, Everett fires him. That's what he would do with anyone else, but the difference is that Randy shows up to work the next day like nothing happened. He works hard when he's here, and those times that he's not, we all kind of pick up the slack a bit. Mostly it's Bob and Rich though. So we all do this dance that sort of keeps them both satisfied. It's a complicated and finely tuned dance they do, but it works. So far anyway."

Neil nods. "Sounds good to me."

"It does?"

"Sure, why wouldn't that all work?"

She frowns at him. "As a matter of fact, it does in its own way. I guess I was just expecting a different reaction from you, that's all."

"You mean because I'm a newcomer and from 'south.'"

"Things are different here."

"I agree."

He studies her closely. "OK, now that we have established my greenhorn status, maybe you can help me out with a couple of things. When he's like he is now, feeling good and all, he said he can see or understand things that aren't real but they still make sense to him. I'm having a difficult time sorting through that whole idea."

"Yeah, I don't know how to help you with that one. Ideas that come from something that he knows doesn't really exist. You've got me on that one, but you know what's really interesting to me?"

"What?"

"Sometimes before something happens, an accident, some boat will come in all beat up from weather and he gets what he calls a bad feeling. It's almost like he knows some things are going to happen before they do. I don't tell everyone this because it sounds so weird."

"Strange you should say that. When he was talking to me, and that one-legged raven, it was about how we better start shopping for cars because he's convinced the road is coming."

Kasey looks disturbed. "Aw, shit." She sits heavily in her chair. "That kind of progress will be the end of him." She adds, "A lot of us really."

"Huh." Neil walks over the window and watches the men work for a moment. "As long as we're talking about the margins of behavior, can you tell me something?"

Kasey is staring at the floor.

"Randy was talking to that raven for a long time, and it sure acted like it was listening. Was it?"

"What the hell are you asking?"

Neil shrugs. "I don't know, but it sure looked like it was listening."

"Do you do drugs?"

"Drink some whiskey once in a while."

"For breakfast."

"Hardly ever do that."

Kasey stands watching Neil with renewed interest. "I don't have any idea about that, but I will tell you one thing that seems a little odd to me. Randy has lived here for years, and as far as I know, he hasn't told me or anyone else what he told you this morning. I don't get that at all." She frowns. "How about we let this subject rest for a bit? It's getting a bit peculiar."

"Good idea."

"I have to get to work."

"I have one more question."

"Just one?"

"You're an Indian, right?"

She laughs and slaps her leg with some invoice she just picked up. "Where have you been? You're supposed to say 'Native American,' you dolt."

Neil tries to apologize. "Oh, sorry, I didn't mean anything—"

She waves her hand. "It doesn't matter. I was just messing with you. To tell you the truth, I don't pay much attention to the terms. I just figure everyone wants to be treated fairly, that's all. Besides that, I can tell in about one minute if someone doesn't like Indians."

"Sure."

"Not many of us folks where you come from?"

"Some, not many, I guess."

"You don't know any though?"

He thinks for a moment. "I spent one summer on a railroad section gang. Mostly Navaho worked on the crew. Leonard Husky, one of the guys I worked with, and I became friends. We didn't talk much, drank some beer when we had a day off, but mostly we just worked. So actually I know two Ind—Native Americans."

"Who's the other one?"

"You."

She laughs again. "Well, it's a start."

He watches her over the top of his coffee cup as he takes a sip. "I know you have a boat coming in, but when we get some time, maybe you could explain some things to me."

"For instance?"

"I'm way out here on the edge of nowhere. Next stop, Russia. It occurs to me that I don't know much, don't even know what I know for sure, but I do know there's a whole bunch of stuff I don't know, and I don't want get embroiled in some situation out of sheer ignorance."

"We'll see."

"I don't want to hold you up here, maybe later."

"We'll see. Go on, I need to get to work."

"I've just watched some guy have a conversation with a raven, who I thought was listening. That's a little odd, to say the least."

"You're a little odd yourself."

"You'll get no argument from me on that subject. All I want is just to get my feet on the ground, fit in the best I can."

"Are you sure you're a schoolteacher? You don't seem like a schoolteacher."

"That's another question I don't have an answer for. I guess we'll find out when the kids show up if I can teach or not."

Kasey shakes her head. "I guess we will."

The office door swings open, and Everett walks in.

Kasey says, "What are you doing here? You look like death warmed over."

"I'm tolerably tired, all right, but I heard on the radio at the house the *Sea Roamer* is coming in to unload."

"Should be here soon."

Everett walks out the door, moves through the totes, checks out the ice house, and hobbles down the ramp to look at the fuel pumps. When he returns, he says to Neil, "Nancy's boy Mike is sitting down there at the float in Owen's skiff. Why don't you go talk to him? I think he needs someone to talk to."

"What?"

"Go on, we need to get to work here anyway. I can see you're distracting my help." He raises his eyebrows at Kasey. She turns quickly to her desk.

Neil is still standing, puzzled. Everett waves his arm at him. "Go on."

When Neil walks down the ramp, Mike and the red aluminum skiff have drifted away from the dock. Mike is sitting, one hand on the tiller with an angry look on his face, staring at the bottom of skiff. Neil sits on the bucket Randy has been sitting on and watches. A small eddy in the tidal current moves the skiff closer to the float. As the skiff comes to rest against the float, Mike doesn't notice. He stays in the same position, unaware of all else. Neil stands and ties the skiff to the bull rail with one of the dock lines and says, "Hey there."

Mike jerks upright, looking about, and begins to get his bearings. "Oh, hi."

"You're Owen's grandson, right?"

Mike nods.

"You're the new deckhand."

Mike looks more dejected. "Doesn't look like that's gonna happen."

"Why not?"

"It's a long story."

"School doesn't start until September. Tell me if you want."

Words come spilling out of Mike's mouth in a torrent of rapid succession. He talks without pause until he runs out of breath. "Grandpa had this stroke, but he went ahead anyway and got this contract to get some logs that were lost in a storm. The logging outfit said they didn't think he could do the job because of his stroke, so they said he had to get someone to run the tug that was just as experienced as him because they thought he couldn't find someone with that much experience that would take a job like this, but they didn't know about Mom, who grew up doing all that stuff. She has worked years on the tug with Grandpa, so she came to help even though she already knew it wasn't going to work even though she told me and everybody else I would be the deckhand. She no doubt knew it wasn't gonna work out because I couldn't do the heavy work that needs to be done."

Mike puts his head down, takes a deep breath, and forges on. "She just wanted to patch some things up with Grandpa because she never did like growing up here, and she always was saying it was medieval. She is all pissed off because she never did have a normal childhood, whatever the hell that is. Now she thinks driving to work every morning on a jammed-up freeway and being late to work because of traffic jams and yelling at people in other cars is normal. That seems really strange to me, but what the hell do I know. I'm just a kid, but I wish I had never heard the word *normal*."

He takes another deep breath. "She and Dad are talking about getting him in an old folk's home before he kills himself trying to do something he shouldn't, and I wanted to come so bad she couldn't leave me home. I can tell they don't want to tell me right out that we can't beach-log. They keep saying 'If you can do this or if you can do that,' but I can't do 'this' or 'that,' so I guess I'm screwed on the deckhand deal, and everybody at school thinks I'm up here on a tugboat, beach logging, but it took hours for me just to drag some boom chains out of the boat shed and put them on the deck of the boat." Mike is done in, more dejected than ever.

Neil says, "You know, I have the same kind of problem right now."

Mike looks puzzled.

"Oh, not with beach logging, but with the 'normal' thing. Now that I think about it, it's been going on for quite a while."

Mike is frowning again.

"Tell me about beach logging."

"This logging company lost a bunch of logs in a storm, I guess, somewhere near a place called El Capitan Passage. I don't know much about how it works, but as far as I know, we're supposed to go there and get them off the beach at the high tides at the end of May or June. We make some sort of raft with them and take them to the logging company and then they pay us some money to do all of that."

Neil asks, "How long do you think that will take?"

"It's not going to happen."

"If it did, how long?"

"Grandpa said a couple of weeks, maybe a little longer, could be a month, I guess." Mike looks as if he's going to cry but suddenly straightens up and looks directly at Neil for the first time. "Wait a minute, didn't you just say that you weren't doing anything for the next couple of months?"

"Yes."

"Maybe you could be a deckhand too." He looks hopefully at Neil. "That might work."

Neil holds his hand up toward Mike. "Hold on there, I thought we were just having a conversation. In the first place, you don't know anything about me and I know even less about you. Nothing personal, but it also sounds like I'd be walking right into a complicated family situation. That sounds like it could get pretty uncomfortable very quickly. It's nothing personal but . . ."

Mike slumps back on the tiller. "Yeah, you're right. It's not like Mom and Grandpa are yelling and screaming at each other. It's just that I think they're convinced that this thing isn't going to work. All of that will be OK. It's not like we're in crisis or anything like that. We all like each other, but I sure would like a shot at being a deckhand. I can learn about the boat and work on it and stuff like that. I guess I can go back to school and technically say I worked on a tugboat, but it won't be the same. It's disappointing."

One of the dogs that have been sleeping on the dock waddles past the fuel pumps and pees on a piece of Styrofoam.

Mike looks away to the entrance of the Cove then begins to untie the dock line. "I better get going."

Neil asks, "Where's your grandpa's place?"

Mike throws his head in the general direction of the back part of the cove that is spotted with small islands and reefs. His eyes are moist. "Back there."

Neil takes a deep breath. "I guess it wouldn't hurt just to talk to him."

11

Going North

Liz walks through La Conner daily. She has annoyed some of the restaurants so regularly that people start leaving the room when she walks through the front door. She calls the unemployment office in Anacortes, but they won't send her the proper forms since she doesn't have a permanent address. The woman on the phone goes silent when Liz tells her she doesn't own a computer and is living on a boat. The woman finally agrees to send the forms when Liz gives her the street address of the La Conner post office as her own. When she fills them out and comes to the segment on work history, all she's able to put down is "fishing."

She continues to comb the area for some kind of work. Finally, she convinces a building contractor to hire her to clean up one of his construction sites. She starts work after the subcontractors have gone home for the day, picking up scraps of wood, wire, insulation, and whatever else has been discarded during the day. She likes the job; the pay is cash under the table, and she works by herself. There's nobody else to deal with. She keeps thinking Eric will show up at the boat some evening; it would be nice to have someone to talk to.

One day she's sitting on deck, having a cup of coffee, and a large man in Carhartt canvas bib overalls, covered in grease, climbs over the railing. "Hi, you must be Liz." He holds out his hand. It's large and meaty; he's smiling. "I'm here to work on the engine. I'll try not to muck up the galley when I walk through." He laughs aloud.

Liz says, "Let me know if I can give you a hand."

"You a mechanic?"

"No."

"Thanks for the offer but probably not." He reaches over the railing, lifting a large metal toolbox from the dock. "I'll try to stay out of your way." He disappears into the wheelhouse.

The captain calls later that day to ask if the mechanic has shown up yet. She says he has and is working. "Could you keep track of his hours so I'll have a general idea of what this is costing?"

"Sure, and another thing, how much longer do you want me to stay on the boat?"

"Do you need to leave at any certain time?"

"No."

"Any luck on a job yet?"

"Not much going on here, stuff is shutting down for the winter."

"When the mechanic is done, I'll be moving the boat to Blaine. You can stay on the boat here if you want, but there will be quite a bit going on. I'm going to have the back deck replaced. You're welcome to stay though."

"I'll think about it."

"Just let me know."

She goes to the engine room; the mechanic lies next to the engine, grunting as he reaches, straining to loosen bolts that hold the oil pan in place, dropping them into a tin coffee can. They clank as they hit the metal bottom. There are hand prints on his coveralls, which are now impregnated with oil. There are also some new smudges on his face and arms of rust mixed with oil. He talks without looking at her as he continues to remove the bolts. "What do you want?"

"The captain called to see how the job was coming along."

"You mean if I had even showed up yet?" He chuckles.

"Well, that too, I suppose."

"Tell him I'll have the pan off and the pistons out today. I should have the cylinder sleeves out tomorrow, and if everything else is good, I should start putting things back together by Friday, if the head is good."

"He asked me to keep track of your hours so he would have some idea of how much money he needs to come up with."

The mechanic stops ratcheting the bolts and lies silent for a moment. "By the time I get the cylinders out, I'll have close to ten hours in it." He mumbles to himself, "You can tell him it will be pretty close to the ten thousand dollars I originally estimated, unless the head is cracked. That will cost another thousand or so."

"OK, I'll tell him."

"I'll write down my hours and leave them on the galley table if you want."

"Sure."

She turns to leave.

"You fish in Alaska?"

"Yes."

"It's always been a dream of mine to fish in Alaska."

"It was?"

"Yeah, but I never could make it work." He has a half smile on his face.

Liz leans against the workbench to listen. "Why not?"

"That's a very good question. I have all sorts of reasons, of course. I've a good job, and as you probably know, there ain't no guarantees in fishing. Then I got married and had a couple of kids, told myself that it wouldn't be a responsible thing to do. You know, just pack everybody up and take off. The kids need to be in good schools. It's a long way from family. Would it be safe? Christ, I had all kinds of reasons why I shouldn't go north." He stops to rub an oily hand on his chest, first the palm then the back. "It just seems like once a person starts thinkin' like that and gets a bunch of reasons why they can't do somethin', then all the reasons why they should seem to disappear. You know what my best excuse was?"

Liz shrugs. "Nope."

"I got to thinkin' that what really counts are the things you do, not the things you don't do. I said to myself, how do the things you don't do count? 'What you don't do counts for nothing, it's meaningless, because it never happened,' I said. But if a person really thinks about it, how does not doing somethin' count for anything? How stupid is that? I couldn't begin to list all the reasons I had for not goin' north, but I had a lot of them. The problem was, they never did keep me from wantin' to go or from being sorry I didn't.

"Now I'm tied real tight to things, like a house mortgage and a loan on a new car. In a few years, the kids will be goin' off to college. That all takes money. So here I am, bendin' wrenches and covered with grease to make all of that work. Don't get me wrong, it's an OK life and I love my family, but I still think about it, livin' up north, I mean. What the hell? I could have made it work in Alaska. When I boil everything down to the bottom of the pan, it's still a real regret. I guess most people regret the things they didn't do that they could have done, don't they?" He tries to clean the oil from his hands with a rag from his hip pocket but just manages to smear it around. He looks sad.

"I suppose they do."

He looks at Liz. "What're you doin' here? You part of the crew?"

"No, I just caught a ride south."

"For the winter?"

"I'm thinking about staying and finding work."

"You mean so you can be like all the other faceless commuters living in houses that look pretty much like all of the other houses."

Liz looks away.

"Listen, lady, this ain't none of my business, and I got no reason to talk to you like this, but what you're sayin' doesn't make any sense to me at all. You've already done the hardest part—you've gone north and made it work."

"It doesn't seem to me like it worked out that good."

He points a greasy finger at her. "Now listen real close to me. Nothin' ever works out like you think it's gonna when you start out. That's just the way of things." He looks at her. "I can tell by just lookin' at you that you're plumb worn out, I mean exhausted. I'll bet you been through a rough patch. My guess is you been workin' your ass off and haven't had any time to look at yourself from a distance.

Maybe all you need to do is heal up a bit, then you'll start thinking stuff through."

Liz sighs. "You're right about that, I mean working."

He says more gently now, "A person doesn't make very good decisions when they're worn out, affects their judgment." He nods slowly. "I'll bet that right now you have learned one of the most valuable lessons a person can learn."

"I have?"

"You bet, you've learned what not to do. That means a lot."

"It does?"

"Bet your ass it does, if you're smart enough to learn from it, and my guess is that you are. Change your plan. People change all the time. Keep the good stuff, get rid of the bad stuff, for example, getting rid of Whatever-his-name-is.'" He smiles a big, toothy grin.

"How did you know there was a man involved?"

"Just figured, I'm not as dumb as I look." His grin gets bigger.

Liz laughs. "I've already done that."

He is still lying on his back by the engine but rolls and looks at her. "Just for the sake of conversation, let's say you decide to go back to Alaska and fish. What would you want?"

"A nice, well-maintained troller big enough to fish on the outside waters when the fish were there. Nothing fancy, but it would have to be a good sea boat, a rig I wouldn't worry much about in tough weather. It would need to be fiberglass. With a wooden boat, I would always wonder about springing loose a plank in heavy seas, and they're a lot more work. Yes, a fiberglass hull would be nice."

He peeks around her as if he's looking behind her. "I don't see an anchor tied to your ass. Go get one."

"I don't have that much money saved."

"Git some."

Liz gives him an exasperated look. "Damn it, look at me. I'm starting to draw a close bead on forty years old, and when you get right down to it, I don't have shit."

He stops smiling. "So what? In ten years you'll be fifty years old, and in twenty years, you will be sixty years old, and sometime after that you'll be dead. So what? What the hell difference does it make how old you are? Gettin' old is what happens to all of us, better make what time you got left count."

Liz is slightly puzzled at his bluntness.

"Were you partners with Whatever-his-name-is?"

"Yes, but the boat is worthless."

"How about the permit?"

She perks up. "I do own half the permit, but he doesn't have enough money to buy me out."

"We're just talkin' possibilities, let's be clear on that. You know, just kickin' some ideas around. They might be good ones or not, OK?"

"OK."

"Him not havin' any money is not your problem. That would be his problem. Tell him he better git some or you're gonna buy him out."

"I don't have that kind of money."

He thinks for a moment. "Do you have any rich relatives?"

"As a matter of fact, I do, but I'm not going to borrow any money from her."

"Does Whatever-his-name-is know you have a rich relative?"

"Yes."

"Then how would he know you couldn't get the money to buy him out?"

"He wouldn't."

The mechanic shrugs. "Make the offer, what the hell, a little motivation never hurts nothin'. Besides that, you have years of experience, a record of fishing. That counts a lot. Sometimes Co-ops and processors will help out with financing permits and boats, then you sell all your fish to them. The fisherman's Co-op in Sitka is a good example of that. They would like to have all your business."

"You know a lot about fishing. I thought you were just a mechanic."

"Mechanics are like doctors. People seem to tell them everything, you'd be amazed. Besides, we're just talkin' here, right?

"Thanks."

"Nothin' to it, ma'am, just talkin'."

She leaves to take a walk to think things over. When she returns, there is a grease-smudged note on the galley table: "Total hours: 10–6 today. Didn't charge for the advice."

That evening, Liz sits on the fantail, sipping a drink while she watches the evening light, when Eric's skiff makes its curved approach to the boat from the other side of the narrows. He pulls alongside and ties the bow line to a turnbuckle. Before he climbs aboard, he peers over the railing and says, "Now that I'm no longer a stranger, you probably won't tell me a bunch of personal stuff you don't want talked about all over town, right?"

"We'll see, come aboard and I'll give you your allotment of one beer."

He scales the side of the boat and sits lightly on the rail as if he can move quickly if he needs to; it's a posture of casual guardedness. There's something about him Liz can't quite make out, put her finger on, something elusive. There's a wariness about him, an edginess that reminds her of something wild.

A few years ago, she and Gordy were anchored at the mouth of a stream to ride out a storm. She needed to get off the boat for a while, so she took the punt to shore and hiked up a game trail that followed alongside a creek, just to get off the boat for a while. The small pools and the soft sounds of the water moving over the rocks making riffles were comforting. She was by herself; it was quiet.

As she stood under the limbs of a large spruce tree, watching for fish in the shallows, a wolf appeared, seemingly out of nowhere, just across the stream from her. His coat was thick, almost white with gray-tipped hackles on his back and the tip of his tail. One second it wasn't there and the next it was standing, sniffing, listening, watching. It moved upstream along the water's edge. She stepped slightly sideways to keep it in view. The instant she moved, it was gone, in the blink of an eye, leaving nothing but silence, not a sound. For a moment she wondered if it had ever been there. She made her way, more stealthily now, up the trail next to the stream. She came to an area where the thick brush opened up into a small muskeg where parts of the moss were torn up. There was deer hair and blood in the muddy ground where the moss had been; blood was pooled in a large paw print. Some berry bushes were torn and broken, showing signs of a struggle. She couldn't get out of her mind how the wolf had disappeared like smoke, how it still might be nearby, looking and waiting. She stayed standing there for the longest time at the edge of the muskeg, looking at the tracks and blood and hair, afraid to move. She is staring at Eric.

He asks, "What?"

"I was just thinking that you're likely a careful man."

He answers evenly, "Very." He waits for the rest of the conversation.

Liz is tempted to say more about what she is thinking, but instead they talk about how the engine rebuild is progressing. She relates her conversation with the mechanic.

Eric says, "I agree. You look a little better than the last time I saw you but still a little worn out." He pauses. "Are you going to call What-ever-his-name-is and put a little pressure on him about the permit?"

"I must admit, the idea appeals to me."

"Then what?"

"To tell you the truth, I haven't thought the whole thing through that well, but if he does cash me out, I'll still face the problem of getting enough money together to buy my own boat, if that's what I decide to do. It's sort of odd because I had given up on that ever happening quite some time ago, you know, ruled it out. But now if it's a real possibility, I might change the way I think about that whole deal. I can't say for sure."

"I'm thinking you can make him buy you out."

"How do you know that?"

Eric shifts his position slightly and looks over her shoulder at the narrows. "I've done things like that before."

She watches his face, and for just a moment, it becomes inflexible. When he looks back at her, he smiles. "Sounds to me like there's still some things about fishing that still appeals to you, some things you miss—maybe?"

She chuckles aloud. "Sure, some thoughts have crossed my mind, but by the same token, the way back seems littered with difficulties, and the idea of changing my life and living south seems different now that I'm actually here. I'm caught between right now.

"I still imagine I could get fixed up, buy some new clothes. A new hairdo and some makeup would do wonders. All have to do is just fit in, quit swearing, practice making conversation about the evening news or some local problems"—she raises her finger for emphasis—"the weather and how it's changing, all of that stuff is always good for a conversation. I bet if I just asked someone, 'What do you think causes global warming?' I could get by with hardly being noticed, no problem. Everybody else in the room would talk for hours. Yep, that part would be easy."

Eric watches her with the hint of a smile. "But? Sounds like there's a *but* in there somewhere."

"Yes, there is. *But*, after careful consideration, I've come to the conclusion that the most difficult thing is, I would have to change the way I think. Could I go to work every day and never be outside, have everything laid out for me? Decisions all made? Live in an apartment house? Christ, the list of the things that would be confining goes on and on. Could I eventually convince myself all of that would be OK? If I can't change the way I think, I'll never fit in down here. If I can't fit in, I wouldn't make it. So then the question becomes, How do you make yourself interested in something you're not? If I can't change the way I think, then I would be just pretending, and that's how I got in this situation in first place, by pretending things were going to change and be better at some point. Well, they didn't." A slight smell of the ocean drifts over the deck. Liz grits her teeth in a peevish way. "I'm working on making better decisions.

"You know, early on I had some reservations about Whatever-his-name-is, but I wound up talking myself out of them, just hoping things would get better. I just wasn't honest with myself. I tried hard to make things work anyway. I don't want that to happen again, so I don't think pretending would be a very good idea. Do people do that just to get along, to make a living? How would they do that? Listening to that mechanic was disturbing."

They sit in silence in the growing darkness, saying nothing. She goes to the galley to get another shot and holds another beer out the door toward him.

"No thanks, I'm good."

She returns to sit and says, "What are your plans for the winter?"

"I'll finish up some work on the boat, then I think I'll head back north and fish for winter kings. It's hard to say right now. If what's on my list to fix is all I have to do, then that should work, but who knows what I'll run into."

"Sitka Sound, sometimes that's real good in the winter."

"Yeah, or maybe out of Harbor Cove. That's pretty handy if there's some fish around. With the Mercantile right there, you can tie up at the dock at night, take a shower once in a while. Pretty easy pickins' when the fish are in."

Liz agrees, "We fished there a bit, never did hit it big, but at times it was pretty steady. Don't burn much fuel."

Eric nods in agreement.

"That sounds like a tough trip north though, fall storms and all of that? I get a little jumpy just thinking about Queen Charlotte Sound in October or November."

"I won't be in a hurry."

"Geez, it still sounds like you could get your butt kicked."

"If it takes a month or more, I don't care. Besides, it's too early to tell. We'll see how it goes with getting the boat in shape."

"So off to Sitka if Harbor Cove doesn't produce?"

"That's to be determined. It can get a bit gnarly in the sound in the winter as well. This being a new boat for me, I'd like to have one season under my belt to get the kinks out of it before I go off shore. The Cove would be a good place to get that done. The mail plane comes in a couple of times a week. That would make getting parts easy. I've heard the price might be ten dollars a pound. A person wouldn't need many fish to make things work at that price."

"Yeah, we fished there. We didn't stay long, but we did sell a few fish to Everett." She smiles. "The whole place is a bit eccentric, but I think you'd fit right in."

The statement puts him on alert, but she continues, "I've only seen you a couple times, so maybe I shouldn't be saying this, so put this down under first impressions."

"Go ahead."

"Sometimes you seem quite civilized, but somehow I get this feeling that maybe there are some parts of you that aren't. Is that a fair assessment?"

"Yes, I think it's safe to say that part of me is civilized."

"What about the other part?"

"It's not."

"And?"

He looks at her with those unblinking eyes and changes the subject. "I just bought this boat a couple of months ago and am going through everything, getting it shipshape before I go fishing. You know how that goes, when you're trying to fix the hundreds of little things that you don't want to go wrong once you start catching fish. If I can get a leg up on that stuff, maybe I won't have so much to do when I'm dead-ass tired or in the middle of a storm, or worse yet, when a good bite is on."

Liz agrees, "I know exactly what you're talking about. It seems like that's all I've been doing the last few years."

"It's a big list. In addition to all of that, I need to do some sanding and painting, but I can see I'm running out of time. I could use a hand, you interested?"

Liz doesn't respond for a moment. "I don't know. I wasn't expecting something like this."

"If you're interested, I'll pay you twenty bucks an hour, and you can fit it in around your job at the construction site. I can pick you up in my skiff, just give me a shout on channel 10 or your phone."

She says, "I can always use the money, and I don't need to show up on the construction site until all the subs leave, around five or so. Actually, I could be later than that and work after dark. The site is well lit. I could work for you all day."

"However you want to organize it is fine with me."

"I'll check with the job foreman, but I'm sure that'll work."

Eric's boat is a thirty-eight-foot double-ender. It sits heavy in the water and has an eight-foot beam. When Liz walks across the deck, it barely rolls under her weight. She's sure it's a boat that will sit steady in tough weather. The galley is well laid out, and the table drops down between the seats to make an extra bunk. The whole boat is well kept. Eric watches her as she inspects.

She says, "Now this is just about what I had in mind for a boat. This is the kind of boat I wanted. This is really nice, Eric."

"Thank you."

"Where's the sander and the sandpaper?"

He motions her out to the back deck and points to a gear locker, and inside is a rotary sander. She begins sanding the hull as she stands in the skiff. He says, "There's lunch meat and cheese in the fridge. The bread is in the cupboard above the stove, if you get hungry. There's coffee on the stove." He disappears below deck.

She continues to sand, stopping only to change sandpaper. She falls into a rhythm of sanding one section of the hull from the waterline to the cap rail, making sure she has covered the entire area, then moving forward to the next. Every day it doesn't rain, she's there working. She progresses from the hull to the outside of the wheelhouse to the bright work and finally the decks. In two weeks, anything that can be sanded and prepped for paint and varnish is done.

The next morning, when he arrives to pick her up, a light rain begins to fall. She says, "I can't paint today."

He looks up at the clouds. "Yeah, it looks like it's going to be around for a while, but why don't you come on over. There's quite a bit of stuff on the inside that needs either fixed or at least looked at."

"Sure."

The trip back to his boat is wet. They shake water from their clothes before entering the galley. She removes her boots and places them by the stove. The wheelhouse is warm, relaxing. He withdraws a piece of paper from his shirt pocket, lying it on the table, smoothing the wrinkles out with his fingers. "These are some things I've written down as they occurred to me. I've started to work on some of them, but I have this sense that I'm missing some stuff. I think I've looked at it too long and can't see it right anymore. What I'd like you to do is go through it and then walk through the boat and write down anything else that occurs to you that might need repaired or replaced."

"You've picked the right woman for this job. I've spent the last few years on a boat where everything always had something wrong with it." She goes down the list with her finger, muttering to herself, sometimes nodding and sometimes shaking her head. "All right, I'll have some questions as I go along, but I'll get going on it."

When she looks up from the paper at him, he asks, "How long do you think it will take you to finish up the painting and varnishing once the weather clears up?"

"Figuring a few days for rain, me moving back and forth between the outside and this punch list, I would say ten days or so. That's if everything goes smoothly, which it never does, and that doesn't include if we need to order parts and how long they take to get here. There's bound to be some stuff we don't know about. You know how that goes once you tear into something. How all that grows on you once you start."

Eric slides his coffee cup aside, placing the punch list under it. "When's the captain going to move the boat to Blaine?"

"He hasn't put a date on it."

"Have you made any decisions about trying to live in America yet?"

"No, but I think about it constantly, go back and forth on it. I'm dead serious when I say the main reason I'm here, in this fix, is that I seem to have really poor judgment. At this point, I sort of feel like any decision I make will be the wrong one." She makes a grim sort of chuckle. "To be honest with you, I'm pretty jumpy about the whole thing."

"I can see you are, and I don't want to weigh in too heavy on this. The last thing I want to do is influence you one way or the other so take what I'm about to say at face value."

She looks at him suspiciously.

"I called Everett, the old guy that buys fish at the Mercantile, and he said that the rumors are true, that king salmon are going to be selling for ten dollars a pound this winter. So I think it could be a good winter, work out of Harbor Cove, fish short days, tie up to the fuel float most every night, make some money." He smiles.

She sighs. "I have to tell you that sounds really good right now."

He looks at her with his unblinking eyes. "You know I've always fished alone, and that is something I enjoy but lately I've been thinking that maybe having some help would be nice."

Liz sits up straight. "What the hell are you talking about?"

"Just what I said. Having some help would be nice, and to be quite honest with you, having someone to talk to once in a while would be great, would beat sitting around staring at my nose all winter."

Now Liz laughs and slaps the table. "Now I'll tell you what. I've met some smooth talkers in my day, but you are in your own league. So, what you're saying is that having me around would be better than sitting around looking at your nose all day?"

He blushes. "What I meant to say is that I think you would be good company, and I would be a whole lot less lonely. Even if you put that aside, it makes sense to have someone onboard that can plug right into the routine, no break-in time, no having to tell you how to do every little thing. You know what a weather report means, how to anchor, how to navigate. Those kinds of things take years of experience to get good at. You already know that stuff. I don't want to take advantage of your situation. I mean, I couldn't afford to hire someone with all of your skills. But if you decide not to stay south, this might be a start toward your getting your own boat, get a little money together. It would be a great deal for me."

"What about the other stuff?"

"Like?"

She points at the bunk in the fo'c'sle. "What about the other stuff? Pretty quickly the other stuff will have to be dealt with."

"Yes, you're right about the other stuff, and I have thought about that. As far as you being something other than just a deckhand is unpredictable, it will just have to work out, or not. The deal I'll make you is this: I'll pay 20 percent after food and fuel. I can ask you to leave without giving you a reason. You can leave without giving a reason."

Liz watches him closely.

"Think this through carefully."

"I will."

"The last thing I need or you need is to get halfway to Alaska or halfway through the season and have things go sideways between us. You'd still be looking for work, and I would still need a deckhand. I'm not telling you anything you don't know already, but any trouble on a small boat isn't worth putting up with. It's the worst possible situation."

"I agree."

Eric stands and fumbles through the cupboard above the stove. He sits back down with a pint jar, placing it on the table in front of him. He reaches in his vest pocket and pulls out a wad of one hundred dollar bills and counts out one thousand dollars, stuffing it into the jar. "This is not a bribe or anything remotely related to it. This is for a plane ticket to wherever you decide to go if things aren't working out the way you want. Just take it and go, get on the radio and call one." He slides the jar to the center of the table.

Liz says, "I'll think about it."

Eric goes on, "The details will take care of themselves. If you decide to go, we'll know if we like the deal by the time we get to Ketchikan, then take it from there."

"I'll think about it."

"When we're in Ketchikan, we can drop in on What-ever-his-name-is and see if he can buy you out. You can bunk here in the galley. If it all goes sideways, you can come on back here. I think you're in a pretty good situation. You have my offer on the table. Your sister as an emergency backup. There's all kinds of loans and grants if you wanted to go back to school. You can do what you're doing now and work odd jobs until something else comes along. Those are all good choices, but I also want you to consider my offer. I'll only ask one thing."

Liz says, "I was just thinking there might be one more thing."

"Here's the deal. Please don't come with me if it's not your first choice of all the choices you have right now."

"Now I have one more thing."

"Shoot."

"I don't have a clue if I will take your offer of not, but if I do, you must promise me that you won't pretend with me, no matter what. Just give me the straight stuff, unvarnished. I'm a big girl, I can take it whatever it is."

Eric says, "Not a problem, now let's get to work on that punch list, that is, if you're coming back tomorrow?"

"I'll come back tomorrow, but let's give this talk of going north a rest."

"Perfect."

For the next few days, she works on the punch list while Eric makes himself invisible. One day she comes out of the engine room with a bilge pump hose in her hand to sit on the hatch cover. An older native man comes to the boat. He asks in a soft but direct way, "Is Eric around here?"

"He's in town getting groceries and some parts." She holds up the hose.

The man nods but doesn't say anything.

She asks, "Are you an Alaskan?"

"From Kake."

"How long have you known Eric?"

"Quite a while."

"Do you trust him?"

"Yes." He turns to leave.

Liz calls after him, "He asked me to go north and fish with him. Do you think that's a good idea?"

The man turns and watches her for a moment. "If you want to." He turns and walks away. When he gets to the top of the ramp, he meets Eric coming the other way. She studies them as they talk. Eric is holding a sack of groceries in one arm and gesturing with the other. The older man stands quietly listening.

When Eric comes down the float, he's smiling. He jerks a thumb over his shoulder. "I fish with his son when I'm in Cross Sound. He just came by to say hello." He climbs aboard and sits on the other side of the hatch cover.

She turns to him. "OK, let's talk." She can see him go on high alert. "Our conversation about going north was a good one, I think. The only thing that stands in the way is I still don't trust my own judgment. My past history with What-ever-his-name-is is living proof of that. So I'm not sure I would recognize a good deal right now if one bit me on the nose."

Eric says, "I would help you with that if I could, but my guess is that you're going to have to work through that yourself. Do you think that's a fair statement?"

"I do."

"OK, so in the spirit of trying to improve my poor judgment, I've decided to express all of my thoughts as clearly as I can. You know, as the old saying goes, 'Just hew to the line and let the chips fall where they may.' If it works, it works. If it doesn't, it doesn't, got nothing to lose at this point. Wouldn't you agree?"

Eric nods.

"I have a couple of questions I'd like answers to."

Eric cocks his head to one side.

"Have you ever had the feeling that there's something sort of floating around in the back of your mind that you need to remember but you don't know exactly what it is, you can't pin it down?"

"Yes."

"I've had one of those feelings about you since we first met, and I think I've finally put it in its place, but I need you to verify it for me." She can see him crouch a bit.

He stays silent.

She goes ahead. "All of the years I fished were mostly spent out of Ketchikan or Wrangell. A couple of years ago, we spent most of the winter in the Basin in Ketchikan, tied up to the transit float. Sometime in midwinter was this incident. It happened over on float five, down toward the end of the float on the breakwater side. The way I heard, it was that this man 'disappeared' off his boat. Nobody seems to know what happened for sure, but they never did find his body."

Eric continues to watch with unblinking eyes, but now they have a feral look to them.

This disturbs her some, but she forges ahead. "His boat came in from up north somewhere that fall, maybe Valdez or Seward. He was a rugged sort of guy, and his son was on the boat with him, stuck to himself. He always looked pissed off to me. Soon rumors began going around on the dock that he was beating his son up pretty good. The kid had bruises. There was all kind of talk and, of course, different versions circulating around about how folks were afraid to talk to the authorities, because if the guy got wind of it, he might just leave and the kid would be worse off. As I heard it, folks might be afraid of him as well. He was a big, rough type of man, so nobody wanted to mess with him.

"Then the rumors became specific. They said that a man from the fishing boat *Gull* killed him and even more specifically stabbed him in the heart with a knife. I don't know how someone would know that unless someone actually saw it happen, but none of the guys would say anything because they thought the guy deserved it. Nobody seemed to know because nobody ever found the body. Some folks even said, when the cops were investigating, they weren't very enthusiastic about figuring it out because when they found the kid, he was in pretty tough shape.

"That was your boat, Eric. It was tied up to that barge-like affair that had that old weather vane on it that said 'Smoke dope' on one side and 'Jesus Saves' on the other, you know, Big's barge. You were there all winter. Now, none of what I said has any verification and I'm not saying I believe any of it, but you see why I needed to bring the subject up."

"You're asking if I killed that guy?"

"Yes, that would be a good thing for a girl to know if she was thinking about fishing with such a person, don't you think?"

"Yes."

She waits for a moment, but he remains silent. "Well?"

"The first thing you need to know is I would never and haven't ever harmed someone I care about. So even though you're asking the question suggests that you think there is a strong possibility I did kill him, whatever my answer is, it seems you will always have that thought lingering around. But I will say that as far as you being in danger from other human beings, myself included, you couldn't be with a safer guy." Eric smiles. It's a satisfied, warm smile that catches her off guard. "That's as close as it comes to getting your question answered."

"Swear to God." She raises her right hand.

"Yes, swear to God."

"One more thing."

"Shoot."

"Sometimes you remind me of some sort of wild animal, like a wolf or something."

Eric squints his eyes. "I like wolves."

She squints back at him. "Do you growl in bed?"

"You know, sometimes I do. It depends on what's going on."

They both laugh. It can be heard clear up on the street, then Liz says, "OK, let's get that damned punch list done and get out of here."

The punch list continues to grow. The more they fix, the more they find what needs done. When the seine boat moves to Blaine, Liz moves on the boat with Eric. When the construction job ends, they both spend all their efforts on the boat. After Christmas, they wait for a dry day or two to put the boat on the grid, check the zincs, running gear, and to bottom paint. As they poke and scrape with putty knives at the spots missed by the power washer, Eric finds that the cutlass bearing is worn. Checking further discovers the prop shaft is slightly bent.

That night, sitting at the galley table, Liz asks, "What do you think about the prop shaft?"

"I wish I would have known that when I bought the boat, but that's a done deal. Nothing I can do about it now."

"Think you can get by another season the way it is?" She has an anxious look on her face.

Eric waits a moment then says, "We've had this conversation, and I believe I said I didn't want to have to fix things or worry about them getting fixed once fishing started."

"It might take a while."

"Yeah, I guess by the time I get ahold of someone to remill the shaft and then put it back in, that will take the better part of a month. In addition to the shaft, I'll need to get the reduction gear checked. It's been out of alignment for God knows how long, the gears could be worn."

"Sounds expensive."

"Bound to be."

Liz offers, "I have some money saved, so I can help out with the food and stall rent. Seems only fair that I should. It'll be a while before we get back north."

"Sure, that'll be great."

"Shit."

Eric smiles. "That's the only word for it."

That night Eric lies in his bunk with his arm covering his eyes but not sleeping. He flinches as a finger pokes him in the ribs. Liz is standing next to him. She says, "I was wondering if one of these little bunks could hold two people."

He says, "I think it's possible, but we might have to experiment a bit."

She curls her lips and bares her teeth and makes a low guttural growling sound. "Grrrrrrrrrr!"

It's the middle of March before the boat's ready. They leave the next week well before daylight. He leaves the running lights off until they are well clear of the harbor. When she asks him why, he says, "It's nobody's business when I leave."

12

A Letter Home

Nancy sits at the kitchen table, watching Owen and Mike as they stand on the dock next to the tugboat. Then she looks back at the pencil and paper that lie before her on the table. She has a wry smile on her face as she picks up the pencil.

Dear Ed and Marcia,

This seems odd sitting down with a pen and paper to write a letter, can't remember the last time this happened. I thought about just calling on the phone at the Mercantile. You remember how it sits right there by the till in the grocery store, the most public place in the Cove. But I thought it's hard enough to keep your personal stuff personal here without engaging in public telephone conversations.

When we landed on the mail plane, the whole crowd that hangs out on the fuel float was standing there to greet us. I was taken aback at how they were all so happy to see us. They were particularly glad to see Michael. They all called him Mike. He now wants to be called Mike because he thinks it sounds like a better name for a deckhand on a tugboat. More on that later.

Another thing that has occurred to me is that it's pretty clear I hadn't really thought through any of the details about how I would feel when I got here. I just wanted to get this over with so I could get back home. Somehow I thought that most of the fuel float outfit would have moved on or be dead. Some have moved on. Tom died, you remember the guy that lived on the little sailboat by the Saloon. He lay there for a few days before anybody checked on him—gruesome.

They explained the severe details in such a matter-of-fact way that I just stood there and nodded my head; it sounded so very reasonable. I kept saying things like, "Oh, that was a good idea," when they considered sticking him with a pocket knife to let the gas out. Michael—excuse me, Mike—was standing right there next to me. He listened to all of that and didn't even blink. I really don't know how I expected him to react, but I expected something different from both he and I.

One of new guys came rowing in one morning in a plastic punt. His boat burned up in Rocky Pass. It took him a day and a night to get to the Cove. Anyway, he's hooked up with Mary. He has built an apartment in her boat shed. They seem in love. Sometimes at night they will play music and dance in the boat shed; it's wonderful. He'll fit right in.

Since then I've found out that, and this is where I'm beginning to have some serious struggles with myself, Mike hasn't behaved anywhere close to how I thought he would. The prime examples are, he doesn't miss having a cell phone, video games, or any of that. I figured this would be a big wake-up call for him, you know, the whole gambit of him having to deal with the remoteness. The little things like using the outdoor toilet. You know how I'm always saying that using electronic devices makes shallow thinkers. It seems like I need to recalculate that whole deal. OK, OK, I can hear you saying things out loud to yourself, like your current favorite: *"She's not always right, but by God, she's never in doubt."*

I figured he would be more than ready to go home by now, but it seems like there is another Michael lurking around in that shaggy red head. He is determined to make this whole idea of beach logging work. I was so sure he would spend a few days here and then couldn't wait to get back home. Jesus, Ed, he's been working his butt off, and to be quite honest, I've found out there's a big gap between what I thought he was capable of and what he's actually capable of, and to top that off, I didn't have a clue how he thinks or even what he's thinking. I'm just beginning to sort my way through that whole deal.

The good news is Dad and I both agree that we can't go ahead on beach logging. We just don't know how long it will be before Michael will accept the idea. We're thinking maybe we'll just go get some logs for firewood in the skiff and that will do for a beach-logging experience for him. I think eventually he will feel OK with that. He can hang out with Dad, have some great pictures to show his friends, get to mess around on boats, have some stories to tell. I can see now that Dad knew we could never pull this off. I think his motives have been the same as mine.

We all needed to spend some time together. Well, I didn't even want that if I were being honest with myself, but here we are.

Dad has Michael, now known as Mike (sounds biblical?), on this sort of training regime, kind of a deckhand boot camp. He told him that there is this list of things he needs to be able to do if we're going to be able to get those logs. But we both know that's not going to happen. He's just too young to do all of the heavy lifting, not to mention run a chainsaw, and rafting logs would be completely out of the question. Mike must know this, but he's determined to give it his best shot. I worry that he will wear himself completely out, but he has told me not to help. He spent all night, one night, last week dragging a stack of boom chains out of the boat shed, down the dock, and put them on the deck of the boat. He would *not* let me touch them. He did let me hold a flashlight and listened to me when I told him to wear a life jacket. Jesus! Ed, you should have seen him. His hands were all bloody; it took him until after midnight. He was barely able to walk back to the house. The only time he really got pissed off is when I tried to help him. To be honest, he sort of reminded me of myself when I get all snarly. I haven't seen him like that before.

OK, here is another one of my disconnects. He didn't complain or bitch or moan, not one time, *not once*! So how is it that getting him ready for school in the morning is like pulling a bad tooth? Why all of the routines we go through just to get him in the car?

Dad and I have both been bluntly honest with him about the chances of this not working. Are you sitting down, because this gets even more muddled. Mike told me he will be disappointed and he knows his grandpa is trying to make this work but will understand if it doesn't. I didn't need to explain any of this to him; he had it all figured out before I had a chance to talk to him. Needless to say, he's way more perceptive than I have given him credit for, which I suppose makes me not very perceptive. How long has he been paying such close attention to so many things while I have been locked into the idea that he can't even brush his teeth correctly? There are some loops in the wire here, Ed.

Last week Dad showed Mike how to run the skiff, so he's been to the Mercantile a couple of times by himself to get fuel and groceries. He loves the skiff and is being very responsible. He asks all the right questions and doesn't seem to have the slightest inclination to be reckless, so Dad has given him the OK to go out by himself as long as he stays in the cove. When he goes out poking around or to the Mercantile, he must tell us beforehand and check in every hour on channel ten. A life jacket is mandatory, of course. I predict that before long, he'll be asking to go farther out.

I dread the thought of him being out in Sumner Straits by himself, but we are doing our best to get him ready for being out in water like that. Dad and I are drilling him on things like listening to the weather reports, how the waves change when the tide changes, how to get water out of the carburetor, how to make a fire with wet wood, what to do when nothing works. You know, all of those little things that can make the difference between spending a miserable night on the beach and not getting home ever.

Thinking about all of that makes me sick to my stomach. Of course, it didn't even occur to me until now that Mike would even consider wanting to be on his own in this country. So now I have fallen into this routine of becoming a major league "pesterer." I give him a constant barrage of "What if?" or "What do you do if?" questions. Michael, sorry Mike, is very patient with me and just nods his head in agreement at all of my suggestions and doesn't argue at all. That makes me really nervous, because what he's really saying is he's going to go ahead with the whole idea anyway.

So here I am, as usual, taking complete responsibility for everything, sound familiar? I lie awake at night, rehashing all of the details and all of the things that can possibly go wrong. As you can probably tell from the tone of this letter, it's driving me a bit mad, but you know how things can go wrong in this country in just the blink of an eye. By the same token, I'm stuck because I can't let Mike know how anxious I really am. I don't want him to get scared. It might force him into a bad decision at a time when he needs be thinking clearly. It's just that he doesn't have any idea of what he doesn't know. I guess I didn't either when I was learning these things, but that seems different to me. Do you think that was different? Do you think Dad went through all of this with me? He must have. I mean, what the hell else would he have been thinking?

He doesn't ever talk to me about things like that. The closest he has ever come is just the other night when he explained to me what a terrible father he had been. If I were completely honest, I would have to say that I've had similar thoughts, but when he said it, it didn't translate the way I thought it ought to. I felt he shouldn't be saying things like that, but he said it in such a way to let me know that he has recognized all along how I've felt about growing up here, a subject we haven't ever talked about and I'm sure we never will.

Since I decided to come back, even before leaving Lynwood, I have been having these conversations with myself about how I would see things after all of these years. I'm struggling with conflicting notions, i.e., how I'm seeing things and how I thought I would see things now that I've arrived.

All these years, I was convinced I knew exactly how things were here. They were like I thought they were, right? I relied on that, my own little collection of personal, rational data. The groundwork for how I feel about growing up. Does anyone question that? Now what? I'm rambling on here, aren't I?

My memory for the physical things seems to be quite accurate—the house, the tugboat, and the Cove in general. The Mercantile hasn't changed much. It just needs to be painted and maybe fixed up a bit. But how many of my memories are self-serving? Have I somehow just chosen to remember those things that support how I already felt? Honey, I'm having a hard time with myself. It seems like I've built this fence of sorts around myself, and I'm finding a bunch of holes in it.

Now, something else to stack on the pile. Just after we arrived, Dad, Mike, and I went to a community meeting. This is just one more thing I'm still trying to digest. I was right in the middle of trying to sort all of these other things out when the Forest Service flew in and held a public meeting at the school. The new schoolteacher just arrived a few days before, so he was sort of the host. For some reason, he came early. He doesn't even know if enough kids will show up to have a teacher.

The Forest Service guy got up and said that they plan to join the Cove with the rest of the island with a road connecting Harbor Cove with the existing road system. He went on at great length about all of the advantages a road could offer. How things in general would be easier and safer, cheaper to live. A great improvement for everybody. Nobody knew quite what to say, could have heard a pin drop in there. Then Dad forced him to say what the real reason for the road was. The road would run right next to a future timber sale that abuts to Harbor Cove. So as it turns out, the real reason was to create access to that timber sale. Then the guy still went on trying to convince everybody how much better things would be with road access. It all went downhill from there. He was basically saying they would be better off being more civilized. There wasn't anything particularly sinister about the guy. Dad has known him for years, but everybody was stunned.

Most of the folks there weren't completely sober, but the points they made were all valid because they were all related to the main reason they were living here, which is because it is "uncivilized," and how a road would bring all of those ideas and views that they came here to escape. But here's where it got a bit creepy for me. One of the guys from the Saloon said,

"Why would the folks here want to deal with a whole bunch of rules and ideas that were meant to instruct them how to live their lives?" Right then, that made complete sense to me, and here's another interesting thing: I got all pissed off just like I do in freeway traffic. Then it hit me that I was agreeing with him, agreeing with the very things I had always said I didn't like about this place. And then I thought, what the hell am I doing? I thought my damned head was going to explode. Coming back here has been way more complicated than I could have possibly imagined.

I have to close now. I just went to the stove to get a cup of coffee, and when I looked out the window, Mike, our son the deckhand, is coming up to the dock, and in the skiff with him is the new schoolteacher. Mike is talking and waving his arms a mile a minute. I better see what's going on.

Love, Nancy

13

The Basin

It's midday when they arrive in Ketchikan and tie up in Thomas Basin. Liz and Eric have been underway or at anchor for two weeks during their trip through Canada. It's been a continuous routine of listening to daily weather forecasts, adding new things to the punch list, trying to stay ahead of the repairs. It's an exercise of constant assessment. How hard will it blow in the anchorage? How well will the anchor hold? What will the next day's run be like?

Many of the bays that used to be good anchorages are filled with fish farms. As they enter these bays at the end of a long day, they are often met with a man in a skiff that explains where the lines holding the net pens in place run under the water to anchors. Sometimes there is room to anchor; sometimes there isn't. If not, then they move on, trying to find a spot before dark. It's constant low-level tension, and weather that can change in a matter of minutes.

When the boat is tied, they both begin to settle down and allow the fatigue to engulf them, then they go to the forward bunk and fall into a deep sleep.

In the morning they walk up town to get some breakfast, and on their way back, they begin to see people they know. One of those people says to Liz, "The *Silver* is down at city float, been there since December."

"So it's still afloat?"

"It always looks like it's not going to make it through the winter, but Gordy puts it on the grid like he does every year, smears some concrete in the seams that are still leaking and he makes it through another year. I wouldn't go to the fuel dock in it, but he keeps it floating somehow."

Liz smiles. "That's not going to change. One of these days, he'll put it on the grid and it'll fall apart."

When they arrive back at the Basin, they stop by Big's barge. Big is a short but large man who is still wearing his grease-stained life jacket. He's quick to explain to anyone that he always wears a life jacket because he's too fat to get out of the water if he falls in. His plan is to yell and scream until someone comes to help. He is also quick to explain the he doesn't think it's a very good plan but at least it's some sort of plan.

They go in and have coffee warmed up on a barrel stove. On top of the stove is a piece of rusty sheet metal folded to make a platform. On the platform is an aluminum saucepan containing boiled water and coffee grounds. Unwashed coffee cups are scattered on floor and perched on the windowsills. He grabs two of the cups and peeks into them. As he peers into one of them, he raises his eyebrows then wipes it out with a paper towel. The coffee is very strong and very bitter.

They fall into the usual conversation, catching up on the local fishing and harbor news. Big glances back and forth between Liz and Eric, recognizing they are traveling together; he doesn't ask for any details. Liz understands what he's thinking and says, "Eric and I are going to rest up here for a bit then head on up to the Cove and do some day fishing. If the prices are good and if there's a few fish around, we'll stay there until we get the kinks out of Eric's new boat, maybe head to Sitka after that."

Big offers, "For some reason, that Bradfield run of kings is really early this year. It might be worth your while to make a few drags there at Onslow and Eagle Island before you move on."

Liz says, "Wow, that is early. Who told you?"

"Mike, on the *Tracy J.*"

"Well, he's fished a long time, he'd know."

The conversation goes quiet for a moment, then Big asks, "Liz, you still own a piece of the *Silver*?"

"I'm half for the boat and the permit, why?"

Big looks a bit nervous. "It ain't none of my business what you do." He glances at Eric. "But, in my opinion, Gordy, he ain't doin' very good."

"What do you mean?"

"The boat's in worse shape than when you left, and as you know, it wasn't in very good shape then." He takes a deep breath. "The other thing is that he's been drinkin' pretty good, spends most of the day, beginnin' about lunchtime, drinkin' beer up there at the Potlatch, and then I seen him lyin' on the dock the other night passed out drunk. He'd pissed himself." Big holds his hands out in front of him and bows his head a bit. "I don't mean to be talkin' him down or anything like that. Lord knows I ain't a good example for nobody, but it's just I never did see him like that before. The only reason I'm sayin' anything is that I was just thinkin" that you might want get some sort of deal with him settled before he comes up missin'. He might fall off the dock and drown or something like that." Big looks instinctively at Eric. "If he's dead and owes a bunch of money, then gettin' your share of the outfit is gonna be a long, slow process. I was just thinkin' . . ." Big glances again at Eric. "It ain't none of my business, I'm just sayin', that's all."

They all sit quietly staring at the floor, thinking. Eric says, as he motions around the room at the old rusty folding chairs and the five-gallon bucket upside down in one corner, "Looks like your morning coffee get-together is still going on."

"Yeah, it's mostly the same as when you were here that winter."

Eric stands. "Thanks for the heads-up on Gordy."

Liz adds, "We appreciate it."

Back at Eric's boat, he asks, "What do you think about what Big said?"

"I don't think Big is a gossip or would say those things just to be mean. Otto has always liked to drink, although he never did when we were out fishing, but he'd go on a bender once in a while when we came to town to sell."

"What do you want to do?"

"I think Big's right. I'd better go take care of business, but I'm not very good at confrontation."

Eric smiles. "Well, you might as well try it. You don't have anything to lose."

She frowns.

"Just go and talk about getting your share. If he gets owly, ignore him, but don't get off the subject."

"OK, in any case, it needs to be done," she says as if she is trying to convince herself.

"Do you want me to go with you, or do you think he might resent it if you came with another guy?"

"I would feel better if you came along. Who I'm with would come under the category of being none of his business."

Eric adds, "It's better to show up at a meeting with more people than the other guy."

They walk to City Float in silence, past the cruise ship docks and through the tunnel. As they go down the ramp, they can see the *Silver* docked at the bottom. There are piles of gear stacked on the dock. Gordy is pawing through a box filled with odds and ends of gear—flashers, spoons, and a couple of lead balls. He doesn't notice them until they are standing next to him. When he does, it startles him. He jerks upright and takes a step back. "You shouldn't creep up on a man like that!" Then he recognizes Liz. "Where the hell you come from?"

"La Conner."

Gordy looks back and forth between Liz and Eric and says, "Huh, that didn't take you long."

"I've made some changes, Gordy."

"What besides him?"

"I'm working on having better judgment. I'm trying to change the way I think about stuff."

"You mean you're not going to just drag up and leave town because the things get too tough for you?"

Liz pauses for a moment. "Or maybe not get myself into those situations in the first place. Let me see if I can give you an example. I think I can put it in terms you'll understand. I want you to buy me out of my half of the boat and the permit, and I want the money by this September. That will give you this season to get the money together. How's that?"

"You don't deserve your half. You just took off, and now you all of a sudden show up with this guy. Everybody knows about him, and think you can buffalo me into selling just like that."

Liz looks at Eric; he has a tight smile on his face. Just the bottom half of his front teeth are showing. It's a smile that's without humor. His eyes have that feral look about them. She holds her hand up. "Just give me a minute here, Eric. It's just that he doesn't quite get it yet." She turns back to Gordy. "You will be required to sell."

Gordy is frowning.

"If I don't have the money for my half of the boat and permit by the end of coho season this fall, let's say September 15, then I will put a lien on the boat and permit that will tie the boat up to the dock until you do pay me. Now if that doesn't appeal to you, then I will buy you out."

"What if I don't want to sell to you?" he says smugly.

"I will force the sale in court. It's my legal right as a partner in a partnership."

"We ain't got nothin' in writing."

"That doesn't matter. I can still force the sale."

"Half of this," as he gestures to the boat, the bilge pump comes on, "won't get me enough money to get another boat and permit."

"I know."

Gordy juts his jaw out. "Shit, you don't have no money neither."

"There's a really easy way to find out how much money I have if you meet me tomorrow at the Potlatch Tavern there in Thomas Basin. Bring the permit and the title of the boat and I'll pay you off. Let's say 10:00 AM. I'm sure we can agree on a price. In fact, I'll tell you what we'll do. You tell me how much you think it's worth, then I will say whether I'll buy or sell. If I think the price is too high, then you can buy my half, and if I think it's low, then I'll buy your half.

How fair is that? That's fair, right? That way we can't jack each other around."

Gordy takes a step back. He's frowning again. "How'd you get that kind of money?"

"That's none of your business."

"It's that rich sister of yours, isn't it?"

Liz shrugs. "Like I said, that's none of your business."

Gordy squints at her. "I think you're bluffin'."

Liz doesn't change expression. "There's only one way to find out, Otto, isn't there?"

Eric says quietly. "I think he understands all of this just fine, let's go."

Liz turns to leave.

"OK, OK, I'll have your half by this September."

"Great, I'll go by the office supply store and get a promissory note form. I'll pay to get it notarized."

"Fine."

As they walk down the street, Eric says, "You have been thinking about stuff."

"That was pretty good, huh?"

He laughs. "All that stuff, a forced sale without a partnership agreement, where'd you come up with that?"

"I just made it up." She smiles.

"Yeah, I would have to say that was pretty good."

The next morning at the Potlach Tavern, Gordy comes in and flops down in a booth by the front window and stares sullenly at Liz and Eric, who are sitting at the end of the bar. "Where's the goddamn paper?"

Liz sits opposite him and lays two promissory notes in front of him. He takes one and writes an amount. She says, "OK, looks good to me, you can buy me out." She writes the date then turns to the owner of the tavern, who is sitting at the far end of the bar, looking at his coffee cup. "Hey, Garrett! Are you still a notary?"

"Yep, it's my only claim to anything respectable." He reaches behind the bar and grabs a small box with his seal inside, comes to the table, and stamps the promissory notes. "There you go."

Liz stands, handing Gordy one of the notes. "This is a personal note, Gordy, which means if you don't pay, I can come after anything you own, not just the boat and permit."

"What!" Gordy looks at Garrett with uncertainty.

"That's right."

As Liz and Eric start to leave, Gordy lumbers over to them and reaches out his arm, pointing at Eric. "You put her up to this, didn't you?"

Eric looks at the finger pointing at his chest then back at Gordy. "Listen, Gordy. This is a good deal. You've both agreed on a fair price, and that's how business is done."

Gordy raises his voice, and the noise in the bar stops. "You didn't answer my question!"

The little half-tooth smile comes on Eric's lips. Liz says, "Let's just go."

They start toward the door. Gordy moves closer to Eric, still pointing his finger. Eric makes a short step to his left, still smiling, and raises his arms to his chest. He is now standing at the outside of Gordy's raised arm and pointing finger. Gordy tries to move his arm, but Eric just holds it in place with his upraised hands. Gordy tries to push him back but can't. Gordy looks confused.

Eric speaks in a low, slow tone of voice. "Gordy, please let this go. We are just trying to leave, but if you touch me again, I will break your wrist."

"What?"

Eric nods at him. "It will really hurt."

Gordy looks at his wrist. "Just like that, huh?"

"Yep."

Gordy sits on a barstool and looks at Eric then back at his wrist. "Huh."

Eric grimaces, with his eyes all crinkly. "Nothing personal."

Gordy continues to stare at his wrist. "Yeah, OK."

Eric and Liz leave.

When they leave for the Cove, they stop at Point Onslow and make a few drags at Eagle Island, but it produces just one small shaker. On the next good day, they run all day to the Cove and tie up at the fuel float just as it's getting dark. In the morning, they go to Everett's office. Kasey is hard at work on her computer. Everett is just hanging up the phone. He looks up at them. "Goodness me, haven't seen you folks in a while."

Eric says, "It's been a bit, all right."

Everett looks at Liz. "Where you been? Word is that Gordy's been fishing by himself."

Liz looks a bit chagrined. "Aw shit, Everett, I won't bother you with the details, but I went south and figured on staying there, but I couldn't pull it off. I'm gonna crew for Eric, maybe get my own boat in a year or two. I made a half-assed attempt to get something going down south but am pretty sure that wouldn't work out."

"It's good to see you."

Eric says, "Hey, Kasey, how's it going?"

Kasey waves her arm in the air without turning around. "I'm fine, but they're gonna build a road to Harbor Cove."

"What the hell for? Nobody here wants a road."

"Logs."

"Logs?"

"Yep, that's it, but according to the folks in Juneau, it's not just the logs. It will bring us access to all the modern conveniences, like driving to the grocery store, the dentist, all those things normal people do."

Liz asks, "They said that?"

Kasey turns and points directly at Liz and, with mock enthusiasm, says, "And best of all, we can now own cars! Can't you see it now?" She turns to point at Everett. "Hey, boss, we can become some sort of tourist destination. What do you think?"

Everett shakes his head. "I try not to think about it."

There's knock on the window. Randy motions Everett outside and begins talking immediately. "We have that last load all done and the totes stacked over there by the ice machine. We left some room for you to get to the compressor if you need to. We're all ready to unload the next boat when it comes." He waits for Everett's approval.

Everett peers at him over the top of his glasses. "That's great, Randy, I like that. The next boat will be here in about forty minutes. Why don't you guys take a break." He pats Randy on the shoulder.

Randy takes his rubber gloves off by pulling one finger at a time, slowly. He calls out to Rich and Bob, "Everett says we have another boat in about forty minutes, break time."

Randy nods confidently at Everett then strides off to join the other two men.

When Everett returns to the office, Eric asks, "How's Randy been doing?"

Everett shrugs. "He's having a good day today, but overall, he's been having a hard time. He's been talking to that one-legged raven that hangs around here a lot. I think he's worried about who'll come here on that road. He barely makes it here now. If it changes much, he won't make it at all."

Kasey offers, "I guess that's so for all of us to one degree or another."

They all stand not looking at each other.

14

Deckhand Training

Nancy is walking down the pier when Mike and Neil tie off the skiff. "Who's this?"

"This is the new schoolteacher, Neil."

Nancy nods. "Neil."

"Ma'am."

"So what's going on?"

Neil looks at Mike. "We were just talking at the fuel float. He seemed a little upset. He wanted to show me his grandpa's place. I hope that's OK."

"Upset?"

"Yeah, Mom, upset that the beach-logging thing ain't gonna work. You know that. Grandpa knows that, and I know that. You're just giving me things to do that I can't do so I'll be the one to say it ain't gonna work. It gets you off the hook for having to disappoint me."

She looks at Mike with incredulity. "Oh, you think so, do you?"

Mike smiles. "Yep, I sure do. It's OK, Mom, but now, as long as I have you on the defensive here." He points at Neil. "Neil here isn't doing anything until school starts."

"What?"

Neil interrupts, "Mike, I told you what I thought about that idea."

The three stand looking at each other, when they here the distinctive sound of Owen clunking down the wooden planks behind them, swinging his bad leg awkwardly. "What's goin' on? Who's this?"

Nancy says, "This is Neil, the new schoolteacher."

"Oh right." Owen reaches out his hand and shakes Neil's hand. He holds it for a moment, feeling it. Mike begins to say something, but Owen raises his hand to silence him. "Yeah, I heard you guys talkin'. He's' not doin' anything till September." Then to Neil, "Schoolteacher, eh?"

"I don't know for sure. I haven't taught yet. We'll see, I guess."

"What you been doin' lately? Your hands don't feel like you're some sort of scholar with all them callouses."

"Been working at a sawmill."

"Doin' what?"

"Dry chain."

"Workin' your way through school?"

"Yep."

"Tell me what else you done to get yourself through school." Owen's statement is on the verge of demanding.

Nancy is looking peculiarly at Owen. "Dad, you don't even know this guy. You're being rude."

Neil says, "It's OK, we're just talking, I don't mind."

Owen persists, "What else?"

"Let me see, worked on a section gang leveling railroad track and replacing ties, worked on ranches, worked in the woods, worked at service stations at night, stuff like that."

Owen has been leaning forward, listening. Now he lurches upright and clatters down the pier to the stern of the tugboat. He points to a large metal jack lying up against the gunnel, tied to a cleat with rope. "Now if you worked on the railroad, you can tell me what that is, right?"

Neil looks at it for a long time then says, "Huh?"

"Well, what is it?"

"Dad! Stop this right now!"

Mike joins Neil and Owen, peering at the jack.

Neil looks at Owen. "I know what it is, but I can't figure out what it's doing on a tugboat."

Mike says, "It's a jack, right?"

Owen asks, "What kind of jack is it, Neil?"

"It's a railroad jack. It's the same kind of jack we used to level track or replace old ties. So what's it doing here?"

"Sometimes we have to move a log by hand, git it off a rock or somethin' like that."

Abruptly, Owen's demeanor lightens as he turns and points at some boom logs. "You see those logs there with the big round holes in the ends?"

"Yes, I see them, looks like somebody used some sort of auger to drill those holes."

Owen is quick to answer, with the beginnings of a smile on his face. "Those are boom logs. Now tell me this. If we got out somewhere and we needed to make a couple of more boom logs and all we had was a chainsaw, could you, using a chainsaw, make holes in the end of some logs like that?"

"Well, the holes wouldn't look that nice, but sure, I think they would be close enough to work." Neil points to the boom chains on the deck. "I assume those chains on the deck there with the large circular link on one end and that tang on the other go through those holes to tie the logs together?"

Owen turns first to Neil with a smile on his face. "Schoolteacher, huh?"

"We'll see."

Now Owen turns to Nancy and Mike, who are just now beginning to understand what's been going on. "Oh, I think he'll do just fine."

Nancy says, "What the hell are you talking about?"

Neil scratches his head studiously. "I believe I've just had a job interview."

"Dad?"

Owen turns to Neil. "Oh, one more thing, are you a drinkin' man?"

"Once in a while I am."

"Whiskey?"

"Not a lot and not too often, but yeah, I am."

Owen turns to walk back to the house. He has a small spring in his step. He begins slapping his right leg with his good hand. "Yes, siree, he'll do just fine!"

As the screen door slams behind Owen, the sounds of laughing and his hand slapping his leg continue as he moves to the back of the house. The three of them stand watching in startled silence. Nancy stares after him with a worried look on her face. Neil is wary, glancing alternately from the house to Nancy. Mike is grinning with excitement. He can't stand still.

Neil is determined not to be the first one to speak. *Just wait a minute and see what happens here.* He watches Nancy closely.

She turns to look directly at him. "Aw shit."

Neil says, "OK, I get it." He turns to Mike. "Mike, take me back to the Mercantile."

Mike is speechless; he begins to melt. It begins with his face and neck, moving down to his shoulders. He droops forward. Neil kneels in front of him, putting one hand on his shoulder. "I am truly sorry, my friend, but as good as all of this sounds, it seems like I have stumbled into a situation here that is way more complicated than yanking a few logs off the beach. If I'm the only reason this whole idea is going to work, then I don't want that kind of trouble."

Mike looks away; he is inconsolable.

Neil looks at Nancy. "If someone gets hurt, when someone gets angry, if things get snarly because we are tired and working all of time, then what?" He points at the tugboat. "That is a pretty big boat where I come from, but my best guess is it's a small place for four people to live. Even if we are all reasonable people, which I'm sure we are, that's a tall order. So here's the deal. If the only reason this thing happens is because I happen to stumble along, when things start to go sideways, guess who everyone is going to be looking at?" He points his thumb at his chest.

Mike walks slowly over the planks in the yard and sits on the edge of the front porch, holding his head in his hands. Nancy is watching him closely.

Neil thinks back about taking George to the hospital and having to deal with his mom and her friend Irene and then George's wife. How the more he became involved, the more convoluted things became; how there were no solutions; how it all just rolled along on its own. He says, louder than he intends, "How in hell do I get myself into these things?" He looks at Nancy, shrugging his shoulders, holding his hands up in front of him.

Nancy begins shaking her head vigorously as if she is trying to rattle some thoughts into their proper sequence. She frowns at Neil. "All right, goddamn it! You are absolutely right. Everything you have just said is the truth, spot on! Except the thing is, none of this is your doing. As a matter of fact, I want to thank you for being so nice to Michael. You don't even know us. Most people, even people we know, wouldn't have done this much. Of course you're correct. This has turned out way more convoluted than I ever imagined, so much for thinking I was in control of anything."

"You're welcome."

She glares at Neil and speaks in clipped tones, "OK. How about this? This is my deal—all this is my idea." She points to the boat, to Mike, and to the house. "And it's not turning out at all the way I thought it would or the way I wanted it to turn out. In fact, it is turning out just the opposite of the way I wanted it to turn out, and right this moment, I can't imagine what the hell I was thinking." She deepens her frown. "What was I thinking?"

"Got me."

She points at Neil. "None of this would have happened if I hadn't agreed to help my dad complete this contract for recovering these logs. I won't go into all of the details, but that is it in a nutshell. I didn't want to, and I still don't want to but here we are." She waves her arms around in frustration. "So you really aren't the catalyst for this. I am. I just need to take responsibility for it. Shit-oh-dear." She stops to gather herself. She turns to Mike, "Michael, you listen closely to what I am about say so Mr. Osborne will have a witness."

Mike looks up expectantly.

"OK, Mr. Osborne, here's how it works. The main reason I'm here is because I have the skill and knowledge to operate a tugboat and my dad can't do all of that anymore, so I'll make all of the decisions related to work, and I'll accept the responsibility for the results, plain and simple. All you have to do is what I tell you to do. If anything happens, it's on me. Win, lose, or draw, you walk on out of here with no strings attached, maybe even with some money in your pocket, maybe not, but as far as anything else goes, you're clean as in hygienic, uncontaminated, sterile, spotless. You just walk and do whatever it is you're going to do. That's it, period!"

Neil stands silently.

"Mr. Osborne, you need to decide about this now before I change my mind."

"So what you're saying is that all I need to do is what I am told?"

"That's correct."

"That sounds just fine to me."

"One more thing."

"It seems like there always is."

"Have you really done all of those things Dad asked you about?"

"I did."

"No bullshit?"

"No bullshit."

"Those seem to be unusual skills for a schoolteacher."

"I'm not a schoolteacher."

"What?"

"I haven't taught school yet. I might not be any good at it. If I'm not very good at it, I really won't be a schoolteacher. At least I won't be a very good one, which would just like not being one at all, I would think. I might wind up working in the woods or back at the sawmill. I just don't know yet. We'll just have to wait and see."

She shakes her head again. "OK, OK." Now she speaks but to no one in particular. "I can't believe I am even saying this." She turns and points at Michael. "You take Mr. Osborne down to the boat and show him around, and you tell him everything you've learned."

Michael leaps to his feet, grinning from ear to ear. "Yes, ma'am" He runs over the planks in the yard. They make that squishy sound as water squirts out from underneath. He grabs Neil by the hand, pulling him down the dock. Nancy watches; Mike begins talking fast and loud. "This tugboat is fifty-two feet total length and forty-nine feet at the waterline. It's made with old growth fir ribs and planking. It was built in 1911. Several planks have been replaced with other kinds of wood, but not many. It has an 871 GMC diesel engine. The prop shaft is four inches. I don't know exactly how big the propeller is, but Grandpa says it is a big damn thing." His voice dies out as they disappear into the wheelhouse.

She hears her dad laughing behind her. He is standing on the porch with a big crooked grin on his face, leaning against the doorjamb. "I knew you would do it. I didn't know how, but I knew you would do it. You always have a way of getting things done. Way to go. We are going to get those logs and have a good time doin' it." He slaps his leg using his good arm. "Yes, siree, and make some money in the process." He tries to hop up and down but almost falls because his one leg doesn't work right.

Suddenly the engine on the boat roars to life. Black smoke boils out from underneath the bucket that covers the exhaust stack. Nancy looks startled. "Dad, did you teach Mike how to start the engine?"

"No." He laughs again. "You better get down there and get your crew lined out . . . Captain."

She walks quickly toward the boat. "Michael, what do you think you are doing!"

They talk loud over the sounds of the engine.

"Starting the engine."

"Grandpa said he didn't teach you how to start the engine."

"He didn't, we just figured it out."

In frustration, Nancy rubs her face with both hands. "*Do not* put it in gear. It will tear the dock apart!"

Neal pokes his head out of the wheelhouse door enthusiastically. "How many PSI should the oil gauge be reading?"

She frowns at him. "Forty pounds."

He disappears for a moment then returns. "What should the engine temperature be?"

"Somewhere around one hundred eighty degrees."

Neil turns his head and yells, "Forty pounds on the oil! We'll keep an eye on the water temperature as it warms up."

Nancy leans forward closer to Neil. She points her finger in his face. She repeats, "Do not—I repeat, *do not*—put the boat in gear. Somebody get up on the wheelhouse and get that bucket off the smoke stack."

Neil comes out on deck and holds his hands up in the air. "OK, OK."

"Say it."

"What?"

"Say it to me."

"Do not—I repeat, *do not*—put the boat in gear."

"Neil, this is serious stuff."

"Yes, it is, and we don't want anyone to get hurt."

"Correct."

"Kind of exciting though." He smiles eagerly.

"Just remember, do exactly as I say."

"Yes, ma'am. Hey, Mike, did you hear what your mother just said?"

"Yes."

Nancy points to the bucket, and Neil scrambles to the roof of the wheelhouse.

Nancy is muttering under her breath as she goes back to the house. When she enters the living room, she catches a glimpse of her dad as he leaves through the back door. She sits in his easy chair, molding into the cushion caved in by his shape. Scattered around the chair on a small table is a wide-ranging assortment of her dad's personal stuff. A small stainless steel shackle sits on a hand-held calculator. A tide book and an empty tube of super glue lie side by side; some of the glue has dripped out of the tube and is sticking to one of the pages. Several stainless steel screws are in small pile off to one side. There was a roll of black tape that is mostly used up, and a tablet that has some notes and scribblings. The writing is uneven and scrawling; there are a series of labored unfinished sentences, but the words peter out to nothing, thoughts unfinished. At the bottom of the page is one word—*gone*. She turns and stares at the back door; it's slightly ajar.

After several hours of poking around in the tugboat, Neil and Mike emerge out on the deck; Neil is taking notes, and Mike is pointing and talking. Finally they sit down with Nancy and begin to ask all their questions. The list is long; she finally says, "That's enough for now. Keep your list, and we will go through them again as they come up."

Mike takes Neil back to the Mercantile. Randy, with the crew, is still busy weighing and icing fish. As Mike leaves in the skiff, Neil waves. "In the morning." He turns back to the ramp. Kasey waves from the railing. "I thought you were kidnapped by pirates or something. Where have you been?"

"Well, I'm not sure how to explain it, but it looks like I am going beach logging with Owen and Nancy."

"Come on up and I'll buy you a cup of coffee." In the office they sit. Kasey chuckles. "Well, I was right then, some pirates did get you."

"Pirates?"

"A beach logger is as close as you can get to being a pirate these days. I have known Owen and Nancy my whole life, well Owen anyway. Nancy's been gone quite a while. By golly, for being a flatlander and just getting here, you have settled right into things."

He repeats, "Pirates?"

She nods. "I don't think Owen has ever captured any ships, cut anybody's heart out or anything like that, but beach loggers are known for, shall we say, pushing the boundaries."

"I'm going to need some details."

"This will take a while."

"Oh right, you're working, we can do this later."

"When are you going start logging?" She is nodding her head and smiling.

"When this month's high tides happen. I think that is in a week or so."

"Right, OK, I can give you a general idea of how it all works right now if you don't mind the interruptions."

"Go ahead."

"To begin with, having a permit to beach-log only allows logging on one specific section of beach. Most of the beaches in Southeast Alaska are permitted to different people. That means, by law, you are allowed to beach-log just that section. But if a log is in the water, floating, it's anybody's log, and even if it isn't in the water, nobody can tell where it came from, so once a log is in the raft, it's yours. Sometimes somebody will grab a log from a beach that is permitted to someone else. You know, this country is a long way from nowhere. The chances of getting caught are pretty slim. Any log harvested by a logging company is branded on the cut end, but nobody pays much attention to that when they are buying them, or they'll cut a couple of feet off the end to get rid of the brand, but still a person gets real sensitive about somebody stealing their logs. There have been shots fired over that, as you might well imagine.

"Then there are trees that have been blown down lying halfway in the water. If a tree is still connected by land, it belongs to the state of Alaska, unless it can be cut off, limbed, and put in the raft before anyone gets caught. Actually, that holds true for any tree. If it's in the water or not, if it gets cut down and limbed, as long as they can get a line around it and yank it down to the water, it's theirs. Just rub the stump with dirt and pile some brush on it, it will be quite a while before anyone can tell what's going on."

Kasey stops and thinks for a moment. "I don't think there'll be much of that going on with Nancy in charge. She just wants to fill her dad's contract and go home, but most of the time, that's the way it works. That brings me to something else. Owen's logs are at the west end of El Capitan, where it enters Shakan Strait, right?"

"I'm not sure, but that's the name Mike's been using."

"Well, Owen's beach permit doesn't cover that area."

"How can he log it then?"

"When he heard about the raft breaking up, he went right to the head office of the logging company and had them write a contract to recover those particular logs. Legally, those logs still belong to the company, so they can make any arrangements they like. That supersedes what the beach permit covers."

"Sounds like trouble to me."

"Ted Wills is the guy that has the permit for that section of beach. He and Owen have already had words. Ted is pissed off beyond description."

"Does Nancy know this?"

"Got me, but she has known Ted for a long time. It won't be the first time they've had a dust-up over beach logging."

"Huh."

Kasey says, "And one more thing."

"What?"

"If Nancy is the same Nancy that folks talk about, you need to know that she has a pretty short fuse on her."

"Thanks, I'll file that away for future use." Neil sits silently staring out the window. A small grin flickers on his lips.

Kasey asks, "What?"

"I didn't say anything."

"I can hear you thinking, but I can't make out what you are saying."

"What an odd thing to say." He shakes his head.

"Well, what are you saying to yourself?"

He chuckles. "Last winter I had this conversation with myself. You ever have conversations with yourself?"

She hesitates, looking at him sideways. "Sometimes, I guess, but I'm not sure that's what I'd call it."

Neil emits a small gurgle. "So here I am, clear out in the middle of nowhere, getting ready to go beach logging, something I didn't even know existed as of yesterday, with people I hardly know. As it turns out, one of them is a woman who hasn't done this in God knows how many years. Now I learn that she might be some sort of Kathrine of Padua."

"Who?"

"Aw, nothing, a character in a play. I normally don't remember things like that, but the character reminded me of my aunt Mildred.

"Back to your original question. Not so very long ago, I was asking myself, how do people wind up the way they do? Is it chance or circumstance, or you know, just plain luck? Does a person have any control over any of that, or does shit just happen? I've wondered about that for some time now. Anyway, that's what I was thinking."

"I think you're very peculiar."

"I've known that for a while, but what do you think about what I just said?"

"I'll get back to you."

Kasey turns her chair back toward where the men are working and yells through the open door. "Hey, Rich, is that a fish ticket sticking out of your shirt pocket?" He looks down at the blue piece of paper and nods. She holds one hand out and motions him over with the other; she takes the paper. "I don't want some fisherman yelling at me that he didn't get paid because you lost his fish ticket." She motions him back to work. "Go on." The paper is soaked with water and fish slime; she reads it carefully then presses it flat on the top of her desk. She stands at the window, watching the crew as they ice fish and move the full totes into position to be loaded on the packer when it arrives.

Neil asks, "Where's Everett?"

"He's back at his house, resting up. His hips are giving him problems again."

She goes to stand in the doorway. Randy is working alone, talking to himself, gesturing with his hands, nodding while he is lying ice in the open bellies of fish. When he looks her way, she motions to him. "Randy, nobody's called in on the radio to say they are going to sell this afternoon, and the packer won't be here until tomorrow afternoon, so why don't you take the rest of the day off."

He ceremoniously removes his gloves, dips them in a bucket of disinfectant, walks down the ramp to the fuel float, and sits on his blue bucket next to the pump shack. After a few moments, the one-legged raven lands to sit on the other bucket opposite him. Randy begins to talk so softly he can't be heard. The raven rubs his beak on the edge of the bucket.

Kasey continues to watch him. "He's having an off day."

Neil says, "Well, I think I'll call it a day, get something to eat and some rest."

Kasey nods. "I hope I didn't complicate things for you. I just thought you would like to know what the deal was."

"No, I appreciate it." As he walks past Randy, he acts as if he doesn't know he is there, but Neil can see he is gesturing as if he is trying to make a point.

The next morning, Neil wakes to a loud banging on the front door of the school. "Hold on, I'll be right there!" He dresses as he stumbles through the classroom. Mike is waiting impatiently.

"Hey, Neil, Mom is going to take us out on the tug for a training session. We're going to count the logs. She says it'll take a couple of days, so bring your personal stuff.

"Right now?"

"We'll feed you breakfast while we're under way. Grandpa and Mom are at the Mercantile right now, fueling up."

When they arrive, Nancy and Owen are on deck, waiting. They quickly untie and idle out into Sumner Straits. The sky is clear and the water flat calm. Neil stands next to the rail, taking in the view. The skiff bobs in the wake, tethered with a towline.

Nancy interrupts his thoughts, "This is a great day. It really doesn't get any better than this, but you don't want to be out here in a storm, particularly down here where the tides run hard out of Sumner Straits and collide with the ocean. When it's like that, being on this boat would be like riding a toothpick. It's violence in its purest form." Her tone is matter-of-fact. "When you're out in a storm like that, there's nothing you can do about it. It's loud, it's nasty, and all you can do is hang on." She sweeps her arm toward the horizon. "There, that island, do you see it?"

"Yep."

"Well, the next stop after that is Japan."

"Now that you put it that way—"

"Do you get seasick?"

"I don't know. I've never been on the ocean before."

Nancy looks disturbed, then she rubs the middle of her forehead just above her eyebrows with her index finger. She takes a deep breath. "Oh right, I forgot. Well, we do most of our work in protected waters, so we can choose when we tow the raft to town." She is momentarily overwhelmed thinking about what lies ahead, knowing Mike and Neil's confidence is born of youth and inexperience.

She quickly recovers. "Here's the deal. You and Mike need to learn as much as you can as fast as you can. As soon as possible, both of you need to be able to independently run this boat, and I don't mean just turn the wheel. I mean know all the shit there is to know." Then she contradicts herself. "There is too little time to know all there is to know. That takes years. But, for example, you guys need to know enough so that if I told you to take this boat to Wrangell, you could do that without running into a rock and sinking or getting lost. Get the idea."

"Yes, I do believe I understand what you mean."

She turns into the wheelhouse, knowing that he doesn't really understand; he just thinks he does. "OK, let's get started."

Neil and Mike stand behind her, as she takes the helm from Owen. He stands behind her, with Neil and Mike looking over her shoulder. She starts with the radio, what channels are for boat-to-boat talk, and to use channel 16 for contacting other boats only. Conversations with other boats are for other channels. On the overhead is a rack of rolled-up paper charts, stuffed under two rods that have been screwed to the ceiling. She sorts through them, muttering names and numbers, pointing with a finger as she looks. "Hah, here's the one we'll need. It's of Shakan Strait. Dad, take the wheel while I show these guys how to read a chart." She unrolls the chart on the galley table. "Here is Harbor Cove, and right back in here is the house. Now I want you to find out where we are right now and continue to know where we are from now until we get to Shakan Strait, which is where the logs are. I want you to be able to tell me the name of any landmark I point to. You always need to know exactly where you are. If the cloud cover drops or if the fog rolls in and you can't see land, then you need to be able to set a compass course based on your location." She places her hand on the chart to disconnect them from their investigations. "I can't tell you how critical this is."

"But, Mom, we have the charts on the electronic navigation system." He points to the screen hanging from the overhead.

"Well, sometimes the electronic systems don't work, and it's generally when you need them the most. Those charts, at least the ones we need now, should be ingrained in your mind."

"I'll bet Grandpa has a whole bunch of these in his mind."

She nods and looks at her dad at the helm; her expression turns to apprehension. "OK, you guys go out on the back deck and work out a system to help each other study. Remember, when I point to something, I want you to know what it is and where it is in relation to the boat."

They go out on deck to stand by the cable drum and eagerly return to the charts. She stands behind Owen at the helm. His heading isn't to Shakan Strait; it's to the west side of Warren Island to the open ocean. She checks the electronic chart then his heading again. She looks wistfully at him.

He speaks, "How is your crew training program going?"

"Oh, I think they'll be fine. They're working hard at whatever I ask, and they're excited to make all of this go well, and if I remember Shakan Strait correctly, the beaches are pretty good, not many rocks for logs to hang up on. The logging part should be pretty straightforward, and I don't care if we get all of the damn logs or not. If we just get the easy ones, it's OK by me."

"Sure, I think that's right, should be pretty much trouble-free. You betcha."

She watches him closely. "We can make the raft right there at the entrance to El Capitan Passage. It's always protected at that old village site there on the south side."

"Sure, you bet that'll work good. That's a good spot." His answer is hurried.

"How ya feeling, Dad?"

"Fine, yeah sure, just fine."

"Great."

As they pass the marker buoy at the Barrier Islands, it's far to the port side of the boat. She goes to the aft deck and leans against the bulkhead, trying to gather her thoughts. After a moment, she peeks through the wheelhouse door to see that Owen is still way off course. She takes a deep breath and says loudly, "Mike, Neil, would you come here. I want to show you something." She stands by the deck winch. They arrive, standing, waiting for their next assignment.

"I'm going to hurry your training along faster than I wanted, something has come up."

Neil responds, "Whatever you say, Captain." He nudges Mike with his elbow.

Mike jerks upright. "That's right, Captain."

She takes a moment to calculate for any sarcasm in their response then continues, "I know that you guys have only had a half an hour or so to study your chart, but do you know where we are?"

They both look quickly around, look at each other, and nod. Mike says, "Yeah, we know where we are."

Neil chimes in, "Right." Neil points, "Those are the Barrier Islands. Over there is Warren Island, there Cape Decision. That's a buoy marking some rocks, and it blinks four times every eight seconds." Then with a smile, he points to the horizon. "And there is Japan."

"Where are we going?"

They both say proudly, "Shakan Strait!"

"And where is Shakan Strait?"

The simultaneously point ninety degrees off to the port side. Slowly their looks of accomplishment fade to mystification.

Neil asks, "We are going to Japan?"

Nancy looks sad. "You guys are exactly correct on identifying all of those waypoints, but I don't think Dad has any idea where he is."

"What!"

She holds her hand, palm out, to calm them, to keep them from talking too loud. "I've been watching him since we passed Hole-in-the-Wall. He hasn't looked around or changed course in the least. I don't think he has any idea where he is right now or where we are going."

"What're we gonna do, Mom?"

"I don't know for sure, but for now, I am going to tell him you guys are going on wheel watch. You need the practice anyway. Make your turn slowly and head for the entrance of the bay. It will be easy with the electronic chart. Just keep it in the middle, no surprises there. I'll check on you once in a while, don't be afraid to ask for help."

They both nod vigorously.

She goes to stand by her dad. They talk for a while, then she motions at them to come forward. She says, "I turned the autopilot off, so you are on manual steering. We'll get the rest figured out as we go."

Owen smiles and goes to the back deck and sits on the rail. Nancy sits next to him. "What's going on, Dad?"

He speaks to her in measured tones. "As you have probably figured out by now, I have no idea where we are. Since the stroke, my sense of direction is completely gone. I can make my way to the Mercantile in the skiff, but that's about it. I wondered when you would notice. I just get locked up somewhere in my mind. I seem to know what's going on, but for some reason, I just can't find a way to get out of it." He shrugs then perks up. "You know you used to say I had this compass somewhere in my head and it was never wrong?"

"I do remember that and remember it well. It was pretty amazing. I can't remember it ever failing us. I haven't thought about it for years, but I do remember. It saved our bacon several times when we were in the skiff, in the fog."

He looks up at her. "The compass in my head is gone. I know we're not on the right course. I kind of know where we are, but I just can't reason my way out of it. I keep thinking that if I can just make one small connection, a first step, that would trigger other steps, that I can find a thread that would lead me through the confusion. But it seems like the harder I try, the harder it is to get out of it, even to say I need some help. After that, I go to panic mode, afraid because I can't say anything, afraid you might not notice, panic at the thought I might hit a rock—all of this is going on inside my head, and I can't get out of it."

He sags forward, resting his hands on his knees, then perks up immediately. "Hey, things worked out, and here we are." Then in direct contrast to his recent confusion, he very clearly describes in great detail where he thinks the logs will be distributed within the bay. "You know there's that huge back eddy at the old village site, then the tide splits there as it comes out of El Capitan and heads up toward that old marble mine. There will be few logs up that way but not many. Most will be scattered out this way. You know, I bet it wasn't a storm at all that broke up that raft. I'll bet they damaged the damn raft, bouncing it off the rocks, towing it through El Capitan."

Now he turns to Nancy with complete candor and says, "I know how hard it was for you to come back and do this. I truly didn't think you'd do it, knowing how you hated the place and all of that. Not in a million years did I think you'd come back and we would get to take Mike out and do this, not to mention he would like it. And that teacher, what's his name?"

"Neil."

"Yeah, Neil. He is just a bonus."

He claps his hands together. "Oh yeah!"

Mike calls from the wheelhouse, "This electronic chart is different colors—blue, white, green. What does that mean?" There is a small pause. "Captain."

"Just keep the boat icon in the white. I'll be there in a minute." Then as an afterthought, "Be sure and cross reference to the paper charts."

"Yes, sir," they say in unison.

She looks back at Owen. He is gazing out over the water, rubbing his hands together. The tug makes its way into the sheltered waters of the bay, and the ocean swells lie down to flat water. Individual logs begin to appear randomly scattered along the eel grass and gravel beaches. Most are single logs, but there are a few bundles at the old village site. Nancy takes the wheel. She puts the boat in neutral and lets it drift to a stop.

Neil says, "Man, that is a bunch of logs!"

Nancy comes to the wheelhouse. "I'll stay at the helm. Mike, you and Neil count the logs. I just want a rough idea of what we are up against here. I'll do the same. There's a spool of nylon twine in that tool box on the back deck. Cut a piece and tie a knot for every ten logs." They all stand in silence, counting. The boat drifts slowly in the tide, and they soon gather to compare notes. Owen sits contentedly on the rail, smiling.

Nancy calls to him, "Dad, did the contract you signed with South Cape Logging specify how many logs were in the raft?"

"Maybe it did, but I don't remember. It doesn't matter anyway, don't even care." He giggles.

Again Nancy massages that spot just above her eyebrows with her index finger.

Mike points. "Hey, look, there's a skiff coming this way." From between two small islands, an aluminum skiff is headed directly for the boat. The starboard gunnel, at the bow, is a bent and crumpled mass of metal. As it comes close, they can see an older man hunched over the tiller. He's wearing wool bib overalls with red suspenders. His hat is jammed onto a head of bristly white hair that sticks out in all directions. He guides the skiff directly to where Owen is sitting on the rail. "Damn you, Owen, my permit is for these beaches. Those logs are mine."

Owen just laughs and waves his arms as if to say "Go away."

Nancy comes to the rail. "Ted Wills, is that you?"

The man looks at her with a frown. "Yeah, who the hell are you?"

"Nancy."

The man studies her for a moment. "I'll be damned." Then he recovers slightly. "Well, it don't matter who the hell you are. He still don't have a permit for this beach. So he can't log it."

"What are you talking about?" She turns to Owen. "Dad?"

Owen says, "It don't matter what he is says. Those logs are mine."

"You old bastard, you had a stroke and you don't know squat. If you ever did, you done forgot it all by now anyway—brain damage. You got yourself brain damage. You're out here thinking you can get these logs when they are really mine. Not only that, you got shit for a crew, some snot-nosed kid who don't know his ass from a hole in the ground, some woman who's been in America for the last twenty years, and a damn schoolteacher who don't know a pickaroon from a jackknife. Why don't you just give it up?"

Neil walks to the rail, raising his voice. "Here's the deal. The logging permit for this beach may belong to you, but the logs belong to Owen because he has a separate contract with the logging company. They own the logs, and they have contracted with Owen to recover them. It's all perfectly legal."

Nancy is frowning as she looks at Neil. "Is that right?"

Neil nods, and Owen laughs and says, "Yes, Siree!"

Nancy turns to the old man in the skiff. "Looks like it's a done deal, Ted."

"If you touch those logs, there will be trouble. I'm telling you that right now!" He points at each of them with a threatening finger.

Neil leans over the railing and speaks directly to Ted; his voice is low and soft. "Well, what do you say we get started right now?" He finishes by nodding slowly.

"What?"

Neil's voice gets lower and softer. "Let's not screw around, no need to wait. Might as well get on with it."

Shocked by Neil's abrupt change in demeanor, Nancy says, "Neil, that's enough, you let me handle this."

"Yes, sir."

Ted wheels his skiff into a tight turn and speeds away. Mike runs to the rail to stand beside Neil. He shakes his fist at the fleeing skiff. "We'll beat you like a rented mule, you old fart."

Her voice louder now, Nancy says, "Michael, you shut up!"

Nancy stands agape, trying to figure out what just happened. Her finger automatically goes to her forehead. She takes a deep breath. "Neil, is what you just said about the contract with the logging company true?"

"Pretty sure."

"And where did you learn that in your short time in Alaska?"

"Kasey told me."

"Dad, is that true?"

Owen slaps his leg and giggles. "Yes, sireee, that is a fact."

"Well, I guess we'll go with that for now."

She turns to Mike. "Like a rented mule? Where in the world did you learn that?"

He points to Neil.

Her eyes shift to Neil. "You need to let me deal with this. I don't want any trouble out here in the middle of nowhere. Let's just keep a lid on it. We're going to try and get a few logs and call it good. Neil, this is serious business. If trouble starts out here, there's nobody else to take care of it but us. I mean, that's it. Just keep a lid on it, OK? No need to get your nose out of joint and get something started. Please remember, we're just going to get some of the logs, and I don't even care if we get them all. Then we're going to get out of here."

"Sure."

"I need a cup of coffee."

In the cabin, she turns the drip valve on the stove for more heat to boil water. She hears Neil and Mike talking; she hears the word *pirates* several times. As the water is heating, she peeks out on the back deck. Mike is grinning from ear to ear.

"OK, you two, I want you to get in the skiff and see if we missed any logs on our count that might have drifted into some of the smaller bights and back bays. Then I want you to take a run into El Capitan Passage to see if there are any hung up in there." She points to the red day marker at the entrance to the narrows. They scurry to the skiff. She calls out, "Wear your life jackets and be careful."

They respond casually, "Yeah, sure, OK."

She stomps out and stands on the stern, pointing emphatically at them as they start the outboard. "Listen, you two, this is no bullshit. You wear your life jackets, or you aren't going anywhere, got it?"

They raise their hands in submission and quickly put on life jackets. "Anything else, Captain?"

"Yes, there is, as a matter of fact." She points to a small island to the north. "You see that little island right there? The one with the big white rock just above the tide line?"

They both nod.

"If my memory serves me correctly, there is a pretty good anchorage just there on its west side around that point, and unless I miss my guess, that is where Ted Wills is anchored up. Now I am telling you in no uncertain terms to stay away from him and his boat. This isn't some game we're playing here. We are a long way from help of any kind, and he knows it. We don't want things going sideways on us out here. Just don't go near him, and if he shows up, come back here. There isn't any point in antagonizing him, just let it go."

Owen pipes in, "It's a big, old wooden tug. It's in tough shape. The planking above the waterline is patched with pieces of plywood put on with screws and Splash Zone. It leaks like the Nile River runs through it; he has to use starting fluid to start it because the engine is in such bad shape. Damn thing smokes like it's on fire, must have holes in a couple of pistons."

Nancy looks directly at Neil and Mike. "Just let it go."

They nod again.

"Promise me."

They say together, "We promise."

"All right, get out of here." Then suddenly says, "Wait!"

"What?"

"I'll leave our radio on channel 10 just in case you need to get ahold of us."

"OK."

"Remember how to use the radio? Everyone listens to channel 16, remember that?"

Mike says, "Mom, we got it."

She waves them away with both arms.

They race off to the south side of the bay, hugging the beach, slowing as they get close. Mike is at the tiller. Neil occasionally looks over the side, checking for shallow water as they get closer to shore. She suddenly thinks of two or three more things she should have told them and sags against the drum. The tug is still drifting in the tide. Owen clumps with his uneven gait to the foredeck and releases the anchor. The heavy chain rattles and bangs as it moves over the bow roller; the sound echoes across the water. The boat swings around as its weight comes against the chain; it rides quietly there in the slight breeze.

When he returns, Owen finds Nancy sitting at the galley table, staring at her coffee cup. He sits opposite her. "You can't tell them everything. It won't mean much to them anyway. They just have to do and find out what works and what doesn't."

"But, Dad, they could get hurt, or worse than that, they—"

"I know that, believe me, I know that."

She thinks a moment. "Must have been the same with me, eh? You know, Dad, it seems like several times since I have been back that there are a lot of things I either didn't remember or have chosen not to remember or maybe even adjusted my memories to support my own thoughts."

"Don't be so hard on yourself. You were just a kid. Nobody knows what they don't know. You're worried, and not without reason, but one thing I do know for sure. If they see that you're scared, then they'll be scared, and person don't make very good decisions when they're scared, generally makes things a whole lot worse. They need a captain that has confidence in them. Now, you need to lie down in the one of them bunks and get some sleep. You look all worn out. I'll keep an eye out for Captain Kidd and the other pirate."

She falls asleep almost as soon as she lies down. Owen goes to his spot on the back deck and sits.

It's toward sunset when Mike and Neil return. Nancy makes it a point not to be at the rail, waiting, when they return. She's sitting with a cup of coffee as they come into the galley. Mike talks excitedly. "Mom, I want you to know we did exactly as you told us. Didn't we, Neil?"

"Yes, we did."

Nancy sees them glance at each other. "OK, but what happened?"

"We went out to the mouth of the bay just like you told us and were counting logs, but when we got to the end of Hamilton Island, we decided to go around the far side to see if any logs ended up in that direction."

"I hadn't thought about it, but that was a good idea."

"We didn't go behind that little island with the white rock, but there's another anchorage back there, and that's where Ted Wills is. We just came around the point, and he was right there, so we turned as quick as we could and got out of there. I'm pretty sure he didn't see us. We didn't do it on purpose, did we, Neil?"

"No."

Nancy says, "Don't worry about it. That's a small deal. I just don't want to have any more confrontations with him."

"But, Mom, he has some of our logs. I couldn't tell how many for sure, but it looked like eight or ten."

"How could you tell they weren't some other logs? You weren't close enough to see the brands on the cut ends."

"No, but—"

Owen speaks from the railing, "Did they still have most of the bark on them?"

Neil responds, "Yeah, they did."

"They're our logs then, because they haven't been on the beach long enough to get rolled around and knock the bark off on the rocks. He's been out here getting what he can, but he's slowed down because he is working by himself, and the tides have been wrong."

"See, Mom, he is taking our logs, that old bastard."

She ignores his cursing. "Let's not get all excited about this. It's just a few logs, and I still don't want to get in a confrontation over a few logs. The plan is still the same; we are going to get how ever many logs we can get without anybody getting hurt. If he gets a few, I don't care."

Mike is incensed. "But they are our logs!"

Owen says, "Your mom's right about not getting involved in some feud out here in the wilderness. Things can go bad in a hurry. By the same token, the tides are on the rise from now to the end of the month. It's only going to get easier and easier for him to high-grade our logs. If we wait until the first of June like we were gonna, there might not be many logs left."

"Dad, I don't care about that either. He can have the logs. I just don't want anybody to get hurt."

They all sit in an awkward silence until Neil says. "I have a couple of thoughts." Nobody speaks, so he continues, "They could wait if you guys want to just have dinner and deal with this later."

Silence.

Taking the silence for license to go ahead, he says, "I don't know, but it seems to me that if we wait too long, like Owen says, we might have just a couple logs left. I guess that's OK, but at some point, you would have to wonder if the effort is going to be worth the price of the fuel or what we have gone through up to this point. If that's going to be the case, we might as well go home and go fishing.

"However, Owen, you and Nancy will have to decide if this would work or not. We could take off tonight, go back to the Cove, get the boom logs, the chains, chokers, and whatever other gear we need. We could be back here by midday tomorrow, ready to go. I'm guessing that running at night isn't a problem. If we could do that, then at least our presence would keep him from stealing our logs, and we could take our time and practice on some of the easy ones. Then all would be ready when the tides are at their highest. What do you think?"

Nancy gives a deep sigh. "What's the weather forecast? Has anybody listened to the weather?"

Owen says, "I think it's pretty good. Somebody better check it though, just to be sure."

She stands, "Mike, you go ahead and start the engine. Neil, you go with Dad. He will show you how to operate the anchor winch. I'll check the towline on the skiff." She talks directly to Neil and Mike. "This means we will be out here working an extra week or ten days more than we planned, don't forget that."

Mike tries to hide his enthusiasm. "Not a problem for me."

Owen turns and clumps across the deck. "Come on, Neil, I'll show you how to pull the anchor."

"Hey, Mom, you and I can do wheel watch. I think I have the thing about the different colors figured out. The darker the blue, the shallower the water, right? Hey, wait a minute, there is some green here too. What's that all about?"

Nancy dutifully goes to stand by Mike as the boat heads for the mouth of the bay.

They arrive in Harbor Cove in the middle of the night. Nancy decides that even though it will take more time than planned, they won't begin preparations until 4:00 AM when there's full daylight. Mike and Neil connect the boom logs with chains, while Owen and Nancy collect food and supplies from the house. By midday they are ready to leave except a quick trip to the Mercantile for Pilot Bread, peanut butter, and strawberry jam. When they return, Mike waves an envelope in the air as he approaches. "Hey, Mom, we got a letter from Dad." She eagerly tears it open.

Dear Nancy,

Marcia and I read your letter. We thought you would go up there, just visit a little bit. You know, get reacquainted with your dad, find a way not to go logging, and come home. Looks like things have become way more complicated than that; we don't even know where to start responding to your letter but will get that figured out by the time you get home.

We will get a bunch of books on how to get in touch with your inner feelings. In fact, we intend to lead the charge on the inner feeling front. When you get home, we will fix you right up. But for now, we do know that if anyone can get it all sorted out and make it work, it's you. Don't take any guff from your crew.

Love, Ed and Marcia

PS: Marcia has decided that a good way to finance her college expenses would be to learn how to be a pole dancer. It's probably good money, and she could hide the tips from the IRS.

She begins laughing so hard the letter shakes in her hand. Mike looks at her questionably. "Your dad and your sister are in their 'We think we are funny mode.' She hands him the letter; he laughs before putting it in his hip pocket.

That evening, they are anchoring in Shakan Strait. The boat rides at anchor in the growing night. Blackness comes quickly and relentlessly after sundown. It has a tangible thickness to it that makes it absolute. They all sit sipping coffee on the back deck in silence.

Owen is the first to speak. "Better get a good night's sleep. We're gonna need it." He disappears into the fo'c'sle.

In the morning, Owen lays a choker out on the deck; it's made with a twenty-foot cable. He demonstrates how the ball and socket work and then tries to show Mike and Neil what a rolling hitch is and how, if you rig it correctly on a log, when it's pulled, it will roll it up from the ground and not into the ground, making it easier to get the log down the beach and less likely it will hang up. "It's just the direction you put it on the log that makes it work right."

Mike and Neil look puzzled.

"Don't worry about it. Once you do it, you'll understand how it works." He continues, "Now you don't just hook onto the log and start yanking. You hook the log you want to yard down the beach to a log that is floating in the water, then you yank on the floating log and use its weight to yard the other log."

Mike asks, "Why can't you just pull it off with the big boat? I mean, this boat can pull a lot, right?"

"Well, it can, but if what you're pulling hard and the log gets hung up on a rock or something like that, you might rip the winch out of the deck or a cleat, if you're tied to that. It's a wooden boat."

"Oh, right."

"Or you might break the cable, and you don't want the end of a broken cable flying around, might get someone killed."

"Does that happen?"

Owen looks directly at him. "Listen, Mike, your mother is right. Now that we are actually getting started on the operation, you need to remember that all of the concerns she has are real and both of you guys need to remember that. Just take it easy and try not to do anything stupid. Maybe a better way to put it is, don't try to do something before you know how." His voice has an edge to it. "If you have any questions, just get on the radio and ask me or Nancy."

They spend the next couple of days anchoring the boom logs at the most protected end of the anchorage. It will hold the logs that'll make the raft. They anchor a single boom log halfway down the bay, which is for attaching each day's recovery, saving long individual tows to the raft. On the third day, they're ready. After breakfast, Nancy says, "Neil, you and Mike take another run down toward the mouth of the bay and try to pick out a few logs that will be easy to get, a smooth beach without any stumps or rocks to get hung up on. When you get back, we'll relocate and start to work."

When they are gone, Nancy asks her dad, "What do you think of this whole operation?"

He shrugs.

"I need to know what you think. I know that you have some gaps here and there from the stroke, like your sense of direction is gone. And I noticed you aren't reading much when you used to read more than most people."

"You probably saw that book by my chair in the living room, lay there in the same spot unopened."

She nods. "I have also noticed that the gaps that you have are few and isolated, but your judgment is still good. You still have your way of assessing people. For instance, you knew instantly Neil would be able to work out as a deckhand, not just that he could do the work physically but that he would not be trouble or afraid of work. That's pretty good. I sure didn't pick up on any of that. So what do you think, should we take the next step?"

"We'll take it slow, like you've been saying, but we have to go ahead. Those guys have been working their asses off, doing everything we told them to do. If we can get a few logs off the beach, easy ones, and they continue to learn like they have been, I think we'll be just fine."

They both turn at the sound of the skiff approaching. "Sounds like they are back already." Puzzled, she goes to the back deck.

Neil begins bellowing before the skiff reaches the boat. "We need some help here!" His clothes are dripping wet. Mike is sitting in the bow with both hands, slumped forward, grasping his forehead, blood dripping between his fingers. They lift him to the deck. Nancy pries his hands away from the wound. There's a gash that runs over his left eye down to the top of his left cheek. Neil grabs the first-aid kit and rolls Mike on his side to keep the blood out of his eyes. Nancy works quickly, wiping away the blood, checking to see if any bone is showing. After a moment, she says, "It's not too deep, it just looks bad. Head wounds bleed a lot."

"What happened?"

"We beached the skiff on that stretch of beach on the south side of the entrance to the bay, just this side of the west end of Hamilton Island. Mike was waiting in the skiff while I went up the beach to check out a log up at the high-tide line. I was most of the way up to the log when I heard the sound of a motor running. When I turned around, here comes Ted Wills, full speed in that old beat-up skiff of his. He came right at our skiff. Mike saw him and stood up to see what was going on.

"He never did slow down, just kept coming. At the last moment, Mike realized, and I realized, that he wasn't going to slow down or stop. About the time, I started running down the beach and yelling. Mike sat down and grabbed the gunnel to brace himself. The collision almost flipped our skiff over. It knocked Mike to the bottom of the boat. He was smart to have braced himself." Neil points to V-shaped dent in the side of their skiff.

Nancy asks Neil, "What happened to your fingers?" The three middle fingers on his right hand are swollen and bruised.

"I ran down the beach, got to the skiff just after the collision. He was just backing away, yelling and screaming about us stealing his logs. I got my hands on his skiff. If I had been a couple of steps quicker, I would have had him. He hit my hand with a gaff hook."

"Are any of your fingers broken?"

He sticks out his middle finger. "This one was out of joint, but I popped it back in. They're kind of sore, don't think anything is broken. Get me some tape. I'll just tape them together and see how it goes."

Nancy very calmly and evenly turns to Mike. "Were you unconscious at all?"

"No, I don't think so, didn't even hurt that bad now that I think about it."

"Neil, do you think Mike was unconscious?"

"No. He was right back on his feet, yelling and screaming. I had to hold him down. He wanted to chase after Ted Wills and do him in. Me too, but I thought Mike might pass out from the loss of blood. I didn't know for sure how bad he was hurt."

"Michael, tell me where are we?"

"What do you mean?"

She points at the boat. "Right here right now, where are we?"

"Alaska?"

"No, I mean this very spot."

"Shakan Bay."

"What are we doing?"

Mike begins to get angry. "We are going to get some logs off this beach if that old fart ever leaves us alone."

"I think he's OK."

Neil grunts in pain as he begins taping his finders together. He turns and talks directly to Nancy. "Here's the deal, Nancy, I'm not going to let this go. I know I promised that I'd do everything you told me, but I can't let this go. This is now a private matter. This requires a personal visit to Mr. Wills and sort him out. I am going see to it."

Nancy raises her hand and starts to say something. Mike interrupts, "Me too." When Mike stands, he's a bit wobbly. As Nancy watches him struggle to gain his balance, an odd look comes over her face. She looks back and forth between Mike and Neil then turns to her dad and just looks at him for the longest time.

He watches her for a moment then says, "Oops, I think we are in for it."

She turns back to Mike and Neil. "I couldn't agree more. This has become very personal. We have just had a change of plans. We're going to pay Ted Wills a personal visit. Now this is important, guys, you still need to do what I tell you, and if and when we are done you don't like the results, then I will be open to any other suggestions." Her manner is detached but dark, her voice thick, disconnected. She seems alone. Then she says in a very, almost uninterested tone, "Do exactly as I say."

"OK."

Owen says to Nancy, "Can you keep this under control?"

"What?"

"Your temper."

"I'm not making any guarantees."

He looks troubled.

"Dad, would you get us going here and pull the anchor?"

She goes to the wheelhouse and starts the engine. It grinds briefly then roars to life. She returns to the deck. "Neil, you and Mike take the skiff. Follow me. When we get to where Ted is anchored, you just stand off from us and wait until I tell you what to do. Stay clear out of the way. Got it?"

They nod.

The small flotilla makes its way through the bay, an old man limping on the deck eyeing his daughter carefully, with tangible concern; a middle-aged woman who doesn't want any part of what she is doing or setting out to do but is consumed by threats to what is hers; a teenage boy, his mop-like red hair blousing out in all directions with butterfly bandages stitching a cut that runs from the middle of his forehead, around his eye, and down his left cheek; a schoolteacher who hasn't taught school and doesn't even know if he can, caught up in this whole undertaking because he doesn't have anything else to. The boat idles down the bay, dwarfed by the scale of the landscape. There is no hurry. It's just happenstance, a collection of ideas and plans gone awry, out of kilter moving on their own muddled momentum. Someone watching from a distance would likely think they're out for an afternoon cruise, a family outing—a cruise to enjoy the day.

When they round the point and turn back toward the small bight where Ted Wills is anchored, Nancy moves the boat closer into shore so it will be more difficult to detect their approach. She comes into a small bight to find the old black tugboat resting at anchor. She takes her boat out of gear, and because it's a heavy boat, it continues to move forward, steadily slowing. When it comes within yards of the other boat, she starts blowing the ship's horn at long, harsh intervals. After a moment, Ted Wills comes stumbling out on deck. His pants are drooping and his suspenders hanging down. He sees the bow of Nancy's boat aimed directly at midship of his; it's still moving slowly forward.

"What the hell do you think you're doing!"

Nancy pokes her head out of the wheelhouse window and says nothing.

"Just a damn minute here, you're going to ram my boat!" He fumbles with his suspenders, trying desperately to keep his pants from falling, but in the tenseness of the moment, he can't quite get them in place. In desperation, he holds his pants up with both hands.

Nancy leans further out through the open window of the wheelhouse. Her voice is harsh, but her tone is matter-of-fact. "Yes, I am. You're a miserable pile of weasel shit. The only reason I don't shoot your worthless ass right now is that lead and powder cost too damn much." As the bow touches his boat, he is jarred off his feet, falling to the deck. She shifts her boat into forward, pushing his sideways. It swings on the anchor, moving toward the shoreline.

She points to the gravel shoreline beyond his boat. "I think it's time you did a little bottom work on your boat. How about I scrape the barnacles off for you?"

He stumbles to his feet. "No, no wait!"

"Ted Wills, you are just a little bit of nothin', whittled down to fine point, worthless." Now there is the sound of gravel growling on his hull.

He is frantic. "No, no, don't. I don't know if this old hull can stand the weight!!"

Owen is standing beside Nancy; he says very carefully, "Don't sink his boat." She doesn't even know he's there. He shakes her shoulder hard. Finally, she looks at him, but her eyes aren't focused.

"DON'T SINK HIS BOAT!"

She puts her boat in neutral, but the momentum continues to push him farther up on the gravel beach; his boat tips and begins to roll on its side. "You want trouble, mucus brain. Well now you've got trouble. I should just do you in right now, but that tub of rust and rot you call a boat isn't worth a match and a can of gas." She revs the engine, blowing black smoke in the air out of the smoke stack.

He raises both hands, letting his pants slip to his knees. "Take the logs." He points to the small raft of logs.

She backs the engine off to an idle, puts the engine in gear again, pinning his boat to the beach, rolling it again until the port gunnel lies on the beach. She walks to the back deck. Neil says, "Mike, did you hear that? Mr. Wills said we could have our own logs back, such generosity." Back in at the helm, she increases the throttle, pushing his boat a few more feet up on the gravel bar. It's perched there, rolled precariously on its side, eventually coming to a stop.

Owen grabs her arm and shakes is hard. "NANCY, THAT'S ENOUGH—STOP!"

She leans on the brass shifting arm, again putting her boat in neutral and leans out of the wheelhouse window. Her arms and shoulders are now hanging out. "Ted Wills, you listen very closely to what I'm about to say! If you are lucky, your boat will float off this beach in two or three days. The tides are on the rise this week. If it doesn't and it sinks right here, that's fine with me. Either way, I don't give a shit! But if it floats, I want you gone. I don't want to ever see you again—EVER! If you see me in town coming down the sidewalk, you best run and hide! If you ever come anywhere near my friends or my family again, I will cut your liver out and eat it in front of you while you are dying!"

He stares at her.

"Ted, tell me you understand what I just said, because if you think this is idle talk or some sort of exaggeration, then you are making a serious error in judgment. Tell me you understand."

He continues to stare.

"TELL ME!"

"I understand!"

She backs away from his boat. Mike and Neil are standing, looking at her in shock and astonishment. She nods at them and says in a normal voice, as if nothing has happened. "It's OK, just go ahead and tow those logs to where we're making our raft and put them inside the boom logs." She nods her head in that direction.

When their skiff comes up next to the log raft, Neil lifts a pickaroon in the air and flourishes it before he sticks it the anchor log. He says in a loud voice while looking Ted Wills direction, "Now let me see. Is this a pickaroon or a jackknife? By golly, I do believe it's a pickaroon. Hey, Ted! Isn't a jackknife one of those little things that you fold up and put in your pocket?" There is loud solid thunk when he sticks it in the log.

They drop the tongue end of the boom chain through the augured hole in the end of the boom log and begin towing the small raft out of the bight. Nancy backs away from Ted's boat and waits until Neil and Mike disappear around the point. As the boat turns to move away, Ted is straddling the tilted cap rail of his tug as someone would ride a horse. He points at Nancy. She is pointedly ignoring him. "Owen, what the hell!"

"She's always had a pretty good temper on her, Ted."

When they're anchored up back at the village site, Mike and Neil return from rafting the logs. Nancy, as if nothing significant has happened, asks, "How are you feeling, Mike?"

"Pretty good."

"Neil?"

"I can work."

"Neil, where do you think we should start?"

"That spot where Mike and I were this morning would be a good spot. The beach is smooth and has a pretty good slope to it, a good spot to learn how to tie that rolling hitch and rig up that log we are going to use to pull from."

In the morning they begin, and they begin slowly. Owen patiently points out the details, warning them of potential problems. They work their way from the entrance of the bay, back to the village site where they're rafting the logs. On the third day, they see Ted Wills leave, headed north. They watch the trail of exhaust from his smoke stack; it slowly shrinks to nothing.

Over the next two weeks, the log raft slowly grows, and as the tides get higher, the job gets easier; the single logs float at the high tides. The days are long, and there's daylight for the evening high tides. The log raft steadily grows. When the equinox tides peak, there is one bundle of logs that will not float. Under Owen's instructions, Mike and Neil, standing on the uphill side, cut the steel banding with an ax. The logs make a low rumbling sound as they slump to the ground. Late one afternoon, when they are making ready to work the high tide, a Coast Guard patrol boat comes into the bay. It launches a smaller boat that approaches Mike and Neil and Owen as they work. A young man stands in the bow. "Good afternoon."

They nod.

"This is a safety check."

They nod again.

He proceeds through his checklist, marking off items as they are produced—a life ring, a warning device. The warning flares are out of date, but he lets that go when they say they will replace them on their return to town. Then he asks, "Was there some trouble here a couple of weeks ago?"

Owen speaks, "What do you mean?"

"We received a call. Some guy said someone pushed his boat up on the beach, threatened him. Would you guys know anything about that?"

"That would be Ted Wills, I bet."

"Yes, it would."

"I have known him for years, and he is a well-known exaggerator."

"He seemed very upset."

"He had some of our logs, but he agreed to give them back, so we agreed not to press charges. As far as we're concerned, it was a misunderstanding and it's over. I can show you the contract for recovering the logs if you want."

"He made some serious accusations."

"Well, like I said, he is a well-known exaggerator, and I don't know much about this sort of thing, but I would think he would need some sort of witnesses or something like that so's someone, like yourself for instance, would know for sure that he was tellin' the truth. I don't think there's any witnesses around here that would say that his story held much water." He turns to Neil and Mike. "Is there, boys?"

"Nope."

The young man waits a moment; he hands them a slip of paper. "Here's a receipt showing you have had a safety inspection, so if you get boarded in the next month or so, just show them this."

"Thanks."

"Get those flares replaced as soon as you can, OK?"

"You betcha."

The closer they get to the end of the job, the better Mike and Neil become. The last few days Owen stays on the tug with Nancy as they recover the last of the logs. They stand on the bow when the raft is ready, looking.

Neil says, "I know it's just bunch of wood, but I got to tell you, this has been real interesting."

Mike asks, "Now what, Grandpa?"

"Well, normally we would tow this raft to the mill in Klawock, but to tell you the truth, I'm not feeling so hot right now and the hard part is done, so I'm gonna have the logging company send one of their tugs up to get 'em. I'll have them take the cost of the tow off the total contract."

Nancy looks worried. "Dad, what's going on?"

"Mainly I'm just worn out. If we spend a few days moving this wood down through El Cap., I won't get much rest, and if the weather comes up, it'll take longer. I won't sleep at all."

They head toward Port Security and are all lost in their own thoughts. It's a way of being by themselves after weeks of living close together, in small space. As they leave Shakan Strait, Owen takes the binoculars and limps out on the back deck. After a moment, he says, "Better come take a look at this." They all collect on the fantail; he points to the far hillside beyond Harbor Cove. "You see Mt. Calder?"

They nod.

"Take a line from the summit at about four o'clock down to the flat spot just above that shoreline that has that stretch of sandy beach. Look uphill a bit in that stand of second growth trees." He hands the glasses to Nancy; she studies the spot. She hands them to Mike. As he watches closely, he says, "Those trees are moving. What's goin' on?"

"They've started."

"What?"

"The road."

"That's a large track-mounted backhoe pioneering the right of way. The drill rigs and excavators won't be far behind."

Neil looks puzzled. "Did anyone take away from that meeting the idea that they were going to start that road anytime soon, let alone this summer?"

They all shake their head no.

They arrive in the back bay at Harbor Cove just after dark. Nancy and Owen spend the night in the house. Mike and Neil stay on the boat.

In the morning, they walk up to the house. Owen is sitting on the front porch in a rocking chair. "Hey, Neil, I'll get your check when I get paid. You've earned a full crew share. There'll be four shares; two for the boat and one each for you and Mike. Nancy said she didn't want hers, and I figure I didn't work enough to earn one. Neil, that might mean you'll make enough to get you through the winter if we don't get enough kids to open the school this fall. Well, that is if you shot a couple of deer and canned up some salmon, you could make out OK then figure out somethin' come spring."

"To tell you the truth, I didn't even think about how much money I'd make, but that will sure take the pressure off."

15

Leaving

"Mike, you take Neil back to the Mercantile, been good workin' with you, Neil. Come around for coffee once in a while and let me know how the battle against ignorance is goin'."

When they get to the fuel float, Randy is sitting by himself, staring at the water.

When Neil enters the office, Kasey looks at his rumpled, unwashed clothes, sweat stained and dirty, then at the beginnings of his scruffy beard. She laughs. "Ahhh, here he is, back from the briny deep. You smell like you've been working hard."

For some reason it hadn't occurred to Neil that he hadn't taken a bath for two weeks. He instinctively takes a sniff of his armpit then takes a couple of steps back.

Kasey waves her hand at him. "Don't worry, I'm used to it. Some of these fishermen smell like they haven't washed for a couple of years. Add a little fish slime to that and it'll just about burn the old nose hairs."

Neil doesn't know how to respond, so he remains silent.

Kasey continues. "The word in town is that Nancy went off on Ted, and he was lucky to get out of it with all of his body parts." She chuckles. "Do you really think she would eat his liver?"

Neil shakes his head. "To tell you the truth, right at that moment, I wouldn't have bet against it. Jeez, word gets around fast."

"There's a lot of country here but not many people, and Ted went right to Wrangell when his boat floated, got drunk, and started shooting his mouth off. It's all over Southeast Alaska by now. He was probably trying to get some sympathy, but I think it had the reverse effect. People know him pretty well."

"I'll bet that's why the Coast Guard dropped by to see us."

The radio crackles. "Mercantile, Mercantile. This is the *Loon*. Are you there, Kasey?"

"Loud and clear."

"We're just out front of Beauclerc—headed your way—should be there in a couple of hours."

Kasey turns back to Neil. "How's Mike?"

"It scared the hell out of us at first. There was a lot of blood, but he's just fine. He'll have bit of a scar. He was worried about that, but I advised him to go with it. I mean to go back south with a bunch of stories and a scar to prove it, that's perfect. I told him to milk it for all that it was worth, might be a babe magnet. He perked right up. I also told him to give up the information grudgingly. It'll have a way better effect."

Kasey stands and faces Neil. "I need to get back to work, so why don't you get cleaned up and let's make a time when we can talk without so many interruptions."

As he begins to leave, she says, "Randy's been saying for days that the road is coming. You guys see anything down towards El Cap?"

Neil nods his head. "Sure enough, there's a track-mounted backhoe pioneering a road just south of Mt. Calder."

When Neil walks past Randy sitting next to the fuel pump, he says, "Hey, Randy, how's it goin'?"

"Not good, roads comin'."

As Neil idles past the Saloon, Arlo is there sipping on a morning beer, blowing smoke from his roll-your-own, watching it drift away.

The next day, Liz and Eric come to the Mercantile to sell fish. After the fish are unloaded, they scrub the hold and take on a new load of ice. They tie to the float, get something to eat, and fall asleep for several hours. When they wake late that afternoon, the full crew is at the Saloon. Their conversation is uncommonly loud. People are talking over one another, waving their arms. Liz and Eric watch for a moment then get a six-pack of beer they have been icing in the hold. They set it on the table then sit and listen.

The conversation rages on: "That geek that came here from the Forest Service sure as hell forgot to tell us that the road was a done deal. How chicken shit is that?"

"Why did he even hold a meetin'?"

"Good question."

Arlo asks, "What're you guys gonna do?"

"Whatta mean 'What're we gonna' do?" There's a harshness to the question.

"Well, I guess what I meant was, are you gonna stay here and just put up with whatever happens, or go someplace else or move to town and get job drivin' cab? Hell, I don't know. I was just askin'."

"Oh, you mean, are we gonna go to town and try to be 'normal'?"

The conversation stops. They all sit in silence for a moment, then someone says emphatically, "Maybe I'll just go down there and put a seal bomb in the fuel tank of that backhoe."

Arlo says, "I don't know about that. Someone might get hurt or killed."

"So what?"

Eric says from his seat at the edge of the gathering, "Bad idea."

Someone offers, "I don't see why. A person could just slip in there on a dark night and blow the damn thing up. If someone's in the way, that's just the way it goes."

Eric says, "It's still a bad idea."

The man begins to get testy, "You keep sayin' that. Suppose you tell us why it's such a bad idea."

Eric asks quietly, "You ever kill anybody?"

The gathering is startled at the question, but more than that, by the calm manner in which it was asked. "No. Why?"

"It's not as easy as it sounds."

The Saloon goes dead quiet.

Someone asks very softly, "It's not?"

"No, it's not, and besides that, you've already made a serious mistake."

"I have? What would that be?"

"You sat here and just told a bunch of people that you were going to do it. If you were really serious, you should've just kept your mouth shut."

Abruptly the conversation changes to other things, and then people make excuses to leave. Soon Eric and Liz are sitting alone. She says, "To be honest with you, Eric, I'm very fond of you, but when you talk like that, you make me nervous."

He looks at her evenly and says, "Just trying to help out." They continue to sit alone as darkness comes to rest over the fuel float. He drinks a second beer before they return to the boat.

As they get to the boat, she nods at the second beer in his hand. "Big night for you."

"Yep."

They leave the next morning just before daylight to catch the morning bite. That afternoon, a summer storm comes through, kicking up white water in Sumner Straits and pounding the Cove with heavy rain; the temperature drops. Mike shuffles his way from his bedroom in his cut-off pants and red suspenders for a cup of coffee. Owen and Nancy are sitting by the woodstove. Its warmth penetrates the far corners of the living room. They turn in their chairs when they hear him approach. Owen studies him. "How ya healin' up, Mike?"

Mike instinctively feels for the scar above his eye. "Pretty good, I think."

Nancy asks, "Are you putting that face cream that I gave you on it? It'll help get rid of that scar."

"Sometimes."

"It'll help that scar go away." She persists.

Mike smiles. "Neil says he thinks it will attract girls, so I need to take that into consideration."

"Attract girls?"

Mike flexes both arms and struts toward his mother. "As in babe magnet, Mom."

"Oh, great."

"Hey, Mom, I have another idea."

"Wonderful," she says sarcastically. "What is it?"

"Let's not tell Dad and Marcia about the scar. What do you think? We can just spring it on them when they meet us at the airport. I'll wear my deckhand outfit." He motions to his clothes.

"That has possibilities, but I'm going to reserve judgment on the 'babe magnet' issue."

Mike pours a cup of coffee from the enameled tin coffee pot sitting on the stove. Owen turns to Nancy. "When you leavin'?"

"On next Thursday's mail plane. We can catch the afternoon jet to Sea-Tac, be home for dinner. Pretty easy."

"You could hang around here for a while?"

'I know I could, Dad, but my boss has been really good about giving me some time off, more than he should have really. I don't want to take advantage of that."

"Sure, I get that."

"We have a big house, Dad, there's plenty of room. It'd be an easy thing for you to be there."

A crooked, sardonic grin appears on Owen's face. "I guess it would be foolish of me not to admit something like that is coming down the road and probably sooner rather than later, but it's damn hard for me to think about it. I guess I'll just put it off as long as I can. Dying right here would be fine with me. We'll just have to see what happens. The older you get, the fewer choices you have. That's the part I hate the most. I'm gonna put it off as long as I can. Whatever it is I'm gonna do."

Nancy says, "How about if I buy you a satellite phone so I can check on you once in a while?"

He thinks to himself for a moment, staring at the rain as it pelts against the window. "I suppose that would be OK as long as you are the only one that has the number."

"Well, the kids and Ed, of course."

He glances at Mike. "Sure."

The three of them listen to the rain and wind, then Owen's eyes light up. "Hey, Nancy, does Marcia have to go to some sort of training to be a pole dancer?"

Mike laughs aloud. Nancy says as she chuckles, "That would be another reason I have to get home."

Catching the spirit of the change in mood, Mike says, "Grandpa, what do you think about my scar?"

"I think you're on the right track."

Nancy stands. "I give up. I'm going to take the skiff over to the Mercantile and make some plane reservations, then I'm going to go see Mary and Ralph. I haven't had a chance to see much of them. We've been busy, and they keep to themselves pretty much anyway."

As she starts for the door, Mike calls after her, "Don't tell Dad anything."

"OK, OK."

When Nancy walks onto the front porch of Mary's house, the door is open but there's nobody home. She goes to the boat shed. Mary and Ralph are sitting in canvas chairs, drinking coffee. "Hey, Nancy, how's it goin'?"

"I'm getting ready to go south, just made reservations on Thursday's mail plane. I thought I'd come by and visit some before I took off."

"Cup of coffee?"

"Been drinking coffee with Dad and Mike."

"Pull up a chair." Mary motions to a plastic lawn chair nearby.

Ralph stands and takes off his hat. "Ma'am, we heard you jerked the slack outta Ted."

"It had to be done." Nancy changes the subject. "What do you guys think about this business with the road coming?"

Mary and Ralph glance at each other. Mary says, "It will sure enough change things. I suppose we'll just wait and see how it goes."

Ralph says, "Gonna be hard on some folks. I expect the police will be droppin' by just to see what's going on. They let a bunch of stuff slide now 'cause it cost so much to get here, be cheaper by car."

Mary looks thoughtful and turns to Ralph. "Will the cops be after you?"

"Maybe."

"Anything serious?"

"Nothing that would be much over thirty days or so."

Nancy asks, "If you decide to move, do you have any idea where you will go?"

Ralph says, "We been told there's some patented land up there at Port Conclusion, an old cannery site or mining claim, thought we'd run up there in the skiff and take a look, just in case. You know, some sort of backup plan. Be hard to leave this place though, got things just about the way we want 'em. That don't happen very often. Matter of fact, it's a first for me." Mary reaches out and touches his arm.

They all sit looking at the water, then Nancy says, "Better get going and start getting organized. It's back to America for me—house to pay for, kids in school, and all that. I been gone a month or so, and Ed is most likely in full rut by now, pawing in the dirt and blowing snot." They all laugh. Nancy waves as she leaves.

Ralph says, "I guess we'll see you when we do."

As Nancy walks down the fuel float, Randy is standing by her skiff. He says as she approaches, "Well, the question is, what's everybody going to do now?"

She says, "What are you going to do?"

He raises his chin, making a gesture of aloofness. "Can't get that one out of my mind, of course. I suppose one has several choices. I could start taking some medication. Done that before, and although I'm still pretty weird, I don't think anyone could single me out as being much different than most other lawyers. I'm guessing I'd fit right in. It's a depressing thought though. I could stay right here until word got out that there's some weirdo that talks to ravens at the Cove. I don't know if that's considered a threat to society or not, probably. I think if they caught me on a really bad day, they might pack me off somewhere—for my own good, of course. How does the saying go? 'A danger to myself or someone else.'

"Everett says I can stay here and work as long as I like, but when the road comes, I don't think he'll have the same influence on things that he does now. He's done way more than his part, keeping me going as it is. I'd be up shit creek already if it weren't for him."

On Thursday they all gather on the fuel float, waiting for the mail plane, standing apart, talking about the weather. But that topic is just a distraction from what is always on everyone's mind—the road. Some of them take frequent trips in their skiffs to check on the progress of the backhoe that's pioneering the road. The last report was, "It's just up there on that flat spot behind Calder Bay." The Saloon crowd are generally listless and subdued. Some of the conversations are mere murmurs. When the sound of the plane's engine is first heard, they cluster closer to Nancy and Mike.

"Take care of yourself."

"Good to see you again."

"Back to America again."

Owen says, "You'll be glad to get home, see Ed and Marcia and out of here I bet."

She says as she wraps his good arm in hers. "To be honest with you, Dad, that's exactly how I thought I would feel, and I still do, but damn it anyway, this is way harder than I thought it would be." She looks at him sternly. "I'm sending you a satellite phone. I want you to keep it with you at all times. You call me anytime you want, it's on me.

He nods and says vaguely, "Sure, sure."

"I mean it, Dad."

"I know you do."

Mary steps forward. "We'll check on him once in a while."

They all step back from the bull rail as the plane cuts its engine and docks. Kasey and Rich begin unloading the freight and mail, calling out names that are written on envelopes and boxes.

Nancy takes her dad by the shoulders. "Just come and live with us. It'll be an easy gig. We all think it would be great. You have to believe me when I say we would enjoy having you around. Wouldn't we, Mike?"

"Damned right."

Nancy frowns at him. "Michael, you are going to have to clean up your language. Your teachers won't put with that kind of shit!"

Mike points at her and smiles. Owen says, "You're on thin ice there, Nancy."

"OK, OK, but, Dad, let's not get off the subject here. It would be a good idea for you to move south and live with us." She's on the verge of pleading.

Owen pats her on the shoulder. "I'll need to think about it, but that sounds like a real good idea. You know with the stroke and all that." He points to his left arm. He laughs. "Might start droolin' any day now."

Nancy stares at him. "Just give us the word. We'll come get you."

"You betcha."

When they climb aboard, the pilot quickly unties from the float. Someone pulls on the tag line that hangs from the wing, turning the plane toward open water.

The engine roars to life, and the plane does a step turn on one pontoon through the mouth of the Cove. When it turns downwind, both Nancy and Mike take a last look over the wing. As Mike turns to look forward, he sees his mother's eyes are moist. He waits until she turns forward then says, "He'll never move south, will he?"

She sighs deeply. "No, what's going to happen is that the next phone call we get, someone will be saying, 'Your dad died.'"

The drone of the engine takes over.

Ed and Marcia meet them at the luggage carousel in Seattle. Marcia is appropriately shocked. At first she just frowns at Mike's work pants that are cut off short just below the tops of his BF Goodrich rubber boots. As he comes closer with a smirk on his face, she sees the scar on his face. "Holy crap! Michael. What happened to you! Your face is ruined! Dad, do you see that?"

Ed looks at Nancy then points at Mike. "What?"

She says, "It might take a couple of glasses of wine to get through it all, but right now, I need a hug."

On the ride home, Nancy sits right next to Ed. She's quiet. Mike and Marcia huddle in the back seat in animated conversation. Ed strains to hear what he can. At one point, Mike raises his voice and says excitedly, Ed can hear him say, "Then she says, 'I'll eat your liver while you are lying there dying!'"

Ed looks at Nancy. She says, "We'll talk later."

"Sounds like this might take at least three glasses of wine."

16

The Road

Toward the end of August, a delayed run of coho arrives. There is the late flurry of activity. Everyone is tired. The fishing has been lingering on alternately without any fish for days, then a fresh batch will show up. They are late, but they are big fish that average ten to fifteen pounds. The end of the season is hard. It's already been months of long days and not much sleep. Randy, Rich, and Bob woodenly move through their routine of weighing and icing fish in weary, silent automation. They have pointedly not discussed the coming of the road and the inevitable arrival of society. On the sunny days, morning fog hangs to the mountaintops then flows silently down the slopes like thick water.

Arlo arrives at the same time most every morning to ceremoniously light his roll-your-own cigarette, blowing smoke in the air, saying "It's fine day, ain't it?" to nobody in particular.

Everett comes through the office door and sits heavily in his chair and stares at the clutter on the top of his desk for a long time. Kasey watches him. She can't tell if he can't focus or if he is just overcome at the prospect of having to deal with it.

"Hey, boss, you OK?"

His shoulders jerk back as if he is startled by the noise. "Huh? Oh yeah, I'm fine, just worn out, I guess. Been a long season. They're sayin' there's still fish on the outside ten or so miles off shore. Looks like this might go on into September, maybe later.

"Boss, you've got some big, nasty bags under your eyes. You better take a couple of days off, get some rest."

"I can't seem to make myself do that."

"In my opinion, you don't try very hard."

"Yeah, can't argue that."

She says pointedly, "I can handle this just fine."

"I know that."

"Well?"

He doesn't answer, and they both go back to their work. A short time later, he says, "Speakin' of people workin' too hard. I was walkin' by the office a week or so ago, and I heard you and Neil talkin'."

Kasey turns in her chair and says accusingly, "Oh, you did, huh?"

"Now I wasn't eavesdropping or anything like that," he says defensively. "Not on purpose anyway."

She squints at him, stands at the counter, and leans forward.

He says, "Don't try to change the subject. You were just sayin' that I was workin' too hard, but I heard you tell him that when you got some time, you and he would sit down and talk. You done that yet?"

"No."

"He's a good guy."

She says, "He must be. He got along with Nancy on that boat for a few weeks."

"So... Better get goin' on that deal."

"You're just trying to get me hooked up with someone you think will be here for a while so I won't leave and you won't have to break someone else in."

"There's some truth to that, all right."

Kasey says, "I'll make you a deal. If you stay home for two days and don't come to the office, then I'll make some time to get together with Neil." Kasey sticks her hand forward. "Shake on it."

He offers his hand. "Done. How about tomorrow? What's scheduled for tomorrow?"

"Damn it, that's not the deal. It doesn't matter what's going on. You just go home and stay there. That's it."

"OK." He abruptly stands up. "I'm goin' back to the house. I'll see you in a couple of days."

"What the hell, you mean now?"

He waves as he goes out the door. "Bye."

She rushes out the door after him. "It's eleven o'clock. You've already worked a half a day today, so figure that into your two days!"

"OK."

She stops and looks puzzled. She follows him out behind the store. He's limping past the generator shed, starting up the trail to his house. "You mean you're really going to do it?"

"It was your idea. Don't forget our deal." He disappears up the trail and into the bushes.

Kasey yells, "You set me up, didn't you!"

She can hear him chortle. The phone begins ringing in the office.

A few days later, Kasey has just finished her lunch and is preparing quarterly reports when Everett arrives. He goes to the window that overlooks the fuel float and taps on it loudly then motions Kasey to join him.

"What?"

He points. When she looks, she sees Neil sitting in a plastic chair on the fuel float, reading a book.

"Go on down there and talk to him."

"I'm right in the middle of the quarterly reports."

"You don't have to spend all afternoon down there. The deal was you'd just arrange a time so you guys could talk a bit, that's all. It doesn't have to work. Maybe he's some closet weirdo that's more interested in studyin' the breeding cycle of herring gulls or somethin' like that, who knows? The deal wasn't that this had to work. It was you two would just talk."

Kasey turns and leaves.

When she walks up to Neil, she says, "I've been busy, but Everett saw you down here and reminded me we were going to try and find some time to sit down and talk." She points to the office window. Everett is smiling his gap-toothed, tobacco-speckled smile; he waves.

Neil waves back. "Hey there, Everett."

Kasey says, "To be honest, he's kind of engineered this thing."

Neil smiles. "Ah, so you're being bribed or coerced."

"No, I've just been too busy. Let's do this. If there isn't a boat unloading around noon, I'll shut the office down, we can have lunch."

"Sure, you want to try for tomorrow?"

"You bet."

As an afterthought, she asks, "Do you have any idea if there will be enough kids to have the school open?"

"So far there isn't."

She says, "The official count is sometime in late October, so all you need is for a couple of more kids to sign up and stay in school until then and you're good to go. I know of at least two who are working as deckhands. I'm pretty sure they'd be willing to sit in just long enough for the final count. I'll talk to them."

"Sounds good."

"You might have to be a little creative when you take attendance, but that generally works out. We've done it before."

"Whatever's customary. Sounds like these kids have given up on school. What's the deal there?"

"They seine for salmon during the summer then start early in the spring for the herring roe fishery. In good years they make a lot of money. Most years they'll make way more than you do."

Neil says, "Good for them." He smiles at Kasey. "Now there's something else I need explained to me, being a flatlander and all."

"Shoot."

"Just to be clear, you and I are going to have lunch a few times so we can talk?"

"Yep."

"I might be rushing things a bit, but if we were somewhere in America, at some point, I might be inclined to ask you to a movie or out to dinner, you know, something like that. Dinner maybe?"

"Yep."

"Is there some sort of Harbor Cove equivalent to that phase of a relationship?"

Kasey thinks for a moment. "Come by for lunch tomorrow." She turns and walks up the ramp. When she enters the office, Everett's sitting at his desk, but she knows he's been watching at the window. She goes to her desk and begins work.

"Well?" he asks.

"I've filled my part in the bargain. He's coming by for lunch tomorrow, and by the way, I don't want you hanging around here eavesdropping. You go home and have lunch with your wife. Take a nap."

"OK, OK." He pauses. "Anything else?"

"He wants to take me to the movies and dinner."

Everett laughs. "Well, it's a good start."

The days grind on. Fish keep showing up, and work continues. Neil comes to the office for lunch a couple of times, but they agree to wait until the season is over to talk.

The conversations at the Saloon that had been centered on progress of the backhoe have all but ceased. All the talk hasn't changed anything. Then one day, the season is over with the announcement on channel 16: "The silver salmon troll fishery will end at midnight on Tuesday." A couple of boats trickle in with partial loads to sell then leave for home.

Kasey tells Rich, Bob, and Randy that since they're not processing fish, there isn't enough work to keep them all on; she only needs one man. They can decide who that will be. That afternoon, when everything is cleaned up and stowed away, she brings them a six-pack of cold beer. When they finish, Bob comes to the office. "None of us wanted to stay, but I drew the short straw."

"We appreciate it, Bob."

Bob stays at the counter, shifting his weight from one foot to another.

Kasey says, "What is it?"

"Well, you know when I said you was lookin' good and all that stuff earlier this summer, I didn't mean nothin' by it. I was just tryin' to flirt a bit, in a funny way."

"I appreciate you saying that, Bob, no hard feelings on my part. The blow-up doll was pretty good, I thought."

"Yeah, you got me on that one. I put it in the corner of the porch, and my dog chewed it all to pieces before I figured out who I was gonna spring the same trick on."

She changes the subject; there's concern in her voice. "Has Randy mentioned anything about what he's going to do when the road comes?"

"You know he hasn't, and we don't ask. Rich and me have wondered about that but agreed not to say anything unless he starts the conversation. We'd like to know of course, but it's really none of our business. But have we noticed he's been talking to that bird a lot more lately. That's not a good sign, at least that's what Rich and I think anyway."

"No, it's not good."

"I did ask him if he ever thought about taking some pills or somethin' like that to help him sort things out. He said he tried that a few times, but it made him feel peculiar, said he feels more normal without the drugs, just being the way he is now. I don't know what to make of that. He's been like he is now a long time, I suppose."

"Sounds like he's in a tough spot right now." Kasey looks out the window and watches Randy clean a tote.

Bob says, "Another thing is, he hasn't said anything about hunting. Usually one of us will go with him to get a few deer for winter, hasn't said a word about that. He'll need deer meat this winter."

"What are other folks saying about the road? Any idea when that backhoe will get here?"

Bob makes a helpless motion. "In my opinion, they're pretty jumpy about the changes that might be comin'. For one thing, if the cops start showin' up on a regular basis just 'cause they can get in their rig and drive here. I got nothin' against cops, and to tell you the truth, I think they'll just come here, look around, and leave.

They got better things to do than hassle a bunch of bums like us, but sooner or later, somebody's gonna drive in here from town or maybe even America and complain that they saw some rough-lookin' people sittin' around, being messed up right in the middle of the day. Drunk in public, I think, is the term. Or maybe they see a doe hangin' on somebody's porch and it ain't doe season. That's just a start. At some point, they's gonna be letter to the editor about how folks at the Cove aren't conducting themselves properly, I'll guarantee it. Then a concerned citizen will call the cops and say, 'Why aren't you doin' your job?' Then they'll have to do somethin'. It'll take some time, but it'll happen."

Kasey says, "That fits the pattern, all right."

He sighs. "Back to your question, a week or so I guess, the backhoe that's pioneering the right-of-way should be here."

"How about you and Rich? What about you guys?"

"Rich hasn't decided yet. He thinks, if he has to, he can go to someplace, maybe Wrangell, clean up his act a bit. He thinks he can fit in, maybe. I told him he should just stay here for a while and see how it goes. See how creepy things get. He could hand troll in the summers, be by himself."

"And what about you, Bob?"

"Oh, I'll stick it out here. If nobody finds out my real name, I'll be OK."

She says sharply, "Don't be saying that where people will hear you!"

"You're the only one that knows."

17

Breakfast

The last quarter mile of road goes quickly. They have all been hearing the backhoe's engine rumble and the tracks clanking for a couple of days. Now it's there, stopping on a flat piece of ground just behind the Mercantile. The entire cove has gathered to watch it approach. The group is standing just downhill from the machine. A short wiry native man leaves the machine idling, crawls out of the cab, and stands on the track. He looks down on the group. "Hey, Kasey, how you doing?"

"We've been better, Jimmy. How's your mom doing?"

"She's had to get a wheelchair."

"Tell her hi for me."

"Sure."

Jimmy talks to the whole group. "Kasey's my cousin. We grew up in Klawock together."

Someone says, "Yeah, we know."

Jimmy takes his cap off and rubs his head. "Come on, you guys, I'm just a backhoe operator. I had nothing to do with deciding to put this road in here. I've got three kids, a wife, and a house payment." He pats the side window of the backhoe. "This pays the bills." He climbs back in the cab, swings the machine around, and leaves. The gathering drifts away one by one.

A few days later, someone asks, "Has anybody seen Randy?"

Arlo checks his house. When he returns to the Saloon, he says, "He's gone, all his stuff is gone, his skiff is gone. No note, no nothin'." When he tells Everett and Kasey, they look grim.

Everett says, "That's about the last thing I wanted to happen. Ain't no way he can make it on his own. He ain't nowhere close to being ready for winter."

Kasey asks, "You seen Neil?"

"A few hours ago, he was sitting in the library, readin' another book." Arlo shakes his head. "That boy's gonna wear out his eyeballs."

Kasey marches out of the office and around the edge of the Cove, climbs through the bushes and onto the boardwalk. When she reaches the school, Neil is still sitting in the library building at the reading table. He looks up when she comes through the door. "Hey there, Kasey, good to see you."

"You are a good guy, Neil."

"Thank you."

"I think I'll take you up on that offer to go to the movies and dinner."

"Oh, I'll bet that there has been some sort of substitute devised over the past few years."

"It goes way farther back than that."

"Seriously?"

"Oh yes. It's an ancient tradition that actually started in my family. Nobody knows how far back it goes. Like the dawn of time, maybe."

"What is it?"

"Breakfast."

"I never would have guessed."

She smiles a bright white smile. "It has to take place fairly early in the morning, but the preparation takes several hours, so it has to be done the night before."

He asks, "So what's for breakfast?"

"Bacon and eggs."

He says, "I suppose pigs and chickens do go back a long way."

"Yes, it sure seems like that."

He stands and goes to her. "When do we begin the prep work?"

She says, "How about right now?"

Epilogue

Eric and Liz leave. They are seen occasionally on the fishing grounds, and word of their whereabouts filters back to Harbor Cove through other boats. They do return to Harbor Cove to sell when they are in the neighborhood but seldom stay more than overnight. As they begin to winter fish, they are seen less and less. When they come to town to work on the boat or sell fish, they only stay long enough to get those things done then leave immediately. When they aren't fishing in the winter, they anchor in some remote area.

Liz begins a trap line mainly as an excuse to get out in the skiff and run the beaches. "Just a reason to get out on the water. I never seem to get tired of it," she says. Eric tags along with her because it's not a good idea to be in a skiff alone in the winter. He helps skin the animals and stretch the hides. They keep the money they make from trapping in joint account. They can't decide what to spend it on, but once in a while, when they're in town, they will have a nice dinner and an expensive bottle of wine.

She keeps the money she gets from Gordy in another account, but the subject of getting her own boat never seems to be discussed much. "I don't know," she says when he asks. "You know I have such poor judgment that it's hard to decide." There is a hint of a smile on her face. As a general rule, she never talks about the future and he never talks about the past.

Kasey tries hard to locate Randy without success. There are rumors. Someone may have seen him in Sitka or heard he's living by himself somewhere in South Chatham. Some say up in Afflac Canal or just north of No Name Bay in a small cabin, but she never can pin him down. She asks Everett so frequently that finally he tells her he saw him on his last trip to Seattle, and he seemed fine. He says Randy told him he was getting some help and was working as a paralegal in a law firm there. Everett couldn't remember which one. "Had a whole bunch of names," He said. She broke down in tears because she knew he was lying.

Neil stays. The two kids that filled in the enrollment quota showed up, so school started in the fall. They dropped out the day after the count. Later on in the year, the Southeast Island School district wrote him a letter and let him know that they knew he has artificially padded the enrollment. He can't tell if his job is in jeopardy or if they are just covering their ass in case it becomes an issue with State Department. Sometime toward spring, he begins visiting Owen and spends hours asking questions about tow boats and beach logging. He consistently repeats those conversations with Kasey to see what she thinks.

A few years later, a young couple from California drive to Harbor Cove in their new SUV with *off-road capability*, because it's at the end of a road in Alaska. They park in the dirt parking lot on the flat spot just behind the Mercantile. When they walk through the breezeway that separates Everett's office from the grocery store, they begin snapping pictures of the bulletin board and the dogs sleeping on the floor. At the end of the breezeway, they stop at a large sign that says, "DO NOT ENTER. THIS IS A WORK AREA—DANGER!" There's another sign on the door of a small office; it's handwritten: Stay Out!

The deck before them is jammed with plastic totes. Two men are working at a hanging scale, weighing and icing fish. They are in full rain gear that is covered in fish scales and slime. One has scraggly blond hair and is nervously glancing behind him as if something threatening might be there. When the woman raises the camera to take a picture of them, he reaches out and pokes the man he's working with. When the man looks at him, he nods at the camera; they both quickly turn their backs.

As they turn to leave, the woman says as she points, "Look at that raven. It's been injured. It only has one leg. Do you think it'll be

OK? Maybe we should call somebody when we get back to town to see if it needs rescued?"

The man says, "Sure."

When they drive away, an old partially filled box of McDonald's french fries is lying where their car has been parked. The raven flaps over to inspect, quickly eating the remaining fries. When he's finished, he turns the box over and over again, looking for more.

About the Author

My wife, Pat, and I have lived in Alaska for fifty years. We have done a variety of things to make a living—taught school, commercial fished, and owned and managed small businesses. One of which was a construction business that operated in remote locations. For forty of those years, we have lived on a small island, Pennock, which is about a mile by water from Ketchikan; a boat ride is the only access. We have spent the past twenty summers living remotely on a boat throughout the Alaskan Panhandle, as far from town as we can get.

Our home is in Whiskey Cove, named because it was a transfer point for Canadian whiskey during Prohibition. Seven or eight people live in Whiskey Cove, depending on the time of year and how bad the winters are. This story and characters reflect our associations and experiences in the Panhandle.